THE ENOCHIAN APOCALYPSE SHOW

A GAME OF LOST SOULS
BOOK ELEVEN

LISA SILVERTHORNE

AWARD-WINNING BESTSELLING AUTHOR

LISA SILVERTHORNE

THE ENOCHIAN APOCALYPSE SHOW

A GAME OF 11 LOST SOULS

**Can Jack and Talia save the world—and their happily ever after—
from Lucifer's deadly vengeance?**

Lucifer's nefarious plan materializes after he breaks the Seven Seals and unleashes Seven Hell princes on Earth, triggering the apocalypse. With High House in smoking ruins and the Gates of Hell open, Jack and Talia must fight for their lives and the fate of Heaven and humanity.

Forced to wage separate battles, Jack fights to stop the Seven Travelers from unleashing their demonic payloads on Earth while Talia takes to the skies in a fierce air battle to stop Lucifer's Dark army from taking control of Heaven.

When Lucifer sets his sights on destroying the Maker's Thrones and killing the Maker, Jack and Talia must defend the uppermost reaches of Heaven to prevent the destruction of all existence. As the clock ticks down to the end of the world, Jack and Talia must fight for their happily ever after and battle Lucifer to save everything from the King of Hell's deadly vengeance.

THE ENOCHIAN APOCALYPSE SHOW

Copyright © 2023 by Lisa Silverthorne
Published by ElusiveBlueFiction.com
Elusive Blue Fiction Logo designed by Samantha Romage

Cover Design and Book Layout by Lost Souls Studio
Cover Imagery by Benny Productions, Brusheezy, Creative Fabrica, Creative Market, Chesire Studios, Deposit Photos, Dreamtime, Obsidian Dawn, Pixabay

ISBN-13: 978-1-955197-41-0 (Hardcover)
ISBN-10: 1-955197-41-5

ISBN-13: 978-1-955197-42-7 (Trade paperback)
ISBN-10: 1-955197-42-3

Novels by Lisa Silverthorne

Standalones:

ISABEL'S TEARS

LANDFALL

PACIFIC BLUE TATTOO

A Game of Lost Souls series:

THE CINDERELLA HOUR

THE PRINCE CHARMING HOUR

THE EVER AFTER HOUR

THE FALLEN HEARTS SEASON

THE RISING SPIRITS SEASON

THE ETERNAL SOULS SEASON

THE ROYAL WEDDING HOUR

THE HEAVENLY HONEYMOON HOUR

THE DIVINE NEWLYWEDS SHOW

THE CELESTIAL COUPLES SHOW

THE ENOCHIAN APOCALYPSE SHOW

Curse and Crown series:

THORN & BLADE

FORTHCOMING!

A Game of Lost Souls series:
The Angelic Anniversary Hour, Book Twelve
The Perdition Picture Show, Book Thirteen

Curse and Crown series:
Storm & Steel, Book Two
Dagger & Flame, Book Three

The Spiral series:
Ruin, Book 4
Descent, Book 5

The Resurrectionist Papers:
Corpses Delicti
Stiffed Again
Cease and Deceased

SCIENCE FICTION WRITING AS **L.S.** SILVERTHORNE
Experiencing True Purple series:
Cipher, Book 4
Renascence, Book 5

THE TALLEST SPIRE IN HEAVEN WAS GONE. DESTROYED WHEN LUCIFER'S Holy Firebomb blew up in the Cloud Chamber. Disintegrating most of the spire and decimating the smaller spires around it. Damaging the Archive's nearby shorter tower, the last remaining spire in the center of lower Heaven.

Talia stared in horror as she circled the smoky air where High House had once stood. Where the Archive teetered in the air currents, blackened, and covered in ash. The last remaining spire aloft.

All of the others had crumbled.

Tears turned to crystal and slid down her cheeks. Where were all those angels? She shuddered as the realization began to burn through her numbness.

Where were the seraphim? The cherubim? All the Watchers!

She held in a sob. And Poor Oseira. Who'd been injured, weakened by Lucifer's earlier assault on Heaven. Only to become prey for Procel's transference attack that had come from Hell.

Smoke drifted like spirits across Heaven's lower spires, skies dark and acrid with the smell of ozone, charred grass and stone still smoldering as Talia flew low over Eolowen, the grand hall undamaged by Holy Fire. And she was grateful for that bit of good news which was in short supply right now.

The eerie silence made her uneasy. Made the feathers ruffle across her wings. A cold chill quivered through her chest.

No songs carried along the breeze. No soft serene melodies lilted across Parrish blue skies that had turned a dirty grey now. Not a single note hung in the air to comfort them in this dark hour.

Azrael and three archangels flew beside her, the returning assault force still behind them, shocked silent at the devastation that Lucifer had wrought through Oseira using transference.

Before Lucifer escaped Hell and set the apocalypse into motion.

Like Talia's guard, the other archangels of death and their squads were ready to rescue any survivors and gather anything left of value within High House. And prepare to save what little they could of the Creation—now that Lucifer was free.

It was Earth's darkest hour.

Talia still felt terrible for poor Oseira. She hadn't asked for what happened to her. Had she known that she'd been carrying stores of Holy Fire into the Cloud Chamber? Ever since Samael's escape?

Oseira had been the closest angel to the blast. There would be no resurrecting her from the spire. So many other angels inside High House and the Cloud Chamber had met that same fate.

Tension and sorrow hung thick throughout the Heavens, the tinny resonance of the seven trumpets still sharp on the wind as Heaven prepared to send the first flight of angels.

To pour the first bowl of pain onto the Earth: Sickness.

And the billions of humans below had no idea what would soon befall them. And she felt powerless to stop it.

Especially with Lucifer's Hell princes about to walk the Earth and deliver seven payloads, one after each flight of angels touched the Earth.

Seven Travelers. About to unleash seven deadly anguishes on the Creation while Light and Dark battled for ultimate control of what remained. The Maker had not started this war with the Dark yet, but now, all of Heaven and Hell would be forced to fight it, with Lucifer leading the Dark in an assault that would dwarf his previous march on the Heavens.

Why hadn't the Maker intervened? Stopped Lucifer from unleashing the end of the world? Harming all of His Chosen in such a sudden and painful manner?

This time, Lucifer had a huge army, the entirety of dark forces at his command. And he had all his powers back. Heaven now knew that meant everything. Including those powers once given to the Maker's most powerful angel. Were they the powers of the Light Bringer? About to be used in Earth's darkest moment? Leading the darkest forces of vengeance and retribution—reserved only for the Maker?

With Heaven's forces scattered, destroyed, and in disarray, they had to regroup quickly while all of Heaven prepared for the seven flights. Talia's guard had to prepare for the sixth flight: the Enochian apocalypse. Where more angels would be lost than had fallen during the Rebellion. And somehow, with everything stacked against them, the angels had to defeat this overwhelming Dark and save the Creation at the same time.

It was an impossible task.

Where was the Maker? Why hadn't He contacted the lower reaches of Heaven? Sent them orders? Directed them?

Her anger spiked. Why did the lower Heavens have to flail in the stark cold of His silence when the end of the world was at hand?

For Heaven and the Creation? She didn't know anymore.

As she gaped at the destruction blanketing Heaven, she realized that all the upper-ranking angels had been aloft in High House. She winced. In the Cloud Chamber. Heaven's upper reaches must be in as much turmoil as they were down here. And probably protecting the soul portal and the Maker's Thrones.

Those were Lucifer's ultimate targets.

She bit her lip. Maybe the silence meant there was no one left to answer the calls for help?

And that terrified her.

Nevertheless, she sent up an urgent prayer, to send help and leadership downward. To help them fight through Armageddon when they hadn't even been trained to handle it yet.

Leaving the entirety of Heaven's death angel guard alone to flounder and fight an overwhelming force of evil would topple the lower Heavens.

And bring Lucifer to the edge of the Maker's Thrones.

Jack landed below her at Eolowen with Berith, but the rest of the assault force pressed onward to rescue angels and save what could be salvaged from the spires.

And learn how much of Lucifer's claims had been true.

Jack was distraught over Lucifer using him to escape Hell and start the apocalypse. And he was worried sick about what that meant for his world. Berith promised to watch over him until Talia returned.

But the Heaven that Talia knew had changed forever.

Tall, black thunderheads hung above once pristine, sparkling white buildings and the memory of tall, delicate spires, much of the grounds and the square coated in ash. Around the spire's rubble, once-white buildings and towers still burned, angels of death and Watchers struggling to smother roiling Holy Flames that required angel light to extinguish. Thick coils of black smoke merged with fleecy alabaster clouds floating above the smoldering crater that had once been the highest spire in Heaven—High House. And turned them grey and foreboding.

Heavy black clouds gathered all across Heaven, thunder and lightning filling the hefty, ominous silence. Accentuating the palpable absence.

Tears trickled from Talia's eyes and turned into crystals that rolled down her cheeks as she and Azrael circled the smoking crater where High House had been.

High House was gone, its spire reduced almost entirely to rubble, the Cloud Chamber a memory. She couldn't process it yet. And there had been no sighting of seraphim in the skies...or most of the cherubim once present in the spires. They were silent. Absent. Along with dozens and dozens of archangels, hundreds of angels, and hundreds of Watchers that had been in High House.

"Azrael," she said with a hiss, gripping his arm as she hovered above the blackened hollow below. "Where are the seraphim?" she asked in a broken voice. "And the cherubim?"

He shook his head, pain sharp in his charcoal grey eyes. "I don't know, Talia," he said in a quiet voice. "I don't feel their presence any longer. The Book of Creation was in the Cloud Chamber. I fear they were all destroyed in the blast."

Unlike Eolowen's terrace where she'd brought back several angels from oblivion, not even a glimmer of light reflected from the ash and destruction below. There was no way to bring these spire angels back, not even with her resurrect power. She felt miserable. Sick. As soon as casualties were healed, she and Berith would search for any traces of angel light, no matter how slight, and attempt to resurrect them.

Azrael sang a clear, aching requiem that floated above the smoke and ash and devastation. Somber tenor notes in a minor key that carried on the air currents across Heaven, delivering the horrible news about how Lucifer had used transference and poor Oseira to destroy the spire. Start the apocalypse.

As his dark Enochian melody drifted across Heaven, she heard the wave of grief met with whispers of retribution that quickly became a determined harmony beneath Azrael's dirge. An unstoppable rhythm that echoed across the Heavens.

Filling the horrible silence.

He also sent up a prayer to the Maker, asking for guidance and wisdom in this bleak time for Heaven and the Creation. And finally, in a commanding melody, he instructed all able angels to regroup at Eolowen, where the entirety of the death angel guard would assemble for further orders. If there were any cherubim or seraphim left.

But the silence that greeted them was painful. Alarming. The intense but comforting presence of the seraphim was strangely absent, the supporting harmonies of the cherubim extinguished. And still, not a sound from the Maker's Thrones.

Or the Maker.

Across from where the spire stood, the blackened Archive spire was badly damaged and teetering. Talia had no idea how it had remained standing so close to High House. The buildings and smaller spires surrounding High House had been obliterated, but somehow, the Archive survived.

"Death angels!" Azrael shouted. "We need to shore up the Archive spire before it topples. Get everyone out."

Daidrean and Laialus blinked toward the unsteady, soot-covered white spire, using their angelic powers alongside three squads of death angels. Rebenya took dozens of Watchers and flew inside the damaged spire to search for survivors. And lead them to safety.

Talia gripped Azrael's sleeve, her wings beating hard against the smoke and grit clogging the air currents, making flight difficult as thunder rolled across the Heavens in menacing waves.

"Do you want my squad at the Archive spire, too?"

He shook his head. "No, we may need your rare angel powers for survivors."

"Azrael, where is the Maker?" she cried. "If ever there was a time to address His angels in the lower Heavens, this is it. The apocalypse is in motion, all seven seals broken, and we know the Maker didn't set it into motion. High House is gone and the Archive is badly damaged—"

She gasped, thrusting her hand over her mouth. The Scribe! Pravuil had gone to High House to escort Oseira back there. Her eyes flooded with tears. Had he been in High House when the Holy Firebomb exploded?

"What's wrong, Talia?" Azrael asked as he took hold of her hands.

"The Scribe," she said in a thin, broken voice. "Azrael, he escorted Oseira back to High House when we left to rescue Berith."

The archangel's face turned pale and he let go of her hands, lifting another painful song across the lower Heavens. Begging Pravuil to check in with Eolowen. Or him.

Azrael called for the archangels and they blinked through the ranks to float in front of him. Sidriel looked shaken, her grey eyes glassy, long white hair blowing in the wind as she glanced at Turiel with his lion's mane of white hair, and then Ramiel who looked terrified, his gold eyes filling with tears, spiky white hair disheveled.

The archangels looked at a loss, confused as they looked to Azrael for guidance. They handled human deaths, not this.

Soon they'd have their hands full with the apocalypse. But this? Assuming command of the lower Heavens against the entirety of the Dark? Without the guidance of the seraphim and cherubim? They were lost.

But Azrael had stepped up—like he always did.

"There were so many Watchers in the spire, Azrael," Ramiel lamented, his voice filling with despair. "So many!"

The Heavens looked dim and foreboding, so much of its light extinguished by Lucifer's Holy Firebomb.

"What do we do now?" Turiel cried, glancing at the halted column of death angels fanning out across the dark skies. "With no seraphim and precious few cherubim, who will lead the coming war?"

Azrael held up his hands. "Everyone, regain your composure. I called for all survivors to regroup at Eolowen. As soon as we've assessed how many archangels, cherubim, and seraphim remain, we'll figure out our next course of action."

"Azrael," said Sidriel, her voice steadier, charcoal grey eyes bright against her ebony skin. "What happens with the flights of angels that must answer those trumpets? When each flight visits the Earth, one of the Seven Travelers will begin their terrible journey. And there aren't enough of us to stop them."

Talia's gaze returned to Azrael. The archangel of death looked focused, his charcoal gaze steely, silver black hair fluttering against the tops of his soot-grey wings. They were all looking to him for leadership and he was answering that call. None of them knew how to handle the breaking of the seals and the trumpet blasts, much less calling together the seven flights of angels. Or how they would engage Lucifer's forces in the skies above the Earth. But she knew that it would take Lucifer time to gather his Dark army.

The most immediate threats were the Seven Plagues and the Seven Travelers. Abaddon couldn't stop the Hell princes from leaving Hell, if he even knew who they were, and he couldn't keep those gates closed now that all seven seals had been broken. At least not to the Seven Travelers.

The only way to close those gates was to stop the Seven Travelers from delivering seven payloads to Earth and defeat Lucifer and his army. Unless the Maker intervened. They needed to talk to the Scribe—but she feared him lost now, along with so many other angels.

To save the Creation, they had to stop the Seven Travelers. To save Heaven, they had to defeat Lucifer's Dark army before the seventh flight of angels poured out its final bowl of destruction on Earth. The seventh flight was death for humanity.

The sixth flight was the Enochian apocalypse for angels. And it was the last point that they could save Jack and humanity.

Jack. Her heart fluttered against her chest. He may be the last source of seraphim power left in Heaven. Without seraphim, Heaven couldn't hope to defeat Lucifer's Dark army.

She looked upward, past the thunderheads and the smoke. Toward the upper Heavens, her heart heavy. Why hadn't the Maker responded? Sent His Throne angels through the portal to help His angels down here? Or at least give them some guidance.

Those questions haunted her.

Were all of them surrounding the portal as the last protection for the risen souls? Leaving everything below that portal as a sacrifice to save them? That thought terrified her.

"Thank you for your leadership, Azrael," said Sidriel as she turned toward the death angel forces surrounding them.

Azrael sang out an intense baritone melody.

"Everyone, search for survivors. Bring them to Eolowen where we have healers. We'll regroup there and assess what's left of our forces. Figure out how to stop the Seven Travelers and defeat Lucifer's Dark army."

Over four hundred angels of death and their accompanying Watchers dispersed over the smoking devastation to search for survivors.

"Sir," said Talia, "It's a good thing we took three guards of death angels and a massive complement of Watchers to assault the Gates of Hell."

Azrael frowned, glancing at her and then the other archangels. "Why do you say that, Talia?"

"Who knows how many we would have lost here—when Lucifer's Holy Firebomb ignited."

"That's a good point, Talia," said Sidriel with a nod toward the hundreds of angels of death that had descended through the smoke and ash toward the ruined spire and surrounding rubble that used to be buildings. "Thankfully, we still have an army left to answer Lucifer's forces now."

Azrael shook his head. "It's not enough, Sidriel. Lucifer has thousands and thousands of demons. Legions. Not to mention all the damned souls in Hell and the fallen angels at his side. A third of Heaven's angels fell with Lucifer and are still loyal to him."

"Regardless, it's a start," said Sidriel. "And it's better than what we might have had if we hadn't helped you rescue Berith."

A brief smile touched Azrael's dark expression.

"It is a start," said Azrael, charcoal grey eyes narrowing. "But we have to build a much bigger army to defeat Lucifer. "If he unleashes hordes of greater demons, we have to have cherubim to defeat them. And without seraphim support...I fear the outcome of this battle."

Talia patted his sleeve. "We still have Jack and his seraphim powers, sir."

A grin lit the archangel's face.

"Jack!" he cried. "His seraphim powers may be all that stands between us and Lucifer, Talia. I want a squad guarding him at all times. We can't lose those seraphim powers."

"Or Jack," Talia added.

Jack Casey meant everything to her. Besides, his seraphim powers were fragile. They had to protect him if they wanted access to those powers. He didn't have an unlimited reserve of Holy Fire like the seraphim, but he did carry their powers. She had seen him lay waste to half of Lucifer's previous army, take down Devourers, and match Lucifer blow for blow.

A pained expression pinched Azrael's face.

"Yes, of course, Talia," he said. "Forgive me. Jack isn't a weapon to use and discard. He's a human being and one of the Maker's cherished souls. But those seraphim powers of his might stop Lucifer in his tracks."

"He's a devastated human being right now, sir," she said with a sigh and motioned toward Eolowen. "He's blaming himself for starting the apocalypse and for letting Lucifer trick him into releasing that monster from Hell."

Azrael looked sad now.

"There is no way that Jack could have known. None of us knew. Now that Lucifer is free, Jack is in grave danger. I don't want either of you going anywhere without a squad at your back. Is that clear, Talia?"

She nodded. For Jack, she wouldn't argue that protection.

"And thank you for bringing Berith home to me," he said in a soft voice, his charcoal grey eyes turning glassy. "You and Jack gave her back to me and I'll always be grateful for that."

"You fought for Jack and me, sir," she said in a quiet tone. "Over and over. It was our turn to fight for you."

He blushed and cleared his throat as he returned his attention to the archangels.

"Sidriel, I want to know where Samael and his remaining guard are," the archangel ordered. "Ramiel, put your Watchers on Samael's trail and sing out if you locate them. I want to know if he's fighting beside Lucifer or sitting out of the fight." He turned toward Turiel. "Turiel, I want that Book of Secrets located. And all of you, be on the lookout for Pravuil, the Maker's Scribe. Everyone else, help locate survivors. Dismissed."

Sidriel and her guard blinked toward the ruins of the spire alongside Turiel and his guard. Ramiel and his Watchers moved toward the Archive.

"All right, Talia, send the guard down to the spire ruins and we'll start searching for any angel light still shining. Only after survivors have been found can we turn this into a resurrect search."

She nodded, the thought of that work grim. It meant looking for any splash or smear of light and then trying to resurrect the angel attached to it. But she'd examine every single stone remnant if it meant the chance of resurrecting a lost angel. If Jack had been lost out there, she'd turn over every stone and scour every bit of ash to bring him back.

"All right, guard," Talia sang out in crystalline soprano notes. "We're charged with searching the spire." She winced at the massive piles of once shiny white stones, shattered, blackened, and smoking across the crater below. "Look for survivors and remnants of light. Turn over every stone when it is removed. And don't forget the lower levels."

"Talia, have you seen how high the debris stands?" Muriel asked. "It may have filled up every part of those lower levels.

"If we have to dig out every single stone of that rubble, we'll clear it all. We have to know if anyone escaped into the lowest hollows of the spire." Talia pointed and blinked. "Break into your squads, tight formations, and let's move! Before the first flight of angels takes off for Earth."

Muriel, Anahera, Kesien, and Deemah gathered around her, wings nearly touching. Talia sang out a command to blink and together, they shot downward onto the blackened ground and crumbled white stones.

"How could any angel survive a blast of Holy Fire this massive?" Muriel lamented, brushing sable hair off her shoulder as she engulfed the stones in Holy light.

Talia summoned transference and lifted the first layer of stone out of the pit. She placed it on the ground beside the crater. Revealing more hard-packed stone and rubble. She winced. And handfuls of burnt wing feathers. They littered the stones.

Using resurrect, Talia searched the wing feathers and layers of stone for any flickers of light. Finding two.

Focusing on the light, Talia cast resurrect, cycling through blue light, red, yellow, green, and then frosty white until she brought back a Watcher. The young coppery-haired angel was overcome with emotion. She gripped Talia's hands, tears running down her face, and chirped a quick thanks before taking to the air to find the other Watchers.

"Azrael, I've brought back a survivor," Talia announced.

Ramiel blinked toward the terrified young Watcher and wrapped her in his wings, leading her away from the devastation.

"Thank you, Talia," said Ramiel.

Talia nodded and returned her concentration to the debris and the faint impression of light.

The other wisp of light was much more difficult. She fought shadows and uneven glimmers of light until a burst of gold light shot up from the crater and a cherubim stepped out of it. He was as tall as Kesien and had short, spiky white hair, gold hawk-like eyes, and a commanding presence. But his wings shuddered and he collapsed.

"Easy, cherub, you need healing," said Talia, lifting him out of the crater onto ash-covered grass.

"Thank you," he muttered. "I'm Cabriawn. My squad and I were just leaving the spire," he said in a tired voice as he rubbed his forehead, his halo beginning to pulse with gold light. "I was on flank, headed toward the main portal in the center of the spire when everything exploded and collapsed around me." His brow furrowed, gold eyes filling with sadness. "My squad. The spire...and all those angels." His eyes turned watery and his wings began to shake. "The seraphim..."

Talia sang a calming, healing melody and Cabriawn settled back into the grass, folding his wings protectively around his shoulders as he stared at the rubble and ruined buildings where the square used to be. His white robes were ashen and torn in several places, his white armor dented and covered in ash.

"We are still searching the debris for survivors," said Talia, motioning toward the crater. "I wish I had news about the seraphim, but it doesn't look hopeful."

"What happened in there?"

Cabriawn was a cherub. He might be one of the highest-ranking angels left in Heaven's lower reaches. He needed to know what happened.

"Lucifer used a rare angel power on a cherub."

Cabriawn's eyes widened and he sat up straight, staring at her, wings shifting nervously around his shoulders.

"What? Lucifer? On a cherub?"

Talia nodded. "Yes. He forced his will on the cherub and made her carry a massive cache of Holy Fire into the Cloud Chamber. Then he used the rare angel power of transference through a fallen angel to make her set it off."

Cabriawn gaped at her, his face shadowing with fear. "No...is—this true? He controlled a cherub? From Hell?"

"Unfortunately, yes, it's true." She bowed her head. "When Lucifer was ready, he sent Oseira into the Cloud Chamber to ignite the cache. It destroyed the spire almost completely."

"But why?" Cabriawn demanded. "Why?"

Talia pulled in a heavy breath. "To destroy the Book of Creation—and the first seal. Cabriawn, he set off the apocalypse."

For several moments, the cherub couldn't speak, couldn't react. He stared at her, unblinking, trying to process everything she'd told him, but it was all so overwhelming.

"But only the Maker can break the first seal!" His face was pinched, a mixture of dread and grief spreading across his long, angular face.

She had to tell him how it was possible, to make him understand the dire situation Heaven was facing right now.

"A while back, Lucifer engineered a Phoenix Shift and got his powers back. Everything, Cabriawn. Including his power as the Maker's most powerful angel. His left hand. The angel that the Maker had trusted to break the first seal in the event that He could not."

Cabriawn looked panicked now, his gaze flicking around him at the ruins and the devastation.

"This is the worst news you could have given me," said the cherub, glancing up at the dark sky as thunderheads rumbled across the Heavens. "We've even lost the quiet peace of blue skies and white clouds."

"There's more," she said and he stiffened. "The seven trumpets have blown and the Gates of Hell have opened. Lucifer is now free with all his powers and we're facing his overwhelming Dark army when the sixth flight of angels descends on the skies above Earth."

He looked ill now. "The Enochian apocalypse," he mumbled. "Much more than a third of Heaven's angels are foretold to fall in this battle of light and dark. Much more than during the Rebellion."

She nodded. What else could she tell him?

"And the Seven Travelers will soon set out from the Gates of Hell for Earth, each with a deadly payload to unleash on the Creation after each flight of angels. If they aren't stopped, they will destroy everything the Maker created. And Lucifer's Dark army will destroy the lower Heavens after Lucifer eliminated the seraphim and most of the cherubim here."

"What?" Cabriawn shouted. "All the seraphim? Are you certain?"

"We're combing the rubble for them or enough light to use resurrect on them," Talia explained above the shifting of heavy blackened stones and debris as angels of death lifted them out of the crater. "We're down to angels of death, Watchers, and a handful of archangels. As far as I know, you're the only cherub we've found so far —unless your squad is still on patrol."

Cabriawn hurriedly closed his eyes. "Let me search for their brands."

He was silent for several moments until a smile lit his face. "My squad—they're still out there! Patrolling the Gates of Heaven! They're safe."

There were five angels to a squad, so Heaven had five cherubim including Cabriawn left. That would make a big difference.

"What a relief!" Talia cried and relaxed her wings against her back. "They'll be needed in the fight with Lucifer, Cabriawn. Everyone's been instructed to regroup at Eolowen, so we'll know how many angels are left and we'll try to form an army without seraphim. A cherubim patrol will be invaluable."

He nodded and reached out to grip her hand a moment.

"Thank you, Talia," he said with a brief smile. "I'll join up with my squad and we will fly to Eolowen and start organizing a defensive force from the survivors."

"Be safe, Cabriawn," she said as he struggled to his feet and spread his wings.

"You, too," he replied and took to the air, soaring toward the Corridor of Pervasive Light.

When he disappeared behind a tall thunderhead, dark skies swallowing up his sparkling white wings, Talia blinked back into the crater and began poring over more stones and rubble for smears of light.

It seemed like forever before the guard had removed enough debris to locate the lowest chambers of the spire. Or more hard-packed rubble. In that lowest chamber, Archangel Raziel had used some dark power to chain the seraphim and cherubim down there with a Devourer of Angels. Where Jack had blocked Azrael and her squad with a ward, preventing them from entering the cavernous area while he fought the Devourer. Azrael and the squad had been furious at him, but Jack managed to defeat the Devourer and save the cherubim and seraphim in the process.

There was a slim chance that some angels had fallen from the spire and landed below, in the lower level blocked by enormous piles of debris. Only through transference could she clear all of this stone. If angels had to carry it out of here, it could take weeks. With transference, it might take hours.

Azrael was at her shoulder as Muriel and Kesien hovered above a small, spiraling hole that dropped deep into darkness.

"You think anyone's really down there?" Muriel asked, glancing up at Azrael.

"Let's find out," said Azrael.

He sang out a call into the opening as Deemah and Kesien removed more debris to widen the hole, but it was still only inches. Seeing darkness beneath those stones—and not more stone—gave her a little hope though.

They waited for a chorus, a song, or even a single note in response. One that would let them know that someone had survived Lucifer's Holy Firebomb.

But all that floated back was silence. Pure. Total.

Until an alto melody floated through the air, startling them. Survivors!

But then she realized that song had come from Eolowen. It was Berith.

Talia frowned as Azrael's expression darkened.

"She's saying that something's wrong with Jack," said Azrael.

Her heart began to race and for a moment she couldn't breathe.

"Is he hurt? Or sick?" Talia demanded, singing back her response.

It seemed like forever until Berith's warm and familiar alto notes hung in the wind again.

"Talia, he's…struggling," Berith intoned, the notes sounding urgent. "Please come back to Eolowen. I don't know how to help him. And Azrael, there are dozens and dozens of distraught angels here looking for leadership. Please come back, too."

Talia didn't know what Berith meant about Jack, but it frightened her. Besides, the redeemed angel of death wouldn't have called them back to Eolowen if the situation hadn't been urgent. Berith didn't panic. She'd spent enough time in Hell to know when something was dire and when the situation was just difficult. Especially with the seraphim in danger and critical rescue efforts underway.

Jack was the love of her life, but his seraphim powers were necessary to rescue angels. His pain made her chest ache.

She had to go back.

Talia turned to Azrael.

"Sir, it's Jack—I need to go to him."

"Of course, Talia," said Azrael. "But I want your squad beside you. Take them and return. I'll have Daidrean oversee the rest of the guard and focus their efforts here at High House. As soon as they're back removing rubble, I'll be right behind you. To direct the surviving angels and check on Jack. We need his help, too."

She nodded and called formation.

In moments, Muriel and Anahera blinked beside her. Kesien and Deemah were at her back in another moment.

"Talia, what's wrong with Jack?" Muriel asked.

She shook her head. "Berith didn't say. Just that I needed to return to Eolowen. With Azrael."

"Hope the kid's okay," said Kesien as he brushed a tangle of black curls out of his eyes. "He went through a lot at Lucifer's hands this time."

Talia was afraid that Lucifer had done something else horrible to Jack down in Hell and they were just now discovering it. Like a soul tether or something worse than marking him for every Hell creature to locate across Heaven and Earth. Maybe he'd been injured in the confrontation with Lucifer and had just told someone? She winced. Or collapsed.

Either way, she had to get back to her husband. Fast.

2

Jack was devastated.

The memory of Lucifer's escape burned through his exhausted brain. But even worse was the realization that it was all his fault. Had the start of the apocalypse also been his fault?

He didn't know anymore.

After flinging his Eternean armor across the small white bed in the round room, he paced back and forth. He trudged onto Eolowen's terrace, hands shoved in his Levi's pockets, short grey robe fluttering over top of his green Henley. His Eternean sabatons clacked against the stones as he dodged the growing number of angels flocking to Eolowen.

Avoiding Berith.

Everything was in chaos.

Heaven burned, the spires destroyed, and Holy Fire still alight across rooftops and in the trees surrounding buildings and gathering places. The smell of smoke was husky, pungent, and had an ozone stink that clung to everything. The skies were stormy and dark, thick with smoke as thunder cascaded across the Heavens in a dire warning. Lightning flashed.

He'd never seen storm clouds over Heaven before today. Except at Heaven's forge.

The dozens and dozens of ruined, smoldering buildings on the horizon made him shiver. The tallest spire was just...gone. And all those angels.

He winced. The thought was terrifying. The Archive spire was the only one left standing and it was tilted, wobbling. Everyone at Eolowen feared it would soon topple, too.

And he couldn't help but feel responsible.

"Jack," said Berith, landing in his path as he headed back into the round room for another lap.

Her dove grey wings folded against her shoulders, her rose-gold halo surreal in the growing darkness across Heaven.

"Talk to me, Jack. I can feel how troubled you are. This wasn't your fault."

What could he say? Of course, it was his fault.

Lucifer was loose because of him. About to lay waste to the planet. His world. He'd caused all of it, but he couldn't stop it. And Lucifer would kill millions. Dude hated humans, blamed them for everything bad that had ever happened to that douchebag—especially Jack.

He shook his head, stepping around her, and then dodged flocks of angels landing all around him on the terrace.

The second most powerful being in the universe, blaming powerless humans for his first-realm celestial problems. And the moment Jack stepped out of Heaven, Lucifer would destroy him. Slowly. Painfully.

Everything was upside and inside out now. And he couldn't fix it. Any of it.

He slowed his pacing to a crawl, suddenly feeling out of breath and suffocated by the smoke blanketing Heaven like fog. But that didn't help. His arms and legs barely responded now. Stiff and aching, he turned away from Berith and staggered into the round room.

He needed to sit down. Or fall down.

The Heavens swayed in front of him, growing darker and more confined, and he struggled to inhale. His mind began racing. Racing with numbers. Filling with every melody and every lyric ever written. Bursting with data and images like his omnificence power was stuck in fifth gear. Like every sound ever uttered or generated had piled into his head, like the Number Four bus out of Santa Monica.

He clutched his head, his heart pounding as angels flew in and out of the round room, blinking onto the terrace and inside Eolowen where Zephana and her forge angels still congregated in the nave, outfitting angels with better armor.

The round room quickly filled with casualties from Lucifer's Holy Firebomb, spilling into Eolowen's long nave and all the other rooms inside the grand hall.

"Where are the healers?" Jack called out. "And the cherubim!"

Berith and Talia had healing talents and so did angels of death, but the cherubim had been Heaven's main source of healers. Until they got blasted into angel confetti alongside the seraphim in High House.

Would angels die because there were no healers?

He felt like a *Monday Night Football* announcer, reading from cards he didn't write about a game he'd never watched. Kind of like the first couple of episodes of *The Divine Newlyweds Show*. Saying things he hadn't even thought about or asking questions that didn't concern him.

What was the matter with him? He was just a spectator for this game.

God, he felt so responsible for all of this death and destruction! What did Talia think of him right now? He'd been more like that out-of-control dick he'd been that first season of *The Cinderella Hour*, battling addiction, his own ego, and that last step toward oblivion. He probably didn't seem anything like the dude she'd married right now. Lucifer's fallen angel puppet. Procel made sure that he was paranoid, out of his mind, and craving flake.

So, what was the matter with him now? Now that Procel was way too far away to use transference on him. He sighed. Like Oseira? Damn. Dude could probably still reach him here, too.

Talia was probably sorry she married him now. Probably wanted nothing to do with him anymore. Somehow, he had to prove to her that he was worth marrying. That loving her had been the best part of his life and he never wanted to lose her. But now that Lucifer's bachelor party was in full swing and headed for Earth to destroy it, one Hell prince at a time on Hell's worst pub crawl ever, Jack feared that he'd die and be forever separated from her. Since Lucifer was on his own deadly pub crawl—destroying everything in his path.

"Jack, you aren't listening to a word I've said!" Berith shouted from somewhere behind him.

"You asked if I needed healing," he said, not turning around as angels rushed past him at all angles. "But I'm good. There are tons of injured angels that need healing right now. Not me."

Watchers. Angels of Death. Archangels. All of them surged past, blinked in front of him, and shot through the rooftop portals. Azrael had called out to all of the lower reaches of Heaven, telling every angel that had survived the blast to regroup at Eolowen. But cherubim and seraphim voices were terrifyingly absent from the wild angel chatter coming across the air currents.

It was like a multi-layered choral performance. Beautiful, but he had no idea what they were saying. At least not right away. It was like the meaning began to slowly seep into his head along with all those angel songs and notes. That he'd never heard until now. He didn't understand the notes, but they were beginning to create strange meanings inside his throbbing mind.

Wait a minute. How was that even possible? He didn't speak angel notes.

Things were coming at him at light speed. From every direction. Blindsiding him sometimes and other times, it seeped into his head like a slow-moving rain.

He frowned and kept pacing, his wings flexing and twitching at his shoulders as he made another lap around the round room despite the chaos of angels writhing through the space.

Wait, how did he know all that? Had Berith told him?

But Jack hadn't even heard her ask if he needed healing. Much less Azrael's songs resonating across the Heavens.

"Jack, you're hurt," Berith replied, stating a fact. "Now, please, let me treat you."

"Berith, there are tons of other angels that require healing," he replied. "Treat them. I'm good."

"Jack Casey, don't you walk off! You're in shock and you need healing. Now, sit down on the bed and let me heal you."

His chest felt like a ton of stone sat on it, making him struggle for breath. The white stone walls were closing in on him, heat and darkness suffocating. He drew in a hot breath of air and it hurt his lungs. He gripped his chest, trying to breathe, but the ethery ozone stench of Holy Fire burned up the oxygen.

What was happening to him?

He sucked in another breath of air. That breath hurt, his lungs fighting to try and expand.

Was this Lucifer's doing? Was that douchebag using transference to transfer all of these horrible sensations onto him until they killed him? No, Lucifer was down on Earth. And Lucifer seemed to have other things on the agenda before killing him. Besides, if it was Lucifer, he'd have popped into Eolowen to gloat or at least call Jack's phone to revel in his attacks.

No, this felt different somehow. Strange. Like he'd picked up someone else's memories or his omnificence was out of control.

Kind of like how he felt right now.

An explosion hammered his head and he froze, arms splayed, trying to sort out the noise and the direction, and brace for the pain.

Like a massive steamroller, an explosion rolled over the spire. Buildings exploded like popcorn around it. Stone crumbled. Falling... falling into darkness!

Bright white fire detonated, shaking Heaven as it burned like a fuse through the cloying darkness.

He couldn't move.

He dropped to his knees when a massive white light blinded him in a blast that made Hiroshima look like a 25-watt lightbulb.

"My eyes!" he said with a gasp.

"Jack?" Berith called out.

He felt her arms around his shoulders, holding him up.

"Jack, talk to me! What's happening?"

He gulped air, smashing his hands against his eyes as they burned and watered, the tremendous roar of the spire toppling all around him. Stones smashing stones. Scattering dust, ash, and angel light. The thick cover of smoke choked off the Heavens. White-hot columns of fire shot upward in massive jets of flame, burning the sky, and setting the clouds on fire.

But his skin felt like jet fuel burned across it, scalding, and flaming with fire that wouldn't go out, fire that ignited from Heaven's Holy flames and burned through everything. Rock, buildings, trees—and High House. But even worse than his skin flaming with jet fuel, his head was inundated with music. An explosion of melodies, major keys, minor keys—and choruses like the whole of Heaven had screamed in agony at the same time and begged for help. For mercy.

For the Maker.

"Make it stop!" he said with a gasp, his eyes clamped closed.

He clapped his hands against his ears. It was the worst concert he'd ever unwillingly attended. Like opera, country, and death metal made an album together and then a high school choir sang along to it at a karaoke bar. But worse than that.

And still, the music rose around him in endless layers. From every angel that passed over Eolowen. Every angel on the terrace and in the rolling meadow outside.

"Make what stop?" Berith asked, her clear alto voice steady despite the fear rising in her tone.

Oh, God, not more angel notes!

"Jack, you're scaring me. What's happening?"

"I—I don't know, Berith," he said with a groan. "The sound and the noise…it's everywhere. It's stabbing my brain with thousands of needles. And bad music." He brushed his hands frantically down his arms. "And I can't get the Holy Fire off my skin…it's burning, it's burning!"

"What Holy Fire?" Berith asked. "Jack, there isn't any Holy Fire. What are you talking about?"

"Jack!"

Talia's soft soprano voice rang through the room, fearful and frantic, joining the thousands of songs, harmonies, melodies, and discords tearing apart his brain. But he was so glad to hear the comfort of her voice.

He couldn't open his eyes past slits. They stung and ached, flooding with tears if he opened them any wider.

In a whisper of wings, Talia was in front of him, her hands cool against his face, fingers stroking his hair.

Through the watery haze in his eyes, her luminous grey gaze, wide and fearful, encompassed him. Her raven black curls were soft and windblown from blinking across the Heavens to Eolowen, her winter-pale skin like moonlight. She just took his breath away.

"You're the most beautiful thing I've ever seen, Talia," he said in a hushed voice, wanting to stroke her soft skin and kiss the rose-petal blush of her full lips.

But the music wrapped around him in tightening layers again. Thousands of threads of melodies and trills and chords that became a crushing sonnet overwhelming his head.

With everything that had happened during *The Divine Newlyweds Show* and with Lucifer, he felt like he'd been away from her for months. He just wanted to hold her in his arms and watch the sunset or sleep curled against her in his old, creaky Murphy bed. Or hell, wrap her in his arms and watch Wildebeest migrate on that studio trailer sofa in Burbank. It was mid-July. They'd only been married since May. And in less than a month, he'd turn twenty-seven. He wanted time alone with the love of his life for his birthday.

If they lived through the apocalypse.

Talia's voice joined the chorus of music until it all became a screeching roar. For what felt like forever, it was all he could hear, but then Talia's soprano voice cut through the well of noise.

"Jack, please—tell me what's happening?" she said, her voice sharp now.

She was scared and she didn't understand what was happening to him any more than he did.

He shook his head. "Don't. Know."

Berith's clear alto voice joined Talia's.

"Jack, I've applied so much healing light to you that you're glowing gold, but it doesn't seem to help."

"Here, let me try," said Talia, her voice quivering as he felt her cool fingers against his fever-hot skin.

"Azrael, I thought he was blaming himself for what happened in Hell," said Berith. "Thought he needed some support, but it's more than that. I don't know what's happening."

He was blaming himself. Because it was his fault.

"Jack," Talia said in her calm, patient angel of death voice as warm healing light washed over his flushed face. "Tell me what you're feeling right now. What are your symptoms, lover?"

He was struggling to breathe, the air burning hot, scalding his lungs with every painful breath.

"Hurts to breathe," he said in a tight whisper. "Too much ash and smoke. Holy Fire's burning my skin, my eyes. And it's so dark, walls are crushing me."

"He sounds delirious," said Azrael in that commanding archangel tone.

Berith's hand pressed against his forehead and he winced. His skin hurt all over.

"He doesn't have a fever, Azrael."

Talia stroked his hair and he wanted to lose himself in her touch, forcing the pain into the background as he tried to push it all backward, tamp it down, and climb out. But he was drowning in it.

"Jack, where do you hurt?" Talia asked him in a soft voice.

"My skin's on fire," he moaned, still trying to brush away the Holy Fire clinging to him. "Eyes are burning. Ears hurt—from all the music. Walls are closing in…lungs are on fire."

"Azrael, it makes no sense," said Talia, glancing at the archangel. "Jack, I'm going to use transference to see if Procel is connected to you. I'm sorry, lover—this may hurt."

He nodded and pulled in a breath that ached all the way down.

"Let's get him onto the bed," said Azrael. "Kesien, some help here."

"On it, sir," said Kesien, his baritone voice soft and calm.

Jack cried out when they lifted him off the stones, wheezing, and trying to catch his breath, but the soft bed beneath him eased some of the ache.

"What's wrong with the kid?" Kesien asked.

"Not sure yet, Kesien," said Berith.

"Okay, he didn't respond to my calling him kid," said Kesien, frowning. "At all. This is bad."

He shook his head. He didn't have the breath to respond.

Talia's hands pressed against his forearm and cheek and he braced himself for that horrific pain he'd felt when she'd pulled out Procel's meat hooks once before. He'd blacked out it was so bad.

"Good news, Talia," said Azrael somewhere off to Jack's right. "Cabriawn and the guard rescued another cherub from the spire wreckage–after Berith brought her back with resurrect. "Janaelis. They're working on trying to heal her now."

"Sir, any news on God's Scribe?" Talia asked.

A pall hung over Eolowen.

"As far as we know," said Azrael in a pained voice, "Pravuil was still in the spire when the Holy Fire explosion hit."

"Poor Pravuil," Talia said, her voice breaking. "I'll miss him so much."

Jack felt sick, his heart hurting. He'd loved that cranky old Scribe. Dude was the best. Told it straight and went out of his way to help. Helped him and Talia when it really mattered. Dammit!

And the roar of songs and refrains wrapped around his brain again. In a cacophony of noise that made his head want to explode. Why couldn't he make it stop? Why?

"I can't find a single connection from transference, Jack," said Talia, hands caressing his face and hair. "Berith, can you help me heal him?"

"Of course, Talia," said Berith, and Jack felt her hands press against his shoulders. "But it wasn't helping him when I tried before."

"And I have no one to consult," said Talia, sounding rattled now.

"Someone that can help him. I need a cherub healer, Azrael! Someone from the Archive that can help. Hold on, Jack—please."

He felt her sit down on the bed and wrap him in her arms.

"There isn't a mark on him, Azrael," said Berith as her warm gold healing light engulfed him again. "No sign of fever or illness or injury. I confess…I'm stumped."

After a few minutes of warmth, Berith's healing light went dark.

His breath heaved again, each one smokier and hotter than the last until he was gulping air.

"What about a human doctor?"

Muriel's voice joined the chorus in the round room, barely audible above the droning wave of music threatening to swamp Jack's brain.

"Wouldn't help," said Berith. "My rare healing gift is the strongest in Heaven at the moment and I can't heal him."

"Maybe this isn't something you heal?" Kesien offered.

Azrael's brow furrowed and he exchanged an uncertain glance with Talia.

"Explain, Kesien."

"Maybe Jack isn't ill," he said and motioned toward the rooftop. "Maybe his newly awakened transference power is acting on the devastation around him?"

"You mean like experiencing what happened in Heaven?" Muriel asked.

"That's an interesting theory, Kesien," said Talia. "It does seem like he's mirroring the trauma, doesn't it?"

"Could his mirrored powers allow him to experience everything you witnessed at the spire, Talia?" Berith asked. "Caused by this new transference power?"

"It's possible," said Talia, the fear in her voice receding. "But now that I'm back in Eolowen, shouldn't everything I saw already be fading?"

A surge of Holy Fire shot through the core of Jack's being.

He screamed, arching his body against the blast that seemed to go on and on and on.

"Jack!" Talia cried. "Jack, tell me you're all right…Jack!"

He rode out the wave of heat and pain until, finally, the agony receded.

"By the Maker!" Berith cried, shuffling back from the bed.

Talia froze, staring at him, her mouth gaping, eyes filled with terror. Kesien and Muriel looked horrified.

His skin burned, eyes aching from the bright aura of blue light that had engulfed the round room. He opened his eyes a little wider than slits but immediately wished he hadn't. His arms glowed with strange blue symbols that covered his hands and fingers. They were all over his skin. Like some sort of angel pox. Craziest tattoos he'd ever seen.

"What the devil?" Azrael cried, reaching out toward Jack's neck.

"It's Enochian," Talia said with a gasp. "All of them are Enochian letters."

Gently, Talia brushed her fingers across his right hand. The symbols burned with blue light, pulsing as some ciphers darkened and others grew brighter.

"Every time the light pulses," said Talia, "The symbols make a new word. Like something's trying to make a sentence."

"Read it, Talia," Muriel cried. "What's it say?"

Talia watched the flash and pulse of symbols. Jack couldn't see them all and even if he could, he had no idea what they even meant. Just like the notes that Talia and the guard sang.

Wait a minute! The notes.

Was that the music he was hearing? Overloading his brain with melodies, but they weren't melodies. They were voices. Messages that he couldn't understand. But somehow, they were speaking through him. Trying desperately to communicate.

"They're…trying to communicate with me," Jack said in a shaky voice.

"Pretty direct with these symbols," said Kesien, hovering beside Talia and Berith.

Jack shook his head. "No, the music." He groaned. "Inside my head."

"The symbols say…trapped below spire. Suffocating. Holy Fire still burns. Walls are crumbling. Save us."

"Jack!" Azrael cried, kneeling beside Talia. "What music?"

"In my head," he said with a moan. "Can't shut off the tunes."

Talia's eyes widened. "Sir, the music—the Enochian tongue! Jack calls them angel notes. Whoever's trapped below the spire has been calling out to Jack. Through Jack."

Jack pointed at the neon blue symbols covering his arms. "Whoever it was got tired of phoning me and decided to text me. Or rent a billboard. Tattoo it on my forehead."

Azrael was grinning now. "That's right, Jack. And seraphim are the only angels I know that can do…this. And last time they had to send a message, they sent it through Jack."

Azrael lifted his voice toward the rooftop and sang out a long string of tenor notes, quickly joined by Talia's soprano harmony. Together, their haunting melody lilted across Heaven.

In moments, Jack felt the music and the Holy Fire and the burning air dissipate. He pulled in a deep cool breath and sank back against the bed's softness as the glowing blue symbols faded from his skin.

"Is that better, Jack?" Talia asked, stroking his hair again.

He nodded. "Much better, babe," he said with a jarring sigh. "Much, much better."

She smiled and then leaned down and gently kissed him.

"It was Seraphina, Jack. Her song was lost among the overwhelming number of voices calling out for help across Heaven. So, she sent her message through you. There are a handful of angels trapped below the spire. It's going to take a lot of effort to free them."

"Muriel," Azrael called out. "You and Kesien assemble the squads while I confer with Berith, Sidriel, and Turiel. Anahera! Find Ramiel. There's a lot of rubble between us and the bottom of the spire. It will take a heavenly effort to remove it and reach those survivors."

"Right away, sir," said Muriel.

Muriel and Kesien blinked up to the rooftop and onto the terrace.

"Berith," Azrael said as he cupped her face with his hand. "My beautiful, loving Berith, I never thought you'd be at my side again."

She smiled and slid her arms around him, pressing a kiss against his mouth.

"Thanks to you, Talia, and Jack—and the guard—I'm home again. And I hope to stay by your side for eternity."

He leaned down and kissed her. "We'll need your healing talents at the spire."

"Gladly, Azrael," she said. "Let's go talk to Sidriel, Ramiel, and Turiel and get started removing the remaining rubble."

Azrael glanced over at Jack. "Jack, as soon as you've shaken off the effects of Seraphina's message, we'll need you onsite, too. In case she needs to communicate through you."

"I'd really prefer a text message—on my phone," Jack replied.

Azrael smiled. "I'll tell her. But we may need your seraphim powers to cut through all of that hard-packed debris."

He nodded, relieved that the awful pain and heat and claustrophobic spaces had receded. But he wished his guilt had fled along with it.

"Give me fifteen minutes, Azrael," said Jack. "And I'll be ready to fly."

Azrael blinked up through a portal onto the rooftop and sailed over the terrace. Berith patted Jack's leg.

"Your color is starting to return, Jack," she said with a motherly smile.

"Blue isn't my color," he said.

"Rest until we're ready to fly to the spire," Berith said, chuckling.

"Yes, Mother," he said with a smile. "I mean that."

Berith grinned. "You're sweet. And thank you both for bringing me home again."

Jack gave her a quick nod. "I couldn't let that douchebag hurt you, Berith. Or keep you trapped back in Hell." His gaze fell from her face. "Even though it's my fault he escaped."

Berith gave Talia a concerned look. "Talia, explain to him that isn't true."

"I will. Thanks, Berith—and welcome home."

Unfurling her wings, Berith rose on the warm air currents and flew onto the roof. She lifted into the dark, smoky sky and flew toward the meadow.

"Talia," said Jack in a pained voice. "How do I fix this?"

She ran her fingers through his bangs. "Fix what, lover?"

"I let Lucifer escape," he said. "Did I cause the apocalypse, too?"

He groaned. Couldn't wait for the paparazzi to get hold of that headline. Much worse than the key bump photo they'd taken of him in his set trailer.

Talia's arms tightened around him.

"First of all, you didn't let Lucifer escape. You had no control over what happened, Jack. And second, no. You didn't cause the apocalypse. As soon as we rescue Seraphina from the spire ruins, we'll all gather here at Eolowen and plan our response to what Lucifer's started."

He looked up at her again.

"How do we fight a dude that's the second deadliest being in the universe? And his massive army?"

"With everything we've got, Jack," she replied without even an eye blink. "The army of Light must face the army of Dark in the skies above the Earth and defeat the Dark before the seventh flight of angels touches your world. And the Seven Travelers can't be allowed to deliver their payloads upon the Earth either."

Army of light facing the army of dark? That made his heart hammer against his rib cage.

Talia was a soldier of the light. Heaven would demand that she fight in that war. He couldn't stand it if Azrael called her away from him to fight Lucifer and he couldn't fight at her side. And protect her. She was a seasoned soldier, an angel of death who'd spent centuries fighting darkness. He was a twenty-six-year-old actor—with wings, halo, and seraphim powers. This war was way out of his league. But he'd go out of his mind worrying about her. And then there were the Hell princes. Seven Travelers with seven payloads. That had to be stopped…somehow.

Then he knew. He'd have to stop the Hell princes while Talia fought Lucifer's forces. And his heart hurt worse than it had the day that Heaven called Talia home to fight again.

"This is a war where I can't stand beside you this time," he said, his voice breaking. "Isn't it?"

She sucked in a pained breath, her eyes turning glassy.

"Yes, Jack," she said finally. "It will be too dangerous for even a human with seraphim powers."

"I'm gonna be sick," Jack muttered.

Her arms tightened around him, pulling him closer. He slid his arms around her and buried his face against her raven-black hair that smelled of rose petals and cool rain. This time, she had to battle Lucifer and his army without him.

And there was nothing he could do to change that.

"I can't stand the thought of being apart from you, Jack," she said, tears threading down her cheeks and turning to crystals. "Especially with everything at stake."

He pulled in a pained breath, slipping on his game face. For her, he had to suck it up and hold it all inside.

"I'll be fighting Hell princes," he said. "Gotta stop them from dropping their payloads. Gonna have to throw my own party with Gianni, Banks, and probably even Rachel. That's gonna suck."

But her reaction made him stop talking. She looked sad and worried.

"I should be at your side, battling the Hell princes, too," she said. "But it will take every angel left in Heaven to stand against Lucifer's Dark army."

He lifted her chin and gave her an urgent kiss.

"And the moment we're done with those Hell princes, I will find you, Talia and I will fight at your side against that douchebag Lucifer and his demons—no matter the odds. I'm sure you dudes can still use my seraphim powers."

She nodded, the tears continuing to cascade down her cheeks. She pressed her face against his hair and he felt her trembling.

"Let's rest for now, Mrs. Casey," he said. "And then we'll rescue Seraphina and plan the worst Welcome Home party that Lucifer's ever attended."

He felt her smile. "Can I bring the murder marbles this time?"

He laughed. "Mrs. Casey, we'll bring enough murder marbles for everyone, this time. It'll be the highlight of the evening."

She huddled against him and he closed his eyes, hoping to slough off the effects of Seraphina's message before they set off to rescue her. Maybe they'd get lucky and find all the seraphim alive? And maybe a bunch of cherubim, too?

Because right now, the bulk of Heaven's army was the death angel guards and a handful of cherubim. And one seraph. Would that be enough to defeat Lucifer's massive demon army? Combined with all of those fallen angels and damned souls?

If the Maker decided to sit this one out, they'd need a miracle to succeed.

3

Seraphina's rather direct messages through him. The seraph had to be badly injured if she chose to send a message that way through Jack. Would Seraphina be in any kind of shape to fight Lucifer? Lucifer was probably counting on that Holy Fire blast destroying all three seraphim. If Seraphina was too injured to fight, would Jack have to carry the seraphim powers into the battle for light and dark?

A battle that might get him killed?

But he couldn't be in two places at once, battling Hell princes on Earth and Lucifer's Dark army up here. Not even with omnificence. He was probably safer down on Earth trying to stop the Hell princes...and as far away from Lucifer as she could get him.

Unfortunately, that decision was out of her hands. It would wrest with Seraphina as the highest-ranking angel in Heaven. Not even Azrael could make that decision.

Right now, they had to concentrate on rescuing the seraph from below the spire. Once Azrael and the cherubim had conferred with her, they would have a plan of action.

Regardless, Talia needed input from the Archive. Why had Pravuil escorted Oseira back to High House?

She yearned for his counsel right now.

Jack seemed to have made a full recovery from Seraphina's messages. He sat up, stretched his legs, and then his silvery grey wings. She chuckled at his faded Levi's still tucked into his Eternean sabatons, his short grey robe over one of his favorite shirts, a forest green Henley.

Angels rushed in and out of the room, swooping through portals and blinking past the bed onto the terrace as thunder rumbled again. The white curtains surrounding the portal that led onto the terrace whipped back and forth as the wind swept across Eolowen like a dark portent.

Jack didn't seem bothered by the wind. He glanced around the room, his sleepy, pale green eyes smoldering against the bright white-gold light of his halo. His eyes looked so sexy against his tousled, light blond hair, his hot caramel voice singeing her ear as he whispered that he was ready to travel. The buttery cedar scent of his skin made her want to curl up with him right here in Eolowen until the apocalypse had passed.

"Love you, Tal," he said and extended his wings, lifting off the bed and landing beside the fluttering white curtains. "We headed to the pep rally on the terrace or the spire for a remake of Towering Inferno? Or Die Hard?"

Talia spread her wings and flew over beside him. "Pep rally," she said and leaned close enough to smell that touch of warm cedar cologne he wore. Tom Ford, he called it. "So Muriel can tell me which human movie is more painful."

He laughed and lifted her into his arms as he flew through a portal to the rooftop.

"Gonna go with Towering Inferno," he said as the smoky air settled around them. "Because Holy Fire's a bitch to put out. And who's tougher than Paul Newman, Steve McQueen, Fay Dunaway, and William Holden?"

Talia shook her head. "I'll take your word for it."

She had no idea who these actors were, but her actor-husband did. She wasn't sure if she'd have access to any Books of Life and Death from the Archive right now. Angels of death were already struggling to cross over humans right now, in the wake of all this destruction. She'd have to see if she could still access the Books and then consult with Azrael. After they'd rescued the angels from the spire's lower chamber.

"I'd call it an even match if Alan Rickman had been on the same side as Bruce Willis and Bonnie Bedelia," said Jack as he carried Talia in his arms to the terrace. "So, still going with Towering Inferno."

She didn't want to let go of him, but she had to in the face of everything that required attention in Heaven.

"All right, angels," said Azrael from the dais when he saw her and Jack land. "Some good news."

Kesien, Muriel, Deemah, and Anahera quickly surrounded them in tight formation, making Jack the vanguard. They all had standing orders to protect the love of her life at all costs. And his seraphim powers.

A tangle of melodies and harmonies danced along the terrace in the strange, surreal twilight caused by Lucifer's Holy Firebomb. She glanced at Jack who had his hands on her waist. She felt the heat of his fingers through her grey robes and wanted to get him down to his boxer briefs and make love to him, but again, their relationship had to wait. She slid backward until she felt his tall six-foot frame against her back. His arms slid around her and he held her close, pressing his cheek against hers.

"Do you hear that, Jack?" Talia asked, motioning at the white stone terrace, Eolowen looking so dark against the storm clouds. "All the angel responses?"

He shook his head, the wind raking through his light blond hair.

"Not a single note. Thankfully."

Seraphina had completely retreated from communicating through him and Talia was grateful. But she worried about the state the seraph might be in right now. They needed to hurry.

"The seraph, Seraphina," Azrael began, "has been communicating through Jack Casey and has conveyed to him that she is trapped beneath the spire debris. She's still alive."

Cheers rose from the guard, including Jack, his more like a whoop than a cheer. It made her and her squad smile.

"But she sounds hurt, so I need every angel that can lift those stones to return with us to the spire and help dig out the seraph. There are also a handful of other angels trapped below with her, so we need to be quick and open the way out for them."

The buzz of Enochian speech was a rumble across the terrace now, excited voices. Hopeful words.

"All right, break into your squads, death angels. Watchers, fall into formation behind Ramiel. Cabriawn is the ranking officer among us. The rest of his cherubim squad is on patrol which is vital right now. It's our only cherubim patrol that survived the Holy Firebomb. Cabriawn, could I ask that you remain at Eolowen to look after the cherub we rescued from the spire and defend the injured?"

Cabriawn stretched his wings and then folded them tightly against his shoulders. He was as tall as Kesien, but his hair was long and as white as snow, his white cherubim robes in tatters, but Archangel Zephana had already outfitted him with cherubim armor. A silver and gold breastplate imprinted with Enochian symbols of strength and courage. He carried a gold sword on his hip and looked formidable despite being brought back from oblivion only a short time ago.

"It would be my honor, Azrael," he said with a nod. "Since I've just returned from oblivion myself, I think it wise to remain here until I'm certain I'm fit enough for the task. And to lead. But I can heal others while I rest."

Azrael nodded toward Berith. "Berith has a rare healing gift and will work alongside you, Cabriawn."

Berith's rose-gold halo brightened as she nodded at the tall cherub, his gold eyes soft against the twilight.

"Thank you, Berith," he said and bowed. "I hope to learn from your healing expertise."

Berith smiled. "I hope to learn from yours, too, Cabriawn. Thank you."

"In squad formation, angels," Azrael replied and lifted into the air. "It's time to rescue more celestials."

Hundreds of angels gathered into their squads and rose to follow him, wings spread wide, halos burning against the dusky sky.

"Blink on my mark," said Azrael.

Talia turned to Jack.

"I'm holding onto you, Jack," she said. "And I'll blink us to the spire. If I let you do it, there's no telling where we might end up."

He winked at her, that sexy smirk curling the corners of his lips.

"Even if it's the Murphy bed at my place?"

"Unfortunately," she said with a sigh. "Yes."

"All right," he said with a shrug. "I guess we'll go rescue the seraph then."

She slid backward to unfurl her wings and then put her arms around his waist.

"Supremes formation, squad," she said as she and the squad lifted into the air, Jack still in her arms. "Blink on Azrael's mark.

Azrael lifted his right arm into the air. "And...blink!"

The six of them shot across the dark sky along with at least two guards of death angels as thunder shook the Heavens. It was hard for Talia to get her bearings with the spires down, but she used the faint outline of the Archive spire as her guide and blinked across Heaven. Toward the blackened rubble and the crater where the square had been.

She, Jack, and the squad landed at the edge of the crater and quickly joined groups of angels using their Holy light to remove debris. They formed lines to move the broken stones away from the huge depression, lifting the stones with their golden angel light, but it took a long time to shift the loads up and out of the huge crater.

Azrael, Sidriel, Turiel, and Ramiel were in the center, working tirelessly to excavate the unending, hard-packed wreckage. No matter how much debris they lifted out as a chorus of angels, that small hole spiraling down into the darkness remained. Giving them hope that they would soon reach Seraphina.

Jack helped alongside her squad, but he seemed frustrated by their slow progress. Finally, he left her side and approached Azrael.

"Angels, hold your positions," said Azrael, holding up his hand.

"Jack wants to try and use his seraphim powers on this debris. Finish moving whatever rubble you're already lifting and then halt debris removal."

Jack stood motionless, silver-grey wings folded against his back, and watched the last blackened stones land on the edge of the deep crater. When quiet descended and motion ceased, he held out his arms and closed his eyes, calling up his seraphim energies.

The crater began to shudder as sweat beaded across his forehead.

He bent his right knee, arms dipping low like he was scooping out a huge load of wreckage. It didn't seem like an easy task for him. He gritted his teeth as a deep swath of rubble began to glow white within the crater. His body trembled as he lifted his arms over his head.

The stones and other debris resisted at first, but he fought harder until it all broke loose in one mass several feet deep. His muscles corded, his body shaking as he lifted the huge wall of debris and set it on the ground beside the crater.

Angels cheered him. That one load would have taken them hours to displace.

Jack rested between loads as Talia and the other angels resumed lifting and removed more wreckage. When he was ready, Jack signaled Azrael.

"Halt removals again and hold positions. Jack is going to move another load."

When everything was still, Jack fought against the compacted stone and twisted structure, lifting another massive load out of the crater until a dark well began to form. Leading into the spire's lowest chamber. One more giant mass of debris and they should have access to the spire's lower level.

It seemed like hours later when Jack dislodged the most difficult wreckage that had nearly fused into one solid slab as a result of the Holy Fire still burning below. He struggled and tugged, his face a mask of sweat, his eyes narrowed and weary as he fought to free the last of the ruined spire and gain access to the lowest level.

He fell to his knees, shaking, his eyes glazed, teeth grinding together as sweat poured down his face.

"Jack," she whispered, reaching out to him, but Muriel held her back.

"You'll break his concentration," Muriel said in a hushed voice.

"Sorry, Talia," said Anahera, a comforting hand on her wings. "You can't help him right now."

Talia nodded. "I know," she said, wincing, her heart aching as Jack fought his human limitations to lift the rubble with his seraphim powers.

With a determined shout, he slammed his fists against the ground. Unleashing a last burst of seraphim energies to free the debris. He struggled under the massive load to lift it out of the crater and away from the ruined spire, setting it down beside another enormous pile of wreckage.

"Jack, you did it!" Talia cried, rushing toward him.

"Thanks, babe," he whispered, out of breath.

She laid her hands against his chest as he panted, trying to get his breath, and bathed him in healing light until he got up from the ground to stand beside her.

"Well done, Jack," said Azrael, patting him on the back. "Let's open that path wider, angels, and then form a column to descend into the lower spire. Be ready to extinguish any Holy Fire that might still be burning down there. Our goal is to carry out anyone that survived the Holy Firebomb and get them to Eolowen for healing. Is that clear?"

Talia nodded as she and Muriel worked with Kesien, Anahera, and Deemah to roll big stones out of the way, widening the opening, and allowing space for angels to enter. She gazed into the winding darkness. The steps had crumbled, but fortunately, angels didn't require stairs. They could fly out any injured angels and get them back to Eolowen.

"Squad, tight formation beside Azrael. Wait for the signal to descend."

"Shouldn't take much longer to widen the opening," said Azrael. "Only a few minutes now that Jack has removed the bulk of the wreckage."

"Great job, kid," said Kesien as Jack moved into position behind the archangel.

"Thanks, Kesien," Jack replied, winded as he wiped his forehead on the sleeve of his Henley and muttered, "Not your goat."

Kesien grinned and looked satisfied. "Okay, I know he's all right with that response."

Anahera and Deemah chuckled as Muriel moved in behind Jack and rubbed his shoulder.

"Good work, Jack," she said.

"Thanks, Muriel," Jack replied. "That was some hard work. Wonder if that comes easily for a real seraph."

Talia gave him a quick hug and kissed him.

"It would have been difficult work for a seraph, too, lover. You did an amazing job. Saved us a lot of time."

He stood up a little straighter, a smile curving across his beautiful oval face.

"Thanks, Mrs. Casey," he said. "I just hope Seraphina's okay. And I hope she has more seraphim with her. Enough to kick Luci's ass all the way back to his playpen in Hell. I knew I should have brought him a new squeaky toy last time—besides me."

The squad covered their mouths, trying to muffle their snickers. Azrael's steely gaze narrowed as it settled on Jack, but Jack just smirked at the archangel.

"Unfortunately, Lucifer has outgrown his playpen, Jack," said Talia. "And there will be no way to put him back in it unless the Maker intervenes."

Jack set his jaw, those pale green eyes turning fiery. "Then we're just going to have Holy Fire his ass out of the sky until he taps out for real this time."

Talia frowned and cast an uncertain look at Muriel then Kesien. Muriel shrugged.

"I don't know, Talia," she replied. "Even I can't decipher that Jackspeak."

"Translate, Jack," said Talia.

"We aim for those huge black wings and shoot him out of the sky," said Jack, arms flailing. "We bring Luci down and he'll give up. Then the rest of his sore loser demons will follow suit."

Azrael shook his head.

"Sorry, Jack, but Lucifer will fight until there's absolutely nothing left. I fought him during the Rebellion and he was the very last angel to fall from the Heavens. We had him cornered, literally knocking him out of the sky and holding him down. More than a dozen archangels, a dozen cherubim, and six shielded seraphim. And still, he fought. With everything he had as the Maker delivered a blow of Holy Fire that burned away his wings and extinguished his halo."

Jack looked uncomfortable now, tugging at the collar of his grey robe and green Henley underneath.

"Wow, took the Maker and a shit-ton, er boatload of angels to take him down, huh?"

Azrael nodded. "Even without his wings and halo, he fought with everything he had. And by the Maker, he was winning with all his powers. Even when the Maker finally took them, Lucifer still fought like an enraged demon until the seraphim threw him from the Heavens."

Jack looked unnerved now.

"So, you're saying we're totally screwed?" Jack asked finally.

Azrael's expression flattened, but Talia saw the worry lighting his charcoal grey eyes.

"As the Lightbringer, he can restore the wings of his fallen angels, Jack," said Azrael in a dire tone. "That means we'll face all of those angels again. Like we did in the Rebellion. Lucifer's been calling the apocalypse Dark Justice. He's petty enough to see it in that light, but it doesn't change the fact that this will be Heaven's deadliest battle since the Rebellion."

Jack cast an uncertain glance at Talia and then turned back to Azrael.

"So, what happens to my world?" he asked. "We on our own to 86 these Hell princes? Sucks to be human and all that?"

Azrael folded his arms against his chest, his soot-grey wings flattening against his shoulders.

"Despite the Jackspeak, I get your meaning, Jack."

"Glad I didn't have to explain that one to Azrael," Muriel whispered.

Talia wanted Jack to wait until they'd rescued the angels below first, but she understood how distressing these events were for him. He was human. That was the only world he'd ever known until Lucifer dragged him off to Hell and then he escaped to Heaven.

"Unfortunately, that decision is not up to me, Jack," said the archangel, his brow furrowing, eyes narrowing. "Seraphina must communicate with the Thrones first and then convey the battle plan. Without support from the Thrones, we'll be severely outnumbered by Lucifer's forces. He's counting on us to divide our army between Earth and Heaven. One may have to be sacrificed to save the other… I…"

The archangel's voice trailed off and he turned away, wings drooping at his shoulders. His reaction frightened Talia.

"All of humanity may perish, Jack," said Azrael, his voice breaking.

"What?" Jack said with a gasp. "Perish?"

Azrael snapped his wings into full extension, hands on his hips.

"That was Lucifer's plan all along. Force the Thrones to choose between Heaven and the Creation, knowing that the Throne angels would choose their own kind—especially since humans have souls. Unless the Maker steps in to save His cherished humans, I don't see how humanity will even realize that seven Hell princes will soon walk the Earth and drop seven deadly payloads."

Jack crossed his arms and Talia watched as he put on his game face, forcing all weakness and emotion out of his face, those pale green eyes hardening, his mouth pressing into a thin line.

"Exactly what are these payloads, archangel?" he asked, squinting in the dim, smoky light. "What will they do?"

"War, famine, pestilence, despair, disaster, silence, and death." Azrael turned back to Jack, his charcoal grey eyes watery. "Each payload will get successively worse, causing more and more damage." The archangel bit his lip. "Beware the white horse, Jack. It's the final payload."

"White horse?" Jack frowned. "What does that mean? We talking the four horsemen here?"

"Seven, Jack. Seven. Ancients wrote about them as they would travel in their time. In your time, they will use your modern transportation. But the seventh and last Traveler is the deadliest, Jack."

Jack exhaled sharply. "Well, you did call this Traveler death. That's pretty deadly."

"Jack, this Traveler isn't just death. It carries a payload that will finish off everything and everyone that didn't perish at the hands of the other six Travelers' payloads. Killing every last human survivor on the planet. The seventh Hell prince will literally unleash a wave of death upon the Creation. And it will extinguish all life. Jack, it's literally the death of your world."

Jack's face turned stone white, his game face slipping.

"The death of my world?" He could barely speak.

Azrael nodded. "And if Lucifer's Dark army defeats the Light, it's the end of everything."

"Everything?" Jack gasped.

"There would be nothing stopping Lucifer from destroying the protective portal into the upper reaches of Heaven and laying waste to it, including the risen souls. And then usurping the Thrones. Only the Maker has the power to defeat his second in command, Jack. His firstborn."

Jack stumbled back from the spire and slumped against the ruins of a stone wall behind him.

"Colossal vindictive douchebag doesn't even begin to cover it," he said, staring at the debris littering the ground. "All because Luci wanted to be an only child."

"There isn't an ounce of mercy within him, Jack," said Azrael as he moved beside Jack and put his arm around Jack's shoulders. "Especially for humans. And I don't understand why. That's why we've got to work together, angels and humans, to halt the apocalypse and foil Lucifer's plans."

The hint of a smile touched Jack's lips.

"And totally ruin his day. That means humans will have to beat down all seven of these Travelers while the angels beat down Luci and his fallen angel thugs."

Azrael patted his wings and let him go.

"Let's consult with Seraphina before we decide anything, Jack."

Jack nodded, but his quick agreement worried Talia. She could already see the mischievous gears turning in that beautiful head of his, already planning his own assault on the Hell princes. She'd have to keep a very careful watch on him. Make sure he didn't go off like a loose cannon to try and fix this mess. He already felt like it was all his fault. She feared that he'd try to make another sacrifice to fix everything. And she couldn't take it if she survived Lucifer's onslaught and lost Jack in the process.

"Archangel, we're through!" Deemah shouted as she and Daidrean slid back from the rubble, another half dozen angels lifting the last stones away from the hollowed well in front of them.

Talia blinked over to Jack who turned toward the dark edge that spiraled into a smoky, fiery well. It looked like the descent into Hell.

"Look familiar, babe?" Jack asked, his arm sliding around her waist.

She nodded. "Looks like the mouth to Hell."

"Azrael, we ready to do this?" Jack asked, unfolding his wings.

"Squads, I want three team members in each squad to ready their angel light to extinguish the Holy Fire burning below us. Captains, select your angels."

Talia turned around, calling her squad into formation in a quick trill of soprano notes.

Deemah, Anahera, Kesien, and Muriel formed a half-moon around her and Jack.

"I want Deemah, Muriel, and Anahera on Holy Fire duty. You'll be responsible for extinguishing the Holy Fire in our rescue paths. I'll take point and Kesien will take flank. Jack, you'll communicate with Seraphina to find out how many angels are down there. I'll need you to use omnificence to locate their exact positions. We'll be one of several squads down below, so sing out when you locate an angel."

"Can I just shout?" Jack asked. "I'll leave the singing to the experts."

Talia smiled and ran her fingers through his hair. "Of course, lover. The rest of the squad, sing out. Questions?"

Jack raised his hand.

Talia gave him her best angel of death glower.

"This isn't a classroom, Jack. Just ask."

Already the squad was snickering.

"If Seraphina overwhelms me down there, I'm gonna need an Uber to get back to Eolowen. Just sayin'."

"Talia, I volunteer to watch over Jack and report out if he gets overwhelmed by the seraph," Kesien said with a chuckle.

"If she makes him power drunk," Muriel replied. "I volunteer to escort him back to Eolowen. And watch the show."

Jack gave her a sour look as the squad laughed.

"Talia, you and your squad are free to descend," said Azrael as he blinked behind her. "I'll be accompanying your squad down. I need to speak to Seraphina right away."

Talia nodded. "You want to be on point, sir?"

"Yes," he said. "That way you can make sure your headstrong husband doesn't get in trouble on the descent."

Talia shook her head. "Just the descent?"

"Good point," said Azrael, nudging her. "Make sure he doesn't anger the seraph, too."

"Anger the seraph?" Jack shouted. "If it hadn't been for me glowing with her call for help across my skin, no one would have even tried to go down into the lower levels. I think she's gonna be real happy to see me."

Talia tried to keep a straight face, but a chuckle slipped out.

"I'll help him locate any other survivors while you talk to the seraph," said Talia, sliding her arms around Jack and hugging him.

"That's better," he said with a smirk. "A little appreciation for your Enochian mailman, please."

"Come on, lover," she said, tugging him into the air. "Let's go deliver some rescue notes."

"Done, Mrs. Casey."

She gripped Jack's hand as they hovered above the gaping hole and flew downward, dodging debris and bursts of Holy Fire. They passed four levels where the winding stone stairs had crumbled until they reached the bottom of the spire. More than a dozen fires burned with bright white Holy flames throughout the vaulted, dark space littered with white stones and parts of the spire's circular white frame that had collapsed and melted.

Talia called out in a series of Enochian notes that Jack couldn't hear and Azrael joined her as Anahera, Muriel, and Deemah began flooding the fires with angel light. Kesien stuck close behind her and Jack.

"No answer yet," said Azrael, looking concerned.

Jack landed with a thump against the cracked floor and she felt him reach out into the darkness with his seraphim powers.

"I feel a very dim pulse of white seraphim light," he said. "It's a faint glow and a thready warmth, like a car heater on the blink." He held out his hands. "I can feel it sometimes, a touch of heat against my fingers. Like a warm breath."

The dark room was as large as a gymnasium with no ceiling, just a circular well for flight up and down the spire. A series of little rooms ringed the perimeter. Where Raziel had once rigged his sigils to keep that Devourer of Angels caged down here and the seraphim and cherubim prisoners. But the walls of those rooms had all caved in and the darkness was only cut by the many fires burning through the cavernous room.

Talia was at Jack's back, not letting him out of her sight, especially down here with everything so unstable.

Jack halted, spinning around, and moving right. To Talia's surprise, his right hand began to faintly pulse with blue light.

"Jack, she's guiding you to her!"

He grinned. "Guess I'm getting warmer."

When he got to the perimeter where three of the rooms were still intact, walls still standing, Jack pointed at the white stone boulders, three of them, in the way.

"Babe, we can use transference together to move these beasts," he said.

She nodded and focused her transference power on the closest boulder. She felt his power join with hers. Together, they lifted the massive stone five feet into the air.

"Shift it behind us, Jack," she said.

She felt the rock turn and lurch to the right. She smoothed out the path and kept it aloft.

"On three, we let go," she said.

He groaned. She had to hurry.

"One, two, three!"

The enormous stone thumped against the floor, shaking the room.

"Ready for the next one, Jack?"

He nodded, his face looking tired.

They worked together, dropping the other stone beside the first one. One more time, she watched her husband struggle to lift the third stone with her support. But she had to shift it over against the other two because transference was draining Jack. It was new to him and he hadn't had a chance to condition himself to use it. At least it wouldn't make him power drunk.

When the third boulder dropped, Jack's right arm began glowing blue.

"There, Talia!" he cried, pointing to the faint glow at the back of the middle room.

"Azrael! We found her!"

The archangel blinked beside them and led the way through the debris to the felled seraph curled in a ball of fiery white wings.

"Stay back, Jack, Talia," he said, holding up his hand. "Her power will burn you." The archangel threw a gold shield around his body and moved toward the seraph.

Jack had a strange look on his face. His expression blanked and he snapped into a stiff posture.

"She wants me to use some seraphim power I can't pronounce, archangel," said Jack. "It will dim her seraphim light enough to protect us from damage."

"Proceed, please, Jack," said Azrael. "I was planning to risk getting burned to carry her out, but the protection would be welcome."

Jack closed his eyes and pressed his hands together like he was praying. He mouthed words that she couldn't hear until his entire body began to glow with blue light.

The seraph lifted one fiery arm, her sparkling white robes covered in soot and debris, wings looking ragged despite the Holy Fire engulfing them. The blue light lifted from Jack's body and shot through the air, seeping along Seraphina's long fingers until it covered her entire form. Dimming the fire and the heat, encasing the seraph in a shell of blue light.

Only then did Azrael move toward her. Without the trails and auras of Holy Fire that radiated from her form, Seraphina looked like a regular angel except that her halo burned with white fire around her head and she had three pairs of wings at her back, all folded against her shoulders.

"Thank you, Jack," said Azrael as he gently lifted the seraph out of the floor and turned to Talia and her squad. "I am rushing her back to Eolowen and into the care of Cabriawn and Berith. In a private space. Talia is in command, so obey her orders." He fixed Jack with his steely gaze. "That especially means you, Jack."

"Dude, she's my wife. You think I'm gonna disobey an order from my wife and sleep on the couch for eternity?"

The muffled laughter made Azrael smile.

"If I'd known that, Jack," said Azrael. "I'd have gotten the two of you married a year ago."

"Jack? Azrael?" said a thin, broken voice from somewhere beyond where Azrael had gathered Seraphina in his arms.

Jack moved toward the sound and Talia followed.

"Keep talking," he replied. "And we'll find you."

"Jack…it's me. Pravuil."

Talia's eyes welled with tears. "Scribe!"

4

"Dude! Am I happy to hear your voice!"

"Pravuil!" Azrael cried.

"Go, Azrael," said Pravuil, waving him off. "Get Seraphina—safety. I'm…still. Here."

With a quick nod, the archangel lifted into the well of darkness and blinked out of the ruined spire, carrying the seraph in his arms.

Jack dropped to his knees in the dark room below and started lifting rocks and hunks of broken stone. Talia joined him.

"We'll get you out of here in no time, Scribe," said Jack. "Stay with me now."

"Scribe, hang on—please!" Talia shouted.

Jack heaved the rocks behind him, tossing them out of the way until he found the Scribe curled in a ball on the floor, wings torn and broken. Angel light leaked all over the floor, glowing with gold light as a large rock pinned the Scribe in the debris.

He could barely speak.

Talia pressed her hand to a wound at his side that poured out light and enveloped it in gold healing light.

"Hold on, Pravuil," said Talia, doing her best to comfort the Maker's Scribe. "Please hold on."

"Can't. Talk."

It took a few bursts of seraphim power, but Jack got the huge rock off the Scribe while Talia soaked him in healing light.

Kesien blinked beside them.

"Here, Jack," said Kesien who slid his arms underneath the Scribe, gently lifting him out of the darkness. "Let me carry him back to Eolowen."

"All you, Kesien," said Jack, sliding back out of the way, giving the tall angel of death enough room to ease Pravuil up from the rock-strewn floor and into his arms.

Talia kept her healing light focused on the Scribe. His short white hair was in disarray, gold eyes dull which scared Jack. He'd never seen the Scribe look this bad before. And all that light leaking out frightened him.

"I'll be flying beside you, Kesien," said Talia, concern darkening her arctic grey eyes. "We'll take good care of you, Pravuil. We've got a cherub healer and Berith to help us. Hang on."

The Scribe nodded as Kesien extended his soot-grey wings and lifted through the well of darkness with Talia beside him.

"Muriel, take charge!" Talia called out from above.

"On it," said Muriel as she blinked over to Jack.

Jack was relieved that he wasn't alone in this death trap. Lucifer's Holy Firebomb had left so much devastation in its wake. It angered Jack in ways he was just beginning to process. Douchebag had to know what he was doing. To his own kind, but Lucifer was so blind with vengeance, all he could see were the wrongs committed against him. Jack got it and at some level, he empathized with that hurt, but this? No.

This was premeditated. And some real evil Biblical shit.

Either Lucifer was the meanest being in existence or the dude was so blinded with hurt and rage over being tossed aside that he couldn't see anything but that pain. Not to mention insane after an eternity of being banished to a place like Hell. Jack had spent enough time down there to see that most of those demon dwellers didn't have all their hellhounds barking. Did the Maker even see that?

At times, Jack felt bad for Lucifer, but not after this attack. Lucifer had to be stopped and dammit, the Maker was the only one with enough power to take Lucifer down.

And now, this colossal douchebag had started the freakin' apocalypse. It was too much. And he couldn't shake that maybe, he'd helped bring the whole party down to Earth. Worst party ever—especially if they couldn't stop it. Or send the guests of honor back to Hell. Seven Hell princes with seven payloads. Sounded like a bad musical that Taylor Swift and Ed Sheeran got stuck headlining.

Was this the end of the world? It boggled Jack's mind to think about what was happening.

And what was to come.

"Okay, Jack, think you can use your omnificence to find any other survivors down here?" Muriel called to him from across the dark, dusty expanse.

He nodded and sat back on the floor. Holding out his hand, he pointed his index finger at the floor as the tsunami of images and locations and dates pounded through his tired brain. First, transference had sapped a lot of his energy and then using so many seraphim powers had hit him hard. Now, he was using this migraine-creation power. He hoped it didn't make his head explode.

As omnificence touched the broken floor, he felt it bounce through the room almost like sonar, mapping the space. In his head, he watched four figures glow in the dark area.

"I'm seeing four more angels down here," he replied. "But I don't know how to make them visible to you."

"Touch their brands, Jack," said Muriel. "Every angel has a brand that's visible to other angels."

"How do I do that when I can't see those brands?" he asked.

"Touch their foreheads with your seraphim powers. That should definitely light them up for us to locate."

Turning, he moved his left hand slowly as he located the glowing images in his head. He walked toward each image and then summoned his seraphim powers. Reaching out into the darkness and guiding his hand in his head, he touched the first angel's forehead.

"It's working, Jack!" Muriel cried. "I see a brand in the rubble. Keep it up."

"You know I'm gonna be power drunk off my ass after this, Muriel," he said into the darkness.

Muriel chuckled. "Why do you think I accepted this assignment? Ring-side seats to the power drunk Jack Casey show."

Jack rolled his eyes and moved toward the next angel trapped in the rubble. Touched her forehead, alighting a golden brand that burned through the darkness. Her gold eyes and two pairs of wings told him she was an archangel.

The third angel took some work to locate because of all the densely packed debris blocking his path. He had to use transference to shove a boulder out of his way and get close to an angel in eagle form.

A cherub! He touched her forehead, lighting up her brand.

"Muriel! Found a cherub! She's still in eagle form."

"Great work, Jack," said Muriel. "I'll call for a squad to get these two out. You keep searching."

"Roger that, Muriel," he said, his voice sounding more tired than he'd expected.

Again, he focused down his omnificence power, letting it seep along the walls and around the debris until he located three more angels.

"Muriel! Three more!"

"That's fantastic, Jack!"

"Gonna start lighting them up for the squads," he said, sweating, hands trembling as he moved toward the closest angel.

A Watcher sprawled across the debris, his stark white wings leaking light. With a soft touch, Jack lit the angel's brand and turned in the opposite direction. Working his way through the smoky blackness, he followed his omnificence power like a GPS and located an archangel. One set of his wings was crushed, the others blackened with dust and ash.

"Got anarchangel here," Jack said, his voice beginning to slur. "Brand'shlit."

"Jack, you okay?" Muriel asked. "You're beginning to slur."

That out-of-his head, lightheadedness was beginning to settle against his exhausted body, giving him that out-of-control feeling.

"Jusht fine," he replied. "Going after lashtangel."

The room tilted and swayed in front of him as he turned toward the last gleam of light in the cavernous expanse. Another angel trapped by rubble, wings splayed, robes torn, body curled into a ball.

He tried to walk toward the last angel, but he got stopped by a wall of debris that blocked him from reaching her.

"Hic! She'sh trapped behind debrish."

Dammit, that first burst of intoxication was wicked! It washed over him, turning his brain to mush as all his senses went sideways.

He stumbled, the room shifting. Reaching out, he grabbed hold of the wall until the sharp wave of dizziness fled.

"Be careful, Jack," said Muriel somewhere behind him, concern in her voice. "Please don't make me go back and tell Talia you got smashed by debris."

"Just smashed on seraphim powersh. Hic!"

Reaching into the rapidly diminishing well of power that was already circling the drain, he pulled out a glimmer of seraphim light. Enough to power transference and move these massive boulders to get to the last angel. Using the quickly fading remnants of transference, he picked up the first boulder and rolled it off to his left.

His chest heaved. He pulled in a heated breath, fighting the drunken stupor hovering just off stage, and reached toward the next boulder. He sucked in a deep breath.

And shoved the second boulder hard. Off to his right.

That left one boulder.

And he was already power drunk off his ass. Maybe he could move it and light this angel's brand before he passed out.

He had to try.

The room swayed. Darkening.

His head swam. Could barely control his fingers.

With both hands raised, he summoned the last dull glimmers of light across his fingertips. He gave a last exhausted shout and launched the final flicker of transference. Shoving the last boulder somewhere off to his left.

Crawling through the rubble on hands and knees, vision tunneling into a dizzying stupor, he pulled himself through the maze of debris, and around large hunks of white stone until he reached the angel of death lying still on the floor in a sea of dust and ash. His black hair tangled around his pale face, grey eyes slits, light grey wings flat against the floor.

"Muriel…"

God, he could barely speak. He'd never felt so power drunk.

"Angelofdeath," he called out, but it all ran together into a single syllable that echoed around him in tinny layers.

"What was that, Jack?" Muriel asked.

"Angel. Of. Death. Hic!" He spoke each word and paused, to keep them from running into drunkspeak.

"What?" Muriel cried. "You found an angel of death?"

"Yep," Jack replied.

"You suppose that maybe it's one of Samael's guard that was imprisoned in High House?"

"Don'tknow," Jack replied as he collapsed beside the angel of death and clapped his hand against the angel's forehead. "Brand'sh. Lit."

But the world tilted sideways and he was overwhelmed with the power drunk.

In moments, the flutter of wings echoed around him.

"Kid?"

Kesien dropped down beside him, his perfectly proportioned face swimming in and out of focus.

"Uber'sh here," Jack muttered.

"You found a bunch of survivors, Jack," said Kesien, his voice sounding tinny and far away. "Good work."

He felt the distant touch of Kesien's arms sliding underneath him and lifting him out of the darkness.

"Wow, this is the most unfun power drunk he's ever had," said Muriel.

"That makesh sixsh of ush," said Jack.

"Six?" Kesien said, squinting as Jack felt the cool, gritty air against his face.

"Two Murielsh, two Keshiens. Two shuvivorsh."

"I think that means he's seeing double," said Muriel, carrying the unconscious angel of death in her arms.

But he could barely make them out against the dark clouds and his darkening vision.

Jack gave her a big nod. He could barely respond. He was spent.

"Let's blink," said Kesien.

A burst of darkness and wind disoriented Jack for a moment or two until the round room came into limited focus around him. Kesien still carried him and Muriel flew beside him, carrying the injured angel of death.

"Berith," Muriel called. A couple more casualties."

"Jack!" Berith's voice sounded panicked. "What happened?"

"Too many shots," said Jack.

Kesien smiled. "Power drunk's bad, Berith."

"Gonna be his worst one yet, I'm afraid," said Muriel. "But he rescued a bunch of angels."

"I know," said Berith. "I couldn't believe how many your squad brought back." She squeezed his arm. "Good work, Jack. Muriel, there's a pallet on the floor by the bed. Put him there."

The last thing Jack saw was Kesien's smile as he slumped onto the pallet and consciousness left him.

Only after the blackness and swirling had subsided was he aware of the Purdue big-ass bass drum pounding against his brain while his stomach twerked its way into his esophagus. He didn't want to hurl all over Azrael's grand hall, but he'd never been this sick before. Ever.

Just when *Hail Purdue* thrummed through his skull and pierced his temples, the gold and black tide rising, a warm hand pressed against his forehead and the swell of sickness ebbed, the tsunami dissipating.

He opened one eye.

Talia sat on the floor beside his pallet, smiling.

"There you are, lover," she said in a soft voice.

"Gonna…hurl," he stuttered, even the turn of his head making him gag.

The warmth from her hand was gold light that engulfed him, easing the horrible nausea and headache that permeated every cell in his body.

"This should help."

Her voice was a whisper, but the cacophony of noise in the room made his stomach shudder and his head hurt.

In a moment, Berith's smiling face hung over him, rose-gold halo bright, grey wings folded against her shoulders.

"How's our patient?" she asked.

Jack shook his head. "Someone needs to…cross me over," he said in a quiet voice, groaning. "'Cause this hangover's killin' me."

Talia shook her head. "Not happenin', Jack Casey."

Bending over him, Berith laid a cool compress on his forehead and added her healing light to Talia's.

"That should ease a lot of the symptoms, Jack," said Berith, straightening up. "But only if you don't get up."

"Get up?" He frowned. "Dude, I can't move."

She gave him a sour look and he sighed, realizing that he'd just called her dude. With her hands on her hips, she turned toward someone he couldn't see.

"Now, I know he's got a bad power hangover," she said.

"He called you dude, didn't he?"

Jack squinted. Was that Azrael? Didn't sound gruff enough.

Berith nodded.

Another face hung over him. He stared at the short white hair and intense gold eyes. Pravuil. the Maker's Scribe was in the bed beside his pallet.

"Scribe? You okay?" he asked.

The hint of a smile touched the Scribe's moon-pale face. It had lost a lot of that soft luster that most angels had, like moonlight. It clung to their skin, giving them an ethereal, dewy cast. A hint of it had returned to the Scribe's face and Jack felt relieved. He'd looked dull and frosty at the bottom of the spire. With all that gold light leaking from both wings.

"Doing much better thanks to Berith and Cabriawn," he said in that hurried, clipped tone that was coming back into his voice. "And your wife."

"Mrs. Casey's slappin'," he replied.

The Scribe frowned, eyes narrowing, and glanced at Berith and then Talia. Both of them shrugged.

"Someone, translate please," he said finally.

Jack sighed and rubbed his left eye. "Awesome, dude," he said as his head began to throb again. "Means she's awesome."

Talia put her arms around him, helping him sit up.

"Thanks, lover," she said and kissed him.

It hurt, but he kissed her back.

"Yes, she is, Jack," said the Scribe. "Talia, I felt your grief and concern for me every time you were at the spire searching for survivors. I'm touched."

She bowed her head. "You're very special to me, Scribe," she said and finally lifted her gaze. "You're…slappin'."

Jack couldn't help but laugh. She sounded so unsure when she said it.

"Best. Wife. Ever."

The Scribe squinted at him and pointed a finger. "Felt yours, too, Jack," he said in a quiet voice. "Thank you."

Jack felt the heat rise in his cheeks.

"You just made Jack Casey blush," Berith said with a laugh that infected Talia.

Jack shrugged. "I got nothin'. Yes. I was worried and upset, too, Scribe. Busted."

His confession brought a grin to the Scribe's face.

"Well, it was nice to be missed. Now, I need to get my keister out of this bed. Now that that putz, Lucifer has set the apocalypse in motion. Who does that? Now, we've got time's biggest mess to deal with—and seven flights of angels." He sighed, rubbing a hand over his face. "And seven Hell princes to neutralize."

"Six," said Azrael somewhere behind Berith.

"Six?" The Scribe's brow furrowed. "What do you mean six?"

Azrael stepped beside Pravuil's bedside. "Six, Pravuil. The first flight is overhead right now, preparing to take flight."

The room fell deathly silent as all the angels stared at each other, fear shining in their eyes.

Azrael's statement made Jack shake all over. It was beginning. And he couldn't stop it.

"What happens with the first flight?" Jack asked, holding his head.

The archangel looked stricken as he stared at Jack with sad eyes.

"The first flight of angels will pour out the first bowl of pain onto the Earth. That will call forth the first Traveler. The Hell prince will travel to some location and drop a payload into place that will unleash pestilence and sickness on your world, Jack."

Jack winced.

"When does the payload go off?" he asked.

"As each payload is placed," said Azrael, wings twitching at his shoulders. "It will go off within one full day, so you'll have a day and a night at most to stop it."

Without warning, every angel in the room jerked their heads upward. Toward the sky.

Angel notes he couldn't hear.

Talia's eyes turned glassy with tears as Berith pressed her hand against her mouth, arm sliding around Azrael who held her close. Pravuil smashed his eyes closed and bowed his head. Looking ill.

"What is it?" Jack demanded. "What's happening?"

Azrael groaned and stared at the white stone floor.

"The song went out across Heaven," he said. "The first flight of angels is in final preparations. Their flight to Earth is now imminent."

Chills rushed down Jack's spine.

"Excuse me, everyone," said Azrael as angels took flight from the room, up onto the roof. "I'm needed elsewhere."

"I'm coming with you," said Berith, lifting into the air alongside him.

All of the angels took to the air, leaving Jack and Talia alone with the Maker's Scribe.

"Look, Talia…Jack," said Pravuil, rubbing the painful red knot on his forehead. "I don't have to tell you how dire this situation is."

Talia nodded and slid her arms around Jack. He held her close.

"We get it, Scribe," said Jack.

Pravuil pointed a finger at him.

"Jack, it's going to be up to you and your other humans to bring down these Seven Travelers before those payloads go off."

Jack nodded. He'd known this was coming since he'd first learned about these douchebag Hell princes.

"Been expecting this temp gig for a while, Scribe."

The Scribe turned his gaze to Talia.

"And something I don't know if the others are aware of yet, but Lucifer had a very specific agenda when he escaped Hell."

Jack shuddered. Lucifer knew exactly where he was going and why when he blasted out of Hell as all the seals shattered and the trumpets sounded. But Jack had no idea where Luci was going or why.

"He left like he was late for a hair appointment," said Jack, "but I have no clue where he was going or what he was planning to do."

A crafty, knowing smile lit the Scribe's face as he held up a finger.

"Ah, but I do, Jack."

Talia leaned forward, eyes wide. "Tell us, Scribe. What is Lucifer doing while his Hell princes plant destruction on Earth?"

A twinkle glittered in the Scribe's eyes, that dull haze receding.

"I'd bet my existence that Lucifer had a very specific plan in mind. He went in search of something very old and very dangerous to ethereal beings."

Talia shook her head. "What does that mean, Scribe?"

"I've only heard rumors, Talia," he said. "And the Maker has been unusually silent. Worried. All I know is that Lucifer is after something as old as the Creation. And if I'm right, we've got to make sure he doesn't get it or he'll become unstoppable."

The thought of that possibility terrified Jack. He winced and cast an uncertain glance at Talia who was intensely focused on Pravuil.

"Scribe, I have no idea what this could be," said Talia as she got up and sat down on the bed beside Pravuil.

Her face was taut, gaze intense as she gave Pravuil her unwavering attention.

A voice filtered through Jack's head, calling to him in a familiar rusty alto voice. It sent a shiver down his spine.

Jack Casey, we need to talk, said the voice with a thick French accent. *Come to the crossroads. It is urgent.*

"Babe," said Jack, struggling to his feet. "Gonna go out and stretch my legs."

Talia nodded. "Be careful, Jack," she said. "And don't go too far from Eolowen."

He rolled his eyes.

"I'll look both ways before crossing the terrace and everything."

His beautiful wife didn't seem to hear him or she'd have given him that angel of death glare of hers. Just as well. She needed time to talk to Pravuil about whatever quest Lucifer had gone on while he went to talk to an old acquaintance.

At the crossroads.

5

At the only patrol of cherubim left as it passed overhead in a blur of wings—both eagle and angel forms—keeping careful watch over the grand hall. And the lower part of Heaven.

Behind the cherubim flew several patrols of death angels that slipped past the terrace every couple of minutes. The smell of burnt soil hung in the air, clouds of smoke still drifting over Eolowen's once-sparkling white stones, turning the entire area grey and hazy.

Like the rest of Heaven that still struggled to recover from the aftermath of Lucifer's massive Holy Firebomb.

But Jack's attention snapped past the smoke and the patrols. At the ghostly, fierce-winged figures that looked like mist as they descended through the grey haze. Draped in silky robes that hung like vapor across their translucent, ethereal bodies. Like they'd come from the upper reaches of the Heavens—somewhere he'd never been before.

Seven in all. Their halos and eyes burned with white fire.

They looked part spirit, part angel. And the sight of them was terrifying.

More spirit than light, their long, flowing robes fluttered in the wind. Smoky white hair undulated around them like storm clouds becoming thunderheads. Even their wings looked like smoke trailing around them. And their glowing white eyes made them look deadly.

They looked like death itself.

Not at all like the angels of death that helped humans cross over from the physical world into—whatever came next. He had no clue. He wasn't a religious dude, but after everything he'd seen, he knew there was something beyond his world. Beyond his life.

No, these angels looked like they handed out death like party favors. That they could reach out and touch your face and you'd just cease to exist.

They had one job. To end things. He shuddered. Like his world.

Not a trace of humanity clung to these...angels. They had wings, but they were all spirit. Like vapor except for the fierce white glow of their eyes. Each one carried a glittering green bowl in their hands. All celestial badasses. Part of the flock that guarded the upper reaches of Heaven.

More ninja than warrior. More assassin than soldier.

He had never seen this kind of angel before, but the sight of them was chilling. They were portents of doom.

This was the first flight of angels that Azrael mentioned. About to pour out buckets of whoop ass all over the Earth. And leave it to the mercy of Luci's Hell princes. The Seven Travelers, as Pravuil called them.

The thought of this shit actually happening made him shake all over. It wasn't some Hollywood movie or even some script.

It was in-his-face real. And right now, he felt humbled and terrified for the only world he'd ever known.

Jack Casey, the raspy alto voice called to him in his head, in that thick, sultry—and familiar—French accent. *We must speak. Now. Hurry.*

At least he wouldn't have to go hunt down two kinds of angel feathers and some demon scales to summon her with three colors of smoke.

Besides, she was already at the crossroads—waiting for him. This time. And Heaven had enough smoke floating around without polluting it further with demon smoke.

Holding his head, he tried to manage his power hangover headache and turned away from the forbidding celestial beings filling the skies over Eolowen. With all the chaos going on in the hall, they wouldn't miss him for a bit.

He walked to the edge of the terrace and held out his hand. He pointed at the rose bushes framing the farthest edge of the rolling green meadow beyond the grand hall and focused his seraphim blink. Gardenias and honeysuckles sweetened the burnt air.

Taking a deep breath, he blinked across the meadow. Stopping beside the roses.

The soft, cool fragrance helped scrub away the stench of burnt grass and black smoke from the ruined spires.

Thunder rumbled overhead as a haze drifted across the meadow, acrid smoke still filling the once-blue skies. His brain throbbed against his skull after the movement stopped, hitting him hard in the forehead.

He had to take several deep breaths to keep from yakking all over Azrael's roses. After the first wave of nausea had subsided, the pounding at his temples easing, Jack turned his attention to the footpath that meandered away from Eolowen's edge and twisted toward the crossroads.

Focusing his gaze past the footpath, he stared into the distance. He was still dizzy and unsteady, but he had to shove it into the background right now.

To meet with an old enemy.

With a deep breath, he pointed his index finger toward the crossroads and shot forward with another blink. Into the quiet intersection where all of the lower Heaven's roads met.

The movement made him drop to one knee, holding his head again until the spinning and nausea had dissipated.

A plume of red smoke roiled over the crossroads. Enveloping it in a thick screen. Demon cone of silence. But it was smoke instead of that red demon glow that had wrapped around him and the others back on the island during his honeymoon. And in his apartment afterward.

To blend into the smoke and chaos that Lucifer had caused—hide their conversations from that colossal douchebag. And right now, the dude could be anywhere. So, an additional precaution by an ex-first lieutenant that did not want to be found. With the fragile soul of her human lover beside her, she was being extra careful.

Regardless of what she was after, she was risking a lot to come here and talk to him right now. He had to remember that.

"Jack Casey," called the smoky alto voice in that sexy French accent.

Like the rasp of ragged velvet against his throat.

He hadn't forgotten the first time he'd fought the former angel executioner. The sound of her voice was warm, sultry, but it still put him on edge. He'd dreaded those past fights with her—like the one on his and Talia's honeymoon at the San Juan Island cabin. When Lare and Hughes had taken Gianni's new wife, Izzy—after they'd temporarily paralyzed Talia. Leaving Jack alone to fight a legion of demons and Zanth, Luci's new first lieutenant.

With Gianni able to see all those demons for the first time—and Jack's wings and halo. Watching him fight the archdemoness with Holy Fire and murder marbles.

Like that was easy to explain away.

No, he had to explain it all to his best friend while the dude was frantic about his brand-new wife's sudden disappearance.

But ever since Jack had gotten the soul of Zanth's trapped boyfriend out of Purgatory, he and the archdemoness had declared a truce. After she helped him and Talia—and her squad—fight Archangel Samael and his rogue angels of death.

And—Jack's eyes misted—she'd kept her end of the bargain and took him to see his dad in Purgatory.

At first, Jack didn't think he could ever fully trust this demon, but now that she wasn't Luci's first lieutenant and had stood by her word, the archdemoness' top priority was to vanish with the soul of her human boy toy, Tre Sheridan. Besides, Lucifer was busy destroying things on his To Do List and running amok down on Earth. He thought that Jack had ended her anyway.

And right now, even Jack wasn't important enough to make a blip on Lucifer's radar. Yet.

He worried about what Lucifer was ruining on Earth right now. And the day that Lucifer returned his focus to him again. Dude promised to kill him last. That meant Lucifer wanted him to see all the horrors he was about to inflict on the Earth first.

And that thought was truly terrifying.

Jack got to his feet and turned around.

Zanth stood on the other side of the crossroads, wearing a short black dress and shiny black pumps. Her ashen skin made her long, board-straight blue-black hair look so vivid against her shoulders. And dramatic around her face, framing those ruby-red eyes, lined and smeared with black makeup. Her full lips were blood-red like long taloned fingernails that sparkled.

Beside her, Tre Sheridan hung close, his form faded and ghost-like despite his bright sapphire blue eyes and vivid stone-brown hair. Like if Hollywood had done the special effects on Tre's soul.

"Zanth," Jack called and wandered through the red smoke toward her, but he kept glancing over his shoulder just in case this was some kind of ambush. "Tre. It's been a while."

"Oui," said Zanth, sauntering toward him. "You have stormed Hell since we last spoke."

"Yeah," Jack snapped. "I let Luci escape and I caused the apocalypse. It's been a busy week for me. Next week, I plan to start rehearsals and destroy the Earth."

She walked around him, looking him up and down. Like she was expecting him to be different somehow? He chewed his bottom lip. Would she blame him for letting Lucifer escape his playpen?

And for starting the apocalypse?

He tried not to think about it. The thought made him want to hurl. But he couldn't help feeling responsible.

Lucifer led him by the nose through every step of his long con plan, herding him and Talia out of California. Up to the San Juan Islands. And then back to Los Angeles. Giving that bastard time to place the final pieces of his Holy Firebomb in High House and get everything he needed ready for his big, show-stopping reveal.

When he slammed Jack's face right into those gates and broke his tether. Then all seven seals—opening the Gates of Hell. Every step of the way, that bastard had herded him right into his trap.

But what could he do? He couldn't leave Berith in Lucifer's hands, not after she'd betrayed the King of Hell so she and Jack could escape. If he had, that douchebag would have ended her. And him.

"Looks like you two have kept a few steps ahead of Luci's army," said Jack, eager to fill this miserable silence.

Or she'd returned to Lucifer's army and was about to lead him into a brand-new fresh hell.

But his gut told him that wasn't the case.

For the first time since he could see Lucifer and all his demons, the King of Hell had better things to do than hunt him down and try to kill him. Or take his soul.

Now that Luci was free of any shackles and not tethered to Hell, he was pursuing something big. Something devastating—alongside the apocalypse. Not some petty vengeance against one human.

Zanth said nothing as she continued to look him over.

"All right, just say it," he snapped and propped his hands on his hips. "It's my fault that Lucifer's free. I caused the apocalypse."

The archdemoness stopped in front of him, head cocked as her gaze looked him up and down a third time.

"Non, Jack Casey," she said and crossed her arms. "From listening to you, I know that you must feel that way. But Lucifer gave you two impossible choices. Rescue the redeemed angel or forget her. Regardless of your choice, everything would have happened just as it did—except that he would have extinguished the redeemed angel's light. Now, he is playing on your sense of guilt to confuse you. Shuffle you into inaction while he pursues his real objective."

Jack frowned, mouth flattening as he studied the archdemoness who began to slowly pace around him again.

Holy shit. And whatever he was after had to be world-ending. Dire for Heaven, too.

"And…just maybe you know what that objective might be?" Jack asked.

Her expression gave away nothing. He'd expected that game face from her. She had too much to lose—like him.

"Perhaps," she answered.

He stepped in front of her, stopping her from pacing.

"Zanth," he said and laid his hands against her cold arms. "The Maker's Scribe thinks that Lucifer has gone after something as old as Creation. To do what, I haven't a clue. But whatever it is, it's gonna be the worst party ever for Heaven and Earth." He shrugged and let go of her arms. "We're talking generic expired cheese puffs, screw cap gas station wine, and those bargain bin One-Hit Wonders of the 2000s CDs, Zanth. Real horror movie stuff here."

Tre Sheridan snickered but gave Jack an understanding nod.

"Bro…that's a seriously bad party."

Jack gave Tre a sharp nod.

"Worst bad party ever, dude. Trust me."

Zanth nodded. "I do not know about these—human things, but I am almost certain that Lucifer went after an artifact from the Creation, Jack Casey," she said in a soft voice.

"Something the Scribe said was dangerous to ethereal beings," said Jack, his voice sharper. "Something that would make that douchebag unstoppable."

Fear rose in those red demon eyes as Tre began to fidget and finally moved beside Zanth, his gaze flicking beyond the mist.

"Unstoppable?" Tre replied and frowned at Zanth, looking uneasy. "He will hunt us down after the dust settles , Zanth. And you know it. No one gets the best of Lucifer for very long."

Even Tre expected Lucifer to eventually come after them. Or attack them right now.

Jack felt his mouth go dry. Had something lured the three of them to the crossroads for Lucifer? To end them?

"Talk to me, Zanth," Jack said in a soft but urgent voice. "What do you know about this thing that Lucifer's searching for?"

"Tell him, Zanth," said Tre. "Or everything's gonna burn."

Tre had a point about that. If Lucifer succeeded, that bastard would burn everything to the ground. And laugh while it turned to ash.

She grabbed hold of Jack's hands and squeezed.

"Jack, listen carefully. This whole story about destroying the Creation…it is another misdirect by Lucifer. His war has always been personal."

Jack nodded. "Again with the daddy issues. This fight is between him and Dad, right? He just wants to destroy Earth because it's Dad's favorite toy and it's on the front lawn. Luci wants to set it on fire to piss off Dad, but the real fight is upstairs. Isn't it?"

"Oui, Jack, it is a war between father and son. Lucifer and the Maker." She glanced around again.

Probably making sure nothing had rolled up on them. Like Lucifer and his legions of demons. Jack had never felt so unnerved before.

"So, what's Luci after?" Jack asked, his wings twitching against his shoulders.

She let her hands slide away from his and her red gaze got far away, the distance spiraling.

"He has gone in search of an ancient celestial artifact," said Zanth, her voice low and dramatic.

"You mean like the Holy Grail or something?" Jack asked with a frown.

She shook her head.

"Non, it isn't like the Grail cup or anything valuable. He is seeking a…a remnant of the Creation. Something you humans would not recognize, Jack. Nor would most angels and demons."

That sounded ominous as hell. Luci was after some sort of transformer weapon that didn't look like a weapon. But if he found it, it would make him unstoppable.

Tre reached out and rubbed his ghostly hand up and down Zanth's arm in an anxious caress.

"Zanth, please—you've got to find a lead for Jack," said Tre, his face scrunched into a look of fear. "If he's going to fight Lucifer, he's gotta know what Lucifer's hunting for down on Earth."

The former archdemoness was quiet for several long moments as she paced around him, deep in thought, arms crossed. Finally, she moved in front of him, uncrossing her arms as she motioned behind him toward the sprawling meadow that led back to Eolowen.

"I do not know exactly what this artifact is that Lucifer seeks. Or where it might be. But I promise you that I am doing my best to discover what Lucifer is after, Jack Casey," she said. "As soon as I find out, I will call to you again. To come to the crossroads. Perhaps then I'll have a lead or two to follow?"

Jack sighed. He had no choice but to trust her. He had nothing to go on, no leads, no clues, not even the hint of a location. Or what this damned thing was that Luci was trying to find.

While Zanth was gathering information, he'd flood Pravuil with questions and hopefully find something no matter how obscure.

"I appreciate all the help you and Tre can give me," he replied and held out his arms. "Because I've got nuthin' to go on here."

Zanth turned her head and stared up into the sky behind him.

"The angels are searching for you, Jack Casey," she said and stared at him unblinking. "You had better return while I gather what information I can. I will contact you soon."

Tre reached out with both hands and handed Jack two colors of angel feathers and some demon scales. He smiled. So he could contact them quickly next time.

"Appreciate it, Tre, Zanth," he said and took the feathers and scales.

"You're welcome, bro," said Tre as the red smoke dissipated around them.

"Stay safe," Jack called to them.

"You, too, Jack Casey," she said as she wrapped her arms around Tre's waist and slid into the shadows.

Vanishing into the smoky haze that hung across the entirety of Heaven right now.

Jack stuffed the feathers and scales into the left pocket of his Levi's and turned back toward Eolowen. He held out his index finger, pointing at the distant willow tree across the meadow, and blinked out of the crossroads. Past the roses. Over the hilly expanse. Until he arrived beneath the willow tree's delicately curving branches and tiny, spring-green leaves.

He leaned against the trunk as Talia and her squad landed, surrounding him. Followed by Azrael and Berith. He sighed.

And so began the interrogation.

"Jack Casey!" Talia shouted, grabbing hold of his arms. "Where did you go? I've been looking everywhere for you! You know how dangerous things are right now."

"Sorry, babe," he said, shrugging at her. "Had to take a call."

Frowning, eyes narrowed, she pointed at his jeans pocket. "What call? That phone hasn't left your pocket, Jack."

With his thumb, he pointed over his shoulder toward the crossroads.

"From Zanth."

Her eyes got wide as she grabbed him by the shoulders and shook him.

"You just went to the crossroads to meet her? Alone? Without any of the squad backing you up?"

He nodded. "Yeah."

Muriel smacked him on the back of the head.

"You dolt! What if that had been a trap? Huh? Then what would you have done?"

He'd been ready to blink out at the first sign of trouble, but he'd worried the entire trip to the crossroads that this meeting had been a trap or a setup.

By Lucifer.

"Blinked," he answered.

Kesien shook his head. "Would have been too late, Jack, if that had been Archangel Samael. Or Lucifer."

"Relax," he said, holding up a hand. "I'm the last thing on Lucifer's focus list right now. He's got places to destroy, people to end, and some artifact to locate. That will make him unstoppable. Then he'll kill me. I've got what…at least a few days before that happens."

Talia looked furious, her grey eyes burning as she gazed at Kesien and then Azrael.

"Which one of you is planning to yell at him first?" she asked and propped her hands on her hips. "Or should I just start?"

Azrael's stormy grey eyes narrowed as he stepped toward Jack, almost standing on his toes.

"First one's all me," he said. "Jack Casey! What were you thinking?"

Jack winced, his power hangover not handling this situation well, especially his stomach.

"That Zanth had information I needed," he replied in a weak voice, his stomach roiling.

Would the Maker send him to Hell for hurling all over Azrael's Eternean armor boots?

He sighed. He was about to find out.

"With the first flight of angels about to take flight for Earth," Azrael continued, winding up to full-on archangel rant, "and kick off the apocalypse and seven Hell Princes about to wander the Earth with seven payloads, the last thing I need is for you to start a firefight with demons at the crossroads!"

Azrael crossed his arms, glaring at Jack.

"No firefights, sir," he said in a sheepish voice as his stomach shuddered. "Just information gathering. With Luci free from Hell, those demons aren't gonna be organized enough for a firefight yet. Not until he finds this Creation artifact he's looking for."

"And what did you discover about this artifact, Jack?" Azrael demanded. "To make you going off Jack Casey style and making the problem worse worth the effort?"

Jack's eyes narrowed and he stared at the archangel a moment.

"I don't always make the problem worse," he replied.

"Yes, you do," said the squad in unison, including Azrael and Berith.

"All right," he said with a groan. "I'll give you that one, but I found out that this artifact is a weapon. It was part of the Creation and most angels and demons wouldn't recognize it. Or humans."

Azrael turned back to Berith. "Berith," he said in a wistful voice and gazed into her eyes. "Lucifer's after something left over from the Creation—something that most angels and demons have never seen before. Something that was left on Earth from the beginning of time. After the planet was created."

Gazing off into the distance, Berith was deep in thought for a moment.

"Lucifer would have been one of the few angels in existence at that time," said Berith. "Observing while the Maker created the Heavens and the Earth. Watching as the elements of the world came into being and were combined to form everything. What would have possibly been left behind on Earth once Creation was complete and time was set into motion? Very few angels would even know about the existence of such an artifact."

The flutter of wings overhead drew Jack's attention.

Short white hair. Yellow eyes. Archangels' wings.

Pravuil!

"And that's why most of you are coming up empty on this issue," said the Scribe with a growl as he landed beside Azrael in the meadow. "But I was there," said Pravuil. "The only thing I can think of that Lucifer could wield as a weapon would be the tools used to create the Heavens and the Earth."

"You mean like celestial hammers and nails? A divine Dremel tool?" Jack asked.

"Crude analogy, but yes, in a manner of speaking," said the Scribe, putting his hands behind his back as he paced through the grass, wings twitching. "One of those forgotten tools could have deadly consequences if Lucifer got hold of it."

Jack's eyes widened and he gazed at Talia. "Like the Maker's nail gun in the wrong hands? Like Luci's hands?"

The Scribe nodded. "Precisely, Jack."

"So, what exactly is the Maker's nail gun then?" Jack asked. "Luci's gotten way more bougie since escaping Hell. Now, he's collecting rare celestial tools. Being the chief celestial tool and all."

"Not even going to ask," said the Scribe. "This tool may be something that the Maker called the Rod of Creation. It combined all the elements to create the world and the heavens. It is a part of the Maker. And that's very dangerous."

A cold chill rolled across Jack. "Dude, seriously? A part of God?"

The Scribe nodded.

"If this thing is part of God," said Jack, beginning to pace. "Then this thing may have all the powers of God. It might be the only thing powerful enough to get Luci upstairs to the corner office. And that supreme tool on level ground, power-wise, with dear ol' Dad."

The silence that greeted him was paralyzing.

He turned around, eyeing all the stunned expressions. Even the Scribe was quiet, staring at him like he'd just suggested that Luci go pick up this rod of Creation as a welcome home gift when he returned to Heaven after being gone for millennia.

This was bad. Really bad.

"Somehow, we've gotta stop Luci from bringing this welcome home gift home. To his dad."

The Maker's Scribe sighed. "Crude, but true, Jack. If Lucifer gets hold of this remnant of Creation, he could get through the portal into upper Heaven. To the Throne room itself."

Okay, Jack had no idea how it happened, but this new revelation had actually made the already dire situation worse.

Much, much worse.

"So, Pravuil," said Jack as he walked alongside the Scribe, his Eternean sabatons swishing through the tall grass surrounding the willow tree. "No blasphemy intended here," he said, glancing up at the sky with a wary gaze, "but what the hell is a remnant of Creation that powerful doing just lying around on Earth like some garage sale find?"

Pravuil stopped pacing, turning around to face Azrael and the rest of the angels, including Talia who had been unusually quiet.

"That's a damned good question, Jack," said the Maker's Scribe, a grin brightening his face as his gaze shifted to Azrael. "Archangel? Got an answer for that one?"

Azrael looked unnerved as Berith shook her head. He turned toward the Scribe.

"Pravuil, I haven't a clue. That was before my time."

"Mine too," said Berith as she shifted closer to Azrael.

Talia stepped beside Jack, her gaze on the Scribe.

"I do," said Talia.

A hushed silence fell over her squad as Azrael's gaze snapped toward her.

"Babe?" said Jack, gripping her hand. "You do?"

She nodded, her gaze still on Pravuil's face.

"It was something Lucifer said while I was being controlled by Vassago."

Jack felt a chill wash over him. Lucifer had been in her head for quite a while in the Middling. She'd probably heard more than she ever wanted to know about Luci's thoughts. Black as midnight and focused on destroying everything his father held dear.

Pravuil motioned for her to continue.

"He needed Vassago to take my omnificence power. It was a fleeting thought that he didn't speak aloud. Something about needing omnificence to find something lost. Something outside of time."

Pravuil's eyes widened. "Omnificence!" he cried and rushed toward Talia, gripping her arms. "That's why he wanted omnificence. Before he was tethered in Hell, he didn't have all his powers back, so he couldn't sense an artifact outside of time."

"Dude, you're not making much sense here," said Jack. "What do you mean outside of time?"

"After Lucifer got his powers back, we tethered him in Hell," Azrael replied. "Lucifer couldn't use his regained powers to search for the artifact unless he was physically on Earth."

Berith nodded. "Unless he had omnificence."

"But like Jack," said Talia, sliding her arm in Jack's. "I don't understand the outside-of-time reference either."

"Are you saying that when the Maker built my world, He left a couple of sponges behind when He closed up the patient?"

Pravuil chuckled.

"That's exactly what that means, Jack. Rods of Creation were used all over your world. Seas. Soil. Sunlight. All of it focused and created by a series of these well-placed rods. Primordial like the Maker, Jack. Of the same essence. Most were used up and emptied of their primordial cores. A few are dormant. But only the Maker and the Maker's left hand can reactivate these cores."

Jack felt his skin crawl at Pravuil's statement. At last understanding the cryptic details that Zanth had given him. She hadn't been around when Earth was created, but ol' Luci was and he knew where all the duct tape and rebar was hidden. All he had to do was visit these locations until he sensed Dad's kryptonite and he had an unstoppable weapon.

And he was using the chaos and cover of the apocalypse to search for it.

"Holy shit!" Jack cried. "Now that Luci has all his powers back and he's free from Hell, there's nothing stopping that little bitch from going down to Earth and finding one of these live rods. Is there?"

Pravuil shook his head. "No, Jack, there isn't."

He let go of Talia's arm and began to pace, feeling like he was totally going to hurl now.

"And he's gonna use it upstairs in a drive-by on the corner office, isn't he? Because it's Dad's kryptonite. The only thing that can take down a Maker is a Maker's essence. Right?"

A dark expression shadowed Pravuil's face as he grabbed Jack by the shoulders and held him still, but Jack couldn't stop his heart from racing or his breath from coming in gulps.

"Right, Pravuil?"

The Maker's Scribe paused a moment, staring at Jack until finally, he nodded.

"You figured it out, did you?" said Pravuil.

Jack winced and shook his head.

"I didn't want to, Scribe, but it's all there. It all makes sense now." His stomach twisted. "Dude, I'm so gonna hurl."

Sighing, Pravuil patted him on the back as Jack turned away toward the willow tree. He grabbed hold of the trunk and dropped to his knees, tossing everything in his gut that had twerked its way out in an unholy burst of bile and spasms.

He felt a hand on his back, gently caressing as he heaved air now.

If Lucifer succeeded, everything that had ever been built would be destroyed. And on its ashes, Lucifer would erase every last soul from existence and reign over the smoking ruins of angel-land with his demons and fallen angels.

"Is he right, Scribe?" Azrael demanded.

Jack felt healing light wash over him. He glanced up. Talia was beside him.

"Are you all right, Jack?" she asked in a soft, concerned voice.

He shook his head.

"My stomach's better, but I'm not so good at the moment. That little bitch can destroy everything. Like it never existed. And I can't do anything to stop him."

Talia dropped down in the grass and slid her arms around him, holding him tight in her arms.

"We're going to find a way, Jack. We have to."

"Otherwise, it all goes away," he said as he laid his head against her shoulder. "Your world. My world. And us. I'm not going to let that douchebag steal my hard-fought happily ever after, Mrs. Casey."

"We've fought Heaven, Hell, and Earth to stay together."

Jack nodded. "The couple that survives the apocalypse together stays together, am I right?"

She nodded and ran her hand down his back. "You are right, Mr. Casey."

His right jeans pocket began to vibrate.

Groaning, he let her go, dreading a look at his phone's screen. Wincing, he slid the phone out of his pocket. Herb Rutherford's name appeared on the lock screen.

He turned the phone toward Talia. "It's Herb," he said. "Guess he's got news about the new show format I proposed."

But he didn't answer the call. The show was the least of his worries at the moment. The phone beeped, indicating there was a new voicemail, but a bunch of text messages popped up on the screen.

> Jack, the network green-lit the new show format.

> They want us to bring more couples aboard.

> Retitling the show to Celestial Couples Show
> to accommodate couples like Rachel and Eric
> and Ryder Kurland and Claire Olsen who aren't
> newlyweds.

Jack sighed. Dude texted like he was sending a telegram. He almost expected to see the word *stop* appear after any punctuation, like in those old 30s and 40s movies. One last text popped onto the screen.

> Rehearsals start in three weeks at Studio 22.
> See you and Talia then.

Too bad the world could be destroyed by then.

He needed time to go after these Seven Travelers and take them down. What they needed was a good old-fashioned scavenger hunt on the show, one that would get them out of the studio. Hunting Hell princes. He'd have to let Gianni and Banks in on what was happening. He couldn't do this alone. Especially with Talia fighting an air war over the Earth against Lucifer and his demons.

Besides, shit was about to get real on Earth now. Gianni and Banks would see it. Along with everyone else on Earth. But most people would be oblivious. Like who actually expected to see the apocalypse unfold in their lifetime.

If ever.

Gianni and Banks were about to see it all. And help him hunt down and disarm seven payloads. They just didn't know it yet.

A rush of wind ripped across the meadow. A lament in a chorus of harmonies echoed over Eolowen as the first flight of angels lifted their bowls of destruction and flew through massing thunderheads. Toward Earth. Setting the whole apocalypse in motion.

It was on now. And there was no way to prevent it. Only stop it.

He had no clue how to do that, but he had to figure out how to disarm the seven payloads of seven Hell princes in a hurry.

6

DREAD TREMBLED THROUGH TALIA'S WINGS AS SHE LET THEM UNFURL IN a rush of wind as the first flight of angels hissed across Eolowen, leaving behind an eerie green trail of light in their wake.

She had always been told that when the flights took to the air for Earth, and emptied their bowls, the skies across the world below would turn the color of each bowl. The first plague upon humanity was pestilence. And these angels carried bowls that were a sickly lime-green. That meant illness and disease would run rampant when the first Traveler's payload ignited the first plague.

As soon as the angels poured out their bowls, the skies would turn that pallid lime-green. Signaling the first Traveler to leave Hell, bound for wherever ground zero had been designated for the first plague. Only the Traveler knew that destination.

Together, Heaven and Hell would launch the first plague on humanity. Unless they could stop each payload from going off, the skies would remain green and unchanged until the second flight of angels took to the air. Turning the skies black as angels poured out the second bowl of plague—black, for famine.

How would she, Jack, and the guard stop any of this? Much less the apocalypse's devastation.

"Pravuil!" Talia called, but the Scribe was already blinking toward the terrace alongside her silent, stricken guard, heads turned toward Heaven's smoky grey skies.

At the fearsome images of the first flight whose angels looked more like phantoms than Heavenly beings. Long lean bodies draped in tattered bone-white robes that fluttered around them, wing feathers ragged and broken. They looked ill, like the plague of pestilence they carried.

"What is it, Talia?" the Scribe asked, eyes still focused overhead, the silence palpable across the Heavens.

"How will we know when the first plague has been delivered?" she asked, her gaze still on the sky.

"The skies across Earth will turn the sickly color of each plague bowl and then become bright and aurora-intense," said Pravuil as the angel flight disappeared through the smoky haze—on its way to Earth. "*If* the payload goes off. If the payload fails to go off within a day and a night of its placement, then the sky will turn blue again."

Jack blinked across the terrace and stood in front of Pravuil.

"But Scribe, as soon as those angels spill that green shit all over Earth, the first Traveler will be…well, traveling, right?"

Pravuil sighed and glanced back toward the round room, looking almost distraught.

"Not until the sky turns green, Jack. That is the signal to all. But once the Traveler puts down its payload, focusing where the first plague begins, a timer starts. A day and a night to stop the payload."

Jack frowned, chewing his lip. "How do we stop these payloads?"

"Each Traveler carries a demonic coin of sorts, Jack," said the Scribe, looking distracted, his gold eyes weary. "Each Traveler has orders to place the coin at a prescribed location. Drawing the plague to it and the location like a magnet. Take the coin and you stop the payload from activating. But to take the coin, you have to defeat a Hell prince. And believe me, Jack—they won't leave that coin unattended. Or they'll face Lucifer's full and immediate wrath."

"Which is?" Jack fired back.

"A legion of hellhounds and assassin demons will pursue each

Traveler that shirks this responsibility," said the Scribe in a dark tone. "And consume them."

Jack looked frantic, his breathing hurried, and his eyes wide and fearful as he followed the Scribe to the round room's doorway.

Talia felt terrible for Jack, knowing that his world was about to be devastated by seven plagues and possibly destroyed. He'd never faced anything of this magnitude before.

And she knew that he felt responsible—for all of it.

"How do we find out these locations?" Jack asked, sounding out of breath.

The Scribe paused in the doorway, turning around.

"There are seven coins, Jack," said the Scribe, pinching the bridge of his nose with thumb and forefinger. "As each pillar crumbled and each trumpet sounded, a location was sent to each corresponding coin. Based on the events that led up to their destruction."

Jack laid his shaking hand on Pravuil's sleeve. "Dude, how do we find that out? We can't stop these Travelers if we can't locate them and these payload coins."

With an abrupt shift of his wings, Pravuil turned around and faced Jack.

"Each coin leaves a colored trail of celestial light for the Traveler to follow to the appointed location."

Jack nodded. "So, first one's green?"

The Scribe nodded.

"Exactly, Jack. There's a seraph skill that Seraphina and I will teach you—to locate these light trails. Fast."

He squinted at Jack and then gripped him by the shoulders in an almost fatherly way.

"But Jack, I have to warn you. All of these locations will be here in your country, near where you live, because of Lucifer's maneuverings at the Gates of Hell. And his thirst for vengeance against you."

Jack's mouth gaped and Talia couldn't stand his pain any longer. She moved over to her new husband and wrapped her arms around him, holding him close, trying to calm his agitation. His wings twitched and jerked against his shoulders, like he couldn't decide whether to leap into the air after the first angel flight or curl into a ball and rage.

"Jack, it's not your fault," she said against his ear, fingers stroking his hair. "You didn't cause any of this. All of this is on Lucifer."

Pravuil patted Jack's shoulders and let him go.

"Talia's right. Lucifer wanted to maximize your pain, Jack, and focusing the apocalypse right where you live was the best way for him to do that."

"But don't we have to leave?" Jack shouted. "Right now! To try and stop this first traveling douchebag from giving the world Ebola or something?"

Talia's arms tightened around him and she laid her head against his, speaking in a soft, calm voice against his ear.

"When the sky turns green," she said, "you'll know that the first Traveler has passed through the Gates of Hell with their payload."

"But Tal, won't the sky turn green any minute now? Those angels are already on the bullet train south. For Earth."

She'd never seen Jack so overwrought before. Much worse than he'd been at the studio set trailer, trying to fight off his craving for cocaine.

Using her angel of death powers, she enveloped him in a wash of gold healing light that sent waves of calm rolling over him. His knotted shoulder muscles began to relax, the tension in his limbs easing.

He hadn't even noticed the glimmer of gold light enveloping him, his whole focus still on the Scribe and getting these details right. She understood. He'd be fighting a war against these payloads down on Earth, but he didn't realize yet that he wouldn't be alone. She would be with him until the sixth flight of angels took flight. Bringing a plague of silence to the world.

She sighed. And an air war above it, one that had never been seen in ancient or modern times before. Angels against fallen angels and demons. Battling Hellfire with Holy Fire until not a single winged being was left in the skies over Earth. Trying to stop Lucifer's army from invading the upper Heavens.

Somewhere during that battle, the seventh flight of angels would take flight. Bearing the seventh and final plague upon the Earth.

Death.

If no angels were left to stop Lucifer, he would ascend to the upper Heavens through the portal using that Creation artifact and reach the Maker's Thrones.

Laying waste to everything.

She hoped someone was left to stop Lucifer. Someone left to keep him from the Thrones.

And the Maker.

"No, lover," said Talia, holding him tighter. "It is just past sunrise on Earth right now. The angels must wait until sunset to pour out the first bowl. Right, Scribe?"

The Scribe nodded. "Correct, Talia. Sunrise or sunset are the appointed times for unleashing each plague, depending on when each of the angel flocks takes flight."

Jack groaned and patted his right jeans pocket.

"Tal, Herb called a little bit ago. Left a message. Said the new format is a go. We're to report for rehearsals in three weeks. We're gonna have to call in sick due to the apocalypse though."

"That's three angel days from now," Talia said, her gaze narrowing.

She wasn't happy about this new schedule.

He ran a hand through his blond bangs.

"Figures. We finally get the show back on track and it's just in time for the apocalypse. Not sweeps week—the apocalypse. Sometimes, but not always the same thing."

"We'll worry about the show later, Jack," she said, still stroking his hair.

He was trying to be everything to everybody and it was too much for him.

"If I can get Ramiel to loan me some Watchers," said Jack, glancing across the meadow, "I think I can do the show and stop the apocalypse at the same time."

Pravuil's gold eyes sparkled, an amused look brightening his face.

"Hear that, Azrael?" Pravuil called to the archangel who blinked beside the Scribe with Berith beside him.

The archangel nodded, looking entertained.

"Jack's got the apocalypse and the filming of his new show all figured out," said Azrael.

Berith chuckled.

"Then I'll let him handle the rest of the issues up here in Heaven, too," said Pravuil. "Since he's got it all handled."

But Jack's brow furrowed, his mouth flattening into an annoyed line.

"I just meant that if I had some Watchers, we could still film the show while Talia and I went after the Travelers. So nothing else got screwed up. I wasn't trying to—"

"To sound like an arrogant jackass?" Pravuil offered. "Keyword being Jack."

The guard snickered at Pravuil's joke, but Jack got quiet.

Which worried Talia. Jack never hesitated to fire back a response at anybody. In fact, he enjoyed those moments, but he wasn't in any mood to trade barbs right now.

Then she saw the hurt radiate in those pale green eyes.

He pulled away from her. He stared at the angels around him a moment and then turned away from the Scribe and the archangel, blinking across the meadow.

"Talia, what just happened?" Muriel asked, glancing from her to Azrael.

"What's the matter with the kid?" Kesien asked as he turned toward the meadow, watching Jack pace around the rose bushes. "I was looking forward to his response."

Talia shrugged, her gaze shifting from Azrael to Pravuil and then across the meadow to Jack.

"He hasn't been himself since Lucifer escaped Hell."

"Forgive me, Talia," said the Scribe as his gaze tracked past her toward the roses at the end of the meadow. "I was trying to soften the direness of our situation with a little humor at Jack's expense. Not insult our brave little human that has already given so much to our cause. If I know Jack, he's been laying all of this out in his head since Lucifer escaped. And it'll probably work, too."

Azrael's gaze narrowed. He shook his head as he watched Jack pace.

"Jack's never been that sensitive before, Scribe."

"He's worried, Azrael," said Talia. "And he's overwhelmed. Combined with his lingering guilt over letting Lucifer escape and start the apocalypse—it's too much."

"And you get a very troubled young man who feels responsible for all of it," said Pravuil.

"Who doesn't know quite how to handle what's happening right now," Berith added. "And he's got people counting on him down there to keep his show going—that don't know the apocalypse has been launched. And people up here counting on him to stop Lucifer. That's a lot of weight on Jack's shoulders."

Talia nodded. "Especially since he's out of his element. He doesn't know what to do, how to help—and he doesn't know any of the details he needs to fight back."

Anahera landed beside Muriel and snapped her head up, body stiffening, wings frozen as they unfolded to their maximum wingspan. Spread wide like sails in the brisk winds rushing across the grand hall.

"Bring. Him. To me."

Anahera's voice was stilted. Controlled. Echoing a seraph's power. Seraphina. Talking through her.

"Seraphina," said Azrael and nodded toward the meadow. "She wants to talk to Jack. Maybe she can ease his distress?"

Pravuil nodded, head bowed as he stared at the white stone terrace floor that looked gritty and grey from the smoke and destruction.

"Jack's a good kid," said the Scribe. "And he's given just about everything he has for us in this fight against Lucifer. I'll make sure he knows that he's appreciated."

"And respected," said Berith.

"Yes, of course, Berith," said the Scribe. "And respected."

Talia turned toward the meadow, intending to blink to the rose bushes, but a brilliant beam of gold light enveloped Jack and he snapped to attention like Anahera had a moment ago.

She couldn't help but chuckle. Seraphina's messages were always direct and the seraph hadn't wanted to wait for her or Azrael to deliver this message to Jack.

She was delivering it now. Herself. In true seraphim fashion.

"Looks like Seraphina has delivered her own message, Scribe," said Talia, pointing at Jack who had spread his wings and launched into the gritty grey sky. He flew through the smoky haze, over the terrace, and landed on the roof of the round room. And dropped through the portal.

"Let's see what the seraph wants," said Pravuil. "Talia, Azrael, you're with me."

The Scribe blinked through the round room and Talia followed, Azrael behind her. She blinked again, into Eolowen's long nave. A third time, she blinked along the length of the long, white-stone nave and into a small room off to the right.

Where the seraph had been recuperating. Cloaked in a strange blue glow that shielded her true seraph light from the rest of the angels. So they wouldn't get burned by her power.

Talia stood in the doorway as Pravuil and Azrael appeared behind her. Jack stood in the room, arms crossed against his chest, wings flat against his shoulders, staring at Seraphina who floated in the empty room, six wings curved around her, and a gold-trimmed white robe bathed in blue light.

Seraphina's long white curls undulated beneath her white halo that was a ring of Holy Fire, wings glittering with Holy light despite the blue glow containing her full seraph's brilliance. Her eyes were white with Holy Fire, her skin reflecting dark, then light as her seraph's light pulsed around her. Barely contained by the blue glow.

Talia had only seen her once or twice with that seraph's glow in check. But this was the clearest she'd ever seen her before.

Jack Casey. Your role is clear. Your guilt is unfounded.

Jack bowed his head. "Whatever you ask of me, I'll do," he said in a subdued voice. "Except walk away from Talia—I'll never do that."

Talia's eyes welled with tears. By the Maker, she loved this man. Standing in front of a seraph and saying he would never walk away from her. Knowing Seraphina could erase him from existence with a thought.

Love frees all. You taught all of Heaven the meaning of our own words. Only the Maker can change them now.

That made Talia uneasy. But the seraph was right. Only the Maker could separate them now.

"Thank you," Jack said in a tight, quiet voice and put his hands on his hips.

You did not start the apocalypse. Lucifer did.

Jack nodded, but Talia wasn't convinced that those words had gotten into his head yet. Now that he'd even heard them from the seraph, maybe he would believe them.

But time is short. Your world and ours are in danger. You must challenge the Seven Travelers and stop their payloads. While we battle Lucifer's army.

Again, Jack nodded. He'd known that defeating the Travelers would be his fight since the seven seals broke.

But your role as seraph is also needed.

Jack laid a hand against his chest, looking startled.

"Me? As a seraph?"

I am injured and will not be completely functional when the sixth flight takes to the air. A fight I must join regardless.

"What else can we do to heal you, Seraphina?" Jack asked. "Can I use my seraph powers?"

It would take more power than you have.

"But with Berith, Talia, the cherubim, and me—"

There is no time, Jack Casey. And not enough healing. If I should fall, you alone possess seraphim powers. You alone will have the power to battle Lucifer and protect the Thrones.

"Just me?" Jack said in a small voice.

You must protect the Thrones. And the Maker. If they cease to exist, all will cease to exist. All. Will. Perish.

Talia felt a chill rush across her wing tips. Pravuil had once told her that all the Heavens, Hell, the cosmos, and the Earth existed because of the Thrones. If the Thrones perished, everything would disappear.

"Everything?" Jacked cried, eyes wide.

Everything. Stop as many of the Seven Travelers as you can, but you must protect the Thrones. And the Maker. That is your role, Jack Casey.

Jack began to pace now, chewing his bottom lip, wings twitching.

"What happens if I miss one Traveler?" Jack asked.

He already knew the answer to his question. It burned in those pale green eyes. He was confirming that he'd have to let his own people suffer and die if the choice came down to stopping Hell princes or Lucifer from reaching the Thrones. But she knew Jack. He needed to hear someone say it.

She understood. She felt the same way and it twisted her heart into knots for him. To have to make such a terrible decision about his own world. Alone.

Protect the Thrones. Protect the Maker. Everything disappears if either perishes.

"So, me and my kind are just the trash mobs in this first-person shooter?" he said. "I have to choose between humans and celestials? Between Heaven and Earth, that's what you're telling me?"

Yes, Jack Casey. But remember...if the Thrones or the Maker perish, there will be no humans and no Earth to save.

Jack's face scrunched with pain and he bit his lip.

"Then I guess I'd better become the best-damned Hell prince hunter ever. Because I am gonna stop all seven of those douchebags. And I'm gonna stop the King of douchebags, too, before he reaches those Thrones. Or the Maker."

Music flooded the chamber, Seraphina's soprano notes lilting around them in an uplifting melody that brought tears to Talia's eyes. Jack couldn't hear her aria, but it carried across the Heavens and touched every angel. Praising Jack's courage and determination.

"Did I just hear your husband say douchebag in front of a seraph? Twice?" Pravuil asked, leaning closer to Talia.

She chuckled. "You sure did, Scribe. That's my Jack."

"At least he didn't call Seraphina dude," said Azrael.

All three of them laughed in notes that Jack couldn't hear.

"Conversation's not over yet, Azrael," said Pravuil with a wink.

Jack began to pace again. "If I'm on Earth kicking Hell prince ass, how will I know that Lucifer has breached the seal on upper Heaven's portal?"

All of Creation will hear that portal shatter. And feel it.

"How do I find this portal?" he asked.

Your seraphim powers will allow you to blink directly to the portal. You can reach it with a thought.

"Then I'll do everything in my power to stop Luci, Seraphina," he said. "You know I will."

And that's what makes you worthy of those powers, Jack Casey.

He smiled and bowed his head.

Now, I must teach you a power to locate and follow the apocalypse payload trails. Come to me.

Jack hesitated a moment and then stepped forward, the blue shielding light enveloping him as he stood in the pale wash of Seraphina's white seraph glow. All six of the seraph's wings extended to their full spans and began to beat the air around her. Churning more white Holy Fire into being.

But the blue shield of light held it all back, keeping it from setting everyone and the chamber on fire with Holy flames.

Seraphina lifted her head toward the sky, halo spinning faster as she extended her arms wide. Lime-green smoke appeared and vanished. Followed by black smoke. Then red smoke.

Her halo spun faster, a high-pitched hum whispering around them now.

Brown smoke rose and fell between her outstretched hands. Followed by orange smoke and then blue smoke. And finally pure white smoke as all seven steamy colors twisted together in tongues of flame and smoke, writhing into a maelstrom of light and heat and mist.

With a deafening clap of thunder, all of it shot forward and struck Jack in the chest.

He gasped and dropped to his knees as all six of Seraphina's wings folded against her shoulders, the light dimming.

Talia rushed over to him, dropping down on her knees beside him. He looked dazed.

"What just happened?" he asked finally.

The seraphim apocalypse power is now part of you, Jack Casey. Use it to follow the payloads to their destinations. And their Travelers. You will know them by the color of the horse that each one rides.

"Horsemen? Like the four horsemen of the apocalypse? Not riding actual horses though? Right? There's seven—not four? Right?"

Jack sounded tipsy. And confused.

There are seven Travelers. Horsemen as the ancients called them because that's all they had for transportation.

"Jack," Pravuil replied. "They're Hell princes—and smart-asses—so they'll arrive by something that has a horse and a color associated with it."

"Seriously, dude?" said Jack, eyes narrowing.

"Wish I wasn't," said the Scribe with a shake of his head, gold eyes bright. "They're going to flaunt themselves to a world they think can't stop them, Jack."

Looking dizzy, Jack looked over at Talia.

"So, Mrs. Casey, what do you say we take a sunset cruise to Earth and throat punch this first Traveler dude?" Jack asked. "And take down the first payload. Dude's probably driving a green Mustang. That'll give us plenty of time before rehearsals start in, what—two weeks or so?"

She nodded, trying not to laugh. His eyes were crossing. Receiving this new seraphim power had already cost him a lot of energy. And a slight power drunk.

"A sunset cruise it is, Mr. Casey," she said and tweaked his nose. "As long as you let me drive."

"Probably a good plan," he said in a quiet voice. "I'm a little over my limit right now."

Azrael and Pravuil blinked into the room beside Jack.

"Seraphina said that Jack's going to feel a little power tipsy after receiving the new power," said Azrael, a hand on Jack's shoulder. "But he'll be fine in a while."

Pravuil knelt beside Jack. "Jack, you know I was just giving you a hard time about the show and the apocalypse, right?"

Jack nodded. "Sorry, Scribe," he said and ran his fingers through his sexy blond bangs. "Guess I'm just taking this whole apocalypse thing hard. Trying to keep the show going and these douchebag Travelers from destroying everything. So, none of the people I care about on Earth even knows about it."

"So, you think that if you keep your show going," said Pravuil, squinting at Jack, "none of your family and friends will have to suffer through the apocalypse? Or blame you for starting it?"

He bowed his head and nodded.

"I can just hear my mother. Jack Casey, you started the apocalypse! First the drugs and now the end of the world. I hope you're proud of yourself. See what you've done. You've ruined the entire planet. Consider yourself uninvited for Christmas dinner."

Pravuil let out a raucous laugh. "Your mother probably blames you for the Rebellion, too. And Lucifer's fall, starting the whole tempting humans and wagering for souls thing."

Jack sighed. "If blame can be attached, she'll duct tape it right to my forehead, dude. Trust me."

The Scribe got Jack on his feet and put an arm around his waist.

"Well, she'll lose her mind when she finds out you stopped it from happening, won't she? Come on, Jack. Let's get you to the round room. So you can sleep this off."

Jack's eyes were already closing, knees buckling. Finally, the Scribe had to pick him up and carry him out of the chamber and back to the round room.

"Talia," said Azrael, stopping her as she started to follow Pravuil and Jack into the nave.

"Yes sir?"

"We've got to locate this artifact before Lucifer does."

"I've already used my omnificence power to search the archive, archangel," she said. "But there's nothing there about rods of Creation

—even Pravuil looked. I've tried searching for these artifacts with omnificence, too, but came up empty."

Azrael nodded. "Berith never heard Lucifer mention them in Hell either. When you and Jack go after the first Traveler, take your squad with you. Interrogate this Hell prince and any demons you encounter. Use omnificence on them."

"We'll do what we can to squeeze any drop of information from them," said Talia, laying her hand against the archangel's sleeve.

The archangel was silent a moment and then turned away.

"Talia…you know that you and Jack's paths must diverge when the sixth flight of angels leaves Heaven."

She winced at his words, but she and Jack knew this moment would come. That would leave him to battle two Travelers without angelic assistance while she and the guard fought Lucifer's army overhead.

"Yes sir," she said.

"For what it's worth," he said with a sigh. "I'm sorry it's come to this. Know that he will reunite with you and the guard during the seventh flight. After the last two Travelers are defeated."

"I'm counting the moments until that happens, archangel," she answered, doing her best not to tear up at the thought of being separated from Jack.

Especially with the end of the world in play. If it all collapsed, she'd prefer to disappear in his arms, with his touch being the last moment of her existence.

"We must also keep Seraphina well-supported, too. If she falls…"

He was right. If Seraphina fell, Lucifer's army could overwhelm them. And bring down Heaven's entire army. Allowing Lucifer to stroll right to the portal and destroy existence.

"I'll make sure my squad and a squad of cherubim never leave her side, archangel," said Talia.

"Berith and I will join your squad, Talia," he said and took hold of her hand a moment. "You're fearless in a fight—as long as you're not protecting that headstrong husband of yours. So, it's probably best that he not be there."

No matter how much she hated being apart from Jack, she knew the archangel was right.

He let go of her hand. "I need to discuss some things with Seraphina," he said. "You'd best see to Jack."

With a mumbled yes sir, she blinked into the nave and up onto the roof. Blinking again, she landed on the round room's rooftop and dropped through a portal to the white stone floor below.

Pravuil and Berith hovered beside Jack who was in bed, eyes closed. She smiled. Sleeping off the effects of receiving the new seraphim power. She sat down on the bed beside him and stroked his hair, watching him sleep.

And waited for sunset. When the first flight of angels poured out the first bowl of pain—pestilence—upon the Earth. Setting the apocalypse in motion.

7

SOMETIME LATER, JACK AWOKE FEELING A LITTLE THIRSTY AND A LITTLE cold after Seraphina had body-slammed him with a new seraphim power. He sat up, glancing around the room.

Empty.

He glanced at the floor. His blue Vans and Eternean sabatons sat beside the bed. He peeled off the white sheet. He was still dressed in a green Henley, grey hoodie, and Levi's, the short grey angel of death under-robe draped across his Eternean armor that leaned against the wall to his left. The clear gold armor sparkled in the sunlight that filtered through the portals in the high ceiling. Letting in the smoke's lingering haze and stale ash scent, softened by the scent of jasmine and honeysuckles wafting on the breeze.

Outside, the clash of swords and crash of shields was sharp, punctuated with muffled shouts as angels of death practiced maneuvers on the terrace and in the meadow beyond the grand hall. But he knew these were the direst circumstances that had ever brought the angels out to train. They blinked in and out of the drills and Jack wondered how many were leaving to cross over people on Earth.

And he feared there were be a huge number of casualties once these Hell princes got their party started.

His stomach dropped a little every time he saw an angel take to the air. There were a ton of angels of death in Heaven. Not all of them were training at Eolowen right now. Not all the archangels of death got along either. Like those douchebags, Raziel and Samael who were out-and-out traitors.

But Jack wondered about the others sometimes. They each had a hall in the lower Heavens where they trained and fought as a guard unit. And crossed over humans. Azrael's was just the best. And after Luci marched on Heaven, Azrael had proven it when he and his angels stopped Lucifer short of the spires.

He smiled. After all, none of the others had a kick-ass right hand like his amazing wife, Talia. Or the best squad in Heaven.

The flutter of wings passed over the rooftop portals, casting a brief shadow.

He glanced upward.

The cherubim patrol passed overhead, a mixture of angel and eagle forms floating past. Wary. Stern-faced. Worried. This squad was the only one left in the lower heavens. They had rescued a few more, but they still needed time to recover and create a new squad.

In moments, a squad of death angels followed in shiny, clear gold Eternean armor, short grey robes fluttering beneath.

They were on edge, gazes flitting around them, below them. Above. No one knew where Lucifer was and with his full powers returned, the dude was the most powerful creature in existence—besides the Maker.

Why hadn't he shown his face yet? Dude loved to gloat and Luci had waited millennia to rub Heaven's nose in this mess. That unnerved him. What did Lucifer crave more than bragging rights and proving he was right?

Vengeance.

It made Jack shudder. That meant Luci was off searching for the weapon he planned to use against his father, the Maker of All Things.

And if he succeeded...

Jack winced and turned his attention back to the round room. He couldn't think about that right now. Because he was second in line in that high school drama, Berith right behind him, and it would turn horror-movie dark if Lucifer won this battle for everything.

The white stone floor was warm against his grey socks as he got to his feet and stepped over his Vans. He moved over to his Eternean sabatons that sat at the foot of the bed near his breastplate and greaves.

He scowled. And that short grey robe that he despised.

"Talia?" he called.

No answer.

They were all out drilling. Or crossing over souls.

Sighing, he slid off his hoodie and left it on the bed. He pulled the grey robe over his Henley and jeans. Then he grabbed his sabatons and sat back down on the bed, pulling them on over his grey socks and tucking his Levi's into the armored boots. He put the greaves and breastplate on over the robe. With a sigh, he stepped underneath the silky white curtains in the doorway and out onto Eolowen's terrace.

And stepped into the middle of the guard's drills. Sword thrusts and shield bashes.

It made his heart hurt to think about all of them soon to face Lucifer's legions of demons in the air above Earth. Fighting for their existence.

He searched for Talia and her squad. They sparred to the left of Azrael's dais, Kesien fighting beside Talia and Deemah, Anahera beside Muriel and Daidrean as the cherubim patrol passed overhead again.

Laialus dueled Irinas, the death angel that Talia revived from the terrace, and the recovering cherub, Janaelis. Azrael battled Berith, Pravuil sparring with Sidriel, while Turiel dueled Sariel. Other archangels of death had joined them, grey eyes bright and hair charcoal and white as they used flaming Holy Fire swords and shields of light against each other.

He didn't recognize these other archangels, but they had come to Eolowen to drill alongside the other archangels of death, including

Archangel Ramiel who oversaw the Watchers. In the meadow, the Watchers honed their archery skills with lightning and flame arrows. Azrael had become something of a celebrity because of his unflinching resolve to take down Lucifer and protect the Heavens. Dude was like the Captain Kirk of archangels. The Phil Jackson of teamwork and coaching angels to victory.

The sun was so bright today. Had all the smoke finally burned out of the sky? Replaced by that calm, serene blue that had always permeated Heaven's skies?

Jack covered his eyes and glanced skyward.

High above the meadow and the patrols, Seraphina burned above the grand hall like a golden sun, doing sword and speed drills alone. He smiled. She was trying to recover from the Holy Firebomb.

But his amusement fled. All of this training dwarfed the preparations they'd made to storm Hell. And it made him queasy.

How many of them would perish in this fight? And what about the people on Earth? Gianni and Izzy? Banks and Morgan? His sisters. Herb, Devin, Jennifer, and Steve. Hell, Rachel and Eric—and even his mother. How many of them would survive the worst event in human history? That no one knew about.

Could he stop all of it before he lost friends? Family? His stomach twisted into knots and his heart hurt. His wife—the love of his life.

If he lost Talia in this fight, he didn't care what happened to him. He didn't want his soul if it meant an eternity without the woman he couldn't live without. If Talia wasn't here to share it with him, winning had no meaning. He would still help save it, but he couldn't live even a moment in a world where Talia no longer existed.

He winced. No, he wouldn't.

The sky was still a bleak grey, but the smoke and ash had dissipated, a hint of that Parrish blue beginning to soften the grit and the charcoal haze that had covered everything in Heaven. The clouds no longer rose into thunderheads. They were slowly brightening along the edges of the horizon. Even the scent of honeysuckles and roses slipped past the gritty air, the blooms trying to scrub the sky clean of Lucifer's destruction.

He pulled out his phone. No calls. No texts.

But the time made him shudder. It was after 7 PM in Los Angeles. His stomach lurched. The sun would set in less than an hour. Bringing the first nuclear-colored sky of the apocalypse.

If he did this right, no one would know how close the world came to ending. No one would face seven horrible plagues, weird-colored skies of doom, or seven douchebag demon princes throwing shade from seven horse-inspired sets of wheels.

Just another miserable, hot tourist season in L.A.

Kesien blinked beside him and handed him a sword, hilt first.

"We'd love to have you spar with us, Jack," said Kesien. "I hear that the squad's going with you to stop the Travelers."

Jack nodded. "Yep, dude, Mrs. Casey and I are taking the whole family to Amusement Park L.A. After we kick some demon prince ass and take their payload coins. Cotton candy's on me."

Kesien's grey eyes brightened and he smiled.

"I've never taken down a Hell prince before," he said. "Looking forward to it."

Talia and her squad liked taking down demons. Jack was just glad that he wasn't doing this alone.

"Just gotta figure out how to get each douchebag's payload coin."

Muriel was beside him and Kesien now.

"Jack, this may help," said Muriel, leaning on her sword. "Don't forget that each Traveler represents a human sin."

Jack frowned. "A sin? Like Old Testament kind of stuff?"

She nodded as Talia and Anahera joined them. Talia was beside him, her arms sliding around his waist, drawing him into her warm embrace. And for a moment, he felt calm, lost in her touch. Everyone was still safe.

"Muriel's correct, lover," said Talia, kissing the side of his face. "Each Hell prince presides over a sin. So, maybe we can use that sin to manipulate them?"

Jack couldn't stop the corners of his mouth from curving into a smirk.

"So, like greed and lust and gluttony? That type of thing?"

Muriel nodded. "Exactly right, Jack."

"But we need to figure out what sin each Hell prince presides over," Talia added.

Jack pulled her into a tight embrace, staring into her intense arctic grey eyes.

"So, instead of fighting all of them, Mrs. Casey, we feed their sins? And take the coins."

"Exactly, lover," said Talia.

"And with a squad of angels beside you, Jack," Muriel offered. "We should be able to unravel the sins these demons represent. Fast."

"Then maybe we can do this," said Jack in a quiet voice that got a little shaky. "Stop the pain, I mean." He gave Talia an uncertain look. "Can't we?"

Talia ran her fingers through his hair. "We can, Jack," she whispered.

Right now, he needed more than his own shaky self-confidence telling him he wasn't going to screw up the apocalypse. Like he did Luci's escape from Hell.

Kesien nodded and patted Jack's shoulder. "Sure can, kid," he said. "If we work together."

Jack felt the turmoil raging inside him soften. They had a plan now. A real plan. Not just show up and try to waste Hell princes. He just hoped no one stepped into the crossfire.

He'd never fought a Hell prince before. He'd fought Luci and an archdemoness and nearly got his ass handed to him each time. How much worse would a Hell prince be?

"Didn't even object to my calling him kid," said Kesien, suddenly looking concerned. "You must be worried sick, Jack."

Talia gripped Jack's hands, squeezing. "You won't deal with this alone, Jack. I promise."

He leaned over and pressed a sensual kiss against her lips that made her cheeks blush.

"Babe, we can really stop these douchebags from turning Earth into a dumpster fire!"

Anahera took the sword from Muriel and handed it to Jack again. "Yes, we can, Jack. Now, spar with us until it's..."

Anahera's voice trailed off, her gaze darting toward the sky.

Dread chilled his fingertips and blew across the edges of his wings as he followed her gaze.

Like an aurora gone wrong, the skies above Heaven began to change. Like a poisoned well, the grey cast turned sallow and flushed a putrid lime-green, like Linda Blair had mixed the paint this time with a 360-degree turn of her head.

Jack's arms tightened around Talia and for a moment, all he could do was stare at her, his gut tightening with trepidation. The fate of his world was up to him now. Him. A broken Hollywood star and recovering flake-addict-turned-reality-TV star. He sighed. Who planned to act his way out of this mess.

The word screwed didn't even begin to cover it.

His breath quickened and he fought to level out his breathing as the shakes rolled over him.

Somehow, he had to find and stop this first traveler. Pestilence. Before this douchebag demon unleashed something worse than Ebola and COVID-19.

He took a deep breath. Held it. And let go of Talia.

"It's time, Jack," said Talia, reaching over to grip his hand.

He glanced at Muriel and Kesien and finally, Talia. "We ready to splatter this first little demon bitch all over the Hollywood sign?"

Talia cupped his face in her hand. "Just breathe, Jack," she said in a soothing voice. "Let's take back your world from Lucifer."

He closed his eyes a moment, reveling in Talia's touch against his face, and then spread his silvery grey wings.

"Then let's get this party started," he said and slid his phone back into his pocket. "Siri, cue up my demon-splattering playlist. Repeat the first song. Loud."

Electric guitars squawked above a thumping drumbeat that echoed across Eolowen's terrace. Forcing every angel of death to look up.

At him.

No, this was no Heavenly chorus. This was serious, demon-ass-kicking music. It was his party and he was bringing the tunes.

Azrael, Pravuil, and Berith turned toward them. Azrael smiled and gave them a nod.

"Jack's anthem," said the archangel. "Play a round for Eolowen, squad. When you take down that first Traveler."

Jack let a smirk curl the corners of his mouth.

"Come on, dudes…let's go piñata a demon Hell prince and gank his payload coin. Collect the whole set."

Grinning, Talia leaned over and kissed him.

"You heard Jack, squad," she said, stretching her wings wide. "Supremes formation. Close ranks. Jack—and his anthem—is vanguard. Let's go splatter some demons." She bowed to Jack as she rose into the air, the rest of the squad around her. "All right, Mr. Casey, use that new seraphim power of yours and locate the pestilence Traveler."

He glanced at Talia and then at Muriel. Dammit! He'd forgotten to ask Seraphina how to actually use the power. He felt his face redden.

"Uh, Tal…" he said in a quiet voice, leaning toward her. "I forgot to ask her—"

A gold light enveloped him. His body snapped to attention and he couldn't control it as the seraph floated far above him in Heaven's skies.

Concentrate on the color of the plague sky. Will the smoky Traveler's path to materialize. The power is already within you, Jack Casey.

"Thank you…Seraphina," he choked out.

Play your anthem for me, too.

When Seraphina released him, Jack was grinning.

Talia slid her arms around him, eyes wide and filled with concern.

"Jack! Are you all right?"

He laughed. "I'm more than all right, babe," he said and lifted his gaze to the eerie green sky.

Willing the Traveler's path to appear.

It took a little sweat and some intense concentration, but the smoky, electric green path appeared, snaking across the sky, and dropping through the clouds.

Down toward Earth.

"Jack, you did it!" Talia cried and threw her arms around him, hugging him.

He held her tight and then kissed her, letting her go as the squad crowded around him.

"Now, we go kick some Hell prince ass. Party's gettin' started. To the tune of *You Shook Me All Night Long*." Grinning, he pointed above his head at the fiery gold seraph light high above Eolowen. "And this anthem goes out to Seraphina tonight. Seraph, this one's for you!"

When he looked back at the squad, they were grinning. Every angel on the terrace was smiling, including Pravuil and Azrael. Berith's expression was as bright as her rose-gold halo.

"What?" Jack asked as he moved along the smoky electric green trail of smoke.

"He couldn't hear it, could he?" Muriel said, nudging him.

Kesien and Deemah laughed, Anahera grinning as Talia clapped her hands together, a look of joy in her intense grey eyes.

Jack frowned. "Hear what?"

"Seraphina just played your music across the Heavens along with your dedication to her," said Talia, chuckling. "Identifying it as your demon-splattering playlist, Jack. Her laughter was heard all over the lower Heavens."

Talia slid her arms around him.

"I have never heard her laugh before. Ever. Much less echo a song with electric guitars across Heaven."

He couldn't help it. He broke into a fit of laughter, imagining all these angels' faces when they heard an AC/DC song thumping across the Heavens. Played by a seraph. About sex.

"That's slappin', Talia!"

He turned his attention back to the trail of smoke.

"Ready to do this?" he asked.

She nodded and kissed him urgently. "Let's go, squad. Tight Supremes formation."

With Jack in the center, they followed the green smoke through the eerie green sky, through the clouds, hurtling toward Earth. Through the twilight.

He gasped when he saw where the trail led. To Union Station in downtown L.A.

This Hell prince dude was probably more likely to get mugged and have that payload coin stolen by the time they found him. Guess that was Plan B. Or Plan C: send the demon into Skid Row to ask for directions.

One of those plans was bound to strip that payload coin off this Traveler's demon ass.

They landed in front of Union Station, an elegant stucco building with its Spanish tiled roof, terracotta arches, and towering palm trees surrounding it. Eucalyptus was soft against the pungent smell of car exhaust and hot asphalt. The sparkle of the city emanated around them, but the green sky reflected like an aurora, giving the world a sickly, nuclear green color. People kept staring up at the sky as they hurried in and out of the building.

No one paid Jack any attention, their gazes fixed on the strange sky. He hoped with the sky as the main attraction, no one would recognize him or Talia.

Of course, he looked like he was alone, even though he was surrounded by a squad of angels of death. His demon-splattering playlist was still playing from his pocket as he followed the green trail of smoke around the side of the building.

He groaned.

It led to one of the trains paused on the tracks, ready for boarding.

Squinting, he searched for a number. Once he found the train's number, he pulled out his phone and looked up its destination.

He frowned. Cleveland? Who the hell carried the first payload of the apocalypse to Cleveland? Why would they choose Cleveland?

Guess it had to start somewhere.

Jack motioned the squad back around to the front of the building. As he stood beneath the palm trees, wash of green sky unnerving, an old 70s Dodge Colt drove up. Boxy. Pea green.

"That's gotta be our first Hell prince," he said, motioning toward the old hatchback.

Muriel glanced at the sky and then at Talia.

"Okay, angels," said Talia, holding out her hands. "We've gotta figure out what sin this Hell prince handles and fast."

A stocky, ashen-skinned dude with shaggy, dull brown hair, dull brown eyes, and a bored expression stepped out of the Colt. He wore beige dress pants, a beige Oxford, and beige loafers.

Damn. Jack recoiled, the color beige making him shudder. This dude was definitely from Hell.

"So, first we've gotta figure out his sin," said Jack. "Besides poor fashion choices. Then we piss him off enough to see horns. Make sure we're not dealing with some human with no fashion sense headed home to Cleveland. Then we take his payload coin."

Muriel looked sick, shaking her head as the tall, stocky demon approached.

"Wow, that's gotta be Lucifer's doing," said Muriel, looking horrified. "Beige isn't a color. It's just plain giving up."

"It's the color of Hell, Muriel," said Jack with a shiver. "Beige was everywhere. It was so disturbing."

Talia materialized beside Jack and stepped in front of this dude as he approached the train station entrance. As the Traveler got close to the curb, Jack realized that this dude hadn't even looked at the sky once. He didn't seem to care.

That was a bad sign. And a dead giveaway—well, that and the pea-green Colt.

"Excuse me, sir," said Talia, blocking his path.

The demon gave Talia a wary look, glancing at Jack and then back at Talia.

"I'm not interested in anything you're selling, Miss," he said and started around her.

"I'm not selling anything," said Talia, staring into those dull brown eyes.

This possible Hell prince's long, angular face showed no emotion, not even annoyance as he looked at Talia and then Jack. To him, she was just something to go around.

"We're here on our honeymoon," said Jack, sliding his arm around Talia as he blocked the demon's path. "But now, we're on our way back home. To Cleveland. But we're not sure which train to board and this place is so huge."

A hint of annoyance brightened the dude's face. Winning.

"It's clearly marked on your ticket," said the demon and pulled his phone out of his pocket, showing a digital ticket. "See? Right here."

Wow, Luci finally got his demons some new phones since he'd been untethered! Wait until Zanth heard that. She'd be pissed.

Jack pulled out his phone and Talia took it from him. Silencing it. When she showed the screen, a ticket was on it. God, he loved angel powers!

"Here?" Talia asked, pointing.

"Yes," said the demon, relaxing a little. "That's the train boarding shortly for Cleveland."

The dude almost spat the word, Cleveland.

"My comrades all got to go to D.C. or New York City. Or hell, even Texas. Where do I get sent? Cleveland." The Traveler ground his teeth together, lips curling.

Talia glanced at Jack a moment and then back at this dude in all beige. Like Lucifer's demons had dressed him.

Jack had seen that old movie, *Seven* enough times to remember all of the seven deadly sins. He rifled through them in his head: lust, gluttony, pride, greed. He reached down deeper into his memory of the movie. Wrath. That was five. Envy and...dammit! What was the seventh one? Sloth!

Okay, this dude was angry. Possibly wrath. Wasn't pride or gluttony. Wasn't greed or sloth. Could be lust or envy.

This dude was jealous that the other Hell princes got to go somewhere cool. But he had to go to Cleveland.

Jack glanced at Muriel and then Talia.

"Guess your comrades aren't jealous that you're headed to Cleveland, aye?"

"That's it, Jack!" Deemah cried.

"Spot on," said Muriel. "Let's see if he's also horny."

Anahera frowned. "But you just said envy, not lust."

Muriel shook her head. "That was a joke, Anahera. We need to make sure he's a demon."

Jack stepped toward the demon. Who had his hand in his pants pocket now. Looking anxious and angry. About to pull out that payload coin?

Time to turn up the volume.

"Yeah, that's gotta suck," said Jack in a quiet voice, trying to set this demon off. "I mean, D.C. would be amazing! Or New York City."

"Tell me about it," said the demon, eyes narrowing. "So would Texas or anywhere in California. Hell, even Minneapolis would be amazing in August, right?"

"I hear their cheese-stuffed bacon burgers are to die for," said Jack, milking the description. "And those crispy, salty tater tots. Melt in your mouth goodness."

The demon's face pinched with anger, his mouth pressing into a flat line as he gritted his teeth.

"Cheese-stuffed bacon burgers? Seriously?"

Jack nodded. "And think about all the fun things to do while you're in town. Amusement parks. Theatre. Restaurants. Concerts. I hear there's a heavyweight boxing championship match happening this weekend in Minneapolis." He smiled and nudged the demon with his elbow. "Gonna spill lots of blood in that ring, am I right?"

Demons loved fights. And blood.

Jack could see the foam starting at the corners of this demon's mouth, eyes sparking red. At last, two tiny horn buds appeared in this dude's hairline. Score!

"Tell you what, dude," said Jack in a quiet voice. "The missus and I have tickets to Amusement Park L.A. The one with all the rollercoasters. Why don't I give them to you? You can go have some fun instead of taking a train to Cleveland."

"I don't know," said the demon, glancing around him. "I've gotta get there by morning." He pulled his hand out of his pocket and held up a strange tarnished gold coin bigger than a half-dollar. "Have to deliver this coin."

"Cool token, dude," said Jack. "Tell you what, the missus and I would be happy to take the coin with us on the train to Cleveland while you use the Amusement Park L.A. tickets."

At last, a grin appeared on the demon's face. "You know what, I'm tired of always getting the shaft. Deal. When you get there, leave the coin in the men's bathroom at the train station."

Pay dirt! So, that's where the apocalypse was supposed to start. In a grimy Cleveland train station bathroom. Made perfect sense now. This Traveler had to be dumb as a stump to risk Lucifer's wrath—and getting devoured by hellhounds—by handing over this payload coin.

Worked for Jack though.

Talia held out two tickets that she'd materialized behind her back while he bargained with this Hell prince.

The Hell prince tossed the coin into the air at Jack and snatched the tickets.

Jack caught the coin as the Hell prince turned around and headed back toward his Dodge Colt. He grinned as the demon drove away, his pea-green hatchback sputtering.

"Great job, lover!" Talia cried and threw her arms around him.

"Yeah, great job, Jack," said Muriel, patting him on the back. "Let's get out of here with that payload coin."

They hurried around the side of the building and Jack spread his wings, lifting off from Union Station with Talia and the squad. They soared through the eerie green sky back toward Heaven. To await the sky to turn blue again. And the second flight of angels to take to the air.

"Babe," Jack said as he flew beside Talia through a dense bank of clouds. "What is the second plague bowl?"

"It's famine, Jack," she answered as they passed through clouds smelling like rain and rose toward the lower reaches of Heaven. "And the bowl is black."

Eolowen gleamed white through the faint grey haze.

"The second one won't be that easy, will it?" he asked.

She shook her head. "No, we got lucky that Hell prince was one of Lucifer's disgruntled minions."

"And dumber than a stump, too," Jack added.

He'd keep that in mind as they waited for the second flight of angels. He sighed. And for rehearsals to start at the studio. In two angel days.

He landed beside Talia, the squad setting down behind them, all smiles as Pravuil and Azrael rushed toward them through the crush of angels training in the meadow and along the terrace. Seraphina's light was absent from overhead, the faintest hint of Parrish blue peeking underneath the eerie green skies.

Jack knew that if the payload didn't reach its destination in a day and a night, then the skies would return to normal. And the first plague wouldn't fire.

This time.

He gripped the payload coin tight in his fist.

"That was fast," said the archangel as he approached, looking concerned. "What's happened?"

Pravuil looked wary as he blinked beside Azrael.

Until Jack held up the gold payload coin.

"You did it!" Pravuil cried as Jack extended the coin to him.

"This Hell prince was all butthurt because his buddies got to go to more exotic places than he did."

Pravuil lifted an eyebrow. "Where was the first payload headed?"

Jack chuckled. "Cleveland."

"Who drops the first apocalypse payload in Cleveland?" Pravuil snapped as he took the coin from Jack's hand.

"A grimy train station men's bathroom in Cleveland," Jack added.

Pravuil's upper lip curled into an almost feral expression.

"Okay, who drops an apocalypse payload in a grimy Cleveland train station men's bathroom?"

"Wasn't me," said Jack, but then he remembered Pravuil saying that Lucifer had focused the events of the apocalypse on him as some added ~~torture~~ fun. "Or maybe it was?"

Pravuil shook his head. "Relax, Jack. It wasn't you. That putz

Lucifer just honed in on your place in the world as the apocalypse's focal point to punish you further. You didn't choose the payload locations." He sighed. "And there are still six more."

Six…he just hoped he could stop the other six.

His phone began to vibrate in his pocket.

For a moment, he froze.

Was it Lucifer? Calling to tell him about all the people he'd killed? All the places he'd wrecked since escaping Hell?

To make him feel worse than he already felt.

"What is it, Jack?" Talia asked, studying his face, worry burning bright in her intense arctic grey eyes.

"My phone's ringing," he said like it was the end of the world.

With dread, he slid the phone out of his pocket.

Armand Gianni's name appeared on the screen.

"It's Gianni," he said, grinning.

"Gianni!" he said after answering. "Dude, how ya been?"

"Jack?"

He sounded terrified.

"What's up, Gianni?" he asked, his gaze falling to Talia who waited for their conversation to unfold as the rest of her squad returned to training.

"Jack…the sky," Gianni said. "What's happening? It's the story on every news channel, but they all say scientists are baffled. No one knows a thing."

"The sky, it's—" Jack sighed. "It's not good, Gianni. It's uh…the worst thing you can imagine."

"Try me."

It's not like he could just come out and say, *Dude, welcome to the apocalypse! Just dodged the pestilence bullet, but we still have famine, war, and eventually death to look forward to—so, have a good night.*

Cringing, he tried to pick his words carefully.

"Let's just say that in a couple of days, the sky will return to normal."

How did he explain to his best friend that it was the apocalypse without saying it was the apocalypse? That it was nothing to worry about. Yet.

"And then what, Jack?"

"Not over the phone."

"Jack, I need to understand what's happening," said Gianni, his voice intense. "Izzy and I need to understand."

"You will, Gianni," said Jack in his most reassuring voice. But he was talking to another actor—who'd see right through him. "In two weeks. At the studio."

"Two weeks!" Gianni sputtered. "Jack, that's a lifetime from now! Please…let me come over to your place and—"

"Dude, I'm not there right now. Tal and I are…elsewhere. Dealing with…things."

"Jack, tell me what's going on," he pleaded. "I need to know."

Jack sighed and gave Talia his most helpless look. And whispered to her.

"What color is the next sky, babe?"

"Black," she said.

"Dude, after the sky returns to blue. It's…gonna change again."

"What?" Dead silence hung between them for several moments.

"It's gonna turn black."

"My God, Jack—black!"

"If everything goes well, the sky will return to blue again," said Jack, knowing that every word was making Gianni's head explode.

Regardless, he planned to enlist his best friend's help to stop the remaining Hell princes.

"When?" Gianni demanded.

"Before we start rehearsals at the studio. I promise you, I'll explain everything then. But for now, I can't."

"You talk like it's the end of the world, Jack."

Dammit! How did he respond to that?

"Jack? Jack!"

"I'm here," he said in a small, tight voice.

"Dear God…Jack. It is the end of the world? Isn't it?"

He was silent, not knowing how to even start this conversation.

So, dude, now that the apocalypse has rolled into town, I'm gonna need your help shutting it down before Lucifer destroys everything. Cool? Cool!

Gianni gasped. "Tell me, Jack. I have to know."

"Give Izzy my love, dude. And don't give up, okay? I'll see you in two weeks."

"Jack, tell me you're not trying to fix this alone. Whatever's happening, I'll help you. You don't have to fight this alone."

Jack chuckled. "Dude, you may regret those words. But thank you. I am gonna need your help—with a lot of things. Talia and I both will."

"Be careful, Jack," said Gianni. "I love you like a brother, you know that, don't you?"

Gianni's comment choked him up. He pulled in a breath, unable to talk for a moment.

"And you're the brother I've always wanted. Love you, dude. Stay safe. Tal and I will see you and Izzy in a couple of weeks."

"You promise?"

"I promise," Jack said with a chuckle.

"Be safe, Jack. Give Talia my love."

Gianni hung up.

For several moments, Jack stared at the phone until Talia's voice shook him out of his thoughts.

"Jack," she said, her hand rubbing his shoulder. "Are you okay?"

He glanced at her, nodding. "Just worried about my friends, Tal."

But their conversation was cut short as a flock of skeletal, emaciated angels appeared in the skies above Eolowen. The fabric of their black robes hung on them, looking old and tattered, wings skeletal and frayed.

Six in all, they each carried an oversized black bowl in their skeletal hands.

The second flight of angels had arrived. Waiting for some signal to fly over the Earth and drop-ship a load of famine on it.

"So soon?" he whispered, giving Talia an unsettled look.

She looked shocked and horrified at seeing the second flight arrive so soon.

The second flight of angels wailed like banshees on the wind. And waited.

For the next round of the apocalypse show to come back from commercial break.

8

Talia and her squad crowded around Azrael and Pravuil. She was distraught over seeing the second flight take to the skies so soon. The window on the first Traveler's payload hadn't even expired yet.

Why rush the flights out to harm so many humans? Why would the Maker allow it?

It made no sense.

"Why so soon, Azrael?" she cried, motioning at the wraith-like angels streaking across Heaven's grey skies with shiny black bowls in their skeletal fists. "It hasn't even been the full day and night yet on the first plague's payload."

Pravuil held out his hands, looking a little lost as his gaze tracked past them to Jack who paced the terrace behind them. He seemed lost in thought, ignoring the loud clap of blades against shields that sounded more like thunder than drilling angels.

Talia kept stealing glances at her troubled husband who seemed a little shell-shocked at how rapidly everything was happening.

"Angels, I wish I could tell you why," said Azrael, motioning for them to talk more softly. "But I can't. I expected a few angel days before the second flight even materialized, but here they are, marking time, waiting for some divine signal to pour out their bowls upon the Earth." He held up his hands. "It's not my doing."

"For what it's worth," said Pravuil, in a calm but gruff voice. "Even Seraphina is surprised by the second flight's sudden appearance."

"Scribe, does the timetable have anything to do with Lucifer's hunt for this artifact?" Talia asked. "The one we know nothing about."

"It's possible, Talia," said the Scribe as he stretched his wings and floated a foot above the terrace stones, also looking unnerved by the second flight's sudden appearance. "This is the Maker's show. Maybe He's trying to hasten the apocalypse and get the sixth flight in the air?" His brow furrowed as he glanced at Jack again. "To get all of us battling Lucifer and his army sooner. If we take them down over Earth, then the danger to the Thrones is over."

Talia frowned.

The Scribe left something unsaid there and she needed to understand the entire picture.

"Or maybe he's trying to get ahead of Lucifer before that putz gets hold of a rod of Creation."

"But Scribe," she continued. "What if Lucifer is using the sixth flight and the remaining Hell Princes as diversions? Misdirections. Keeping all of us so busy that we can't stop him from locating the artifact and then compromising the upper portal to reach the Thrones."

Her words sent ripples of fear across her squad. And across the terrace, as angels of death stopped drilling and turned to listen.

She glanced over her shoulder. Her words had unnerved her husband who blinked beside her, terror burning in those pale green eyes. His arm was around her waist and she smelled the faint coconut scent of his hair mixing with traces of warm cedar on his clothes. She laid her head on Jack's shoulder, his proximity calming her.

"Wait a minute!" Jack cried, fixing Pravuil with his frightened gaze, and motioned at the Scribe with his right hand. "Are you saying the entire apocalypse is another one of Luci's misdirections?" He motioned toward the sky. "So Luci can pop the soul portal and murder dear ol' Dad while we're all fighting for our lives? So he can just turn around and cancel our service, shutting off the lights on existence? Seriously, dude?"

Pravuil's cheeks puffed out as he exhaled sharply and folded his hands behind his back, still floating above the terrace, wings rustling.

"Unfortunately, Jack—that's exactly what it means. Lucifer has one goal right now. Finding a rod of Creation. And there were several of them. But I believe he's after a special one." His brow wrinkled. "The Omega Rod."

Jack squinted at her, looking more lost and confused than ever.

"The Omega Rod?" Talia repeated. "As in the final rod of Creation?"

"Exactly right, Talia."

"Why the last one, Scribe?"

The Scribe's expression darkened, those gold eyes brightening.

"Because the last rod of Creation absorbed all the remaining power left orphaned when Creation was completed. Much more than any of the other rods, including the Alpha rod which actually has the least power because it was the most measured."

She had used omnificence several times, searching for the rods of Creation, but she had no idea what to look for. Or where to look. And she came up empty-handed.

"Pravuil?" Talia called to him. "How do we find this rod before Lucifer?"

At last, a hopeful look softened the creases on the Scribe's face. "An excellent question, Talia. I've been pondering this subject at length, discussing it with Seraphina, and even the Maker. To find it, we have to recognize it. And to recognize it means that we must locate something with Creation energies."

"Isn't that everything?" Kesien replied.

"Yes, Kesien," said the Scribe as he shifted position to lean against the wall of the terrace. "Everything has these energies, but some things are stronger in them."

"Like the resurrect power?" Jack asked, uncertainty slowing down his words. "It needs five elements from the Creation to cast."

Pravuil's demeanor brightened. "Jack! That's a very good point. It would have most of the rod's vibrations when touched by omnificence, but not all. And we do need all."

"But Scribe," said Talia. "What about using resurrect to find these rods? If we successfully bring angels back from oblivion, their bodies will contain all the elements of Creation, at least for a little while. Elements newly brought together again."

The Scribe blinked across the terrace and gripped Talia's shoulders.

"That's exactly right, Talia!" he said with a grin. "Use omnificence to scan the last few angels you resurrected. Collect those unique signatures and use that Creation pattern with omnificence."

"I'll go find Cabriawn and Janaelis," said Talia. "They were the two most recent angels resurrected. They should still have the Creation elements present from resurrect being cast on them."

"Cabriawn! Janaelis!" Pravuil's gruff, loud voice barked across the meadow and the terrace. "Come and see Talia. Now. Time's short."

In moments, the cherubim appeared to her left. Jack still hovered at her right side, looking a little tired and lost.

"Yes, Scribe, of course," said Cabriawn, catching Talia's gaze and holding it. "Talia, whenever you're ready."

"I'm here, too," said Janaelis as she blinked beside Cabriawn. "Whatever you need, Talia."

"You, uh…need any help, babe?" Jack asked, sounding so sweet.

She wanted to wrap him in her arms and fly away with him to a quiet beach house along the shores of the Celestial Ocean. And disappear from all of this pain and devastation building everywhere.

She didn't need Jack's help to scan these cherubim, but she might need his help to isolate the rod's signature in omnificence. Even if she didn't, she wanted him beside her, wanted to feel his vibrant, electric presence, breathe in his warm cedar and coconut scent. The last thing she wanted right now was to be away from him.

"Yes, lover," she said in a soft voice, staring into the pools of his pale green eyes. "I'll need your help to isolate the rod's signature in omnificence."

He smiled, looking pleased that she needed him. Jack seemed to think that the times she needed him were rare, not realizing that she always needed his presence. His proximity. The heat of his soul against hers.

"Right beside you, Mrs. Casey," he said with a smirk. "Whenever you need me."

"Does now until forever work for you?" she asked, softly kissing his lips.

"That—totally fits my schedule," he replied, kissing her back, his mouth so warm that his lips burned against hers. "Who knew?"

"I did," she said.

She brushed her fingers across the sculpted curve of his jaw and turned toward Janaelis and Cabriawn.

Both a head taller than Jack's six-foot frame, their gold eyes were bright against the grey skies. Cabriawn's white hair was short and spiky but layered down the back of his neck. He had an oblong face, strong jaw, and chiseled features, especially his perfect nose with its gentle slope. He had a nice smile and wide-set eyes.

Janaelis had long white hair that tumbled down her back in soft curls that were so bright against her mahogany skin. Her softly squared face had a delicate nose and full bow-shaped lips, her large almost cat-like gold eyes giving her an inquisitive look. Like she wanted to touch and see and do everything.

Cabriawn smiled and reached out, taking Talia's hand.

"Talia, thank you again for bringing me back from oblivion," he said, his voice a sunny baritone that matched his smile and sculpted good looks.

"You're very welcome, Cabriawn," she replied, glancing over at Jack who looked concerned, watching the cherub with newfound interest.

She chuckled. And a little jealous, those eyes a little greener now.

"If you hadn't brought back Cabriawn," said Janaelis who stepped forward in front of Jack. "He and my squad wouldn't have brought Berith to the rubble and rescued me. Thank you."

"I never want to experience those moments of non-existence ever again," said Cabriawn.

Talia glanced at Jack whose stony expression had darkened. Like he was contemplating a new moment of non-existence for Cabriawn.

Janaelis turned her gaze to Jack, those gold eyes widening.

"And what's your story?" she asked Jack. "You're human, right? With wings and a halo?"

"It's a long story," said Jack, those pale green eyes sparkling, lighting every luscious feature of his handsome face. "Got dragged off to Hell. Played the long con on Lucifer to escape. Trapped him in the Garden. Where he killed me—but Tal brought me back, too."

Janaelis gasped. "You, too?"

Jack nodded. "Seraphina kept my soul in my body long enough for Talia to bring me back. When Lucifer's powers returned, he broke free of the Garden. And hunting me became his life's ambition. So, Azrael hid me in the guard, giving me wings and a halo. Only now, they can't figure out how to take them back. Or the seraphim powers."

Janaelis' eyes got huge. "You've got seraphim powers?"

He nodded. "And Talia's rare angel powers got mirrored back to me."

Janaelis looked at him with renewed interest. "You're a human with all those powers? And you trapped Lucifer?"

He shrugged, looking almost embarrassed now. "An archangel trapped the seraphim in the spire, but the only way they could get a message out without being detected was through me. So, they channeled their power into me so I could rescue them."

"You rescued the seraphim, too?"

"Well, not just me," said Jack with a shrug. "Had Talia's squad and Azrael there."

Janaelis took a step toward Jack, her gaze fixing him with a bold, unblinking stare. Smiling at him in a way that suddenly made Talia uncomfortable.

"You are quite a handy human to have around. Jack, is it?"

He nodded as she circled him. Like prey? A new conquest. A love interest?

"Jack Casey," he replied.

"You're that human actor, right?" she said, taking another lap.

Around her husband.

Jack nodded again. "That's me."

Janaelis halted in front of him, an almost sly smile on her face as she reached her hand toward his cheek.

He held up his left hand, displaying his wedding band. "The married human actor," he said.

The cherub's hand still went to his face, stroking.

"Meet my wife," he said with that sexy smirk that made Talia want to marry him all over again. "Talia Casey."

A confused look touched the cherub's face for a moment. She glanced over at Talia and drew back her hand.

"You married an angel of death?" she cried, brows furrowing.

"Sure did," said Jack. "Azrael, Berith, and the guard attended. Even Abaddon was there. Trying to kill me, but he was there. Tal, show her your rings."

By the Maker, she loved this man!

She held out her hand, showing Janaelis her wedding band and aquamarine engagement ring. And the silver band she wore on her index finger. The silver wedding band that had belonged to Jack's dad. The one that Jack had used to propose to her on a live television broadcast.

Janaelis stared at the rings in wonder. Finally, her gaze met Talia's.

"You actually married a human?" she said. "And Heaven let you?"

She wasn't making a snide comment. Janaelis looked shocked that Heaven had allowed her to marry at all. And marry a human at that.

"Jack seems to have one foot in Heaven and one foot on Earth," said Talia. "He's even stopped aging. But the seraphim have allowed us to remain together—especially after everything Jack's given."

"What about the Maker?" Janaelis asked, glancing from Jack to her. "Forgive me for asking so many questions. I'm just trying to understand."

Jack sighed and got quiet and distracted. Like she felt. The Maker's blessing—or lack of it—was the last thing that could separate them.

"The Maker is aware of our marriage," said Talia, glancing at Jack and then back at Janaelis.

At last, the cherub smiled, but her gaze was all over Jack in a way that made Talia uncomfortable again.

"Well, Talia," she said. "You are a very lucky angel to be with one of the most beautiful humans I've ever seen. Positively breathtaking."

Jack shoved his hands into his Levi's pockets and gazed at Talia, anger burning in his green eyes. She felt his impatience and discomfort, too.

"The human thanks you," Jack snapped.

"I'm sorry, Jack," said Janaelis. "I meant no disrespect."

"All I ask is that you talk to me like I'm still in the room, not talk at me." His gaze had hardened like glass.

"Of course, Jack, my apologies," said Janaelis who turned her gaze back to Talia. "Are you ready to scan us for Creation energy?" And hurriedly changed the subject.

Talia fought back a laugh. Jack had handled that like a professional. And she loved him for it.

"I am," said Talia as she gazed at Cabriawn whose stoic expression encompassed her and Jack both. "I will be using a rare power called omnificence. You'll both feel a soft breeze and some warmth as I scan. Slight movements won't affect my power, but I do need you to remain in one spot until I'm finished."

Cabriawn nodded.

"Understood," said Janaelis and stiffened as Talia lifted both hands in the air.

Calling up omnificence.

She'd never used omnificence on anyone like this before—especially one of Heaven's angels. Much less cherubim. The closest she'd come was searching for Kesien with it, but she'd never actually used the power on him. Not like this.

A soft yellow light misted both angels as she focused the power onto the cherubim who both stood with bowed heads, hands pressed together as Talia dialed the power downward through the endless layers of Holy light that fluttered within all angels. Separated by warm air that filled their bodies from the core of Holy Fire churning at their centers.

Talia pressed harder with her hands, forcing omnificence deeper into their ethereal forms. Into the layers of light. Into the currents of warm air that flowed through every angel. Into the glowing white core of Holy Fire that pulsed like a human heart through celestial beings.

It was the breath of the Maker that set their angel hearts beating and made their angelic lungs channel light and air through their bodies. Giving them buoyancy. Giving them wings. She smiled. And flight.

She focused omnificence deeper. Into that core of Holy Fire. Into the breath of the Maker. Where all the elements of Creation were most concentrated within an angel. And captured the pattern of elements there.

Angels were mostly air and fire. They had blood but it was essentially light. With little bits of earth and water. And the more powerful the angel, the higher the concentration of fire. And for each being, there were some unique pairs of Enochian symbols. Symbols that made each being unique. It was sort of like human DNA.

It took her several minutes to gather all of this code and its temporary levels of Creation elements for Cabriawn and then for Janaelis. When she was finished, she compressed the information into an orange orb of Holy Fire for Cabriawn and a blue orb of Holy Fire for Janaelis. She snatched each one out of the air as it hovered beside its angel and cradled them against her stomach.

"Got them! Thank you both."

The cherubim nodded and took flight, rejoining the patrol flying over Eolowen and Heaven.

"Babe, you did it!" Jack cried, rushing over to her.

"Took a while, but I got all the information." She sighed and glanced over at Pravuil. "But I don't exactly know what to do with it."

"The Scribe will have to tell us," said Jack as he took her in his arms and held her close. "Great job, Mrs. Casey."

She loved his enthusiasm and support. He always made her feel special. And loved. She smiled. Especially when he called her Mrs. Casey.

"Let's take these over to him," she said and took one orb in each hand.

Jack bowed and let her pass, falling in behind her as she approached Pravuil.

"Scribe," she called. "I have the patterns and codes."

She extended both orbs to the Scribe whose eyebrows lifted in surprise.

"You got all of it?" he asked.

Talia nodded. "It's all here."

A grin brightened the Scribe's brooding features. "Nice work, Talia. Let me have a look at these."

The Scribe held the orange one against his temple and closed his eyes a moment. After some silence, he switched it with the blue orb and closed his eyes again. As if reading the information.

"Now, inside this information are Creation codes from those temporary elements in resurrect," said Pravuil, his gaze focused on her. "I need to isolate and gather those codes. They are the most complete record we have right now."

Talia frowned. "Why is that, Scribe?"

Pravuil's wings unfurled as he held out his hands. "Because bringing back those angels with resurrect touched all of the Creation elements—which includes any of the rods still floating around Creation."

Jack looked intrigued. "So, now, you're going to see which phone numbers still ping back after you called the main number?"

The Maker's Scribe stared at Jack a moment, brow furrowing, and then returned his gaze to her.

"Talia, translate please," said Pravuil.

"I think Jack understands that you're going to send out those codes and see which Creation rods respond back."

"Exactly, babe," said Jack.

Pravuil's brow lines deepened as he stared down at the terrace stones for a few moments. Finally, he jerked his head up.

"I don't have the power to search for the rods, Talia."

Talia felt a chill against her wings. If the Maker's Scribe couldn't search for the rods, who had enough power to find them?

"Does Seraphina?" Talia asked.

The Scribe nodded and she felt some of her tension release.

"Seraphina will search for those codes throughout the Creation. By comparing the power in each rod that she locates, she should be able to identify the Omega Rod." The Scribe grimaced, making her worry again. "Unless the Omega Rod is no longer responding."

"Why would it not respond?" Talia asked, laying her hand on Pravuil's sleeve.

He patted her hand. "Let's hope it doesn't come to that."

He was avoiding her question. It was never good when the Scribe avoided a question.

She started to pursue the question, but Jack stepped closer to Pravuil.

"So, if this rod doesn't respond," said Jack, chewing his bottom lip, "does that mean Luci already found it?"

Pravuil glanced from Jack to her and back again. And sighed. "Yes, Jack. That's what it means. Unless it's been destroyed somehow."

Jack's face turned pale. "Destroyed? How could that happen?"

Pravuil grabbed hold of her and Jack and pulled them into the round room. His gold gaze was intense, his face taut, fingers twined together as he studied her and Jack a moment.

"All right," he said, gaze narrowing. "Straight story here. The Omega Rod of Creation is a deadly remnant from the foundational elements of Creation. It causes all the elements to collide and explode, creating the essential components for creating life."

Jack's eyes got huge, his mouth gaping. "For real, dude? Like the big bang or something?"

"For real, Jack," said Pravuil in a hoarse whisper as he lowered his voice. "Like the big bang theory. It is what created the Maker. And it's the only thing that can kill a Maker."

"So, what does this thing look like?" Jack asked.

"A bit like a shaft of corroded iron," said Pravuil, glancing up at the ceiling portals and then around the room. "A bit like metal left at the bottom of the ocean for a very long time. It has a thick metal-like crust over it that protects its core of molten white light. A Maker's essence."

"Dude…that's—nuts," Jack said in a sharp whisper. "Are you saying that the Maker's essence is in his this freakin' Omega Rod?"

"More or less, yes, Jack," said Pravuil. "That's why we need to get to it before Lucifer does."

"Ya think?" Jack cried. "You're right, Scribe. Luci gets hold of that thing and Heaven's screwed. Humanity's screwed. I'm beyond screwed."

Talia put her arms around him and held him close.

"It'll be okay, Jack," she said against his ear. "We'll get to it in time."

A heavy sigh echoed from Jack's lips. "We don't have a choice, do we, Mrs. Casey?"

She shook her head. They had to locate the rod before Lucifer and take it first. Otherwise, Lucifer would become unstoppable.

"Regardless, Seraphina will know what to do," said Pravuil, the volume of his voice returning to normal again. "Talia, I'll let you know as soon as we locate the rod."

Jack had a funny look on his face. His worried expression intensified as he chewed his bottom lip.

"Jack," she said, stroking his hair. "What's the matter?"

"This Omega Rod," he said, his wings shifting against his shoulder blades. "Can Luci destroy angels with it?"

She didn't think so, but she needed Pravuil's input.

"Pravuil?" she called and held out her hand to Jack. "Can you please answer Jack's question?"

"Sorry," said the Scribe as he floated toward Jack, using his wings as rudders. "What was your question, Jack?"

"Lucifer," said Jack, twisting his fingers together. "Can he destroy angels with that rod?"

The Scribe shook his head. "No, Jack," he replied. "Those rods can only absorb Creation light now. And there shouldn't be very many left out there. Two or three at the most. After the Creation, they were left to absorb excess Creation energy so it could be returned to the Maker."

Jack still looked worried.

"I'm taking these orbs to Seraphina now," said Pravuil, lifting off the floor. "Don't give up, Jack and Talia. I'll keep you informed. Now, you two go train with the guard and concentrate on getting hold of Traveler number two's payload coin."

Talia nodded and slid her hand into Jack's, holding his hand tightly. "Will do. Thanks, Pravuil."

"Thanks for setting the record straight, dude," said Jack as Talia led him back out to the terrace to spar with the squad.

But the second flight of angels flew overhead again, bowls raised high as the green cast began to fade from the sky.

Jack gasped and slid his phone out of his pocket.

"Tal, it's now sunset in Los Angeles." His face pinched into a look of misery. "Time goes so fast up here," he said with a deep, jarring sigh. "Has it really been a night and a day?"

She nodded and squeezed his hand. There wasn't a lot she could say to comfort him. She had no idea how he must feel at this moment, knowing what could happen to so many people that he loved.

A deep, bass moan rumbled across Heaven as the second flight of angels circled the dove grey skies, black bowls of the second plague tilted toward the Earth.

With a bone-rattling shriek, the six emaciated angels whispered a lament across the Heavens and flew in a patrol formation and floated like apparitions down through the clouds.

Bound for Earth. To pour out the second plague on the Earth. Famine.

And launch the second Hell prince into action, delivering his payload beneath a pitch-black sky.

They had to find—and neutralize—the second Traveler. Fast.

9

Jack watched Heaven's greyness begin to fade beneath a soft, soothing wash of Parrish blue that seeped through the grey smoke and began to calm Heaven's skies. The blue was probably returning to Earth's skies, too. People below probably thought that whatever had caused that sickly lime-green color was gone now.

Wait til they saw black skies during the day.

He winced, pacing Eolowen's terrace. They had no idea that they'd just dodged a plague of Biblical proportions. And that a worse plague —famine—was on the way and the longer it stayed in place on the ground, the more harm it caused.

He watched the second angel flight hiss across the skies, those black bowls clutched so menacingly in their skeletal hands.

These angel-wraiths and Hell princes would deliver progressively worse things to Earth in the worst delivery service event since Pizza Playpen brought him a pineapple pizza instead of pepperoni.

Okay, so things were much, much worse than that.

Did this famine plague mean interrupting supply chains, killing crops in the fields, and rotting food on its way to groceries and restaurants? Or would all the food just suddenly disappear?

He had no idea how it would all unfold. Or how quickly people on

Earth would feel the pain. He only knew that he had to stop it before it came to that. Before Hell prince number two's payload coin popped off. He wouldn't let anyone on Earth go through that kind of hell.

Then he had to stop the plague of war. And disaster—bowls three and four. He sighed. And stop the three other bowls that came after the plague Heaven called disaster. The ones he had no clue about.

Plagues that Talia wouldn't be here to help him stop. That made him shake all over.

And he wouldn't be beside her to make sure she was all right fighting Lucifer.

Earth's sky was about to turn pitch black. While Traveler Two carried a new payload to another unknown place.

He checked the time on his phone again. After sunset meant this flight of angels would be taking the red-eye to Los Angeles, preparing for a sunrise premiere of this horrid sequel.

Talia slid her arms around him. Startling him.

"Tal, this is all happening so fast," he said, unable to keep the fear out of his voice. "By sunrise, the skies will all turn black, won't they?"

Her face was taut, muscles tightening in her jaw as her expression darkened. Slowly, she nodded.

"Why is it all happening so fast like this?" he asked, but she was already shaking her head. "And will people just instantly start starving if this bastard demon Hell prince sets off his payload?"

Her gaze tracked across the sky as she watched the second flight of angels circle Eolowen again.

"I wish I knew, Jack," she said in a soft voice, her arms tightening around him. "None of this was supposed to happen right now. Or like this."

Jack stepped away from her, holding out his arms as the shadows of the second angel flight passed over him.

"Then why doesn't someone in charge stop this insanity?" he shouted. "Luci is obviously cheating. So, why doesn't the Maker just end this? Full stop. Because it totally wasn't on the schedule this week to end the Earth."

A hand was on his shoulder, squeezing in a supportive gesture.

"Because, Jack," said Azrael, his soot-grey eyes glassy. "The seals have been broken, setting certain events into motion. And those events can't be reset. At least not yet."

"But Azrael, the Maker *made* time! And the planet." Jack replied, turning around, feeling like he was going to hork all over Azrael's sabatons. "Why can't He just do a little rewind? Like you did for Talia?"

Azrael's cheeks reddened.

"A planet-wide rewind of time could very well destroy all of the Creation, Jack," said Pravuil as he hovered behind Azrael who looked relieved at not having to deal with that question. "The upheaval that would cause would require too much energy and force to repair. Too much for the Thrones to bear. It would break them apart and everything would cease to exist."

Azrael's lip curled into a snarl. "Which is exactly what Lucifer was counting on when he set these events in motion. The events can't be stopped. Now, they can only succeed or fail. Otherwise, it all comes apart."

Berith put her arms around Azrael.

"So, you dudes are saying the only way to stop this is to win?" Jack asked, studying Azrael's angry expression and the Scribe's anxious stare.

Azrael nodded. "Exactly right, Jack."

"And it was never about the apocalypse, Jack," Pravuil said with a groan and folded his hands behind his back. "You know that."

"It was always about the diversion," said Jack, his gaze narrowing, Talia beside him again, holding him in a comforting embrace. "With everyone focused on saving the Creation, there's no one to stop Luci from Michael Baying the Thrones. And dear ol' Dad."

Azrael frowned and raised an eyebrow, exchanging a confused look with Pravuil.

"Michael what? The archangel, Michael?"

"More Jackspeak," said the Scribe, groaning as he turned to Talia. "Talia, translate, please."

"I'll call Muriel," said Talia. "That one's beyond me."

"You call yourselves angels of death?" Jack shouted, shocked that he had to explain this remark. "Dude, there are tons of explosions and a body count attached to every one of Michael Bay's films," Jack replied. "Kinda awesome, too."

"Muriel!" Talia called.

In a moment, Muriel blinked beside Talia, looking fearful as she glanced from Talia to Azrael.

"What's happening?" Muriel asked, looking pale and unnerved, sword in one hand, gold shield of light in her left hand.

Azrael glanced at Jack and then fixed Muriel with his gaze. "What does Michael Baying the Thrones mean to you?"

A smile lit Muriel's face as she stared at the archangel a moment.

"Means blowing them up. Haven't you ever seen a Michael Bay film before?"

"See!" Jack cried and hugged Muriel. "Clear as a Midwest summer day."

She blushed, glancing at Jack. "This is about Jackspeak, isn't it?"

Pravuil sighed and nodded. "Talia, your husband is starting to influence the guard."

Jack's gaze snapped to Talia, fearing her response as she smirked at the Scribe.

"Kinda awesome, too," she said.

Jack broke into a fit of laughter and pulled Talia into his arms, kissing her hard on the lips.

"I knew I married the right woman," he said with a chuckle.

Muriel laughed and patted Jack on the back.

"Going back to training, but if you need more translation—sing out."

She blinked across the terrace and into the meadow, returning to Kesien, Anahera, and Deemah who sparred together just below the steps to Azrael's dais.

"Regardless of the Jackspeak," said Pravuil, beginning to drift along the terrace. "You're right, Jack. Lucifer knows that all we can do is stop the stages of the apocalypse now. He's counting on us choosing to selfishly save ourselves and our people, leaving him a narrow window to challenge the Thrones. And the Maker."

Jack propped his hands on his hips and began to pace the terrace parallel to the Scribe.

"And that's why we have to give him the appearance that that's exactly what we're doing, Scribe."

Pravuil halted his wings and landed with a thump on the white stone terrace.

"Elaborate, Jack," he said.

"We keep going after the Hell princes. While we search for the Omega Rod."

Berith looked frightened. "Jack, he knows we're searching for the rods of Creation. He must have some information about the Omega Rod's whereabouts that we don't."

"Question is, where'd he get it?" Jack asked, almost to himself as he continued matching Pravuil's pacing.

"What if that information came from Lucifer's own memories?" Talia replied.

Talia's comment sent shockwaves across the terrace.

Both Azrael and the Scribe were stunned silent, staring at Talia, looking like they'd all just eaten a piece of pineapple pizza, expecting pepperoni. Okay, it was much worse than that, but just pineapple? That's just wrong.

"Talia, you're—you're right," said Azrael, the anger fading from his face, replaced by a touch of anguish.

"How do we get information that only Luci has?" Jack asked with a groan. He moved over to Berith. "Berith, there's no way Luci would share that information with his demons or his Hell princes, right?"

"Something this important?" Berith replied, staring into Jack's gaze. "Never. He'd only share it if his demons needed to know. Which they don't if Lucifer has gone after the Omega Rod alone. No, he'd keep this information to himself because that's also keeping it from Heaven."

A curious smile lit Azrael's face. "But he can't keep omnificence from tracking his every movement. He is an angel after all."

"His Brand!" Talia cried, wings twitching as she unfurled them in the wind. "Azrael! His Brand is active now that he has all his powers back."

Jack thought back to the spire ruins, to the lowest chamber where he'd searched for survivors in all that wreckage. Muriel had him focus on some symbol that burned gold in the dark, in his head when he used omnificence. Could he locate Luci that way? He had no idea what Luci's brand looked like, but the Archive would know.

"We can at least follow his movements," said Berith, nodding as her gaze on Talia intensified. "See where he's gone. It won't give us an exact location for the Omega Rod, but it's better than no information."

But Jack still felt queasy about this plan. They would be at least two steps behind Luci the whole way. If he got hold of that Omega Rod, he could extinguish every angel's light on his way up to the Thrones. And that kind of power in Luci's hands terrified him.

"Who else would have that memory, Scribe?" Jack asked Pravuil who was quiet for several moments.

"You know what, Jack," said the Scribe. "That's a great question. Because the answer is me. I have that memory, too, because I was there." He turned his body toward Eolowen, lost in thought for a moment. "What if Seraphina could somehow...extract that memory from my head? And find out where the Omega Rod is right now."

Azrael's eyes got huge and he turned to the Scribe, hands gripping the Scribe's white robes. "Pravuil? Can Seraphina do that?"

The Scribe nodded. "She can. Don't think she's ever done it on an archangel before. Much less the Maker's Scribe. Might take a while. But much quicker than capturing all of my memories into a story gem and then trying to find one memory. That's my backup plan."

"Then let's get started!" Berith cried, taking the Scribe's arm as she stretched her wings. "Come on, Pravuil. Let's go see Seraphina."

Together, they rose from the terrace and dropped through one of the round room portals. And into Eolowen.

"Tal, where will the second flight pour out their bowl of bad soup this time?" Jack asked, fixing Talia with his gaze.

She glanced at Azrael a moment and then returned her gaze to him.

"The ocean," she said finally and gripped his arms. "Jack, the seas will all turn black when that happens."

Jack gasped. "All of them?"

"All of them," she said. "They're all connected. The blackness will carry off the waves like dust. To the crop fields. Killing your food supplies. It'll make animals sick, too. Tainting their milk and they won't reproduce."

"Everything edible will shrivel to dust and blow away, Jack," said Azrael in a dire tone as the second flight of angels passed overhead again.

He felt the direness of the situation sitting on his chest again. One more angel day until he had to show up for rehearsals at Studio 22 in Burbank. While stopping the other Hell princes. Until the sixth flight of angels emptied their bowl of pain—and filled the skies over Earth with the worst air war between angels and demons ever witnessed. With its seraph general injured and unable to lead the assault.

Leaving his wife and Azrael to lead the fight. Jack sighed. While he was grounded, babysitting demons with emotional problems and an urge to commit genocide.

Sounded like a new streaming series on TVN. One he didn't want to helm.

BY THE TIME the sun rose over the West Coast, and a whole week had passed since yesterday in his time, the second flight of angels descended from Heaven in a trail of black smoke, shiny black bowls cradled against their skeletal chests.

Headed for the Pacific Ocean.

When the sun rose over Santa Monica Boulevard, all six angel-wraiths had poured out their black bowls of sorrow into the ocean. Turning it and the sky inky black. Like a volcanic eruption where ash clouded the sun, turning sunrise to dusk.

Leaving Los Angeles in a panic.

As he and Talia flew into the clouds of blackness, Jack moved as close to her as he could and gripped her hand, using the light of her gold halo to guide him. He pretended it was just night flying in L.A. as Talia's squad appeared around them in Supremes formation.

He didn't hear one single angel note. All of them looked as terrified as he felt, including Kesien who rarely let his emotions shadow his face.

Rehearsals started tomorrow. It seemed so trivial in the face of these Hell prince payloads, but he had to keep his life going. Keep everything moving forward.

Maybe it no longer mattered?

He had no idea, but maybe if he faked normality long enough, everything would go back to normal.

If he didn't have something familiar to focus on right now, he didn't think he could handle this end-of-the-world shit. Or Luci trying to pull the plug on the whole simulation by killing his own father. Didn't Keanu Reeves already do this movie? Way better, too.

Jack sure as hell didn't want to remake it. With demons.

They landed on the beach. Just north of the Santa Monica Pier. It was open, neon lights bright in the inky darkness.

"Wow, the second flight's influence is like flying through pea soup," Muriel replied, glancing around, the black ocean swells pounding the beach.

Staining the sand.

"Jack, can you see the trail leading to the second Hell prince yet?" Talia asked, rubbing his arm.

Jack looked up at the sky and focused on the thick blackness that stuck to everything like someone had spilled motor oil over everything. He closed his eyes, concentrating on the sky and the black bowls that the second flight had carried to the ocean and emptied.

Searching for the trail.

Sweat covered his face like it did when he ran three miles in L.A.'s summer heat. It clung to his skin like a mask, but he held his focus on the blackness.

"Good job, lover," said Talia, holding him tight as he opened his eyes.

Hanging in the skies above the pier, a black smoky trail twisted and turned like a tornado across the sky.

"Thanks, Mrs. Casey," he said with a tired grin and kissed her. "Let's follow this mess to the next Hell prince."

"And waste him?" Deemah asked, her grey eyes sparkling.

"I love a good shield bash," Muriel replied, looking hopeful as she held up her gold shield.

A few people passed Jack as they walked along the beach, staring up at the sky. Looking like they'd just seen all the Baldwins together on the same beach. They mumbled about the darkness, their white sneakers rasping against the sand as they walked toward the pier.

The whole angel squad was visible now, but the handful of tourists and locals walked right past them. Like they'd always been there. Like the pier.

Muriel rolled her eyes. "Only in L.A."

Jack chuckled. Worked for him. At least they hadn't recognized him or Talia.

His phone started to vibrate and he slid it out of his pocket.

A frantic text from Gianni.

> Jack, what the hell is happening now?
>
> It's after 8 AM and it's as dark as midnight

He tapped out a response.

> dude chill 😎 it'll 🌑 by tmrw
>
> cu@studio

Gianni sent a short response.

> 🙏 trusting u

"Ready, Jack?" Talia asked.

Nodding, he slid his phone back into his Levi's pocket and lifted off from the beach, Talia and the squad surrounding him as they followed the twisting black smoke.

South. Jack's stomach dropped. Toward the airport. Where was this demon headed?

Flying along the roads, it took about fifteen minutes to get to the airport. LAX's sprawling parking lots surrounded the terminals like a sea of concrete and headlights. The stream of cars and people and trams was constant. But every person that stepped off a tram or out of their cars stared up at the sky as suitcases rumbled across the pocked asphalt.

Jack blinked across the long-term parking lot. Toward the end of the smoky black trail.

Stopping as a moon-pale woman, about six foot tall and model-thin, stepped off a huge, shiny black chopper with long, tall handlebars, black leather banana seat glistening under the lights. The bike's front axle extended the chrome-and-spoked front wheel far out in front. Giving it a 1970s look. He sighed when he saw the motorcycle brand.

American Iron Horse.

"Not funny, Luci!" Jack shouted at the sky.

The demon chick pulled off her shiny black helmet, revealing a long tangle of blue-black curls that framed her square face, her big eyes blacker than Lare Dumont's soul—owned by Lucifer. She wore tight black leather pants, a black bustier, and black platform pumps. A hunger burned in her eyes, giving them a red glow that made him uncomfortable.

Envy was off the table now.

That left six other sins, but he was betting that hers was either Lust or Greed.

He frowned as she licked her lips, looking him over like a first date —or the bar menu after a cross-country ride.

The Hell princess looked him up and down and then her gaze tracked behind him to Talia and the rest of her squad.

"It's a little late in the year to be casting for Christmas movies, isn't it?" she asked in a rusty alto voice, the touch of a southern accent soft as she leaned against her bike.

"Just finished doing an airport commercial for Christmas in July," said Jack. "Part of California tourism campaign. Made a wrong turn on the way to Sturgis, didn't you?"

She tossed her head back and laughed.

"You're cute. Nah. On my way to New York City actually." She motioned behind him at Talia and her squad, squinting. "What's a little human doing riding around with angels? Your mother Catholic or something—afraid to have fun?" She patted her bike. "Have some adventures?"

Jack frowned. "With demons?"

Her smile didn't waver. "We're a lot more fun than angels, kid," she said.

He felt Talia bristling behind him.

"Except for that torturing my soul for eternity part," he replied. "And my mother wasn't Catholic. Just a narcissist."

He started to insult the demon, too but bit his tongue and didn't call her a narcissist. He still hadn't figured out what sin was her weakness yet.

The Hell princess laughed again and slid a tarnished gold coin out of her pocket, flipping it up in the air and catching it.

Dammit! The payload coin! She was flaunting it at Talia and her squad. Pride?

Jack pointed at the coin. "You planning to buy me dinner before trying to steal my soul?" he asked.

Her eyes sparked, flashing red.

"Mmmm, dinner," she said with a purr in her voice. "Now, you're talking, sexy. Where can a gal get a gourmet meal to remember in this town?" She winked at him. "I hate airport food."

Then he knew. Gluttony. That was her sin. He had to tempt her into giving up that coin somehow.

Those black eyes had sparked. He'd only seen that in the most powerful demons.

"C'mon, kid," she said and sauntered toward him. "I don't have all night. I'm taking the red-eye to New York City," she said with a snort. "Before I make this whole planet starve to death, I want to gorge on the best meal of my life." Her gaze darkened. "Before I have to return to Hell. And don't even try to make a play for my payload coin, angels. I will extinguish your light like a cheap candle before you get halfway to my bike."

"Speaking of cheap candles," Jack replied and nodded at her. "Those eyes of yours have quite the sparks in them. That natural or did Luci inflate your powers and your ego?"

Those black eyes burned red and she glared at him. "You disrespectful little shit," she snapped. "You dare talk about the King of Hell like that?"

"What are you going to do about it?" he taunted.

That smile returned. "Starve you and the rest of useless humanity to death." Again, she tossed that coin up in the air.

Just out of his reach. And if he seraphim-blinked, he might end up halfway across the parking lot. Couldn't risk that maneuver.

It was risky, but he had to try to tempt her into a meal she'd only dreamed of—even if he had to make it up.

"Eat Cheez-Its then, bitch," Jack said, turning away. "And here I was about to tell you about a little gourmet restaurant near Eagle Lake with the freshest trout you ever tasted. I'm sure it's just as fresh in New York. Twelve hours from now."

"Trout?" she said, catching the payload coin in her fist.

He caught Talia's gaze and held it, mouthing the word gluttony to her.

She gave him the slightest nod, her arctic grey eyes a mixture of fury and trepidation. Like Muriel and Kesien beside her. They wanted to take this Hell princess bitch apart, but that just might take the whole squad. Or the entire guard.

Unless he could rain down some seraphim energies on her. Just enough to get that coin. That's all he cared about. The payload.

Showtime.

He whirled around. "Rainbow trout," he said in a wistful voice. "Caught right there on the shores of Eagle Lake. They have these big long teak tables right beside the lakeshore. Set with fine gold and black china. Silverware. Crystal wine glasses, and cloth napkins."

"An outdoor table?" she said, her eyes widening.

Jack nodded. "A hundred flickering candles up and down the table. And as the moon rises above the lake, they cook fresh-caught trout over an open fire. Cooked on a cedar plank. Encrusted with pecans and a bourbon maple glaze. With grilled summer squash, zucchini, and carrots—fresh out of a garden beside the lake. Served with the crispest buttery, lemony chardonnay you ever tasted. Straight out of Napa Valley. Fresh, churned butter from a nearby dairy on crusty, yeasty white bread that tastes like Tuscany if you close your eyes. And just picked mixed greens and herbs with a freshly made Dijon vinaigrette that will haunt your dreams."

The Hell princess' eyes glazed over as she stared at him with longing. And shoved that coin into the right pocket of her leather pants.

Dammit.

"I. Want. That meal." Her ashen face flushed red, those black eyes glowing full-on red now.

Jack shrugged. "But I haven't even told you about the just-baked cheesecake."

"Cheesecake?" she said in a whisper.

"Yeah, just-baked cheesecake with fresh blueberries and a sugar cookie crust."

The Hell princess shuddered, her mouth watering with a hunger that glazed her eyes with longing.

She rushed toward him, grabbing him by his Eternean breastplate. Shaking him.

"You tell me where this restaurant is," she said with a feral growl. "Now. Or you're my appetizer."

He felt Talia and the squad shift behind him, but the Hell princess held up a hand, her murderous gaze still on him.

"One move and I tear his head off right in front of you, angels. I'm not some common demon. I'm a princess of Hell. A Traveler. I'll take all of you apart despite this fancy angel armor."

Okay, so maybe he'd miscalculated this situation a bit. Somehow, he had to get that coin. He had seraphim powers. This bitch might be powerful, but she didn't have seraphim powers. And omnificence.

Could he move like a seraph while being in two places at once?

"Wow, the appetizers," said Jack, holding his right hand parallel to the ground. "I didn't even tell you about the fresh grilled artichoke hearts. Just harvested."

Her eyes got glassy again and she let go of him. "Just picked?"

"Basted in olive oil, fresh garlic," he said in a dramatic voice. "Along with that Napa Chardonnay and grilled fireside. Served with roasted tomatoes, balsamic vinaigrette, and that crusty bread. Or the stuffed mushroom caps."

He called up omnificence and fixed her with his gaze as he described, in painful details, the mouth-watering crab-stuffed mushroom caps. Calling up a solid image of his form in front of her.

When she didn't react, he took a step left and began to separate from his projected form.

No response.

But then he felt her reaching toward him.

His heart hammered his rib cage. And he slid back as she grabbed him by the shoulders, shaking him.

"I. Want. This Meal, human. Now!"

Time to misdirect. He just hoped that Talia and her squad didn't intervene.

He grabbed hold of the Hell princess' cold limbs and used the seraph focus to hold her gaze. He'd seen Seraphina do that to him and other angels.

"Are you sure?" he said in a whisper and let his left-hand slip away from her shoulder.

Falling toward her pocket.

"It's way up north from L.A. though," he said. "East of Sacramento. Small mountain town." He nodded toward the American Iron Horse bike. "That bike won't get you there and back to LAX in time for your red-eye."

He dipped two fingers into her pocket. The Hell princess leaned closer.

"Then I'll fly out of San Francisco instead." Her eyes sparked red again. "Now, tell me where this damned restaurant is or I'll shred you right here, little human."

His two fingers slid around the coin.

He clamped them together and lifted the large coin. Softly. Gently.

"Ever heard of Eagle Lake?" he asked.

He lifted the coin upward. Until it cleared the edge of her leather pocket.

"It's near the Nevada border," he said, pulling the coin toward his Levi's.

"Nevada?" she said, looking surprised, thick eyebrows pressing into a ridge of those black eyes sparking red.

Jack nodded. Sliding the coin into the left pocket of his Levi's.

"It's like six hours from San Francisco. You sure you want to chance it? What if you can't get a flight to New York tonight?"

She grabbed him by the breastplate and lifted him into the air.

"You let me worry about that. Directions. Now. Or I waste you and all these angels."

Talia blinked, the whole squad behind her. Surrounding the Hell princess.

"Let him go," she said with murder marbles in both hands. "Now."

"Or what?" the Hell princess crowed.

Talia lifted the murder marbles to eye level.

"Or I splatter you all over this parking lot and you'll need a couple dozen shuttles to get you onto your flight tonight."

The Hell princess seemed apprehensive of Talia's murder marbles and slowly set him down again.

"Besides, I don't care what you do to Earth tonight, demon," said Talia, glaring at the female demon. "I already rescued the human I want. The others can deal with what's coming. This world's going to be remade anyway. Why should I or my squad try to stop you?"

"Tell me the location of this restaurant and we part company in one piece," said the Hell Princess with a growl.

Jack pretended to be scared, holding up his hands.

"Take Highway 99 out of Sacramento and follow the signs to Eagle Lake, okay? Lakeside Resort. Near Stones Landing."

The Hell princess let go of his breastplate and backed away toward her American Iron Horse chopper. She draped one leg across the seat and climbed onto it.

"All right then," she said and kickstarted the bike. "Have a lovely evening, angels. I know I will—with the meal of a lifetime. Before I starve the entire Earth to death." She grinned. "Kind of poetic, don't you think?"

The bike growled as she stood it up and shot across the parking lot. Becoming part of the shadows.

Talia threw her arms around Jack, holding him tight.

"You scared me to death, Jack," she said with a sigh. "I was terrified that she'd eviscerate you right in front of me. And I couldn't get to you fast enough."

He wrapped her in his arms.

"Sorry, Mrs. Casey," he said as his breathing evened out. "I'd planned to use omnificence, but she kept touching me." He sighed. "So, I did an old-fashioned pickpocket. Had to learn that move for the film, *You and Me*. I played a street performer that pickpockets the love interest, setting off the romance. Long story."

She kissed him again and let him go.

Muriel kicked at the asphalt, gold shield shining on her arm.

"I didn't even get a single shield bash at that demon."

"Sorry, Muriel," he replied, sliding his hand into his jeans pocket to make sure the payload coin was still there. "Next Hell prince, okay?"

"You promise?" she asked.

He nodded. "You and Deemah both will get in a shield bash on the next Traveler."

Deemah's face brightened as she nudged Kesien. "Hear that, Kesien?"

"Can't wait," he said and laid his hand against the gold shield on his right arm.

Muriel glanced toward the shadows and back at Jack.

"And now that damned Hell princess is going to have the meal of a lifetime. Not right."

Jack smirked. "Not exactly, Muriel."

"Why not?"

He laughed. "Because I made that whole place up. It doesn't exist."

"What?" Talia cried, turning him toward her. "You made all of that up?"

"Had to feed her gluttony, so I made up the best-damned restaurant that didn't exist."

Talia burst out laughing, the squad quickly joining her.

"That's beautiful, Jack!"

"By the Maker, I would love to see her face when she doesn't find that restaurant," said Muriel with a grin.

Jack patted his jeans pocket. "And she discovers I lifted the payload coin from her. She'll lose her shit." He turned back to Talia. "That's why we need to have a couple of cherubim there to meet her. So, no one gets hurt."

Talia ran her fingers through his hair. "Very good point, Jack. I'll send up a call to Azrael."

Her mouth opened and she sang out some angel notes that Jack couldn't hear.

"Now, let's get back to Heaven with that payload coin," said Talia. "Muriel, blink us back with your angel of death powers."

Jack gathered in close with Talia and the squad, sliding his arm around her waist as Muriel blinked them back to Eolowen using those almost instant death angel powers.

They materialized on the terrace beneath a pitch-black sky as Azrael and Pravuil rushed toward them.

Jack held out the payload coin. "Here you go."

"How'd you get that?" Pravuil asked, holding it out for Azrael to examine.

He smirked. "Picked the Hell princess' pocket. While I was bullshitting her about a restaurant that didn't exist."

Azrael frowned. "Picked her pocket?"

"I was trying to distract her with omnificence," he said with a shrug, "but she kept grabbing hold of me. So, I picked her pocket."

The archangel put his hands on his hips.

"Jack Casey, how is it that you have a pickpocketing skill?"

He chuckled, holding up his hands.

"Relax. Before you start talking about sending me to Hell, know that I learned it for a movie role."

"A movie role?" Azrael's charcoal grey eyes were intense, brows furrowed.

Jack nodded.

"I don't want to know any more," said Azrael, waving Jack off as Pravuil flew up onto the roof. "Good work, Talia and Jack. Good work, squad."

"Tal," said Jack, sliding his arms around her. "We have to get to the studio now before tomorrow morning, Earth time. Nine-ish."

Talia turned toward Azrael. "Sir, what do we do about the show?"

Azrael seemed torn as he stretched his wings. "Let me consult with Pravuil."

"No need, Azrael," Pravuil called as he flew back down from the round room's rooftop and landed beside the archangel.

Dude looked all kinds of tense. And pissed off. Everything was at stake and Jack had no idea what to do about the show. Put it on hold or pretend like nothing's wrong and keep doing it. There were still five Travelers left to shut down. And that Omega Rod to find before Luci found it.

Squinting, Pravuil turned to Jack.

"Jack, you and Talia do the show. Keeps everything in balance." He wagged a finger at Jack. "And Jack out of trouble. But be vigilant. When you see that sky change color, Jack, use that seraphim power to locate the next Traveler. The fate of your world depends on it." He pointed toward Eolowen. "That comes directly from Seraphina."

"I'll make sure that sky is my primary focus," said Jack and turned his attention back to Talia. "Tal, what does the third flight carry?"

Talia turned toward him, looking concerned.

"War, Jack," she said. "The third angel flight will turn the skies blood red. And they will pour bowls of red into nearby streams."

He frowned. "That means our next Hell prince—or princess—will be traveling in a red vehicle." He sighed. "Named after a horse."

"Demons are so arrogant," said Talia. "Announcing their arrivals like they're untouchable."

Pravuil turned toward Talia.

"Talia, all of that is Lucifer's doing. He's making fun of the prophecies and he's taunting Jack and humanity with the fact that even if Jack sees them coming, he can't stop what's to come."

"Douchebag," Jack muttered and turned his attention to the Scribe. "So, Scribe, was Seraphina able to locate the Omega Rod from your memories?"

"She's still working through them. There are millennia of memories for her to analyze." He folded his hands behind his back. "I just hope we can find it before Lucifer does."

"Me, too, Scribe," said Jack and slid his hand into Talia's. "Ready to head to our set trailer, Mrs. Casey?"

She nodded. "Shall I blink us there, lover?"

He was exhausted. All he wanted to do was sleep beside his wife for a few hours before he had to deal with Rachel and the apocalypse. In that order.

"Please," he said.

"Talia, I'll be in touch," said Azrael who turned to Talia's squad. "Squad, do not leave Jack and Talia's side. And keep watch on those skies. At the first sign of red, you let Jack know. Muriel, you're in charge when Talia is involved in the show."

"Will do, sir," said Muriel. "All right, squad. Blink out to Burbank, California. Four Acres Studio. To sweep and secure the trailer."

"Stay safe, Jack and Talia," Berith called from the doorway of the round room.

"You, too, Berith," Jack called to her and turned to Talia again. "Ready, babe?"

Smiling, Talia wrapped him in her arms and closed her eyes.

Blinking them out of the Heavens and into their Burbank Studio 22 trailer.

Into a legion of demons.

10

Talia groaned. Divinely fixing this trailer back to brand-new was still fresh in her memory. After Asmodeus laid waste to it more than once. After the show had gone on hiatus to retool its premise and get the network to greenlight Jack's new proposed format.

Already, the trailer's high-end taupe and grey finishes were burning from demon hellfire. Curtains and walls scorched and burned. L-shaped kitchen's taupe quartz countertop had already broken and those pristine, shiny grey lacquered cabinets were hanging off their frame. Burning as acrid grey smoke drifted through the trailer. Even the large flat-screen television was smashed, the new taupe couch on fire.

Talia called up a writhing gold oblivion sphere in each hand and flung them into the rampaging tangle of red, leathery minion demons that rushed at them from the shadows. Lurching in all directions throughout the studio trailer. Lucifer's angry lackeys had escaped when Hell's Gates opened and now, they raged through the space with glowing red eyes, horns, lots of pointy teeth, and tough leathery skin.

Maybe Lucifer sent them? Maybe they'd come after Jack, seeking revenge after he'd splattered so many of them? Or maybe Lucifer's bounty on Jack was still active? Regardless, she planned to end this with oblivion spheres.

Murder marbles as Jack called them.

Explosions shook the trailer, tossing a hail of demon parts in a wild spray of red goo from the kitchen to the taupe couch. Even the basket of gold and silver spheres on the coffee table in front of the couch was splattered in demon spray as her oblivion spheres erased demon after demon from existence.

Jack turned around in the smoky haze, tossing murder marbles as the familiar taupe grey walls turned black, remnants of the grey lacquered kitchen cabinets gleaming like embers in the warm overhead lighting.

She glanced down the short narrow hall leading to the bedroom. Where Kesien slashed demon after demon apart with his Eternean sword. Deemah knelt beside him, gold shield bashing demons into the shower to the left and toilet and sink to the right. Asmodeus had obliterated the whole trailer once—almost killing Jack and Armand Gianni in the process.

And it looked pristine when she and the other angels had left it— until demons flooded the trailer. Even now, she smelled a trace of Jack's cedary cologne above the smell of burnt hardwood flooring.

She glared at the floor as she threw another murder marble, taking apart four demons about to swarm Muriel who had her back to them, her shield in constant motion.

That maple flooring had been pristine. And it took a lot of work to celestially replace. But with this trailer cloaked in the blackness of the famine sky, Jack had probably been too much of a temptation for Lucifer's freed demons. Since they could come and go as they pleased.

Another explosion rocked the trailer.

Talia turned.

Jack stood just past the kitchen, flinging handfuls of murder marbles in front and behind him as minion demons mobbed him from all sides. But he was about to get swarmed from above.

"Jack! Duck!"

"What, Tal?"

Talia tossed an oblivion sphere into the tangle of demons descending from the ceiling, about to overtake him.

They exploded in a shower of red spray that splattered Jack head to toe.

She laughed as he made a face and swiped at the spray, those hypnotic pale green eyes so intense against the red demon goo. The wall in front of him was painted red and on fire now.

She sighed. Not a good sign for returning to the show right now.

"Are you okay, lover?" she called to him.

"I'm good, Mrs. Casey," he said and dropped another handful of murder marbles.

The crush of gold light exploded, sending more demon parts in every direction. And flames.

All of the walls burned now, giving off acrid, steely clouds of smoke.

"This—Lucifer's doing?" Jack asked through gritted teeth and gathered more murder marbles in his hands. "Or are they still that pissed at me for taking down the ones that tried to torture me?"

"Probably both, Jack," Muriel replied. "And don't forget, you still have Lucifer's mark AND a bounty on your head. "

The highest one Lucifer had ever placed on a human or angel.

Jack's pocket began to ring.

Startled, he jumped and flung the remaining murder marbles in his hands into the hallway and retreated into the kitchen. Where he reached into his pocket and slid out his phone.

Sympathy for the Devil screamed through the demon-infested trailer, electric guitars scratching against the demon minions' movements.

The sound of that ring made her heart do somersaults now. Lucifer was free. He could ambush Jack in the blink of an eye.

With gritted teeth and narrowed eyes, Jack answered the phone, putting it on speaker as the wave of demons began to subside.

"Luci, how's the vacay going?" he shouted and kicked a demon in the teeth that lunged for him. "I'm sure you've killed lots of tourists and destroyed lots of sights by now. But honestly, I'm hurt that you didn't send me a postcard to talk about the weather or list yet another reason why you'll kill me last and all."

"Jack!" Talia said with a hiss.

He hadn't learned his lesson. He was at it again, taunting Lucifer. Had he forgotten that Lucifer was free? And at maximum power? He could blink into this trailer from anywhere and snap Jack in two like a toothpick. And here was Jack, taunting him into a street fight. They both had seraphim powers, but Lucifer could outlast Jack.

"Jack!" Lucifer cried in that bright, charming British accent. So precise. "So good to hear from you! Thank you for opening Hell's Gates and ushering in the festivities. I hope you're enjoying them. I made sure you'd have lots of fun, local activities to attend. I'm hoping one will manage to kill you, so I can take your soul and torture it for eternity. But no matter. I'll kill you last as planned. After you watch me erase all of humanity. And the Maker—my father."

Jack's pale green eyes were filled with hate as he glared at the phone, his game face mostly intact.

"It's good to have dreams, Luci," Jack taunted, that dangerous, troublemaking smirk curling the corners of his mouth. "And I'm gonna laugh my ass off at you when the Maker yeets your ass all the way back to Hell again. Like the little bitch you are."

Talia blinked into Jack's face. "Jack Casey!" she shouted in a hoarse whisper. "Don't."

"Not this time, Jack," Lucifer said, still sounding so bright and charming, so deadly and edgy with barely restrained fury now. "You will get to witness the end of it all this time. And the rise of a new Maker. One that does not suffer fools like you, Jack Casey. Oh, no...I plan to make a massive example of you to the surviving angels. After I've devastated everything above and below the lower Heavens. A slow, deliberate execution for them to observe."

Jack stared at the phone a moment.

"I'll pull up a chair," said Jack, biting his lip. "Eat some popcorn and watch you fall on your douchebag face. Like you always do. I just hope Heaven has that laugh track installed by then. And ringside seats around the Lake of Fire. Will make it so much funnier to watch you fail."

There was a moment or two of silence.

But the puling of shadow panthers drew Talia's attention.

Six of them. Red eyes shining in the faint light as they approached from the end wall and stalked toward her and Jack.

"Squad, tight phalanx formation," Talia said in a deadly quiet voice. "Protect the vanguard."

Her squad blinked into a phalanx formation, shields raised, swords ready as they moved parallel to the small kitchen.

"Jack…" said Talia, calling up two oblivion spheres. "We've got more company."

Jack cast a casual glance toward her and then returned his gaze to the phone. But then he slowly turned his head back toward her.

And the shadow panthers.

"Tal," he said and called up a big handful of murder marbles. "Duck, please."

Talia folded her body and dropped to the floor as her squad shifted right.

Jack flung the double load of murder marbles over top of her head. Into the glow of red eyes.

Talia rolled her oblivion spheres across the maple hardwood. Into the tangle of shadowy paws that advanced on them.

A string of explosions rocked the trailer. Throwing her and Jack against the remnants of the cabinets and backward. Onto the maple hardwood floor.

Jack nearly dropped his phone but managed to hang onto it. He had just pulled himself up on his knees when Lucifer's voice echoed from the phone. Still on speaker.

"Still there, Jack?" Lucifer replied with a chuckle.

"Still here, Luci," Jack said with a smirk. "Still a pain in your ass."

"Good. Because the only laughter you'll hear is mine, Jack, after my Hell princes and princesses set off their apocalypse payloads and your world self-destructs from war or disaster. Or plain ol' death. I want your kind gone. Forever." Lucifer laughed. "But feel free to enjoy the arrival of the other Hell princes, Jack. It'll be like Carnevále—except no fake masks. And lots of death. It's all real, Jack and they will destroy your world with one of those plagues. You can't stop them all."

Lucifer's delirious laughter echoed through the trailer.

"You watch and see how many of these douchebags I stop, Luci. Gonna be all seven. Can you count that high?"

"We'll see who's laughing at the end of this…party, Jack. I hope *you* brought crisps this time. Shall I hold your beer while you try and stop me? And fail? Miserably."

Jack chuckled. "Oh, I brought chips…and the murder marbles, you colossal douchebag. Before this is all over, Luci, you'll be holding my beer. In chains, bitch. Enjoy the vacay while it lasts and don't forget to send me a postcard highlighting your latest failures. Gives me something to read while I spay and neuter all your Hell princes."

"Oh, Jack, you're so attractive when you're terrified. Brings out the hopelessness in your eyes. Give Berith my love and tell her she'd best take a number. For execution. Ta-Ta, Jack. Must dash. Places to destroy, people to murder, and all. Cheers."

Jack glared at the phone, fighting down an urge to heave it across the room.

"That sonofabitch!" Jack shouted, tossing another handful of murder marbles at a shadow panther that had escaped the flood of murder marbles Jack had already thrown. "Gloating. Like he's already won!"

The lone shadow panther went down and shattered into black smoke. Disappearing.

Talia grabbed him by the shoulders and yanked him against the ruined cabinets as two more shadow panthers leaped at them, claws raised. Missing his throat by a hair.

She sang out a string of notes to the squad.

"Supremes formation. Defend Jack."

Again, another horde of leathery red-skinned demons appeared in the room, lunging for her and Jack. Burying them in another sea of demons.

Until Talia called up a white burst of Holy Fire and slammed it into the writhing tangle of minion demons.

Setting them alight with Holy Fire. They turned to ash and floated away as Jack sat up from the floor and pulled his arms away from his face as her squad formed around him.

Until they got swarmed with more demons.

"Nice burn, Talia," he said with a smirk.

"Thanks, lover," she said as a shadow panther landed on Jack's shoulders.

Jack slammed it against the wall, rolled on the ground, and butted it into the door, but it hung onto him like glue.

He rolled to his left against the refrigerator, trying to shake the assassin demon loose, but its talons dug into his shoulders. It tried to sink its teeth into his arm, but Jack punched its shadowy face until it let go.

The trailer door slammed open.

Jack's head snapped up and Talia turned toward the sound.

Armand Gianni stood in the doorway, a sharp sword in his right fist, warm brown eyes filled with determination.

"Armand!" Talia cried.

"Dude!" Jack called, blinking out of the kitchen toward him.

Jack stood at his best friend's left shoulder, ready to deflect—or end—anything that leaped at Armand.

"You all right?" Jack asked.

"Fine, Jack," he said, swinging that sword in a tight arc around him. "Welcome back to the show."

Jack grinned and patted his best friend on the back before slamming his fist into a demon's face that rushed at him from the shadows.

Armand cut down the next one with his blade, a smile on his face. Talia couldn't believe it. He was enjoying this fight.

Another horde of minion demons popped up inside the trailer and Armand lunged toward them, Jack at his side.

Together, they took down demon after demon, fighting as a team as her squad dealt with another force that poured into the trailer from the bedroom.

Watching Jack and Armand together, she knew they were both enjoying themselves fighting these demons. She smiled. A little too much.

"Siri, play my demon-splattering playlist."

"Which one?" the American female voice on Jack's phone asked.

Armand's eyes narrowed and he gave Jack a funny look. "You've got more than one?"

"You know how many demons I've been fighting lately?"

"Good point," said the tall soap opera star with a nod. "Then the obvious answer is…the loudest."

Jack grinned. "You heard the man, Siri. The loudest metal playlist, please. More metal than the security checkpoint at LAX. Start with Metallica's Seek and Destroy."

Electric guitars overwhelmed the set trailer as another wave of demons materialized around them. But Talia, Jack, and Armand made quick work of them. Talia had just taken down the last demon when her squad fought their way back from the bedroom and blinked onto the charred, goo-slickened hardwood floor.

Muriel looked flustered, gold shield still perched on her right forearm. Kesien looked angry, a fine red mist of demon spray covering him and Deemah. Anahera's short red hair was in disarray, Eternean sword clutched in her fist, wings spread wide.

"You guys okay up here?" Muriel asked, holding up her shield, ready to bash the first thing that moved.

Armand sighed and nodded as he let his sword fall to his right side. Jack held out his hands as Talia moved toward Muriel.

"Dammit, I was ready to give Luci's minions both barrels again," said Jack. "And get through at least one playlist. Siri, pause playlist."

The electric guitars fell silent as quiet descended through the set trailer.

Talia wanted to laugh. Both Jack and Armand looked disappointed.

"We're bummed, Muriel," Jack snapped and let his hands fall to his sides. "But fine."

Armand moved over to Jack. "Jack, the sky is black as midnight. What the hell's going on?"

"Sounds like a perfect night to play some AC/DC's Back in Black and splatter more demons," said Jack and poked Armand's shoulder with his fist.

"You're avoiding my question, Jack," said Armand, letting the sword lean against the wall as he fixed Jack with a serious stare. "What is going on? First, the sky turned electric green. Now, it's black."

Jack reached out and patted Armand on the shoulder. "Relax, dude," he said, a little out of breath. "It'll be blue again by morning."

"You said you'd level with me when you got back to the studio. What's happening?"

Armand could tell that Jack was stalling, playing the whole thing off in that *hey, there's nothing to worry about* way of his. That wasn't fooling Armand Gianni one bit. He knew Jack too well and as an actor, he saw right past Jack's game face.

"Jack," said Armand, gripping Jack's shoulders, his gaze intense. "Tell me what's happening. I have a right to know—to protect Izzy."

"Talia," said Muriel with a groan. "We need to talk."

She nodded toward the bedroom, but Talia didn't want to leave Jack alone in here with all of Hell free and lurking out there. They were knee-deep in the apocalypse and Lucifer was free. She wanted Jack in her line of sight at all times.

"As long as I can still see Jack, but no farther, Muriel."

Muriel glanced over at Jack and then back at her. "Probably a good plan," she said, sounding a little tired. "Lucifer could show up at any moment."

Armand heard her comment, his gaze shooting over to Muriel and then snapping back to Jack.

"I thought you said that Lucifer's trapped in Hell," said Armand, arms crossed, those warm brown eyes hardening.

"He was," said Jack, leaning against the wall. "But dammit, Gianni —the bastard played us."

Armand's eyes widened. "What do you mean *played us*, Jack?"

"We all knew it was a trap," said Jack, exhaling sharply as he fixed

Gianni with his undivided attention, like he was the only one in the room. "But we had to go save Berith. And he used it to his advantage. Used us to be more precise."

"How?" Armand demanded.

Sighing, Jack ran his fingers through his bangs. "Uh, used us to… um—" Jack winced. "Break the seven seals."

Armand grabbed Jack by the breastplate, his warm brown eyes wide with terror.

"What?" Armand looked stunned for a moment. "Break the seven seals! Jack, do you understand what happens when the seven seals break?"

"We get seven trumpet solos?" Jack replied.

Muriel snickered.

"Not funny, Jack," said Armand with a shake of his head.

Muriel laid her hand against her breastplate. "I thought it was funny."

"We get the apocalypse, Gianni," said Jack, giving him a dark expression. "And we get Lucifer freed from Hell. He could be anywhere right now."

Talia returned her attention to Muriel.

"All right, what happened to you and the squad, Muriel?" Talia asked. "It was just Jack and me for that first wave."

"We got a little lagged behind you, only got here for the end of that first wave of demons. Ran into heavy numbers of them on the way here, Talia. And Earth's humans are either intrigued by the changing sky colors or they think the apocalypse is just a rare aurora borealis. Sun's about ready to set, not that you could tell under a black sky. But we need to keep a close watch."

Talia held her breath a moment. "Have the demons attacked any humans? Ramiel's Watchers are in position, ready to defend humanity if needed."

Muriel shook her head. "The demons are rampaging, but not attacking humans yet. Just looting, rough-housing with each other, eating, and drinking—and causing property damage. Kind of like Mardi Gras—with more demons."

So, the apocalypse was just a big party to the demons. Better than them seeing it as a hunting expedition.

"Third flight is in a holding pattern over Eolowen right now," Muriel continued. "According to Azrael anyway. But when the Hell prince of war arrives on Earth, those demons might start attacking humans."

Talia felt her heart sink. That meant the third flight of angels would leave Heaven at sunset, on approach to pour out the red bowl of war on the Earth. By sunrise. That meant an intense red sky in the morning. And hunting down another Hell prince.

"Is this a joke, Jack?" Armand asked, his face turning as pale as the bathroom tiles.

"Wish it was, Gianni," he replied and leaned against the wall.

"Does this mean the four horsemen will bring devastation to our world?"

Jack shook his head. "No. Four horsemen won't destroy our world."

Some of the tension left Armand's taut posture and he relaxed a little, the corners of his mouth lifting into a relieved smile.

"That's a relief."

"Seven Travelers will though. Seven Hell princes unless we stop them. Take their payloads before they ignite."

"What?" Armand looked sick. "Then it's too late. The apocalypse has already begun."

"Phase three, dude," said Jack, sliding his arms behind his back. "Talia, the squad, and I just got back from taking the payload coin from the second Hell prince. Er, princess."

Armand's whole demeanor shifted. "You mean that you and the angels stopped these—these Hell princes from delivering some kind of payload?"

"We sure did, Armand," said Muriel, moving toward Armand. "Jack there actually pickpocketed the second one. From a Hell princess. Took her payload coin. So, two down. Five to go."

The tall soap star whirled around and spun Jack away from the wall, a grin on his tanned face.

"Then there is a way to stop them?"

"Sure is, dude." He motioned toward the ceiling. "By taking their payload coins. By morning, the sky will turn blood red and the third Hell prince will leave Hell. I have a seraphim power now that lets me locate these Travelers."

"What payload does this…Traveler carry?" Armand asked, his expression intense.

"War, Gianni. This Hell prince or princess will bring war if we don't stop them." Jack pointed at Talia and the squad. "When that sky turns red, we'll have to go track down this Traveler and take its payload coin. Each Hell prince rules over a type of sin, so we have to figure out which one and play to their weakness. Somehow."

Armand frowned. "Like one of the seven deadly sins?" His gaze flicked over to Talia and then back to Jack.

"Exactly right," said Jack. "As we figure out each one's sin, we use it against them. So far, we've stopped Envy and Gluttony."

Poor Armand. He was trying to help and understand all of this, but he looked like he was drowning. Way over his head.

"So, this Traveler could represent any of the remaining five sins?"

Jack nodded. "Right, dude. It's a weakness that we're trying to exploit. And I'm going to need your help with the last three Hell princes. Now that rehearsals have started."

He swallowed a breath, his eyes turning glassy and Talia wanted to take him in her arms and kiss her husband.

"It'll be just the humans against the last two or three Hell princes, Gianni," said Jack in a tired voice. "No angels."

Armand gazed around the trailer, studying the squad that had let the tall soap star see them, then her, and finally returned his gaze to Jack.

"Just us?" he said finally. "Where will Talia and the others be?"

"Fighting for everything in the skies above Earth against Lucifer's demons and fallen angels," said Jack, trying not to make it sound like the end of the world.

But she, Jack, and the guard already knew it was the end of the world. Jack didn't call it that to his best friend. Armand didn't need to know that if Heaven lost the fight to Lucifer, everything would be destroyed. So, Jack kept it a little vague on purpose. To protect his best friend.

"And most of humanity won't see most of this happening?" Armand replied.

Jack shrugged and gazed at her for help on that question.

"Armand," she replied and moved toward him. "By tomorrow morning, once the sky bleeds red, another Traveler will carry the plague of war to your world. As a Hell prince or princess, they will be formidable to fight, much worse than that archdemoness you watched Jack fight on our honeymoons."

Jack shifted uncomfortably and his eyes flashed with concern.

Armand looked paler now as he glanced at Jack and then nodded.

"How do we fight something like that without angels to help us?" Armand asked in a deathly quiet voice.

Jack put on that game face and exuded confidence as he clapped Armand on the back, that self-assured smirk on his sexy face.

"Dude, we may not have angels, but you've got my seraphim powers as a backup. And we don't fight them, we match wits with them. They're arrogant narcissists, so we outsmart them. I've even got some ideas on how we break away from the studio using scavenger hunts to disguise what we're really doing. May have to enlist some Watchers to help, too, but Gianni, we can do this."

Jack's rousing monologue gave Gianni hope and he nodded at Jack, the color returning to his face.

"You think so?"

"I know so," Jack fired back. "We've taken down two of these bastards by using their weaknesses against them."

"No angel powers?" Armand asked.

Jack shook his head. "Just mine, dude. And I'm also going to get Rachel Daniels involved," Jack added. "And Banks."

Talia pulled in a nervous breath. His ex-girlfriend was unpredictable and Talia hated when he had to be around her. She liked to hit on Jack even with a fiancé in the picture. Talia was never sure what Rachel's goals were—much less her motivations. But with the apocalypse in motion, she might be the best help Jack could enlist right now. She knew what was at stake and she knew how to fight demons. Like Gianni.

But Mark Banks had no clue that demons even existed. Talia smiled. Or angels for that matter. Still, she trusted Jack's judgment. And when that fifth flight of angels landed on Earth, she had to prepare to engage Lucifer's air forces. Defend the skies from an invasion. The bulk of Lucifer's forces. His Dark army. And still no word from Pravuil on that artifact.

"Hell, Gianni," Jack said as he paced around him. "I could call my mother. She'd scare the hell out of all of them. Might be the best secret weapon we have."

Armand laughed and Talia felt the tension in the ruined trailer level out.

Jack turned to her and smirked, pointing at Armand with his thumb. "Dude thinks I'm kidding."

She shook her head. "He's met her, Jack, so he believes you."

"We all believe you, Jack," Muriel added to chuckles from the squad.

"All right, Jack," said Armand as he walked to the door. "I'll tell Izzy that everything's all right and we'll see you and Talia in the studio at nine A.M. To hear all about The Celestial Couples Show."

Jack walked Armand to the door. "Can't believe they changed the show's title again. Guess it makes sense since not all the couples are newlyweds now."

Armand nodded. "I've heard that they plan to bring in Claire Olsen and Ryder Kurland, too. So, two unmarried couples."

"Dream house is a dream house," said Jack, opening the door that was bent and still smoking. "Don't have to be married to get one. Take care, Gianni."

"You, too, Jack," said Armand.

Jack closed the door and collapsed against it, still splattered in demon goo.

"All right, squad," said Talia as she moved toward Jack. "Let's get this place put back together."

Muriel shook her head and motioned at Kesien.

"Kesien, let's start with the bedroom and work forward. Deemah, you and Anahera start at the far end. Talia can help us meet in the middle."

Reaching out, Talia took hold of Jack's hands and pulled him into a scintillating kiss.

"Just another day at the office, babe?" he asked with that sexy smirk that set her whole being alight. "Except kiss me like that again and I'll be down there helping Muriel repair the bedroom."

She showered him in a wash of gold light, erasing the demon goo from his face and clothes, and then wrapped her arms around him, holding him close.

"Promise?" she asked.

"Guaranteed," he said and kissed her lips, his mouth so hot against hers, hands anxious as he stroked her face and neck.

She wanted to lose herself in his touch, to forget about Lucifer and the apocalypse and the coming air battle with Lucifer's Dark army. Wrap herself in his warm cedary scent and run away with him to some remote corner of the Creation. Where they would both be safe in each other's arms for eternity. Safe from Lucifer's reach. Safe from waves of demons. Safe from any more threats and obligations.

"Tal," he said, his expression suddenly serious as he pulled back from her. "What's the matter?"

"Nothing," she said and stared into those beautiful light green eyes that were full of heat and love and concern for her. "Why?"

He shook his head and held up a clear crystal. "You're crying, Mrs. Casey. What's wrong?"

She didn't realize it until she saw all the crystals at her feet. She couldn't deny it.

"I'm worried, Jack," she said in a hushed voice and pulled him close again.

She needed to feel his heat against her body. His warm embrace. His love that burned hotter than anything in Creation.

"About what, love?" he asked in a quiet voice.

"Worried that Lucifer or these Travelers are going to kill you.

Worried that I won't survive this air battle." She bowed her head, the crystals falling again. "Worried that this is the end of everything and we'll be worlds apart if everything explodes."

His arms tightened around her and he cradled her against him. The beat of his heart quickened along with his breath that hitched. And for a moment or two, he couldn't speak. Finally, he pulled in a sharp breath and laid his head against hers.

"Talia, Lucifer wants me to witness his triumph, so even if he destroys everything, he'll kill me last. Make sure he gets in that last taunt. And I'll make sure that's the last mistake he ever makes."

She didn't know if Jack's seraphim powers were enough to take down Lucifer, but she let his confidence win her over, needing to believe that somehow, the love of her life would survive all of this devastation.

"And those Hell princes only want to drop their payloads and leave, Tal."

His hot caramel voice vibrated through her chest and set her whole being alight. He was so beautiful. And she ached to love him.

He took her face in his hot hands and smashed his mouth against her lips, his kiss so urgent and anxious that it brought new tears to her eyes. They cascaded like sleet around them.

"I will fight to protect my world and Heaven, but Talia, when the guard clashes with the full force of Lucifer's army above the Earth, I will be there—somehow." His voice began to tremble. "And I will fight my way through every single demon to get to you. To make sure that you come home to me." His eyes got glassy, voice tight, and breaking. "Because you are the first and last thing that I love the most in this whole wide world. In all the Heavens. In all those stars overhead. None of them means anything to me if you're not right here beside me, in my arms, to share it."

A tear threaded its way down his cheek. She brushed it away with her fingertips as he pressed his face against hers and heaved a breath, forcing down a sob.

"I love you, Jack Casey," she whispered against his ear. "My husband."

"Now until forever, Mrs. Casey," he said, his voice still shaky. "With everything I've got."

They held each other in the trailer's dim light as her squad rebuilt it around them. Tomorrow would bring war. Then disaster. He might have to fight despair without her. And then silence and death alone while she fought for Heaven.

Somehow, she had to survive the Enochian apocalypse and return to him. It was all that mattered to her. He was all that mattered to her—her husband. The life they'd put on hold to save humanity and Heaven. To stop Lucifer.

But fighting a separate battle away from Jack was the worst hell she could imagine.

Somehow, in spite of being apart, they both had to survive the apocalypse.

11

HEN MORNING LIT THE EASTERN SKYLINE, JACK WAS ALREADY AWAKE. Pacing the small, dark, angel-reengineered bedroom alone. And worried sick about Talia and the sixth flight. Dressed only in grey boxer briefs, blond hair messy, feet bare, and arms crossed against his chest, he walked from the wall to the window. And back again. He closed his eyes a moment, letting the calming traces of Talia's cool rain and roses scent wash over him in the almost-dark room.

Yesterday, after the demon battle that had destroyed their set trailer—again—she'd been terrified. And worried sick. He hadn't seen her like that in a long time.

And it scared the hell out of him.

Most of the night, she was beside him, holding him so close that he felt the rush of air, like breath, through her angel's heart. They'd made love after the squad left them alone and afterward, Talia had wrapped him in her arms and laid her head on his chest. Staying against him until almost sunrise. She'd never been clingy and he'd enjoyed her need to hold him so close for so long. Those were rare moments and he cherished last night.

But it told him how sick with worry she was about this upcoming battle. It was the biggest fight of her existence. With everything at stake. And he'd been out of his head about it ever since he learned that she would have to fight this battle without him beside her.

With so many people he cared about. Muriel. Azrael. Berith. He winced. Kesien and Anahera. Pravuil and Deemah. And so many other angels. He sucked in a breath. It made him ache all over.

He couldn't protect Talia and defeat the last two Travelers at the same time—not even with omnificence. But after she'd revealed her fragile state last night, his mind was already alight with plans to find a way to be in that air battle. At her side.

To protect the love of his life. To keep her safe no matter the cost.

He was gambling with the fate of the world for the love of one angel. One woman. He bit his lip. His woman.

But without her love, he had no fight left in him. Wasn't that worth a roll of the dice? A flip of the coin? The turn of a card?

In his book, he was just one fewer person fighting the last two Hell princes, but if he got more people on his team, maybe it would be enough. While he protected the love of his life in the skies above Earth.

He had some ideas about recruitment, too.

So, maybe this made him less than a hero, but he'd given everything he had for so long. Except his heart. That belonged to Talia. And he refused to give it or her up.

Opening the bedroom drapes wide, he stared out the east-facing window as the first brilliant streaks of yellows, pinks, and oranges flushed the sky when the sun peeked over the eastern edge of Four Acres Studio.

He gripped the curtains, fingers going cold, heart thumping faster as he watched the sky. Waiting for it to turn blood red. Hoping it wouldn't, but knowing that it would turn just like it had turned green and then black.

For the next half hour, the intense sunrise faded to watercolors beneath California's summer blue skies, the soft fleecy clouds making him almost believe that none of this had been real. That the apocalypse and those two Travelers had just been some bad dreams he'd had after Lucifer blew up High House and toppled spires in the lower Heavens.

But like dye bleeding across fabric, the sky began to flush purple as red seeped into the crisp blue. And began to burn blood-red on the horizon. Like someone had murdered the world and spilled its blood across the sky. He turned away from the window.

Dammit! It was real. And it was still happening.

The intense red meant that the third Traveler was on its way to Earth to start a war of Biblical proportions. Unless he, Talia, and her squad could stop it. With Gianni along this time.

The knock on his trailer door startled him.

He grabbed a pair of Navy blue cargo shorts out of the dresser drawer (the clothes he'd brought still where he'd left them from before the hiatus) and pulled them on over his boxer briefs. Before the hiatus, he'd brought a small box of props out of his SUV to the trailer, intending to prank Gianni and Banks—in case things got tense on set. Whoopie cushion, fake vomit, hand buzzer, two-headed coin, can of silly string—anything for a shock or a laugh to break the tension. He'd hoped to lighten the mood on set. Change the energy when things got bad.

Too bad Asmodeus had already pranked him hard with all the bags of flake on set.

Now, with Lucifer and his demons free and that whole apocalypse thing happening, pranks weren't going to lighten the mood this time.

He left the box out on the dresser.

Barefoot, he hurried down the short hallway to the door as someone knocked harder. Longer.

He opened the door.

Gianni, eyelids drooping like he'd been up all night, stood on the top step. His yellow polo shirt was pristine along with his dark grey dress pants and new dark grey loafers. But despite it all, his Cary Grant demeanor held, creases pressed into those dress pants, every hair in place.

"It's red, Jack," he said, despair in his usually calm voice. "The sky is red."

Jack held open the door and motioned Gianni inside. But then he saw Jennifer Collins at the bottom of the stairs, lips pursed, clipboard hugged to her chest as she stared up at the sky. She wore jeans, blue flats, and a long-sleeved turquoise top with matching turquoise glasses that had already slid down her nose. The soothing ocean color made her brown hair look so dark in her usual sleek, tight ponytail.

"What's happening to the sky again?" she asked, looking so lost as she stared up at him.

"It's weird, isn't it?" he said. "But I'm sure it'll clear up in a couple of days. It's probably some aura-like effect from a forest fire or pollution. Or maybe some sort of corona effect from the sun warming different elements in the atmosphere?"

That was a load of bullshit, but if it made her feel better, he'd keep going.

A slight smile curved across her face, some of the tension in her cheeks relaxing. "That's probably it. Thanks, Jack. I feel better. And I came to tell you that we're meeting in fifteen minutes in the back conference room in Studio 22 to discuss new blocking and the new format."

He put on his most relaxed smile for her. "Tal and I'll be there. Thanks, Jennifer."

"Of course, Jack," she said and turned to leave.

Then she stopped and turned around again. Staring at him.

"Nice cargo shorts, by the way," she said. "Could you relay that about the conference room to Armand please?"

He smiled. "You got it. Thanks, Jennifer."

Nodding, she left to visit the other trailers.

He closed the door as Gianni began to pace through the reconstructed trailer. The squad had outdone themselves this time. The couch and large flat-screen TV looked brand-new. He just hoped Gianni wasn't planning to watch another Wildebeest special on it.

"Jack! It's happening. The red, just like you said."

Gianni's voice was a little shaky, but his actor's game face held, giving him that calm, unaffected look that he'd perfected on *The Cinderella Hour.*

Jack nodded. "Yeah, we're gonna need to go after that third Traveler. Right now."

Gianni rushed over to him. "How can we be in two places at once, Jack? Dammit, I know we've got a show to do, but...this is the apocalypse! I think that takes precedence over rehearsals. Don't you?"

Jack laid a hand against his chin, trying to find a way to keep the show going and stop the Hell princes from launching their payloads. Could he use omnificence? For a short while, but it would drain his power fast and leave him power drunk. He sighed. And unable to do the show.

"We can't, dude," he said, beginning to pace.

Gianni paced alongside him. "We'll have to call in sick then. Go after these monsters before they destroy the world."

"So, we go to the rehearsal," Jack said as he thought through the beginnings of a plan. "Fifteen minutes in, one of us gets a call and we ask for a fifteen-minute break."

Gianni frowned. "Then what?"

"We call in Ramiel's Watchers," he said. "They impersonate me, you, and Talia while we find Hell Prince or Princess number three. Take them down. Be back by lunch to spell the Watchers."

Gianni was already nodding. "I like that idea. Like when those bastards kidnapped Izzy and Talia's squad impersonated us. That could work. It's just a rehearsal."

"Cool, let me bounce it off Talia," he said. "Make sure this is gonna work."

Gianni nodded, but he still looked unnerved by all of the chaos and danger. Jack understood. He felt the same way. And all of this could get so much worse.

He hurried down the hallway to the bedroom. But Talia wasn't there.

He called for her three times before the flutter of wings whispered through the room. When he turned around, Talia and her squad stood in front of the window.

"Good morning, Jack," she said and rushed to him.

He wrapped her in his arms and kissed her. "Good morning, Mrs.

Casey," he said, smiling, pasting on his best game face to try and ease her nerves. "Where have you been?"

"Outside," she said and pointed at the ceiling. "On the roof, watching the sky."

Jack sighed. "I watched it turn red, too. Babe, Jennifer Collins stopped by to tell us we're meeting in fifteen minutes in Studio 22. Gianni is out front, scared out of his mind. Don't blame him. I get it. This could be the end of everything."

"Calling a meeting when an apocalypse-red sky appears? That's some sucky management," said Muriel, glancing at him and then at Talia.

"I know, right?" said Jack. "So, I propose that we go for fifteen minutes. Then a phone call leads us to ask for a break. We go after the Traveler and call in Watchers to impersonate you, me, and Gianni. Will that work?"

Talia folded her arms against her chest and paced the room, wings quivering as she pondered his plan. He frowned as he watched her pace. She'd never been someone that paced. Like him. It made him afraid for her. He'd never seen her so rattled before.

"Talia," said Muriel, following alongside her. "The Watchers impersonate humans all the time. They should be able to handle this." She glanced at Jack. "Well, not sure about getting someone like Jack right, but they can do a good approximation of him."

"Is that more angel code for pain the ass?" he asked.

Muriel chuckled. "In your case, yes, Jack."

Not even a smile from Talia. He doubted she'd even heard him. She took two turns around the room and then moved back to him.

"That should work, Jack," she said. "But we're only going to spend about ten minutes in the first meeting. Agreed?"

He chuckled. "Agreed, babe," he said. "No worries."

He wrapped her in his arms and held her a moment or two. "It's all going to be okay, Mrs. Casey. I promise."

She nodded against his shoulder and he felt crystals against his bare skin. She was crying again. He just held her until she leaned up and kissed him. After returning her kiss, he let her go.

"Gianni!" he shouted.

In a moment or two, Gianni appeared in the bedroom doorway. He stepped inside, glancing at Kesien and then Muriel. Anahera then Deemah. And finally Talia.

"Talia," he said in a tired voice. "Will it work to have the Watchers play us? Like your squad played us on camera on our honeymoons?"

Smiling, she took Gianni's hands in hers and squeezed. "It should be fine."

Gianni looked relieved by Talia's response and then fixed Jack with his gaze.

"Jack, I told Izzy everything last night."

Everything? Holy shit. Did her head explode? Like his did the night that two angels walked into his apartment. And then Lucifer.

"Like *everything* everything?" he asked. "Or about the apocalypse?"

A wry smile brightened his face. "Well, she already had some memories of being abducted. Like seeing you with wings, Jack."

"Seriously?" he said with a groan. "She'll never look at me the same again, will she?"

Gianni waved him off. "She knows that you protected her, Jack. And that you, Talia, and—Azrael, isn't it, saved her from those demons." He nodded. "Yes, she knows there were demons."

Jack felt ill. He thought that Heaven had made her forget everything. He had no idea that she remembered him with wings.

"Relax, Jack," said Gianni with a smile. "She knows you're no angel—believe me! She knows better. I told her about the mix-up, so she gets that you're still human. She's just grateful you had those wings when it mattered."

He bowed his head, feeling uncomfortable now.

"She still loves you, Jack."

"Hope so," he said finally.

"I warned her that I'd have to go help you with these Hell princes though, so she'll play along with my imposter—except no kissing, she said."

Jack laughed.

"I had the same rule," said Muriel as she poked Kesien. "I agreed to play Talia as long as I didn't have to kiss Kesien playing Jack."

When Kesien blushed, Jack broke into a fit of laughter.

"Seeing Kesien blush made that story, Muriel," said Jack. "Nice work."

"Okay," said Talia. "So, Jack, use your seraphim power to illuminate the Traveler's trail and then when you're dressed, we'll hurry to the sound stage. And then take down this Hell prince."

Jack opened a drawer and pulled out a faded pair of Levi's. He grabbed another pair of boxer briefs, green this time, and hurried into the bathroom. After brushing his teeth and a very quick shower, he pulled on his boxers and jeans. He slid on a black and white checkered pair of Vans and pulled on a mint green V-neck T-shirt out of another drawer. Then he took a few things out of the prop box and shoved them into his pockets.

Talia was already dressed in an ice-blue T-shirt, black flats, and cut-offs, looking smokin' hot. Waiting for him.

He kissed her and brushed his lips against her ear. "And you're smokin' hot in those cut-offs by the way. Damned apocalypse."

She grinned and kissed him back.

He took her hand and hurried out of the trailer, Gianni on his left, hands in his pockets as Talia's squad took to the air above them. And in moments, a flock of Watchers appeared around the squad. They were smaller and brighter than the angels of death with blond to black hair. Some had eyes like glass and others had deep brown eyes. Some had moon-pale skin, others with tawny skin, and some with skin the color of ebony. Like they'd come from all walks of life.

But crossing over humans changed the angels of death over time. Their skin faded to moon-pale, eyes turning grey, and hair darkening to jet black. Unlike archangels and cherubim with their white hair and gold eyes. All bets were off with the seraphim. They had white hair and white fire for eyes. When they didn't burn so hot that they were just three pairs of wings and white Holy Fire. Well, except for Lucifer who had pale blond curls and crystal blue eyes.

That were red now.

"Did you hear me, Jack?" Gianni asked.

He stopped glancing at the sky and all the angels overhead and turned his attention to his best friend.

"Sorry, what'd you say?"

"I asked if the Watchers were here yet?"

He nodded as Izzy hurried out of the trailer beside his and Talia's and dashed along the walkway toward them. Already, the grey, squat studio buildings cast their stark, cool shadows across the pavement as a golf cart sputtered past. Six crew carried a set backdrop from one building to another as dozens of actors dressed in costumes hurried in and out of the cluster of buildings.

Jack squinted. Looked like someone was filming a western today, judging by all the chaps, cowboy hats, and holsters flashing past.

He kept pace with Talia's fast walk as Izzy took Gianni's hand and huddled between him and Jack.

"Jack," said Izzy, her big, bright brown eyes filled with worry, her bronzed skin soft against the white sundress and sandals she wore. "Are these skies really signs of the apocalypse?"

He reached out and squeezed her hand. "'Fraid so, Izzy," he said. "But we're going to fix that. Don't you worry."

"Just keep my better half safe," she said, breathless, worry spilling out of her usually calm and poised alto anchor voice. "He doesn't have any special angel powers to protect him."

Jack smiled. "Don't worry, Izzy," he said. "If all goes well, I don't intend to fight these bastards. Just beat them with their own weaknesses. So, it's all good."

Talia leaned around him. "And besides, Izzy, there'll be a flock of angels protecting him." She ran her fingers through his hair. "And Jack."

His and Talia's assurances made her relax.

"Then let's do this," said Izzy, a smile lighting her face. "Day one of the Celestial Couples Show. And the next round of the apocalypse."

Talia frowned.

"They changed the show's name," Izzy told her. "Because there will be two unmarried couples on the show."

"Oh, I see," said Talia, winking at Jack. "Glad to hear there isn't the word, apocalypse in the show title."

Izzy laughed.

"No, that would mean Lare Dumont, Nicole Reardon, and Tyler Hughes were back on the show with Rachel," Jack replied. "With special guest star, Erica Thomlin. And I totally didn't sign up for that."

Gianni nodded. "There isn't enough money in the world to get me to do that show."

"Agreed, love," said Izzy as she slid her arm into Gianni's.

And then Jack's. Together, as a single force, the four of them walked toward the door to Studio 22.

Jack opened the door and held it open for all of them. Talia halted, glancing up at the red sky and her squad gathered with the Watchers on the roof of Studio 22. She leaned toward him and kissed him.

"Ready for this new format change, lover?" she asked.

"Ready as I'll ever be," he replied. "With the apocalypse exploding around us. But as long as you're beside me, I can get through anything, Mrs. Casey."

She kissed him again and they walked into the building together, behind Gianni and Izzy.

The studio stage was unusually quiet as they passed through it, stage lights dark, the air smelling like coffee and donuts and sawdust as he walked arm in arm with Talia behind Gianni and Izzy toward the back of the building. To the cluster of four glass-enclosed conference rooms that overlooked the sound stage. The largest meeting room had a new grey conference table and at least a dozen comfortable padded grey task chairs around the oblong table. A flat-screen television hung on one wall, whiteboards covering the remaining two walls, and dry-erase markers in several colors littered the long, grey table.

Herb looked tense as he stood in front of the huge sound stage window, dressed in a midnight blue short-sleeved shirt, baggy grey pants, and black dress shoes. He'd shaved off the remaining hair on his balding head, giving him a more stylish look. Jennifer Collins white-knuckled her clipboard as she stood beside him, pushing those turquoise glasses up on her nose, turquoise top bright against the grey and white conference room.

Steven Kosinski sat in a chair beside them, his long dark brown hair loose at his shoulders, a jean shirt over a burnt orange T-shirt with *The Celestial Couples Show* logo in black. His close-cropped beard hid his expressions, but his eyes had a fearful look in them.

And around the table sat familiar faces. Mark Banks, his spiky, light brown hair shaggy, like he'd just woken up. He wore a faded black Pink Floyd Dark Side of the Moon T-shirt, torn jeans, and tan loafers. Morgan sat beside him, dressed in a red-striped shirt dress, her brown hair longer than he remembered. She held Mark's hand like it was a life preserver.

Rachel Daniels sat beside Mark, dressed in a body-hugging pink lace dress cut halfway up her toned thighs. And a scuffed-up pair of those damned red-soled shoes in a matching shade of pink that probably cost more than his rent for the year. A big pink diamond, at least three carats, glimmered like a searchlight on her left ring finger. Engagement ring at last from Eric Saunders who wore jeans, flip-flops, and an olive-green T-shirt.

Beside Eric sat Claire Olsen, her layered, shoulder-length sandy blond hair highlighted pink and white blond. Still willowy at five foot nine, she'd been a model who wanted to act. Dressed in a fuchsia tank top, jean shorts, and tan sandals.

Jack had tossed his glass slipper with her initials on the toe that first season, along with their million-dollar match, so he could pour his heart out to Talia and tell her that he loved her.

With Claire, it would have been a typical Hollywood life. They probably would have split up a year after the show—if not sooner. There hadn't been any sparks between them. Not enough chemistry for him to have stood on a live theatre stage, offering her the heart on his sleeve.

Beside Claire sat blond-haired, blue-eyed Ryder Kurland, part surfer dude, part CEO. A little sunburned, he looked like he'd just stepped off the beach in a white and blue Hawaiian shirt, tan board shorts, and blue flip-flops.

But the shock came when he saw Tyler Hughes sitting beside Ryder. With a woman that had a familiar face that he couldn't place.

He bristled, his body stiffening as Hughes' gaze shot toward him. But the anger and hatred that had always burned in his eyes were strangely absent.

Talia's arm tightened around Jack's waist as he stared at Hughes. And the pale, lithe woman with hair so black that it shimmered blue, a waterfall of board-straight shiny hair that fell to the middle of her back. Her eyes were the darkest brown he'd ever seen. She wore a royal blue sundress and spiky black heels. Tyler's eyes were beer-bottle brown, brown hair falling into curly locks at his ears and nape, bangs hanging in waves across his forehead.

God, she looked familiar! But he couldn't quite place her.

"Jack," Talia whispered against his ear. "Is that—"

He made sure his game face was immovable. "Sure is, babe."

"Why would Herb allow this?" she whispered.

He smiled at the room. "Guess we're about to find out," he said through that painful smile.

He felt Gianni bristle beside him, but he laid a hand against Gianni's arm, signaling him that for now, it was okay.

"Jack and Talia!" Herb shouted, rushing over to shake his hand and hug Talia like he hadn't seen them in years.

Jack had to bite his lip as the move smashed both wings against his shoulder blades, sending a spike of pain through his back and chest. He sucked in a breath and waited it out.

"Hey Herb, good to see you," he said. "What's it been? Two, three weeks?"

"Good to see you, two," he said and turned to Gianni. "And Armand and Izzy! Welcome back!"

Gianni weathered the hug with his calm Cary Grant reaction as Izzy hugged Herb, a warm smile lighting up her expressive face.

He smelled coffee.

Turning, Jack saw a table against one wall with three silver carafes of coffee and a huge box of donuts. When he glanced back at the conference table, he realized that Hughes' gaze hadn't left him. His former movie costar looked wary and strangely, that look of hatred was still absent from his face.

Had Lucifer's escape been a boon for Hughes (and maybe even Lare)? Letting him escape both Hell and Lucifer's attention? He'd find out as soon as rehearsals started.

"Please, take a seat," Herb replied, motioning toward the table.

Gianni gave him a nod as he and Izzy walked around the table, saying hi to Mark and Morgan and then Rachel and Eric. They said hello to Ryder and Claire and then Gianni's posture stiffened as he approached Hughes. It took a helluva lot of acting on Gianni's part as he nodded at Hughes.

"Banks!" Jack replied and patted Banks' shoulder. "Good to see you, dude."

Banks reached over and patted Jack's arm as Jack moved past Eric and Rachel. Eric gave him a hard, jealous stare as he moved past.

"Hey Rachel," he said, moving past, but Rachel reached out and took his hand, caressing it a moment or two.

Pissing off Eric.

"Good to see you, Jack," she said in that throaty alto purr, her smoky eyes generating heat in his direction.

And more anger from Eric.

Jack ignored her jealous fiancé. Dude needed some anger management classes and a serious reality check.

"Ryder and Claire, good to see you again."

"Hi, Jack," said Ryder as Claire's voice joined his, her arm around Ryder's waist.

These two were tight now. He smiled. And a good match.

Gianni looked furious as he walked past Hughes, toward the next empty chair. Right beside this kidnapping demonic douchebag. Nice.

But Jack rushed ahead, Talia beside him, and dropped into the seat beside Hughes. So Gianni wouldn't have to sit beside the demon that had terrorized and kidnapped his wife.

Talia slid into the chair to Jack's right and held his hand as he turned his acting up to overdrive and turned to Hughes as Gianni and Izzy sat down beside Talia on the right, looking relieved.

"Hughes!" Jack cried, forcing a big grin on his face. "Dude, how are you?"

Hughes looked surprised. Then confused. He cast a sideways glance at the woman beside him and then turned to Jack.

"Jack," he muttered, his gaze flicking from Jack to the table, fingers drumming against the edge of his chair.

The black-haired woman smiled at him and winked. Puzzled, Jack stared at her a moment.

"And hello, Hughes' date. Welcome to the fun house. They don't deliver the keg until noon."

Her smile widened into a grin. "Hello," she said in a soft alto voice.

One word wasn't much to go on, but he couldn't identify the voice. Maybe if he heard her talk more, he'd figure it out?

"All right! Everyone's here!" Herb hurried around the table and plopped into a chair between Steve Kosinski and Jennifer who still white-knuckled that clipboard.

Both Jennifer and Steve looked unhappy. Worried.

Was it the sky? Or Tyler Hughes? Or hell, why not both?

Talia leaned against Jack's ear and whispered.

"Jack, who is that?"

"Wish I knew, babe. She looks familiar…but I can't place her."

"Now then," said Herb, gazing around the table. "I think everyone knows each other." But then the director's gaze settled on Hughes. "You all know Tyler Hughes, but this is his girlfriend, Zoe Tabeau."

Banks looked pissed. Gianni was livid.

"Uh, Herb," said Jack, glancing around the table. "Is this a good idea?"

Herb's relaxed, happy expression darkened as he cast a hard look past Jack at Hughes.

"The network and the crew have had extensive talks with Mr. Hughes, Jack. One unscripted slight toward you or anyone else in the cast will result in his immediate dismissal."

Hughes turned to Jack, studying him a moment. His girlfriend laid a hand on his left arm. Keeping him calm or holding him back? Probably both.

"Jack…I'm sorry. For everything that happened. Armand and Isabella, I know I can't ever make this right, but I'm sorry. You won't get any trouble out of me. I give you my word."

Herb turned to Gianni and Izzy. "Armand and Izzy, will you agree to just try this? See how things go?"

"First whisper of trouble and we're out, Herb," said Gianni in a deadly calm voice.

Swallowing a breath, Herb nodded. "Talia and Jack?" Herb asked. "How about you?"

Talia looked all kinds of pissed as she stared at Hughes and then back at Herb. Gianni was still furious and Izzy looked upset. Gianni moved closer to her chair and slid his arm around her. She leaned against him, keeping her focus as far away as possible from Hughes. Dude had Eternean balls to show up here after everything he'd done.

But Herb signing him to the show was worse. Herb knew most of what Hughes had done. Rachel was enough trouble without having to worry about Hughes, too.

"One insult to Jack and he and I walk, Herb," Talia said, those intense angel-of-death grey eyes piercing as she stared at the director. "Just so we're clear."

Jack smirked as he pulled her into his arms and kissed her lips. "You heard the lady, Herb."

Then he glanced at Hughes, looked him up and down, searching for the burn of red eyes or horns budding at his forehead. But the dude just looked little and sad. He couldn't even see a hint of the demon that had misdirected him, Talia, and Azrael at the crossroads while Archangel Samael broke out of High House and stole the Book of Secrets.

Hughes' new girlfriend looked unaffected.

Finally, he extended his hand to Hughes. "Welcome to the show, Hughes."

Hughes' eyes got huge as the shorter actor looked at him in surprise for a moment or two and then shook his hand.

"Thanks, Jack," he said in a quiet, surprised voice and shook his hand.

He jumped like he'd been electrocuted, snapping his hand back.

Jack cackled and held up the hand buzzer. "Now, we're even, dude. Let's move on."

Everyone around the table laughed, including Talia and Izzy. Finally, Hughes laughed, too and the whole room chillaxed.

"That was so lame, Jack," Hughes said, rolling his eyes. "But funny."

And dammit, Hughes' girlfriend winked at him again.

Why was she flirting with him like this when his wife was sitting right beside him? An angel of death. That could smite her into the dark ages. Guess she didn't know that yet.

He felt Talia's grip on his arm tighten. She'd noticed all right. And she was pissed.

"Now that that's settled," said Herb, his clueless happy look returning. "Let's talk about the new format."

Did the dude not see the sky turn three different colors in the past three weeks? With zero explanation? He either had no clue that the apocalypse was on his doorstep or he didn't care. This was Hollywood. The apocalypse would always come second to getting episodes of this show in the can.

Who cared if there'd be no one left to watch it if just one of those Hell princes succeeded in activating a payload. Just one of the seven would destroy a good deal of the people and the planet. Regardless, Lucifer would exterminate the rest of it on his quest to erase Creation and start over again.

Jack shook his head, frowning at his director. *So, no worries, Herb. Carry on, dude. Business as usual. Step over the bodies and keep filming.*

And speaking of the apocalypse, he, Talia, and Gianni really needed to track down Traveler number three and intercept its payload. Fast.

"Jack," Talia whispered in his ear. "We need to go. Now."

He nodded. "I know. Let him at least explain the new format first. Okay?"

"Two minutes," she said with a stern look.

She was right. He nodded.

Herb stood up, grinning as he faced the cast of the show's new format.

"The network loved the new pitch, so we took a filming hiatus to get the new format in place." Herb held out his hand to Jack. "Big thanks to Jack Casey who pitched the dream home makeover for the Divine Newlyweds Show. But with Eric and Rachel planning their wedding and the network asking for more couples, we renamed the show to The Celestial Couples Show. And added Claire and Ryder, Zoe and Tyler."

Murmurs echoed around the table as Jennifer kept glancing out the sound stage window toward the door. Steve kept sneaking looks at his phone that sat on the table to his right.

Checking his stock portfolio? Or the weather? The sky? Was it raining demons yet? Or just Hell princes?

"So, now, we have six couples vying for a couple's dream home makeover. You'll each pick out a fixer-upper house to get a top-of-the-line makeover. Then each week, the couples will work with a designer and a contractor to do a budget makeover on one room. Audiences will vote on the best makeover. The couple with the lowest score goes home every week. The last couple standing wins the dream makeover and we film its progress each week until the end of the season."

"That's really cool, Jack," said Banks, grinning at him from across the table.

"Good suggestion, Casey," said Ryder as Claire gave him a nod.

"I love decorating and doing renovations, so this will be fun," said Claire, sliding her arms around Ryder's. "With Ryder helping."

Time to suggest a little help for stopping the apocalypse while they filmed the show.

"Herb," said Jack, rising from his chair. "I've been thinking that we can make these challenges more interesting by upping the stakes a little," he said, pacing around the side of the table.

Herb frowned. "How so, Jack?"

"By making each couple go out on a scavenger hunt every week and find one item or piece from a thrift shop or the studio vaults as the inspiration for their room makeovers."

Herb's eyes got wide, so Jack plunged ahead.

"Have us film our searches with Go Pros or drones or something and then you edit the raw footage into the week's episode."

"Jack!" Herb cried, rushing around the table and gripping Jack's arms. "That's fantastic! I love it! Especially the vault idea. Ties it back to the studio." He turned toward Jennifer and Steve. "Steve? Jennifer? Thoughts?"

Jennifer nodded. "Yeah, I really like that, Jack. It would work well in the show, Herb."

Steve was also nodding. "Good ideas. I like having some inspiration for each room makeover. And the raw footage would give a lot more depth to the show."

"Does anyone object?" Herb asked the room.

No one spoke up.

"Okay, then," said Herb, returning to his seat. "Steve, work with Phil and Rhonda on the streaming cameras while I get an okay from the studio on using items from the vault. And Jennifer, coordinate locations with the designers and contractors."

They couldn't wait any longer. They had to go after the Hell prince.

Jack frowned and slid his phone out of his pocket.

"Herb, I've gotta take this call," he said. "It's from my sister. Meredith. Can we take fifteen minutes?"

"Of course, Jack," said Herb, his arms in motion, directing the room to the coffee and donuts in the back. "Everyone, coffee and donut break."

Gripping Talia's hand, Jack held his phone to his ear and pretended to talk to his sister as he walked out of the room toward the studio's stage door.

"Is Gianni behind me?" he asked Talia.

Talia nodded and opened the door for Jack to step out. Into the blood-red haze of the apocalypse sky. He turned left behind the building. Where Muriel and the squad waited. A flood of Watchers crouched on the roof.

"Muriel?" said Jack. "We good to go?"

"Are there Watchers willing to impersonate Jack and me?" Talia asked. "And Gianni?"

Muriel nodded toward the roof. "They're ready to go. After a few minutes, three Watchers will return to the rehearsal as the three of you."

In a moment, Gianni was beside him, looking angry and concerned.

"I can't believe they'd bring Tyler Hughes back to this show after everything he's done."

He still looked furious, those usually kind brown eyes hard and narrowed, his Cary Grant poise slipping.

"We'll keep both eyes on him, Gianni," said Jack, patting him on the back. "He'll never get another shot at harming, Izzy, dude. I give you my word."

"Thanks, Jack," said the taller soap star, squeezing his shoulder.

Talia turned to Jack. "Lover, you need to use your seraphim power. Right now or we'll lose the third Traveler."

Lose him? That thought was terrifying.

Nodding, he turned toward the walkway between Studio 22 and Studio 21 and gazed up at the intense red sky. Calling up the seraphim power inside him.

It took several moments of concentration until red smoke began to materialize in the sky above him. Coiling. Twisting. Like a snake in hot ashes. Until a red loop of smoke lengthened and stretched across the sky, roiling through the sea of red toward the studio's front gates. Disappearing into the haze.

"Got it," he said. "Ready to hit this little bitch in the balls whenever you're ready, Mrs. Casey."

Talia turned to Muriel. "Watchers in place?"

"Ready to roll."

She turned to Kesien. "Kesien, will you carry and conceal Armand Gianni?"

Kesien nodded, his tangle of black curls looking so vivid against the blood-red sky as he lifted Gianni into his arms. Deemah tapped Gianni's shoulder.

"You can use my Eternean sword if it comes to that," she said with a smile.

Gianni's face lit up. "Thanks!"

Jack reached out and stroked Talia's face. "You okay, babe?" he asked.

She nodded, but she was avoiding his gaze.

"Not the answer I was looking for," he said and leaned over, kissing her hard on the lips. "I love you, Mrs. Casey."

Her gaze met his and she threw her arms around him, her kiss urgent and steamy.

"I love you now until forever, Jack Casey," she said and let him go, turning to her squad. "All right, squad. Tight Supremes formation. Jack and Armand are the vanguards. We're following Jack to the target."

"Lead the way, kid," said Kesien as he lifted into the air with Gianni.

"Not your goat," Jack snapped and spread his wings, letting the warm air lift him alongside Talia and the squad.

Kesien was smiling.

High above the studio, Jack turned in a wide circle, wings in motion, and searched for that red smoky trail again. It was hard to pick out against the blood-red sky, but he found it and followed it over the studio building. Up over the main gates and above the streets as it twisted and tangled in the wind.

Shifting toward the Five as the interstate curved north toward the distant hills. They flew past the Burbank airport, the red trail of smoke mimicking the interstate's path.

Was this Hell prince driving to his or her payload location?

He stepped up his pace, flying lower over the interstate until the red smoke curved downward. He groaned. Toward a busy gas station below.

Confronting a Hell prince in broad daylight. That was comforting.

"We need to be careful, squad," Talia announced. "Headed into a heavily traveled location. Lots of humans present. Be ready to intervene on my mark."

As he closed in on the flat red rooftop that shielded the gas pumps, Jack saw a shiny red vehicle. And groaned.

It was a brand-new Ford Bronco.

Okay, this horseman shit wasn't funny anymore.

"Not even slightly amusing, Luci!" he shouted into the wind as he landed at the edge of the concrete framing the busy gas station.

Every one of the twelve numbered pumps was occupied. But he only had one in mind. The red Ford Bronco. Where the trail of red smoke stopped.

"What is it, Jack?" Talia asked, sliding as close as she could to him, wings folding against her shoulders.

The rest of the squad landed behind her. Kesien set Gianni down and Deemah handed him a sheath with her Eternean sword tucked inside. Gianni licked his lips, his warm brown eyes focused on the red Bronco as he fastened the sheath around his waist.

"Trail stops at that brand-new red Ford Bronco, babe," he said. "We can't just lay waste to this douchebag in the middle of a crowded gas and sip."

"The Bronco?" she said, giving him an annoyed look. "Really, Lucifer?"

"I know, right?" said Jack, rolling his eyes. "Can we get even a little creative here?"

Talia stepped over the curb and moved toward the Bronco. "Let's see what we're dealing with."

Jack followed on her left as Gianni trotted beside him. The rest of the squad blinked ahead, taking up positions near the Bronco.

As he and Talia got close, a stocky, sunburned man in a red and black flannel shirt and black jeans walked toward the back. Wearing dog tags and black combat boots. Three-inch horns protruded out of the stringy coal-black hair falling over his forehead. Jack squinted, realizing he wasn't sunburned. He had red skin. Not even trying to hide the fact that he was a demon.

The Hell prince glanced up from the pump as he slid the nozzle out of the gas tank and put it back in its holder.

"Almost finished here," he said.

"Where you headed in flannel?" Jack asked with a smile as he leaned against the pump.

"San Francisco," he said with a leering grin. "Gonna get a little cool there tomorrow. And across the globe."

"Why's that, dude?"

It was freakin' August. And he carried the war payload. How was it going to get cool in San Francisco? Much less the world?

The Hell prince patted the front pocket of his flannel shirt. "Nuclear winter's coming."

The payload coin! It was in his front pocket.

"Is that why the sky's so damned red!" Jack asked, studying the Bronco.

Studying the demon. Looking for the sin this Hell prince oversaw.

"Planning any excursions before you nuke the city?" he asked, keeping his tone casual and unaffected, not wanting to set off this huge demon.

"Going to tour the bay," said the Hell prince as he crossed his arms and settled back against the Bronco's driver's side door.

"Are you into sailing?" Gianni asked. "I usually rent a boat when I'm near the bay."

What sin did this demon oversee? Gluttony and Envy were handled. There was Pride, Wrath, Lust, Greed, and…Sloth. And this dude was giving nothing away.

"No, not really," said the demon, glancing from him to Gianni.

"Well, there's lots to do around the bay," Jack replied. "At least a day or two before you nuke it."

Restaurants were out. That was Gluttony. War and Wrath fit together. Pride maybe?

Jack began to sweat as he walked toward Gianni, casting glances at the Bronco. When he got to Gianni, he turned toward the demon and stared through the windshield of the shiny red Bronco.

That's when he saw the fuzzy red dice hanging from the rearview mirror. Greed! Dude was a gambler. Had to be it.

"House always wins, y'know," said Jack as he slid his hands into his Levi's front pockets and felt for the joke props he'd stuffed there.

"The house?" said the demon, squinting at him.

"Those casinos around the bay," he replied. "Odds are terrible. Dude, at least head to Vegas after you nuke San Francisco. Much better odds."

"Really?" said the Hell prince, looking intrigued.

"Really," said Jack. "Those bay casinos rarely pay out. Hell, I could give you better odds on—" He pulled the quarter out of his pocket. "Well, on a coin flip."

The demon's eyes flashed red and sparked. "You want to wager, little human?"

"Okay, sure," said Jack with a smirk.

"Jack, don't!" Talia snapped, glaring at him.

Gianni was shaking his head. "Don't you dare wager with a demon, Jack. It'll just end badly and you know it."

"Why?" Jack replied and nodded at the grinning demon. "Dude just wants a game of sport. A little wager. That's all." He flashed the coin at the demon. "You toss up the coin and if I guess right, I win."

A twinkle lit the demon's red eyes. "If you lose, I get your soul."

"Fair enough, dude," said Jack.

"Jack!" Talia cried, looking alarmed. "No! NO!"

Jack tossed the coin to the demon who flicked it into the air.

"Heads!" Jack shouted.

Talia froze, terror in her grey eyes.

The Hell prince caught the coin in his meaty fist and opened his hand.

George Washington's face stared up at Jack.

"Heads!" he cried. "I win!"

A dark look shadowed the demon's face.

"What do you want for winning?"

Jack pretended to pace with excitement and nerves around the demon, getting in as close as he could as he stuttered through possible things he wanted.

"There are so many things…"

When he was within a hand's distance of the demon's flannel shirt, he shoved his hand into the front pocket and snatched the payload coin.

"This will work. Thanks, dude!" Jack grabbed the two-headed coin out of the demon's hand and slid both coins into his front pocket.

Fury burned in the stocky red demon's face as he glared at Jack, fist raised, horns sprouting larger out of his forehead.

"You're about to become a dark stain on this pavement!"

Jack stepped back as Talia and the squad surrounded the Hell prince, swords and shields raised. Talia held out an oblivion sphere in each hand.

"Unless you'd like to be removed from existence, I suggest you find someplace else to go. I hear Death Valley is lovely this time of year."

With his terrified gaze fixed on Talia's oblivion spheres, the Hell prince backed away from her. She shooed him away from the Bronco.

"Leave the Bronco," she said. "Just leave. Or be obliterated."

Nodding frantically, the Hell prince, wide-eyed, turned and ran away from the Bronco, disappearing behind the gas station.

She turned around and lunged at Jack. Shaking him hard.

"What were you thinking, Jack Casey!" she shouted. "Taking a massive risk like that!" She shook him again. "What if you'd called the wrong thing, Jack? What if that coin had come up tails?"

He smirked at her, making her madder as he fished the quarter out of his pocket. And handed it to her.

"It's a two-headed coin, babe," he said in a quiet voice. "It can only come up heads."

Slowly, the words sank through her fear and fury until finally, she turned the coin over and over in her palm.

"Jack Casey," she said, looking almost shell-shocked. "You…you cheated."

"Cool, huh?" he said.

"You cheated. You used a rigged coin on that Hell prince."

Her response was beginning to make him nervous. He frowned.

"I'm not gonna go to Hell for cheating a Hell prince and thwarting the apocalypse, am I?" he asked in a quiet voice.

She began to laugh. "You just played another Hell prince. You exploited his greed and cheated him with a two-headed coin."

"That's about right," he said as Talia threw her arms around him.

"You scared me to death, Jack," she said, kissing him. "But that was beautiful, lover!"

Laughing, he held her and spun her around. "Glad you enjoyed that, Mrs. Casey."

But when he glanced over at Gianni, he looked sad.

"Gianni?" he said, squinting as he let go of Talia and laid his hand on Gianni's shoulder. "Dude, what's the matter?"

Gianni slid the Eternean sword out of its sheath and held it up. "I didn't even get to swing it."

That made Jack laugh even harder. The squad and Talia quickly joined him. Finally, Deemah blinked beside Gianni and patted him on the shoulder.

"I'll tell you what, Armand," she said, winking at Kesien. "Why don't you hold onto that sword? For the next Hell prince. Okay?"

Gianni's sad expression brightened. "Can I?"

"Of course," she said. "I prefer shield bash to the sword any day. You keep that for the rest of the Hell princes."

"Thank you," he said, giving it a few practice swings before returning it to the sheath.

"All right, my devious husband," Talia said, caressing his cheek. "Let's get back to the studio before Rachel and Hughes hurt the Watchers."

"Done, Mrs. Casey," he said and kissed her again.

"Supremes formation, squad," Talia said, giving Jack a sideways glance. "Kesien, Gianni is with you. Jack and Armand are the vanguards."

Muriel smirked at him as she moved beside him and ruffled his blond bangs. "Two-sided coin. That was beautiful, Jack."

"Thanks, Muriel," he said. "I was terrified he'd look that coin and bust me, but he was so focused on his own greed that he didn't even think to check it."

"What if he'd checked it, Jack?" Gianni asked.

"If he'd looked at the coin," said Jack, "I planned to grab the payload coin out of his front pocket and fly away with it."

Muriel shrugged. "That would have worked, too."

Gianni's eyes narrowed. "Would have been safer."

"But not nearly as much fun, dude," said Jack.

Talia ran her fingers through his hair. "In the air, squad. Husband."

Smiling, Jack kissed her and then stretched his wings wide, lifting on the warm air currents as Talia floated beside him, gripping his hand. The squad emerged around him and Gianni in Kesien's arms, in a tight circle. At Talia's signal, they flew back south toward Burbank and Four Acres Studio.

12

He'd scared her to death with that little trick.

Talia edged closer to Jack as they landed behind the Studio 22 building at Four Acre Studios. But she should have known that even Jack wasn't foolish enough to wager with a Hell prince, using his soul as currency. She couldn't be mad at him. He hadn't planned that, but if he had, the Hell prince might have suspected a trick if all of them had known about the two-headed coin.

Her nerves were getting to her—as the sixth flight moved closer to launching. She couldn't bear the thought of leaving him behind here on Earth—or the thought that she might not survive the Enochian apocalypse. If she and Berith both perished, there would be no one left to resurrect angels. It took an angel's full power to use resurrect. Could Jack's seraphim powers fuel even a single use of resurrect?

The thought of leaving him forever made her want to fall on her knees and weep.

By sunset tomorrow, the fourth flight would take to the air, pouring out mud-brown bowls of disaster onto the sun. This one would be terrifying to humanity. The sun would momentarily eclipse and then burn bright as the skies turned a deep mud-brown.

Hell prince Four would set natural disasters into motion if his or her payload activated. Hurricanes. Tornadoes. Earthquakes. Even volcanic eruptions and tsunamis.

After rehearsals tomorrow, the sky would change again. And they would go after the next Hell prince. After disaster came despair. Including her own. When they neutralized that fifth payload, she had to leave him behind. She winced. Leave the man she loved more than her own existence to fight the totality of Lucifer's demon army. It might be the very last time she would ever see Jack again and it made her ache all over.

She couldn't halt the crystalline tears collecting on the ground at her feet as she tried to rein in her despair. She wanted to rage and scream at Lucifer, pound him into the earth with oblivion spheres. She and Jack had managed all this time to stay together. To get married and go on their honeymoon. She wanted that happily ever after.

Her hands balled into fists. No. She demanded that happily ever after. They'd earned it.

"Tal? Are you okay?"

His hot caramel voice burned through her chest and sent sparks through her heart. She wanted to wrap him in her arms and fly away. Tuck themselves into a little cottage along the Celestial Ocean's ethereal beaches and let humanity and Heaven take care of Lucifer.

But duty burned through her like Jack's love and as much as the pain of it ached through her, she knew she had to stop Lucifer. Before he erased all of Creation—including her and Jack.

"It's the sixth flight, isn't it?" he said in a soft whisper, holding her against his chest.

She shook her head. "No, it's leaving you behind." Her voice quivered and she couldn't hide her pain or her anguish. "I'm terrified that I'll lose you forever."

His arms tightened around her, his hot mouth finding hers in a frantic kiss.

"Hey," he said, cupping her face in his hands, thumbs brushing away her tears. "You're never gonna lose me, Mrs. Casey."

"But Jack," she cried, tears nearly blinding her. "What if I—"

"You won't," he whispered. "Because I'm gonna be right there in that sky. Fighting beside you. With these wings, I won't let you fall." His face scrunched into a pained look. "But if something happens." His voice began to quiver. "If I can't get there in time…I'll be there to catch you, Talia."

With shaking fingers, she stroked his face, staring into those sexy, pale green eyes that were turning glassy, his bottom lip beginning to tremble.

"Because I refuse to live a single day on this planet without you. You hear me, Talia? Not one day without you."

His frantic kiss burned across her lips and she smashed her mouth against his, wanting to feel his heart beating against her chest. Never wanting to forget the feel of him. The warm cedary scent of his buttery skin. The press of his leanly muscled body against hers. The heat of his hot caramel voice.

He held her, kissing her, and caressing her face for a long time until her shaking subsided and her crystal tears stopped falling. Only then did he let her go, his game face slipping as a tear slid down his cheek. He quickly swept it away, forcing a smile on his face.

"Ready to see the house we're going to turn into our dream home, Mrs. Casey?" he asked.

He'd tried to hold it all together, but she still heard that little hitch in his voice.

"I love you, Jack," she said and held him again, if only for a moment, for the memory of the heat of his love and the rhythm of his heart that beat only for her.

She'd fought so hard to be with him. They started this whole fight against Lucifer together. Together, they would finish it. As a couple.

"I love you more," he said against her ear, chuckling, and gripped her hand.

Together, they followed Gianni back into the building after Muriel gave them the signal that the Watchers were gone.

"What's the next payload?" Jack asked, pulling in a breath as he struggled to call back his game face.

He was suffering with the sixth flight, too. And it hurt her to put him in this position. She also feared that he might do something reckless—or sacrifice himself. He'd done it before and with her existence at stake, she knew him too well. He wouldn't hesitate to save her…any way he could.

"Disaster," she answered. "Tomorrow night at sunset, the fourth flight will turn the skies mud-brown and the sun will momentarily eclipse."

Those sexy green eyes widened.

"Eclipse? Wow."

"We'll worry about that tomorrow, lover," she said, kissing the side of his face. "Let's go see what sort of house we're making over."

Nodding, he kept an iron grip on her hand as they walked into the conference room. Into a tangle of arguments.

Jack stopped in the doorway, watching Rachel and Ryder shout at each other. Claire and Morgan stood by the donuts, a tense conversation in motion. Eric and Banks were in each other's faces, gestures heated, voices loud. Hughes stood against the wall beside his girlfriend, Zoe, eyes wide as he watched the chaos unfolding. Looking confused.

Herb moved around the room from Rachel to Banks, trying to calm the room, but the cast ignored him as tempers flared. Steve and Jennifer huddled against the window, glancing from Jennifer's clipboard to the cast and back again. A mixture of annoyance and worry burned on their faces.

"Whoa! Stop already!" Jack shouted, plunging into the room, arms above his head. "What the hell's wrong with everyone?"

He turned back to Talia. "What did the Watchers do? We weren't gone that long."

Talia shrugged. She had no idea what had happened.

When he moved past Morgan and Claire, Morgan scowled at him.

"Like you don't know?" she snarled, glaring. "Mr. Beach House."

"What are you talking about?" he demanded.

Morgan's hands snapped to her hips. "Just because you thought of the new format and are the big series draw doesn't mean you should get the best fixer-upper. And a beach house no less! Like you couldn't buy one on your own."

Jack burst out laughing. "With what? The piles of money in my bank account? The one the bank closed because it had a negative balance? Or maybe I could trade my Bugatti for it? Oh, wait—I mean my five-year-old Ford. Have you seen where I live, Morgan? The appliances are older than my parents. The amenities include constant cop presence, extra ventilation from bullet holes, and dramatic views. That means copters flying overhead 24/7."

Talia sang out a string of angel notes.

Muriel, it's chaos in here! Find out what the Watchers saw, please?

Chaos? Muriel's alto notes echoed around her. *Are there demons involved?*

No, Talia replied. *Just a bunch of arguments. Aimed at blaming Jack for getting an unfair advantage—which he didn't.*

An air horn screeched through the room.

Everyone turned around.

Jennifer stood in front of the window, clipboard and air horn can in hand.

"Now, everyone just stop and sit down!" she shouted in a firm but shaky voice. "Let's talk about this calmly, please."

Jack turned to Talia and gripped her hand. They hurried around the table and slid into the chair beside Tyler Hughes. His face was tense, his mouth in a taut line, eyes narrowed as he waited. Probably wanted someone to explain why everyone was so worked up.

She didn't understand why Morgan berated Jack about a beach house. Everyone in this cast knew about Jack's money troubles. He finally had his debts paid, including his former drug dealer, and he'd been tucking away paychecks for a few months. He had a good start, but he wasn't a wealthy celebrity anymore with millions in the bank, expensive cars, and a couple of houses. He hadn't been that person for years and he was still getting back on his financial feet.

"All right," Jennifer said and slapped her clipboard down onto the conference table, startling Herb and Steve. "We took everyone's preferences for neighborhoods, types of houses, and needed amenities to heart and worked with realtors all over the area to bring you a short list of properties in your price ranges. So each couple could choose the best fixer-upper for their situations."

The cast was deadly quiet now, everyone looking angry and tense, casting glares at the other couples. Like high school kids.

Talia couldn't believe it. Except for Izzy who leaned against Gianni and looked disgusted by the others' behavior. Gianni had totally disconnected from the pettiness.

Jennifer pointed at Jack.

"And for everyone's information," she said, her tone sharpening, "Jack did not get preferential treatment. His budget for a place was the smallest of all the couples. The most inexpensive house on the shortlist was that beach house. In the least exclusive neighborhood on the list, too."

Talia squinted at him. "Lover, what's she talking about?"

"No clue, Tal," he said. "I don't remember turning in anything about houses."

That was because he didn't. Jennifer had asked for Jack's budget and preferences in a text to his phone just after they returned from rescuing Berith. She'd sent Jennifer a page of notes that Jack had scribbled down about finding a new place. She'd added the words beach cottage and no neighborhood preference.

"Jack, I sent her the notes you'd scribbled down about finding a new place for us. But I added the words beach cottage because I knew that was your dream."

She expected him to get angry. To her surprise, he smiled.

"Really? You gave her a request for a beach cottage with that budget I wrote down?" He chuckled. "That's awesome, Talia."

"It is?" she asked, studying his sexy face and those sparkling light green eyes that were burning bright right now.

"Because it's all I can afford right now and to find a beach house at that price, even a fixer-upper, that's nothing short of a miracle."

Talia smiled. "Maybe it was?"

He thought for a moment and then nodded. "Will have to figure out who to thank." He turned his gaze to Jennifer. "Starting with you, Jennifer. Thank you!"

Everyone began to settle down as Jennifer passed out house specs to each couple and when Jack saw the picture of the cottage and its floor plan, his eyes lit up.

"Tal!" he cried. "Look at it! It's like a 1940s bungalow or something."

"Good eye," Jennifer said with a smile. "It's gotta be taken down to studs, but it'll have two bathrooms and three bedrooms if you win the dream makeover."

He didn't seem concerned. He was thrilled with the price, so maybe he would have enough saved to renovate it into their dream cottage whether they won or not. Talia loved it, too. Of course, she didn't care as long as Jack loved it.

She would hold onto an image of her and Jack living in this beach house, happily ever after. It was the only thing keeping her from falling into a ball of tears right now.

After all the houses had been discussed and any changes had been made, Jennifer emailed schedules for blocking rehearsals and details about the first renovation challenge. A dining room makeover.

She also passed out cameras to each couple. Those Go Pro things that Jack had suggested. In a week, they would film the first makeover-inspired scavenger hunt. Each couple would go into the studio warehouse and pick out one item as the inspiration for making over their dream dining room.

"Is that clear?" Steve asked, walking around the table. "After each couple gets their inspiration item, they'll return to Studio 22 where we have six spaces in back set up. You will work with a contractor and designer to create a dream dining room."

Claire motioned to Steve. "Steve, how long will we have to do each makeover?"

"Good question, Claire," said Steve as he turned in her direction. "Each renovation will happen in the first week of a two-week block. The first week, we will film all of the work and inspirations. So, next week we'll show progress footage and six finished dining rooms to our home audiences. They will vote on the website and then, the next week's show will be a live elimination show. The winning couple, safe from being sent home, will then be filmed at their dream house as we unveil the renovation of their real dream dining room according to the preferences they chose."

The first live elimination show was in two weeks.

Her stomach twisted into knots. By that time, the sixth flight would have begun pouring out blue bowls of silence upon the Earth as the Army of Light faced the Army of Dark above the world's skies. Jack's world would become deathly quiet, the clash between Light and Dark the only sounds heard until the seventh and final flight of angels emptied its plague bowl on the Earth.

Death.

And Jack would be faced with stopping the sixth and seventh Travelers' payloads. Alone. It hurt her chest. How could he and Gianni stop one Hell prince's payload? Much less two? It seemed impossible. And what if something went wrong?

By the time everyone was comfortable with the schedule and filming sequences that started next week, it was late. After hearing the schedule, Jack had gotten quiet. She knew that he was piecing it all together. Knowing that she would be away from him—battling Lucifer's army by the end of next week.

As the red sky began to fade and the blue began to return, she and Jack walked back to the trailer alongside Gianni and Izzy. They said a quick goodnight and continued to their trailer as she and Jack disappeared into their unit.

In the silence and late afternoon light filling the trailer, Jack kicked off his checkered Vans and curled up with her on the studio trailer's taupe couch. He looked as scared and helpless as she felt. He held her close as they tangled together, cuddling, television dark. She didn't want to be far from him.

It made her chest ache to think that they may only have a week left together.

Jack felt time slipping through his fingers, too. She saw it in his face even if he couldn't bring himself to say it. But for tonight, she and

Jack let the approaching doom that they both felt fade with the setting sun and waning apocalypse red.

He held onto her like it was their last night on Earth. As they waited for morning, another rehearsal, the coming approach of Traveler number four, and the fourth flight that would eclipse the sun and wash the sky mud-brown with tomorrow's sunset.

13

LAST NIGHT FELT LIKE THE EVE OF AN EXECUTION AND NOT EVEN sunrise had taken away Jack's feeling that he was losing Talia with every tick of the clock and every march of the days toward the sixth flight's launch.

He couldn't even talk about it. Couldn't plan. Or figure out how to make sure that she came back from this massive air battle against Lucifer's Army of Dark.

This morning, he'd woken up alone, her side of the bed cold and empty. Reminding him of his old empty, broken life that had been spiraling out of control…until he'd met Talia on *The Cinderella Hour*.

She hadn't been beside him for hours and he'd slept fitfully, dreaming that the world had been devastated. He'd searched everywhere for her and couldn't find her anywhere. Not in the spires, not in Eolowen. His apartment. Or even the studio.

He'd flown across the country, landing everywhere in the destruction, where angels had fallen out of the sky, but she wasn't among the lifeless heaps of blunted halos and shredded wings littering the world. He shouted her name until he'd grown hoarse and walked until his feet had blistered. But not a single sound returned to him in the dark, smoking world.

He'd woken himself up shouting. Then found her side of the bed cold.

The emptiest ache he'd ever known trembled through him. Making him curl into a ball under the covers and shake, his eyes filling with tears, and his breaths coming in gasps as he tried to shake off this profound feeling of loss that was killing him.

When he couldn't escape it, he got out of bed and paced the floor, barefoot, in green boxer briefs.

Refusing to give in to this despair. To this sense of dread that he was about to lose the love of his life to Lucifer's assault.

Part of him couldn't voice the fact that he felt like Talia had given up. That she was starting to accept the fact that she wouldn't survive this air war. That she was leaving him and he couldn't stop it.

He balled his hands into fists and beat them against his thighs, the moisture welling in his eyes. His face scrunched against the pain. He struggled to breathe. And he wanted to scream and shout all the way to the Thrones of Heaven that this wasn't over. That they'd taken everything from him but his heart. Talia was his heart.

And he wasn't giving that up. Her up.

Something whispered behind him.

He turned, tears leaking out the corners of his eyes.

Talia stood behind him, watery grey eyes shedding crystals that tumbled down her beautiful, winter-pale face. She pressed her lips into a tight line, the pain touching every stunning feature of her flawless face.

He went to her, throwing his arms around her, pulling her against his bare chest as he pressed his face against hers. Fighting hard not to let his pain bubble up. He did his best to force it down deep, but a sob shuddered out. He bit his lip, wings trembling as his heart hammered his ribs, the pain almost too much.

"I love you, Talia," he said in a tight voice. "And I won't let you go. Won't—lose you now."

Her arms tightened around him and she nodded against his chest, heaving a breath as she began to weep.

It turned him to jelly.

Shoving his pain beneath hers, he stroked her hair and rubbed her back, whispering against her ear not to give up, that he'd fix this.

"I won't let this battle be the end of us, Tal. I won't. You're not going to disappear. I won't let you cease to be, do you hear me?" He brushed the coal-black curls out of her teary eyes. "Look at me," he said in a sharp tone until she lifted her chin, her gaze meeting his. "I won't let you go, do you hear me? No matter what it takes, I won't let you go."

She ran her fingers through his hair, across his face, like she was memorizing the curve of his chin, the shape of his lips, the slope of his nose.

He sucked in a breath. She was giving up. Giving in to an outcome that she'd feared since Lucifer set off the apocalypse.

He made her look at him again.

"I will be there when it matters, Mrs. Casey," he said, the fight beginning to burn through him now. "I. will. Be there."

"I love you, Jack Casey," she said and enfolded him in her arms again, pressing her face against his chest. "Just—hold me...until the sun rises."

He smiled. "I'll hold you until time grinds to a halt." He bit his lip. "To my very last breath."

He carried her in his arms over to the bed and wrapped the blue comforter around them. Leaning against the headboard, he sang *You and Me* softly to her as the sun's first rays crept along the maple hardwood and reached warm fingers toward the foot of the bed. His voice was the only sound in the room except for the steady, persistent tick of the alarm clock beside the bed.

Reminding him that by sunset, Traveler number four would be loose and trying to shake the world apart by setting loose earthquakes, tornadoes, and tsunamis. Pushing the sixth flight, the Enochian apocalypse, one flight closer to the battle for everything.

He swallowed hard, pulled in a breath, and sang the chorus of *You and Me* to Talia one more time as she nuzzled her face against his neck. She smelled like cool rain and roses. Like Eolowen when the jasmine and honeysuckle climbed along the white stone pergola that meandered beside a cool, clear stream. And the breeze that rustled the willow tree's branches. Like everything good in the world. Everything safe and worth fighting for.

And he vowed to fight for her to his very last breath. If she didn't survive the sixth flight, he wouldn't survive it either. He wouldn't settle for memories of the woman he loved. Of flat, distant images taunting him with the life he could have had. Of never touching her again or feeling her warm body against him.

It was happily ever after or nothing.

They made love in frantic touches and urgent caresses, the heat of her skin burning along the length of his naked body as her legs wrapped around his, drawing him deeper, closer as an intense rush of emotion and sensation ached through him. He collapsed against her, his mouth finding hers. Entwining his hands in hers, he pressed them against the pillow, the heat of her body still radiating as the rush of climax faded into her warm embrace and hypnotic grey eyes.

After showering together, he dressed in a jean shirt, faded Levi's, and flip-flops. She put on a jean skirt, black flats, and a purple T-shirt that hugged her lean ethereal body with all its curves and Heavenly glow.

Holding her hand tight, they hurried out of the trailer and walked along the studio walkways that crisscrossed the road and meandered between the long row of squat grey studio buildings. The scent of eucalyptus was warm on the breeze, Cali's early August heat heavy against the crisp blue sky as an airplane buzzed overhead, leaving a trail of white vapor in its wake as he held open the door to Studio 22. They moved past the dark sound stage toward the large conference room in back a few minutes before the 7:30 A.M. rehearsal began.

Another day of bickering and selfishness. It made him ill. Especially with the apocalypse revving its engine and torquing everything into high gear. He was doing everything in his power to get it to throw a rod—especially that Omega Rod that Lucifer was trying to locate.

That even Pravuil hadn't found a single reference to in the Archive spire's chaos.

Jack didn't plan to be here chasing those last two demon asshats when Talia and the whole guard faced the end of their existence in that clash with Lucifer's army.

He wouldn't tell anyone his plans yet. Wouldn't give them time to try and force him into sacrificing Talia to save his world. How could he choose between them? It was the worst dilemma he'd ever faced.

When he and Talia entered the conference room, the scent of bacon made his mouth water.

The table in back was laid out with breakfast sandwiches, three silver carafes of coffee, and mini breakfast burritos. He smiled, remembering the day he'd shown Talia how to assemble them during *The Ever After Hour*. Her reaction when he showed her how they came in their own container (the tortilla) had been adorable and still made him chuckle.

"Babe, they have breakfast burritos," he said and nodded toward the table. "Remember when I showed you how to make and roll them up?"

At last, the hint of a smile softened her worried expression.

"At the beach house and also at the vineyard," she said. "I love how they just roll together."

"That's right," he said, running his fingers through the curls that hung around her face. "We had them at the vineyard, too. Good memory, Mrs. Casey."

Her smile widened at him calling her Mrs. Casey as she followed him to the table. He picked up a plate and took a breakfast sandwich and a mini burrito. She picked up a plate and took one of the breakfast burritos. After grabbing some napkins and some salsa, he moved around the table with Talia beside him. He set down his plate as she slid into a chair.

"Babe, you want some coffee?" he asked.

She shook her head and made a face. She didn't care for most human food, but the burrito still amused her.

"I'll bring you a bottle of water," he said and she nodded.

So quiet that it terrified him. Talia wasn't quiet—especially with him.

He hurried over to the table and said hello to Gianni and Banks who had just grabbed plates, both dressed in casual clothes. Gianni in a yellow polo shirt, dark jeans, and loafers, and Banks in a faded blue *Prince Charming Hour* T-shirt, jeans, and flip-flops.

"Morning, Jack," said Gianni, clapping him on the shoulder.

"Hey, Gianni," he replied as he filled an orange *Celestial Couples' Show* mug with coffee, cream, and sugar.

"How's it goin', Casey?" Banks asked as he grabbed a plate and filled it.

"Good," he lied. "How you doing this morning, Banks?"

He cast a glance over his shoulder at Morgan at the table in a gold and blue striped blouse and jeans. She still looked upset. About the houses, he reminded himself.

"Okay," he replied. "Morgan's still unhappy about the fixer-uppers. I asked Jennifer if they could do another pass for us. In Brentwood. Morgan's got her heart set on that neighborhood."

Gianni carried a plate with two burritos and two sandwiches, a cup of coffee, and a bottle of water under his arm.

"Izzy is starving this morning," he said. "Said she'd get coffee later."

Jack grabbed a bottle of water and followed Banks and Gianni back to the table. As he got to his seat, Hughes and his strange girlfriend arrived. She stared at him, looking so familiar, but he just couldn't place her.

He handed the bottle of water to Talia and took a sip of coffee before taking a big bite of his breakfast burrito smothered in salsa.

After everyone had eaten, Jennifer passed out the script for next week and they went through it as a group, getting a feel for the blocking, locations, and the first scavenger hunt in the studio vault. Jack was relieved that Herb had gone for that part. He didn't know how he'd explain his and Talia's absences. Or Gianni's.

But saving the world took precedence over everything, including this new season.

They broke late for a short lunch, Craft Services providing the food. An incredible stir fry that even Talia liked. Once the food was gone, they kept working through the script's blocking, but as the afternoon shadows lengthened and five o'clock came and went, Jack began to notice the sunlight fading.

He walked out during another break and headed out of the dark sound stage, the smell of fresh-cut grass strong as the maintenance crew roared past his building on a riding lawnmower. He checked his phone. Almost seven.

The sun had sunk low on the horizon, the golden hour giving everything a delicate ethereal glow. Like Talia's healing light.

But that warm, soothing light began to turn rusty. Darkening. Fading.

He held his hand over his eyes and turned to the west. The blue sky was turning grey, like someone had kicked up clouds of dust around the sun.

His stomach dropped.

The sun's light had gotten dull, dimming, looking like a rusted streetlight as a brown haze overcame its fragile gold light. He gasped.

The blue sky was turning mud-brown, the sun becoming a ball of brown mud right before his eyes.

"Holy shit," he muttered, staring at the sky.

All over Four Acres Studio, people stopped what they were doing and turned to stare at the sky. People cried out. Others shouted and whispered, pointing at the terrifying sky that had no explanation. There was no ring around the sun like a total eclipse.

It was all just going dark. Like someone had flung mud at the sun and engulfed the Earth in a persistent silty, sepia-like twilight.

The door to Studio 22 opened behind him, clatter of feet skittering across asphalt, their shadows fading away as the sun's light almost went dark as it slipped closer to the tree line.

"Dear God," Gianni said in an incredulous voice.

"What's happening?" Morgan shouted, sounding panicked. "There's nothing about this on my weather app. Nothing on the news. What's going on!"

Then he felt an arm slide around his waist, scent of roses and cool rain brushing across his senses.

Talia.

He put his arms around her and held her against his chest as the flutter of wings passed overhead. Landing behind the building. Talia's squad.

"The fourth flight has landed," she whispered against his ear. "And another Traveler makes their way to Earth."

He didn't take his gaze off the turbulent sky. "What's the payload again?" he whispered.

"Disaster. Any kind of natural disaster, Jack. If that payload goes off, it could destroy so much of your world. It's going to get hot outside until we shut this Traveler down."

Jack frowned. "You mean like a heatwave?"

Talia nodded. "Exactly."

He felt someone on his left. He turned. Gianni and Izzy. He had Deemah's Eternean sword at his side.

"This is terrifying," he whispered and Talia nodded, stepping out of Jack's embrace.

"We handle this one fast and bring back the sun," she said. "Bring the temperature down."

Gianni frowned. "If the sun's blotted out, how will things get hotter?"

"Don't know, dude," said Jack, "but I can guess it's because this shit's coming directly from Hell."

"Exactly right, lover," said Talia as she turned back to him and kissed him gently on the lips, a smile lifting the corners of her mouth. "It's Hellfire."

He returned her kiss, making her smile deepen.

"Be right back," she said. "Need to talk to Muriel."

He nodded and let go of her hands as she slipped through the crowd staring up at the sky and hurried behind the building.

Izzy stepped in front of him.

"Jack," she said, her warm brown eyes looking terrified. "Do you really think that you can stop..." She held out her hands. "Whatever this is?"

He gave her his most confident smirk.

"We've already stopped three of these asshats," he replied. "This one will put us halfway to stopping these douchebag Hell princes, so yeah, I think we can stop them."

She leaned up and kissed Gianni. "Just bring Armand home safely, Jack," she said. "And kick demon ass."

Jack pointed at her with his thumb. "Dude, you totally married the right woman."

His comment made Izzy laugh.

"Those Watchers did a great job last time," she said. "Even put Rachel in her place once—as you, Jack."

He busted out laughing. "Wish I'd seen that."

Izzy winked at him. "Trust me, it was glorious."

"Attention, everyone!"

Herb stood outside Studio 22, waving the cast over to him.

"What's up, Herb?" Jack asked as the rest of the cast crowded around him.

"Whatever terrifying thing that is," he began, looking unnerved. "We're not competing with it. Go home. We'll play tomorrow morning by ear. See if this mess has cleared up. Keep your phones close."

With that, Herb, Steve, and Jennifer rushed off and disappeared in the tangles of people clogging the studio walkways as Jack felt the air getting a little warmer as sunset approached.

Damn, that was creepy!

In a moment, Talia was beside him again as the rest of the cast dispersed. Except for Tyler Hughes and his strange girlfriend, Zoe who was staring at him again.

"Jack," said Hughes, hands in his jeans pockets as he glanced from the sky to him. "You know what this is, right?"

Time to find out what Hughes was really doing on this show. It sure as hell wasn't to fix up his dream house. In Hell. Dude was a card-carrying demon that had escaped Hell when Luci went on holiday to murder and destroy everything between him and this Omega Rod.

"It's either really slappin' special effects, Spielberg's making a sequel to E.T., or it's the apocalypse," said Jack.

Yeah, he was dialed up to maximum smartass right now. He had no clue what Hughes' agenda was or if he was still Lucifer's hand puppet. And this dude had been nothing but a colossal douchebag to him since he came on this show. Jack fully expected his new girlfriend to burst into flames, turn into Nicole Reardon's demon ass, or morph into Erica Thomlin's red-eyed ugliness.

But the big question remained: was Hughes still waiting tables for Luci?

"Regardless," Jack replied, staring at Hughes. "What are you doing here?"

Hughes' voice dropped to a raspy whisper.

"When Hell's Gates popped open, I ran like the whole place was chasing me. Lucifer didn't try to stop any of us, so right now, I'm free and working for myself." He made a sour face. "But Jack, if Lucifer wins this war, we're all screwed. My only chance of changing anything is if Lucifer loses this war."

Hughes was no fool. He saw what was at stake and that his only way out was if Luci lost this war.

"Look, I know I was a dick to you, Jack," he said. "I did a lot of shit to you over the years, too." He sighed. "And after Lucifer took my soul. If I help shut this thing down, then just maybe it'll shut Lucifer down, too. So, I'm in. Whatever you're planning to do—and I see it in your eyes, bro, I know you're trying to stop this thing—I'm in."

Another recruit to deliver ass-kickings to underprivileged Hell princes. He'd take any help he could get. Hughes would probably stab him in the back the first chance he got, but if he kept the dude on a short leash, then maybe they could take this Traveler down fast.

He turned his gaze to Hughes' girlfriend.

"What about your bae here, Hughes?" He looked into her dark eyes, searching for a glimmer of recognition, something he could use to identify her. "She helping us, too?"

"Bro, that's not my girlfriend," he said, looking worried. "That's…"

Zoe looked at Jack and smiled, batting red eyes at him.

"Oui, Jack Casey," she said in a smoky alto French accent that made him take a step backward. "I am here to help you win, too."

For a moment, he was speechless, staring at her like a middle schooler with his first porn download.

"Zanth?"

She nodded, grinning at him. "Oui. I had to find a safe place for Tre while I returned to Earth to fight this—this mess that Lucifer has started. This misdirection." Her eyes narrowed as she glared at the mud-brown sun and the darkening sepia-brown sky. "Like Hughes, I can only win if Lucifer loses. And that means protecting Tre with everything I have."

In a moment, Talia blinked across the concrete back to him. She wrapped her arms around him and stared at Hughes and then Zanth.

"Mrs. Casey," he said, grinning as he held his hand out to them. "Hughes wants to switch sides and play shortstop for the Angels. And he brought reinforcements. Zanth the archdemoness and former Hell's first lieutenant."

"What?"

Her gaze shot toward Zanth as she studied the archdemoness for several intense moments.

"'allo, Talia, angel of death. Thank you again for reuniting Tre and me. I came with Tyler Hughes to help you stop the Hell princes."

That smoky alto French accent was unmistakable as her features shifted into the familiar ashen skin, bobbed black hair, and darkly sexy face with its pert nose and full lips. She had a thin, supple body with sexy curves and shapely legs. And Talia would kill him if he admitted that Zanth was hot—for a demon.

This was definitely Zanth who had hidden her features underneath a plain human form. He knew she was trying to hide herself from Lucifer's hordes, but he wouldn't say no to her help. Maybe he couldn't trust her all the time (or most of the time), but when their goals aligned, she was a good ally.

Talia's tense expression said everything. She did not like this at all. With a wary glance, she turned her attention to the former archdemoness.

"I know you haven't been in Hell for a while," Talia said, crossing her arms against her chest, "but what can you tell us about the remaining Travelers?"

Zanth glanced at the sky again and fixed Talia with her gaze.

"The Traveler of Disasters is on his way to Earth to unleash unnatural forces into nature. And cause cataclysmic damage and pain. Heat waves. Destruction—as much as possible."

Jack groaned. Talia wouldn't appreciate that response.

"That's it?" he replied. "I could have told you that. C'mon! Talk to us about the important stuff. What sin does this thing preside over? How do we take the payload coin from this Hell prince?"

"Exactly, Zanth," said Talia, her glare more of a challenge. "Either help us or stay out of the way."

Talia was not in the mood to be led by the nose by demons. Giving her the runaround right now was not advisable.

"This Hell prince presides over the sin of Sloth," said Zanth, her voice like worn velvet. "It is indifference. Laziness. Apathy."

"Where is he supposed to deliver his payload?"

Jack figured he already knew since this sin was Sloth, but he wanted to confirm it.

"Right here in your city of angels, Jack Casey," said Zanth.

Just what he expected. Lucifer wouldn't trust a lazy-ass to carry a payload any distance if he presided over a sin like Sloth. Too damned apathetic. Made sense.

Jack turned his gaze to the mud-brown sky and closed his eyes, calling up the seraphim power in him as he concentrated on the brown color clogging the entire sky, obscuring the crisp summer blue and what might have been an intense, radiant sunset.

He kept his focus on that sepia-brown as the seraphim power stirred within him, reaching into the muddy twilight until a smoky brown trail appeared in the sky. Connecting his new raiding party to this next Hell prince.

Some lazy bastard that didn't care about anything. Perfect. Probably expected the apocalypse to come to him.

"Wait a minute!" Jack cried, grinning as a devious plan began to form in his head.

"Uh oh," said Gianni as he turned to Talia. "That look is trouble."

Talia studied him a moment and nodded. "That look has Jack Casey's up to something written all over it."

"No, listen!" he cried, motioning everyone in closer.

"Be careful, love," said Izzy as she stepped away from the group. "If this is one of Jack's crazy schemes, I'll feel better if I don't know about it until it's over. Be safe, Jack and Talia."

"You, too, Izzy," Talia called after her. "We'll bring Armand home safe. I give you my word."

Izzy smiled. "Much less worrying than Jack's word, Talia. Thank you."

Talia ruffled Jack's hair. "See, I told you that you were trouble from the day I met you."

He laughed. "And now, I'm gonna prove it. Okay, listen up. Here's how we're going to get the payload coin from the Sloth demon."

"I've got to hear this," Muriel said with a chuckle to Anahera who nodded, her short red hair blowing in the breeze.

"This will be good," Kesien replied and moved closer.

Gianni slid close to Jack as Muriel and Anahera blinked beside Talia. Hughes and Zanth took a few steps closer, but Hughes looked apprehensive when Deemah appeared behind Talia.

"What's the matter, Hughes?" Jack asked.

Zanth smiled. "I think he is still allergic to angels."

Jack chuckled as Talia broke into a grin.

"That what you call getting curb-stomped by angels these days, Zanth?"

Talia's musical laugh washed over him like wind chimes as her squad laughed with her. Especially Muriel who snorted.

Zanth laughed, too, leaving Hughes to cast a scowl at him.

"Sorry, Hughes," said Jack.

"We're cool, Jack," Hughes replied. "And I deserved that. I did a lot of shit to you and Talia. And to your buddy Gianni and his wife. Tell your wife I'm sorry, too." He fixed Gianni with an unblinking stare. "I didn't have much choice then. But I do now."

Gianni gave him a deep nod as he shifted the Eternean sword around in its sheath.

"Apology accepted, Hughes," said Gianni in his calm, unaffected Cary Grant way. "Thank you."

"Now," said Hughes, pushing up his sleeves. "What's this plan of yours, Jack?"

"Zanth, need this demon's name first and then I'll tell you the plan."

Looking puzzled, Zanth thought for a moment. "It is Havres."

AFTER JACK HAD EXPLAINED his plan and Talia approved it, Kesien carried Gianni as the squad took to the air. Zanth and Hughes lifted off behind Jack, their scaly bat wings in frantic motion as Jack followed the trail of sepia-brown smoke across the sky. Curving toward Los Angeles' downtown. That was congested. Choked with traffic. And lots of tourists. Worst place he could think of to release a disaster payload in L.A.

That made him nervous.

"Trail leads toward downtown!" Jack shouted.

The heat and the soupy brown haze made flying difficult as Jack slogged his way alongside the trail of sepia-brown smoke, sweat masking his face and making his clothes cling to his body. The sepia trail coiled and twisted its way into the center of downtown. Toward the mirrored towers of the Westin Bonaventure Hotel.

They flew low over Harbor Highway toward the sleek, modern-looking hotel with its silvery reflective panels that made the hotel's towers look like a futuristic rocket launchpad. He'd stayed there a few times. Attended a lot of parties held in those suites. And snorted a lot of flake at someone's beach house afterward.

The brown smoky trail swirled toward the sidewalk right in front of the hotel. And stopped.

Guess it was all going down right here. In front of tourists and everybody.

"All right, Muriel," he said, turning toward her as she glanced behind him at the brown smoke undulating across the sidewalk. "Send that Watcher over with the Ford Bronco we took from the last Hell prince."

"Already taken care of, Jack," Muriel said with a smirk and motioned behind her. Toward the curb.

Where the brand-new four-door red Ford Bronco stood. He hugged Muriel.

"Perfect! Thank you!"

She looked a little dizzy when he let go and turned to the rest of his posse.

"Okay, Talia and Zanth—you're with me," he said and motioned them toward the Bronco. "Everyone else, back me up if this goes south."

Kesien nodded and Gianni wrapped his hand around the hilt of his sword. "Be careful, Jack."

"Muriel, you, Hughes, and the squad keep a lookout for…"

His voice trailed off when he saw the vintage 1930s truck pull up to the curb and stop.

"For that."

A boxy old brown truck with hand-painted gold trim and a hood with an old fold-over cover concealing a loud motor and radiator. The wheel spokes were painted red. Even from here, Jack saw the plate on the hood that read, Clydesdale. It looked like it had driven off a Hollywood set. Or straight out of World War I. Classy workhorse truck.

Named after another damned horse.

A tall, thin demon with pale red skin stepped out of the truck, dressed in a black wool coat buttoned up to his chin. Small thin black horns poked out of the demon's ginger-red hair, cut high and tight.

Jack hurried around the Bronco and climbed into the driver's seat as Talia and Zanth slid into the backseat, leaving the front passenger seat empty. Talia and Zanth both changed what they were wearing with the flick of their fingers. Zanth shifted into a short black satin dress with thin straps that hugged her body and showed off her legs.

Talia changed into a short, sparkly red dress with spaghetti straps that hugged her hips and thighs. Showing off her amazing legs.

"Promise me you'll wear that tonight back in the trailer, Talia," he said, glancing into the rearview mirror. "That's smokin' hot."

She grinned at him. "We'll discuss it. In the bedroom."

"Sweet!" Jack said with a smirk and started the engine.

He drove the Bronco up beside the old truck and rolled down the window.

"Mr. Havres?" he called out the window.

The demon turned around and stared at him, red eyes looking confused and intrigued.

"Yes, little human?" he said in a raspy baritone voice that carried. "Living dangerously, aren't you? Didn't your momma teach you not to talk to demons?"

Jack cringed. Not his momma. That woman was more demon than this fool and Nina Westwood would have taken him apart.

"I apologize for being late, sir," said Jack. "I'll be your driver tonight."

The demon's long, angular face scrunched into a confused stare. "Driver?"

Jack nodded. "Of course," he said. "A Hell prince such as yourself can't be expected to drive that old antique anywhere in the city. So, I've procured this brand-new Bronco for your use tonight, sir. In red." He smiled. "I thought you would approve."

The demon glanced back at the antique truck and scowled. He returned his gaze to the Bronco and smiled.

"It's even in my color," said Havres, a smile burning across his stupid demon face and Jack wanted to punch that smile right off his lips.

"Hop in, sir," Jack continued. "And we'll deliver your uh, item in record time and get you on your way home again."

"A driver and human minions…this is great!" Havres exclaimed with a grin, that mouthful of pointy teeth glinting in the sickly yellow wash of streetlights as the apocalypse brown sky and the night sucked up the light.

"One second."

When Havres opened the front passenger door of the truck, Talia crossed her legs, showing off those long, sculpted legs that made Jack's blood boil.

"Oh, sir, please—" Talia called to him in a sexy alto voice as she batted long lashes at this demon and playfully motioned him to the back with her index finger. "Back here."

Zanth took a cue from Talia. When Havres opened the backseat door, Zanth showed her legs as she struck a seductive pose and smiled at the big Hell prince.

"Back here, sir," she purred in that worn velvet rasp, heavy with her sultry French accent. "We will keep you company on the way to your destination."

Jack wanted to smash in this lazy bastard's red demon face as he slid into the backseat between Talia and Zanth and put an arm around each woman. They both cuddled up to him. Zanth stroked his horns while Talia ran her fingers through Havres' wisps of red demon hair.

"Best. Job. Ever!" Havres crowed. "Lucifer's the best. Driver, let's hit it!"

"Where to, sir?" Jack asked, glancing into the rearview mirror.

"Grand Central Market," Havres ordered. "But take your time, kid. I got no schedule tonight."

This demon was dazzled by Talia and Zanth. Talia cuddled up to him, stroking his face, his chest, running her hands up and down the length of his coat as Zanth slowly unbuttoned it, kissing him with teasing kisses. Until this demon didn't know up from down.

Jack drove down Fourth Street and slowly turned left onto Broadway as Talia and Zanth got this demon so hot and bothered that he slid off his coat and tossed it into the floor, pulling Talia and Zanth against his chest. He had a big, fat stupid grin on his face and Jack still wanted to punch his little bitch face.

That was his wife this asshat was molesting.

When the light on Third turned green, he drove through the intersection and pulled over against the curb on the left.

"Your destination, Mr. Havres," he announced.

The demon looked pissed. Sighing, he snatched his coat out of the floor and put it back on.

"Wait here," Havres ordered, glaring at Jack over the seats. "I won't be long."

He was all smiles when he turned back to Talia and Zanth.

"Ladies, I'll be right back."

"We eagerly await your return," Talia said in a sultry voice that about melted this demon's horns.

Zanth ran her fingers up and down Havres' arm. "Don't be long now, you tall, gorgeous demon, you."

Grinning, Havres almost floated away from the Bronco as he rushed down the sidewalk and ran toward the Market. Mr. Sloth Sin himself.

Talia grinned and held up the payload coin. She'd lifted it from him on the drive over.

"You're the bomb, Talia!" he shouted. "Let's blink. Quick. Before he comes back."

"Oui," said Zanth.

Jack threw open the driver-side door as Talia and Zanth shoved open their doors. Talia grabbed hold of Jack's wrist and Zanth's elbow.

"Blinking us out on three," she said. "One, two, three!"

Lights flashed, the world spinning into darkness, but Talia's steady grip on his wrist kept him upright. In a moment, they materialized on the sidewalk beside the antique Clydesdale truck.

Grinning, Talia held out the payload coin as Gianni and the squad crowded around her.

"Way to go, Talia!" Muriel cried, patting her on the back.

Anahera hugged her as Kesien cheered.

"How'd you get it so fast?" Gianni asked, staring at the coin in disbelief.

"Zanth and I pretended to be Havres' dates," said Talia.

"And that is all it took," Zanth added. "I kept him distracted and Talia lifted the coin while he was drooling over both of us."

Talia grabbed Jack's arm and dipped him, kissing him hard on the lips.

"What was that for?" he asked, laughing.

"Incredible plan, Jack," she said and brushed her lips across his mouth. "It was a risk. He could have just been indecisive and slow, but you pegged him as lazy."

Hughes chuckled. "So, that lazy bastard thought you guys were going to do all the work for him?"

Jack nodded.

"What a loser. That was too easy."

"Just the way I like my Hell princes and princesses," Jack said with a smirk. "C'mon, Mrs. Casey," he said and wrapped her in his arms. "Let's go talk about this dress."

She grinned, her hand caressing his cheek. "What do you want to know?" she asked.

"Where the zipper is for starters?" he said with a wicked smirk. "And how it comes off."

"Let's get out of here," said Muriel.

Gianni crossed his arms against his chest, that Eternean sword bobbing at his side.

"When do I get to stab one of these demons with this sword, Jack?"

Jack broke into a fit of laughter. "Okay, next Hell prince, Gianni gets first stabbing priority. Remember that, people."

"Committing that to memory," Kesien said with a chuckle and lifted Gianni off the ground. "Let's get out of here."

"First stabbing priority," Muriel said with a snicker. "I'm so asking Azrael for dibs on that when I get back to Eolowen."

Jack smiled. "He'll know it came from me."

"Boy, will he!" Anahera cried, poking Jack as she unfurled her wings. "He always knows when you instigate something, Jack."

Chuckling, Jack spread his wings beside Talia as Zanth and Hughes followed them into the strange, mud-brown night sky. He flew close to Talia all the way back to Burbank. They set down in front of the trailer. Talia spent a few minutes with her squad and they flew up onto the trailer's roof to keep watch.

"See you tomorrow," said Gianni as he walked toward his and Izzy's trailer that stood beside Jack and Talia's trailer.

"Night, Gianni," Jack called.

"Goodnight, Armand," said Talia, standing beside Jack.

"We will talk about the remaining Travelers tomorrow, Jack Casey," said Zanth in that summer-hot French accent.

"Seeya then, Jack," said Hughes.

Together, they faded into the night as he and Talia hurried into the trailer. Jack grinned as he swept her into his arms and carried her down the short hall. Into the bedroom.

He dropped her onto the bed and straddled her, kissing her hot mouth.

"Now, about this dress," he said, reaching toward the straps.

She pressed her index finger to the dress. And it vanished right before his eyes. Leaving her in lacy red underwear and a strapless bra.

"What dress?" she asked, grinning as Jack smashed his mouth against hers and rolled her under the covers.

14

A NIGHT AND A DAY AFTER TALIA HAD LIFTED THE PAYLOAD COIN OFF the fourth Traveler, the strange mud-brown color left the sky, returning California's summer blue and the bright sunlight to Jack's world.

She and Jack spent the next two days sitting between Gianni and Izzy and Zanth and Hughes while Herb went over every single stage direction in the script. Talia didn't know how Jack sat through this process every time. It made her want to start tossing oblivion spheres. Without the apocalypse exploding around them. But no matter what Herb said, he always brought in a cast that was explosive to Jack. And this one terrified her. Even without Lucifer stirring them up this time, they seemed eager to blame Jack for everything and call him out for things he didn't do.

Morgan Banks had surprised her with her overt contempt for Jack, something Talia hadn't seen before. Mark Banks was one of Jack's best friends and he'd proven that many times, but Morgan had done nothing but cause Jack harm and heartache. Talia hoped Jack didn't lose Mark's friendship over Morgan's immature pettiness.

And then there was Zanth and Tyler Hughes, sitting to Jack's left. Within strike range.

Was it the proliferation of demons running loose around them? Or Morgan's jealousy and pettiness toward Jack? After his former show had offered him more than two million dollars an episode to return, Morgan had hinted that he didn't deserve that money and that he had a condescending attitude toward the rest of the cast. Something Jack had never had. Since Talia had known Jack, he'd always felt like he didn't belong, that he wasn't good enough.

She couldn't help but worry that Lucifer had sent this cast to cripple Jack's efforts to stop his Hell princes. But she also worried that all of this was more misdirection. To keep them all busy and blind to Lucifer's real goals. He'd been so quiet that at times, she'd forgotten that Lucifer had caused all of this.

And that scared her. A lot.

She hadn't heard a word from Pravuil about the Omega Rod that Lucifer sought either. And she couldn't help but worry that Zanth and Tyler Hughes were here to lure Jack into some deadly trap.

At Lucifer's request.

Talia didn't trust Tyler Hughes either. He hadn't proven anything to them yet. They at least had a reason to trust Zanth, the archdemoness but not long term. Zanth had fought Archangel Samael beside Talia and her squad. She'd taken Jack to see his father in Purgatory, giving him a priceless gift. And she'd given them information that had helped shut down one Hell prince so far. But right now, Zanth and Jack had a common goal.

What would happen when those goals diverged?

And then there was Rachel Daniels. A wild card in this strange cast.

Who still flirted with Jack in front of her fiancé, riling up the muscled financial planner enough to want to fight Jack. What motivated Rachel? Had she returned to working for Lucifer? Now that he was free? And where was Lare Dumont?

Why hadn't Jack asked Tyler Hughes about his former *best friend*? Lare Dumont started all of Jack's pain. Instigated it. Planned Jack's death like he was planning a dream vacation. Out of jealousy. Rachel had been just as complicit as Lare Dumont, assaulting Jack after drugging his drinks. Talia would never trust any of these demons. Jack may have inadvertently spared Rachel from Lucifer's contracts, but Talia feared that Jack's former costar would still turn on him like a rabid dog.

She hated the thought of leaving Jack here with these people. She trusted Izzy and Armand to watch out for Jack. And Mark Banks. But the others frightened her. Made her afraid for her headstrong, reckless actor-husband.

Only Mark Banks, Armand Gianni, and Izzy remained above suspicion in her eyes. And she was grateful that Jack had them to watch his back.

Especially when the sixth flight took to the air.

They finished out the week of rehearsals and on the way out of the building, Jennifer informed them of the 7:00 A.M. set call on Monday morning.

If Monday ever dawned.

After tonight's sunset, the sky would turn electric orange and call forth the fifth Traveler. It hurt her heart. It was the last Traveler she could help Jack bring down.

Her eyes welled with tears. And it might be the last time she ever saw him.

She and Jack ate dinner with Armand and Izzy in their trailer where Armand and Izzy grilled salmon and asparagus. Jack brought a bottle of merlot. The four of them laughed, drank wine, and ate a wonderful meal together, and it was the first time she and Jack had had a normal married couple's evening. With their best friends. Something Jack had craved ever since he learned that she was an angel of death.

Angels didn't eat, but she'd loved this night with friends and Jack. She'd savored the wine and the taste of the human foods that Jack loved so much. It brought her back to her favorite seasons of the show. Planning their wedding together on *The Royal Wedding Hour* with so many cake flavors, wines, and mixed drinks. Cooking with

Jack for the first time on *The Ever After Hour*. She swallowed a breath. Before Lucifer had dragged him off to Hell.

She felt that way tonight as the sixth flight drew closer. Restless. Frightened. Grieving. Never wanting to let go of Jack, fearing she'd never see him again. Every time she dreamed of her happily ever after with Jack, Lucifer managed to take it away from her.

This time, she resolved to fight for it with the last flicker of her angelic light.

The sun was setting as she and Jack returned to their trailer, the sky flaming pink, purple, and orange against a bank of clouds on the horizon. But in moments, the orange color began to spread. Overtaking the bright pinks and smoky purples until the bizarre orange color intensified into an eerie neon glow. Setting the sky alight like wildfires burned nearby.

"Talia," Jack replied, his gaze glued to the sky. "What's happening to the sky?"

She winced and gripped his hand. "It's the fifth flight, Jack. Pouring out orange bowls of despair on the Gates of Hell that have overflowed onto the Earth. Day will turn to night and the night will darken with despair."

He looked frightened and a little lost as he stood there staring up at the sky. Finally, he turned toward her.

"Talia, what happens when we stop the fifth Traveler?" he asked, his voice breaking. "Because we are going to stop it."

His eyes turned glassy as he began to shake all over. Like he knew what she was about to say to him.

Forcing a smile to her lips, she put her arms around him.

"Then I have to leave you, lover."

By the Maker, she ached all over, knowing what was to come. Knowing what might happen.

"For a while," he added in a tight voice, his pale green gaze searching her face for a response, for a confirmation that this separation wasn't forever.

Finally, she couldn't let him hurt like this and she nodded.

"Yes, Mr. Casey. For a while."

He bit his lip, fighting back a sob, and held her against his chest, his heart beating so fast and so wild.

And then her squad was on the trailer roof. Blinking to the ground. Zanth and Tyler Hughes were right behind them. Beside them, Armand's trailer door slammed shut, anxious footsteps pounding toward them.

The fifth Traveler was on his or her way to Earth. And they had to intercept its payload. She had to see this through. For Jack. For his world. For Heaven. And somehow, she had to find enough faith to face the sixth flight.

The Enochian apocalypse.

And she had to believe that she would come home to Jack.

He kissed her lips with a desperation that made her chest ache. She returned his kisses, holding him tighter, doing her best to reassure him despite the dire odds. But to protect him, she had to let him believe she was coming home to him.

She needed to believe that, too. It was the only thing keeping her going right now.

"You okay, lover?" she asked, stroking his hair as he wiped his eyes, struggling against his emotions to find his game face.

But it failed him this time as he pulled away, breaths ragged as he tried to quiet the storm of grief rampaging through his head. She loved him more than her own existence, but she knew that losing her would break him. And she couldn't bear the thoughts of his Book of Life and Death ending so soon. Or by his own hand in a headstrong, bitter sacrifice. She had to make sure that Armand Gianni and Mark Banks were here to watch over him.

If she couldn't.

Zanth laid her hand on Jack's sleeve after he finally found his game face and turned back to Talia's squad, Gianni, Hughes, and the archdemoness.

"Looks like it's showtime, people," he said, clearing his throat, sounding distracted as he turned his attention to Zanth. "Zanth, tell us about Traveler number five."

The archdemoness wore a short white satin dress, like the one she'd worn when she attacked Talia and Jack on San Juan Island, Washington during their honeymoon.

"The angel flights have poured out their sorrow on Hell," said Zanth. "And your world, too, Jack Casey. This plague will turn day into night and cast despair everywhere. Your next Traveler is a Hell princess. Called Maraxa. She presides over the sin of Wrath."

Jack stared at Zanth a moment or two, like he was processing everything she'd said, and then turned toward Talia.

"Tal," he said. "Wrath. It's not just anger, is it?"

She shook her head. "No, lover, it is a deep and vindictive rage. It's a desire to punish others. Lucifer is filled with wrath."

"So, this princess is angry at the world and wants to see it all burn. And pay for some slight against her?"

Zanth put her hands behind her back and began to pace. "Oui, Jack Casey. Maraxa hates humanity like Lucifer. She wants to make humans pay for their arrogance. And blames them as the cause of even the angels falling from Heaven. So, she will delight in releasing this payload of despair upon the Earth. She is one of the most difficult Travelers to defeat."

Jack chewed his bottom lip. "Wow, how are we going to stop that?" He rubbed the back of his neck. "What do you think, Talia?"

Something hell-bent on wrath believed their cause was just. One look at Lucifer and she knew how hard it was to dissuade him from believing that he was wronged and humanity should be punished for it.

"Lucifer believes that his wrath is righteous, Jack," said Talia as she gazed up at the sky. "We would never make him believe otherwise."

Jack nodded. "He doesn't believe that he's done anything wrong. Thinks he's been defending himself this whole time."

Zanth leaned against the side of the trailer, staring down at her black stiletto heels.

"Maraxa is no different than Lucifer," said the archdemoness.

"So, no tricking the payload coin out of her hands," Jack said with a sigh.

Zanth shrugged. "Not easily."

"Where is the payload delivery location?" Jack asked.

"Your government capital," said Zanth.

"Whoa, what?" Jack looked frightened. "Washington, D.C.?"

"Oui, the despair will take hold and filter out from there. And no one can stop the devastation and darkness that it will cause."

So, trying to trick this Hell princess was a poor option. And they didn't seem to be able to scam this one out of the payload coin like they had the others. Because this one was a zealot. She believed in her cause and its righteousness to the point of obsession. Like Lucifer.

But maybe they'd still find a way.

"It looks like we may have to fight her for the payload coin," said Talia, hands on her hips as she fixed Muriel with her gaze. "Zealots don't back down. Again, look at Lucifer."

She glanced over at Jack who was beginning to pace, the color washing out of his face. Like her, he knew this would be a tough fight.

"Tal…how do we openly fight a Hell princess?" he asked, motioning at the sky. "Aren't they like right under Luci in the power structure?"

Zanth stepped into Jack's path and laid her hands on his arms, forcing him to look at her.

Talia bristled. She had to remind herself that Zanth loved someone else and wasn't hitting on Jack like she had when she was hunting Jack's soul.

"You are correct, Jack Casey," said Zanth. "Lucifer possesses seraphim powers and more. My powers are similar to an archangel. The closest comparison to their power would be your cherubim. So, this fight will be dangerous."

Cherubim-level power? That was disturbing.

Jack's reaction was difficult to measure though. Talia watched her husband force his game face into place for the benefit of the others, especially Armand Gianni.

But they had numbers on their side. With her rare angel powers, she had some cherubim-level abilities like summoning Holy Fire and oblivion spheres. But even as Azrael's best squad, she knew that one squad of death angels was no match for a Hell princess.

Zanth was a seasoned warrior with archdemon powers. Again, no match for a Hell princess. Even when she joined forces with a squad of death angels.

Talia sighed and the pain washed over her in waves as she studied her beautiful, sexy human husband. With rare angel powers. And seraphim powers.

Only Jack was a match for this Hell bitch. He'd lasted against Lucifer blow for blow and was winning, too. All that the rest of them could do, like it or not, was support him. Protect him. And hope that he didn't fall into a power drunk before taking this Hell princess down.

Not good odds.

"Talia, none of us can go against a Hell princess," said Muriel as she moved beside Talia, gold shield glowing on her right arm. "You know that."

Talia nodded. "I can't. The squad can't. Even Zanth can't. Together, we might keep her busy before she ended all of us. But Jack has seraphim powers."

Muriel looked scared. "But Talia, what if he goes against her and runs out of power? She'd destroy him, us, Zanth, and the world."

"Can't argue with that, Muriel," said Talia as she moved over to Jack and laid her hand against his face. "Jack, only your seraphim powers will be effective against this Hell princess."

He ran his fingers through his light blond bangs, looking worried. "I was afraid you were going to say that." Again, he stared up at the sky. "So, I need to pound this Traveler with every ounce of seraphim power I've got until I can take her payload coin?"

"That may be the only choice, Jack Casey," said Zanth as Jack began to pace again. "If it comes to that, you must challenge her. She will turn down your challenge, of course, so you must be ready to fight for that payload coin. Taking it from her may be our only chance to stop her."

Jack's best friend, Armand Gianni stepped toward him and walked beside him while he paced.

"But Jack, if she believes her cause is just," said Armand, his warm brown eyes intense. "She may not fight with you even if you challenge her. You'll have to force her into combat by trying to take the coin." He glanced toward Talia. "Talia, if all of us rush the Hell princess, can we pin her down long enough to take the coin?"

The hint of a smile lifted the corners of Jack's sexy mouth. "Maybe we can use that somehow? I keep her attention focused on me. Everyone ambushes her and we take the coin."

Zanth shook her head. "If you take the coin, she will either continue to hunt you down or continue fighting you. She will not give up like the others."

"That means we're going to have to kill a Hell princess," said Jack in a dark tone.

He was right. This Maraxa would never allow them to take the coin and not come after them. She'd fight for that coin back because it was the key to her bid for justice. And the heart of the sin she presided over. Besides, she'd be devoured by a legion of hellhounds.

How did they get around a zealot Hell princess?

"Yes, Jack," said Talia finally as she exchanged a knowing look with Zanth. "She would be relentless just like Lucifer."

"How do we kill a Hell princess?" Armand asked as he turned toward Talia, Deemah's Eternean sword on his hip.

Deemah walked over to Armand and tapped the hilt of the Eternean sword.

"That sword you carry can kill a demon," she said and then her gaze flicked to Kesien. "If you're an angel of death. Kesien, what will this sword do in a human's hands?"

Kesien leaned against the trailer and folded his wings against his shoulders as he gazed at Zanth and then at Talia.

"I'm not certain, but I'd guess that sword would still do considerable harm in a human's hands. Gianni could kill minion demons with it. Assassin demons. But kill a Hell princess?" He shook his head. "Don't think so."

Talia stepped between Armand and Kesien. "Kesien's right," she said. "That sword is no match for a Hell princess. Maybe if we add Holy Fire in high concentrations? Lots of oblivion spheres."

"Non, it is not enough," said Zanth as she fixed Talia with her gaze. "Your rare angel powers will damage her, Talia, but to kill a Hell princess? It is not enough."

"Then this kill is on me, isn't it?" Jack asked as he moved beside Talia, his hand sliding up to caress her face.

She laid her hand against his as the fear and pain radiated through her body. This Hell princess wasn't as powerful as Lucifer, but she was just as obsessed. And she could still kill Jack.

Reluctantly, she nodded. "Afraid so, Jack," she said, bowing her head.

She hated being forced to send him into the ring against a Hell princess like this, but they didn't have a choice.

Only seraphim powers could fix this and right now, Jack was it. She didn't even know if Seraphina would be fit enough to fight the Army of Dark when the sixth flight took to the skies. Without Heaven's seraphim, most of the angels were powerless against Lucifer and his highest-order demons.

That had been half of Lucifer's goal when he'd exploded a bomb in High House. Destroy the Book of Creation. Destroy the seraphim in the Cloud Chamber.

Talia didn't know if Heaven's former Lightbringer was powerful enough to defeat three seraphim at once. But destroying the Cloud Chamber meant bypassing that complication. Regardless, Seraphina, in her current condition, was no match for Lucifer alone.

And above the seraphim stood the Throne angels. All eyes and wings. Incredibly fast. Incredibly deadly.

Lucifer had been the Maker's Left Hand once. None in Heaven, not even the Throne angels, were as powerful as Lucifer. None but the Maker.

And now Lucifer was free and had his powers back.

Would this Omega Rod make Lucifer invincible?

Jack turned toward Zanth.

"Zanth, do you agree?" he asked. "Am I the only one here that can end this bitch?"

Zanth glanced at Talia and then back at Jack. Finally, she nodded.

"It would take at least a seraph to bring down a Hell princess."

For a few moments, Jack paced around the front of the trailer and Talia noticed how wild his eyes were as he struggled to get his emotions under control. Finally, he stopped pacing and gazed up into the sky again, hands at his side as he closed his eyes. Concentrating on something.

He was silent and still for several moments until a trail of orange smoke materialized in the sky above the trailer and snaked off into the distance. He'd summoned the trail to follow with his seraphim powers.

He stared at it, like he was surprised by the direction of the trail of smoke. It was bright against the hazy orange sky, leading off to the northwest.

With a sigh, he turned around, that game face intact again.

"So, if this Hell princess is headed to D.C., she'd be trying to get there fast, right?" he said, his gaze moving around the circle of angels, demons, and humans as he held out his arms, waiting for a response. "But no wings, correct?"

Talia turned her attention to Zanth who whispered something to Hughes and then turned back to Jack.

"Fast as humans can travel," said Zanth. "You are correct. She has no wings to fly there, so she would have to rely on your human transportation. I made some…deals to get mine."

"Same, Zanth," said Tyler. "Or rather Lare did."

Jack frowned, his gaze snapping to Tyler. "So, where is Lare, dude? He waiting to ambush me out there?"

Tyler shrugged. "I never saw him when I escaped Hell, Jack. But I can guarantee he didn't stand around and wait for Abaddon to close those gates. He flew."

"So, if you guys have wings," said Muriel, her brow furrowed as she studied Zanth and Tyler. "Why wouldn't these Hell princes make some deals, too? If they're that high up the chain and all."

Zanth gave her a quizzical look. "Lucifer did not want them to have wings because they were ground troops. He wanted to have a formidable force in the air and on the ground. Unless Maraxa has made a deal after leaving Hell, she won't have wings."

The possibility that she could have made a deal made Talia nervous. They had to hurry.

Jack stared at the ground and began to pace again. "So, assuming no wings," he said but stopped in front of her. "She's probably taking a flight, but Tal, wouldn't she do more? If she thought her cause was so *righteous* and all."

His tone was sharp with sarcasm as he crossed his arms, mouth pressed into a thin line, annoyance burning in those pale green eyes. He was out of his element, looking a little lost, turning to her for help. Not caring what anyone thought either.

And she loved him for that.

But Jack brought up a good point. As a self-important Hell princess who saw herself as the Wrath of Hell, she had probably balked at slow commercial flights. No, she probably saw herself like she was a human celebrity.

"You may be right, Jack," said Talia. "She thinks she's a celebrity. She probably hired a private jet to take her to your government's capitol."

Jack grinned. "Tal, a private jet! That's brilliant!" He moved back to Zanth. "Would this Maraxa have seen herself as important enough to hire a private jet?"

Zanth rolled her eyes and gave him a firm nod. "Of course. She would see herself as Lucifer's left hand." She laughed. "But Lucifer prefers his first lieutenants to his Hell princes in battle. His first lieutenants are seasoned warriors that must prove themselves in the cage fights. Hell princes are reserved for situations like the apocalypse and other figurehead duties. Like leading ground troops."

Talia spread her wings and the rest of her squad followed suit.

"Are we heading back to the airport?" Anahera asked, glancing at Talia and then Muriel.

"LAX, right?" Muriel replied.

Jack and Armand stared at each other a moment. Smiling, they turned toward Talia.

"Van Nuys!" they said in unison.

Hughes nodded along with them.

"Van Nuys?" Talia replied, giving her squad a perplexed look.

None of the squad seemed to know what Van Nuys was and she certainly didn't either.

Grinning, Jack and Armand nodded.

"When Hollywood takes a private jet," said Jack, "it's usually out of Van Nuys."

"More privacy. No public," Armand said, nodding.

"Whenever Nicole and I flew private, it was out of Vån Nuys," said Hughes as he slid his hands into his jeans pockets. "Way less hassle than commercial through LAX."

Jack motioned toward Hughes. "I never had the privilege of private jets, but back in the day, Hughes here made a shit-ton of A-List movies, Talia. He'd know."

Tyler Hughes' expression brightened. "Definitely Van Nuys, Talia," he said. "If Maraxa thinks she's Lucifer's left hand, there's no way she's flying commercial." He snorted. "Or economy."

Zanth propped her hand on her left hip. "She should be presiding over the sin of Pride rather than Wrath."

As those sexy, pale green eyes narrowed, Jack pressed his hand against his chin, pacing again as something devious began to filter into his head. Already, she was worried.

He made four or five laps in front of the trailer before he turned around and faced the group.

"Why don't we try playing into her self-importance?" he said finally, glancing around the group. "Zanth, you and Hughes could pretend to be her entourage with me and Gianni as your human slaves."

A spark lit Hughes' red eyes as a smile curved across his face.

"Wait a minute, that's good, Jack!" Excitement burned in Tyler Hughes' demon eyes. "Zanth! We show up, tell her we're her support. We drag along a couple of terrified human slaves, boosting her ego, and walk her out to the plane. Like we're boarding to serve her."

Jack leaped into the conversation. "And then we ambush her. Take the payload coin. Scoop up Gianni and fly the hell out of there like there's no tomorrow."

His wicked grin lit up his whole face with mischief and she wanted to kiss him hard on the lips.

"And Zanth," Jack added. "Maybe she'd be too ashamed to come after a couple of humans, some angels of death, and an archdemoness that got the better of her?"

The longer that Zanth pondered Tyler Hughes' and Jack's plan, the more her red eyes lit up.

Talia felt relieved that Jack might not have to fight a Hell princess. This way, they had the element of surprise on their side. This Hell princess wouldn't be suspicious of Zanth, who could alter her appearance. And likely dismiss Tyler Hughes because he was the lowest of demons in her eyes. Beneath her attention. But two human slaves would probably feed her ego.

"Tyler, that just might work," said Talia. "Including the ambush, Jack. We don't need to kill a Hell princess. We just need to humiliate her and grab her payload coin. That's all. So she won't come after us."

That sexy smirk curled the corners of Jack's mouth.

"And she can't even fly after us."

Zanth nodded. "It is a good plan. She would be humiliated, but locating all of us to try and get the coin back—before we destroyed it —would be beyond her efforts alone." Zanth chuckled. "Without an entourage."

Talia turned to Armand. This would be dangerous for him. He had no special powers and was only as safe as the squad's protection. She needed to make sure he'd be okay.

She reached out to Armand and laid her hands on his shoulders. "Armand, are you sure you're okay doing this?" Talia asked. "This will be extremely dangerous for you. You'll be unarmed and unable to fight against her if all of this goes badly."

Jack waved his left hand in the air. "I vote that we initiate our original plan as our official plan B if this one goes south. If it gets salty, I plan to slam that bitch with enough seraphim powers to send her back to Hell. Economy class. Just so you know."

Muriel and Kesien held their shields over their mouths, hiding their laughter.

Shaking her head, Talia stepped in front of her husband who had that look in those pale green eyes. Trouble. With a capital J and a capital C. But at least he was letting them know what he was planning instead of just springing it on them in typical Jack Casey fashion. And since he was the only one that could take down a Traveler, she was grudgingly on board with it.

"Thank you for the warning, Mr. Casey," she said with a smile and leaned up, kissing his warm lips, making those green eyes turn fire-bright.

She turned back to her squad and the demons.

"All right, Zanth, Tyler," she said. "Let's play into her ego. We'll locate her and land ahead of her on the tarmac. Play out this little scene. If it goes badly, we go with Jack's Plan B. Otherwise, we rely on Zanth and Tyler Hughes to grab the payload coin."

Jack waved his arms in the air. "Hold it! Hold it!"

"What's wrong, Jack?" Talia asked, turning back to him.

"Decide now. Who grabs the coin? Who would be the least sus?"

"Qu'est-ce que…sus?" Zanth asked, her gaze hardening.

Muriel rolled her eyes. "Sus is Jackspeak for suspicious, Zanth."

"Isn't that what I said?" Jack replied with a shrug.

"The least suspicious?" Zanth said with a smile. "Me. Of course. She'll see me as an archdemoness. Her inferior. A mere bodyguard. She would not expect me to dare to take that payload coin. Jack, you and Armand must distract her with some human drama."

Jack and Armand looked at each other for a moment and burst out laughing.

"Dude, you're telling two actors to distract her with some drama?"

"Can you do it?" Zanth asked, looking worried.

This made Jack and Armand laugh harder. Even Tyler was laughing now.

"Zanth, we're actors!" Jack shouted. "We live for this shit."

"It's our life, Zanth," said Armand as he poked Jack's shoulder with his fist.

Tyler Hughes gave her a big nod and Jack motioned toward him.

"Got the third actor involved now, Zanth. Trust me, we got this drama thing."

Talia laughed. Again, she appreciated her husband's considerate nature. He had included Tyler Hughes in that group, knowing Tyler probably felt like an outsider after having his soul claimed by Lucifer and thrown into Hell. And after all the terrible things he'd done to her and Jack. But Jack rarely held onto a grudge. One more thing she loved about him.

"All right then," said Zanth. "When you hear me bring up Lucifer to Maraxa, that will be your cue to start some human drama."

Jack clapped Armand on the shoulder and motioned toward the sky and the writhing trail of orange smoke.

"Let's get this party started."

"Squad. Phalanx formation." Talia lifted into the air. "When we get to the airport, take up perimeter positions near the Hell princess. Prepare to engage only on my mark. Acknowledge your orders."

She listened for each response. When she heard all four, she hovered above the trailer, waiting for her squad to appear in a phalanx line around her. Kesien was first, carrying Armand. Muriel appeared on her right followed by Anahera and Deemah.

Jack appeared behind her, sliding his arms around her waist as he hovered beside her, nibbling her ear, kissing her neck.

Electric sparks shot through her and she wanted to wrap him in her wings and make love to him. She held him close until Zanth and Tyler appeared. Only then, did she give the order to blink along the smoky orange trail that would lead them to this Hell princess. Traveler number five.

Jack led them northwest.

As it turned out, the Van Nuys airport was much closer to Burbank than the Los Angeles International Airport, so they made it there in a little over ten minutes. As they flew over the parking lot, Jack broke into a fit of laughter and pointed at a row of VIP parking spaces. In the middle of the row was an old boxy orange car that looked like it was covered in a fine sheen of dust.

"It's a Ford Pinto!" Jack cried.

"You're serious!" Armand replied as he stared down at the parking lot. "It's an orange 1970s Ford Pinto…incredible!"

"I've only seen that thing on the internet," said Tyler. "Thought they were fake. Didn't they explode if someone rear-ended them or something?"

Jack cackled. "Then we should have just rammed her with the Ford Bronco on the way here. Problem solved."

The three humans broke into a fit of laughter, but the ethereals just looked at each other. Talia smiled. Except Muriel who laughed along with them.

"That should have been Plan A, Jack," Muriel called out to him.

"Damn, you're right, Muriel," said Jack, shaking his head as they banked over the building and followed the trail of smoke onto the dark tarmac. "Missed opportunity."

This airport was much smaller than that huge one with all the lights and runways. And people. Where they had stopped the second Traveler on the motorcycle from activating her payload.

They followed the smoky trail into the dark toward a hangar at the farthest edge of the terminal. Where a small white jet sat on the tarmac, lights twinkling in the sky's orange lighting, windows lit with warm gold light. The jet had a red tail with a big number 60 on it.

Talia landed close to the plane, staying out of sight with her squad as Jack landed beside Zanth and Tyler. Armand hurried toward them out of the shadows and stood beside Tyler as Jack folded his wings against his shoulders. Zanth worked some demon magic and attached some glowing red smoky chains to Jack and Armand's feet. She and Tyler each held onto what looked like red glowing leashes. Zanth shifted her appearance back to the one she had used at the studio, of Zoe, Tyler's girlfriend. Together, with Armand and Jack in tow, they rushed toward the plane with rolling stairs that led up to an open hatch.

Talia stiffened.

As a stocky, ashen-skinned woman with wild strawberry blond hair came up from behind them and rushed toward the stairs. She wore a long white fur coat, a red sequined dress, and black stiletto heels. Her makeup was heavy and smoky, blood red lipstick on her full lips. She was tall, at least six feet, and looked stern as she started up the stairs.

"Maraxa!" Zanth called, letting go of her French accent as she dragged Jack and Armand forward.

Tyler ran behind her.

Talia's stomach twisted into knots. If something went wrong, she only had oblivion spheres and Holy Fire. She prayed they would be enough of a distraction to get Jack and Armand out of there.

The demon Hell princess turned around and glared as Zanth stopped in front of her. And did a deep bow or curtsy. A nice touch. Tyler quickly bowed when he reached the Hell princess.

Then he glared at Jack and Armand and thumped Jack in the chest. "Bow, human scum, in the presence of royalty!"

Armand did a deep bow, turning on a terrified expression. But not Jack. She groaned. Jack was about to start that drama that Zanth wanted.

"A failed actress with bad hair, no tan, and a second-hand fur coat? Seriously? Nah. Not bowing."

Zanth yanked the red leash hard, forcing Jack onto his knees.

"How dare you!" she shouted and pointed over at the Hell princess. "Maraxa is a princess of the Seven Spokes, overseer of the sin of Wrath and the Spokes of Hate and Malice and Premeditation."

It sickened Talia to watch this Hell princess' arrogance and how she puffed up at Zanth's lavish introduction. This Hell bitch needed to be humbled. With some Holy Fire. She just hoped this encounter didn't end with Maraxa fighting Jack. Talia couldn't bear to watch him get torn up in an all-out war with this demon.

"And who are you?" Maraxa demanded, looking down her nose at Zanth.

"I am Royal Coordinator Camia, coordinating human and demon servants," said Zanth who motioned at Tyler next. "My assistant, Forras." She glared at Jack and Armand. "And these embarrassments are human servants that we captured in the city to serve you on your journey to the East."

Maraxa walked toward Jack and Armand. She reached out and lifted Armand's chin, looking him over like a steak at a meat counter. She walked around him, staring at his body, and then walked over to Jack.

Every nerve in Talia's being frazzled, every muscle stretching to its limits, wings taut like rubber bands as Maraxa ran her hands across Jack's face, down his chest and back. Like she was buying cattle.

"They are exceptional, Camia," she said, those red eyes beginning to glow. "They will satisfy me until we land."

Talia smashed her hands into fists. She'd satisfy that demon bitch with some Holy Fire right to the face if she even touched Jack. Or Armand.

"What is our destination?" Zanth asked.

"Washington, D.C. I have procured passage on this luxury jet. It's not much, but it will do."

"Why are we going to the other coast?"

Maraxa dismissed Zanth with a wave of her hand and sauntered toward the stairs but paused, patting the left pocket of her coat.

"I must take care of some urgent business there, so I appreciate your thoughtfulness in gathering a suitable entourage befitting my station."

The payload coin!

Talia gasped. It must be in Maraxa's left coat pocket.

Zanth nodded as she stepped beside Maraxa.

"You are most welcome, Mistress," said Zanth. "Lucifer wanted me to ensure that I attended to all your needs during the apocalypse."

Jack and Armand ran with Zanth's cue.

"I'm not getting on any damned plane!" Armand shouted and grabbed Jack by the collar. "This all your fault! You just had to stop for one more drink, didn't you?"

"My fault!" Jack shouted, shoving Armand backward. "I'm not the one that wanted to cruise for women on Hollywood Boulevard! Like they did in that stupid movie you dragged me to last week."

"You're full of shit!"

"And you're behind the times!" Jack fired back. "Everybody knows you cruise for women on apps, not streets. Well, unless it's Sepulveda Boulevard."

Armand glared at him. "You calling me old?"

"So's your flip phone, dude."

They lunged for each other and rolled across the tarmac, pretending to punch each other.

"Forras!" Zanth ordered, pointing at Jack and Armand. "Beat them senseless for this outburst!"

Maraxa's eyes brightened as she licked her lips. She was enjoying their fighting.

"Not…senseless," she said with a leering smile. "I still have uses for them."

Jack and Armand rolled back toward Zanth as Tyler started slinging that red leash at them. Capturing Maraxa's complete attention.

They maneuvered their tussle closer to Maraxa and Zanth stepped in front of the Hell princess, hands on her in a mock protective stance.

"Stop this!" Zanth shouted. "Right now! Forras, protect the princess!"

"I'm trying!" Tyler shouted and leaped at Jack and Armand. "Stop it or I'll slay you both!"

When Zanth abruptly moved away from Maraxa, Talia knew she'd grabbed the payload coin.

The archdemoness rushed toward all three of them brawling with each other on the tarmac beside the jet. When Zanth got to Tyler, they grabbed hold of Armand, holding him up between them as Jack got to his feet. Zanth glanced at Jack and then Tyler.

As Tyler and Zanth faded into the shadows with Armand, Jack blinked across the tarmac, wings spreading as he leaped into the air.

Talia sang out to the squad to blink and all five of them shot across the sky behind Jack.

Fifteen minutes later, they all landed back at Four Acres Studio in the darkness. When Zanth and Tyler appeared, they set Armand down between them.

Blinking, Talia shot across the pavement and gripped Zanth's shoulders.

"Zanth," she cried, wide-eyed as she stared into the archdemoness' sparking red eyes. "Tell me you got the payload coin."

Grinning, Zanth held out her ashen hand. Where a tarnished bronzed coin the size of a half-dollar sparkled.

Talia grabbed it and held it up to the brilliant orange-tinted darkness.

They'd done it! They'd neutralized the fifth payload. Without Jack having to battle a Hell princess with his seraphim powers.

She threw her arms around Zanth and hugged her. "Thank you!"

Zanth looked surprised as she let her go.

"You are welcome, Talia." She nodded at Tyler, Jack, and Armand who looked tired but pleased. "I could not have done it without your assistance."

"Think that Hell bitch even knows we ganked the coin yet?" Jack asked.

Zanth shook her head. "Probably will not until she steps off that jet in Washington, D.C."

Talia turned to Tyler and hugged him. Then Armand. When she got to Jack, she stared into those steamy pale green eyes. His grin faded to a smile and then disappeared.

"No hug for me?" he asked with a boyish look that melted her into a puddle of need.

She shook her head as she stepped closer to him. And smashed her mouth against his in a bone-rattling kiss that left him weak in the knees.

"I'm good with that," he said in a dazed voice, making her laugh.

Only when his smile returned did she throw her arms around him and hold him close.

"Goodnight, Talia, Jack," said Armand as he started toward his and Izzy's trailer. "I'll see you in the morning. Izzy's probably worried sick."

"Night, dude," Jack called to him. "You rocked that ruckus tonight."

"Think they'll be an Oscar nomination in it for me?" Armand asked with a laugh as he walked up the stairs to his trailer.

"I'm writing your name on the next ballot," said Jack with a smirk.

Armand waved him off and disappeared into his trailer.

"Nice work tonight, Hughes," said Jack, poking Tyler's shoulder with his fist. "You just helped save the world. How's it feel?"

Hughes flashed a shy smile at Jack. "Better than ever," he said. "I hope to do more. A lot more."

"Stellar acting, dude," said Jack. "You still got it."

Jack's comment made Tyler's whole face brighten.

"And Zanth...wow." Jack bowed. "Oscar-worthy. You played that Hell bitch like a pro. Impressed."

Zanth batted her lashes at Jack and Talia fought down her annoyance.

"I enjoyed putting that poser in her place," said Zanth. "Goodnight, Talia and Jack. Tyler and I will see you tomorrow."

"Goodnight, Zanth," said Talia as she tugged Jack toward the trailer door. "Let's go home, lover."

Jack wrapped her tight in his arms, pressing his face against hers. "Gladly, Mrs. Casey. Night, Zanth. Tyler."

Together, with Jack's arms so tight around her, they went inside their trailer. And straight to the bedroom. For wild, married angel of death monkey sex.

BY THE NEXT MORNING, Saturday, the orange sky had begun to fade. Despite her growing restlessness, she fought against her nature and stayed with Jack all night, still holding him close when he awoke before dawn.

"Talia!" he said in a scratchy voice, a shadow of sexy stubble across his strong jaw as he smiled at her. "Good morning, babe."

She kissed his hot lips and brushed a lock of hair out of his eyes, that blond hair messy from sleep. Making him look so sexy. She'd seen images of him with no shirt, this messy hair, and sleepy green eyes on heartthrob posters from his *SanFran Confidential* days. He wore his hair a little shorter than his twenty-year-old sex symbol days. But he was still that lean, sexy blond icon that had captured America's hearts as Detective Davy Pierson.

"Morning, lover," she said, entangling him in her arms and wings as she gave him an urgent kiss, wearing only his AC/DC Back in Black T-shirt.

Fighting back the wave of tears threatening to overflow her eyes.

He didn't know that she was leaving him today. To prepare for the sixth flight that had probably just arrived above Eolowen, preparing to carry their bright blue bowls of pain to the rivers surrounding Los Angeles. Turning the skies into a brilliant, electric cyan that would light up the world like daylight until the sixth Traveler either launched their payload. She winced. Or Jack managed to take the payload coin.

She prayed that she would still exist. That she would see the sky return to its crisp summer blue as the seventh and final flight prepared to pour out the seventh plague bowl from delicate white bowls. Death was the seventh angel flight. Bearing the deadliest human payload.

Deadlier than the first six payloads combined.

His fingers stroked her cheek and she concentrated on his stunning green eyes, strong chin, the upward curves of his hot, sexy mouth, the gentle slope of his nose, and that light blond mop of hair. Memorizing every part of him. Even after a year had passed since she'd first seen him standing there under the hot stage lights, he still took her breath away. He was still the most beautiful man, human, or angel, she'd ever seen.

That sexy smirk lifted the corners of his mouth, pale green eyes twinkling, silvery grey wings flat against his shoulders.

"Since it's Saturday," he began. "Why don't we just...stay in bed, Mrs. Casey? Practice our newlywed couple skills?"

By the Maker, he just melted her into a puddle with his sizzling good looks and that hot caramel voice that burned right through her soul. She ran her hands along the length of his bare chest with its leanly sculpted muscles. To the waistband of his blue boxer briefs.

Somehow, she had to find a way to tell him goodbye.

And join the guard in their final preparations. But just thinking about those words tore her up inside. Stung her eyes with every word she tried to conjure onto her lips.

How could she say goodbye to him? He *was* her life. The reason she wanted to exist.

"Is that a yes?" he said with a chuckle and then a gasp as she pushed down his boxers.

She pressed her mouth against his, kissing him with feverish kisses as she stroked him hard. He rolled the T-shirt over her head, his hands frantic against her body, his mouth pressing against her breasts in fiery kisses as his fingers caressed her skin, sliding between her legs.

His touch was electric, his tongue teasing against her nipples as he shifted on top of her, his body so hot against her skin. She felt the first gentle thrust of his penis inside her, his body rocking against hers, his touch burning as hot as his love. With frantic strokes, he made love to her, the sensations so electric and wild as they shuddered through her body and her wings.

She moved with him, her hands sliding across his naked body, stroking his back and sexy round ass as he began to pump inside her. Harder. Faster. Deeper. Until she was moving in tandem with him, arms and legs wrapped around him as his thrusts sent that white-hot burst of climax shuddering through her entire body. She rocked with him in an urgent rhythm with every wave until he gasped and his body trembled against hers as he found release. Like an intense sprint through a thunderhead.

Until the pounding sensations faded into a warm heat, his body still pressed against hers.

She pulled the sheet across them and closed her eyes, settling against his scorching body as she tried to capture this moment in her head and hold onto the memory of his touch, of his love, like a film in her head.

Her eyes teared up again.

A series of vivid pictures to get her through the battle against Lucifer's Army of Dark. Only after he'd slept and they'd gotten dressed would she shatter her heart into a million pieces and leave him behind to return to Heaven.

And hope against hope that she would survive the sixth flight and return to him.

She held onto him with everything she had, crystals cascading across the sheets as his breaths deepened into a comforting sleep. And she resolved not to let go of him until the absolute last moment.

15

WHEN JACK WOKE UP AFTER HE AND TALIA MADE LOVE, HE KNEW RIGHT away that something was wrong.

Very, very wrong.

She'd been with him all night last night, in his arms before dawn, eager to make love. She'd even snuggled under the covers with him afterward for a long time. Holding onto him in a way that unsettled him. Gave him a hollow feeling in the pit of his stomach.

That he was losing her.

After he'd showered, shaved, and dressed in Levi's and a Henley, he left the achingly quiet bedroom and went to the front of the set trailer, but she wasn't there. It made his stomach drop.

"Talia?" he called.

Not a single sound touched his ears.

No whisper of footsteps on the hardwood. No hiss of water from the shower. No rustle of wings against the cloth couch cushions. Just rigid, unyielding silence that hit him hard in the face. Making his chest ache.

"Talia!" he shouted, his voice echoing through the still trailer.

Like she'd never been here at all with him. Like all of this had been just a dream he'd had. A thin comfort, the memories of having loved a woman so completely hurting deeply as he lay on the floor of his shithole studio apartment, dying of a cocaine overdose. Had it all been a dream?

The possibility terrified him.

He began to sweat, his hands shaking as he rushed back into the bedroom. Searching for a stray wing feather. The jean skirt she wore yesterday that she'd folded and put in a dresser drawer. Anything that told him that she'd been here. And that she planned to come back. To him.

Shaking, he slid open the drawers. Finding the first one on the right—her side—empty. And with each one he opened, his heart splintered into shards.

All of her things were gone!

"TALIA!"

Fear was an arctic chill against his skin as he opened the closet, finding her things gone from there, too.

He ran back up to the front of the trailer. Desperate to find her.

Muriel stood in front of the door, wings folded, head bowed, looking solemn. Distant. Resigned.

"Where's Talia?" he demanded.

He couldn't see through the haze of tears filling his eyes, his chest in knots.

Muriel's expression was stoic as she lifted her head, her gaze shifting past his shoulder, not quite looking him in the eyes. Tearing him apart in a hundred different ways.

He bit his lip to keep it from trembling, but his hands were shaking like he had the DTs, the shards of his heart crunching underneath his Vans with every step he took toward Muriel.

"Muriel! All her things are gone..."

He couldn't breathe. His world imploded around him as the tears leaked out the corners of his eyes. He couldn't hold them back. Couldn't hold them in. Couldn't feel anything but the gaping wound in his chest that shot out his back where his heart used to be.

He sucked in a shaky lungful of air, his breaths coming in gasps.

"Muriel...please."

Tears threaded down Muriel's cheeks as she studied him and the growing puddle of grief and despair he was becoming as the minutes ticked past and the horrible silence grew. The palpable absence he'd dreaded since the moment he knew Talia was an angel.

"Jack," said Muriel, a heavy sigh slipping free. "She couldn't take saying goodbye to you. She said it hurt too much and she asked me to tell you."

"Why?" He raged. "I'm her husband! She's the love of my life. My first and last thought. And she couldn't even say goodbye to me?"

He turned away, covering his face, sucking in air as he tried to hold back the tide of grief and anger tearing its way through his body.

Muriel's hand squeezed his shoulder.

"Jack," she said in a pained voice. "Kesien and I had to carry her out of here and fly her back up to Heaven because she was so distraught. She asked me to remove her things. Afraid seeing them would be too painful for you."

His knees buckled and he grabbed hold of the wall to keep from pitching into the floor.

"It's like…like she was never here at all."

His voice choked out at the end of his sentence and he barely got the words out.

"She sobbed all the way back and not even Berith can heal her enough to get a coherent sentence out of her. She just cries and says your name."

No! He balled his hands into fists and forced himself to stand up straight, wings spreading wide.

"I'm going to her!" he shouted, blinking past Muriel.

She grabbed his arms and spun him around.

"Jack, you can't," she cried. "If you fly to her, she'll never let go of you and Lucifer's army will blast her out of the sky."

"Then I'm flying into the battle to find her!" His voice was hoarse. Broken. "I'm going to be there, Muriel! To protect her! She's my wife!"

He tried to shove past her, but she pushed him backward, away from the door again, her face screwing up with pain.

"You can't stop me, Muriel!"

He lunged again and she forced him backward each time.

"Jack, please—" Her voice was all anguish now, the tears still hot on her cheeks. "Only you can stop the Hell princes, Jack, or your world goes up in flames. And Lucifer gets stronger."

He sank to his knees, the fight knocked out of him. He bowed his head, arms folded against his chest.

"Why?" he raged through gritted teeth. "Why me? When my wife's about to face the worst battle of her life! WHY!"

Muriel dropped down beside him and put her arms around him.

"Because, Jack—only you have the seraphim power to find them quickly. Before they unleash those payloads."

"I could still fight beside her," he said, his voice weakening. "And come back when the Travelers arrive. I could—"

Her hand was against his hair now, stroking.

"Not even omnificence can put you in two places at once from that distance. And you don't have the stamina to fight an air war like this, Jack. She'd be focused on protecting you and it would get her erased. Probably both of you erased. Understand?"

No matter how hard he raged and beat his head against this wall, it refused to budge. He couldn't be in two places at once. He couldn't fight at Talia's side or risk getting her erased.

And he couldn't even say goodbye to the love of his life.

He wanted to curl into a ball and scream until his voice disappeared and then beat his fists against the walls until they shattered.

He couldn't do this. He couldn't just let her disappear in this battle. Out of his life. His heart.

"I can't do this, Muriel," he said in an aching voice. "I can't just let go like this. If she doesn't come back…"

He dropped to the floor, the sobs bubbling up. He couldn't hold them back. Couldn't hold it all inside. This was destroying him and he couldn't even fight back. Couldn't even tell her how much he loved her. How many deaths he would die until she was back in his arms.

And if she didn't come back…

Muriel's arms wrapped around him and she held him until he

couldn't utter a sound, his body collapsing under the massive weight of grief against his soul.

"Jack, the whole squad will be at her side, protecting her because you can't. This battle has always been called the Enochian apocalypse for a reason." She pulled in a shuddery breath. "Because so many angels are expected to fall from the skies when faced with the totality of Lucifer's army."

"Then let me help you fight them," he cried through gritted teeth, his voice thin and desperate despite his best effort to sound strong. "Please, Muriel! With my seraphim powers."

She rubbed his shoulders, shaking her head as she pulled in another breath.

"You can't help us this time, Jack." She sighed. "I don't know if I'll survive this battle. Or Kesien. Or Anahera. Or Azrael and Berith. But if I live through it, I give you my word that I will protect her with my last spark of angelic light, Jack. So will Anahera, Kesien, and Deemah. Besides, you've got to be there to stop Lucifer, Jack."

"Me?"

"Yes, you, Jack," she said, still rubbing his shoulders. "Remember? Seraphina isn't well enough to tangle with Lucifer. We need your seraphim powers. To help us find the Omega Rod before he does. To help us defend the Thrones and the Maker from him. That's what you can do for all of us, Jack. Defend Heaven. If Lucifer succeeds, everything disappears. Don't forget that. Everything."

He sucked in another breath. "By why is the cost so high, Muriel?" he said. "Why do I have to lose everything to help save it all?"

She hugged him. "Nothing is certain, Jack. All we can do is fight this with everything we've got."

She was right. It was all he could do. And he hated it.

"Do we know where the Omega Rod is yet?" he asked, unable to keep the exhaustion and pain out of his voice.

He already felt spent. Wrung out. Lost without Talia.

"Pravuil is still trying to locate it," said Muriel. "He thinks that—"

The horrible sound of *Sympathy for the Devil* rang out from Jack's jeans pocket.

Wincing, he stared at Muriel who looked frightened.

"What does that bastard want?" Muriel replied.

Jack's hand shook as he slid his phone out of his pocket. Like things couldn't get any worse. And now he had to talk to Lucifer when he'd never felt more wrecked in his life.

He answered the call. But there was no more game face. No more jokes. No more smartass left in him. He could barely summon the energy to answer it.

"Jack?" Lucifer's precise British accent was sharp and loud as he put the phone on speaker. "Jack? Are you there?"

"Luci," he said in a faded voice.

"Why, Jack—what's the matter? Are you ill?"

Every word cut through him and he couldn't muster the energy to counter this maniac. It was all spiraling out of control and Jack couldn't stop him anymore. Lucifer was the second most powerful being in the galaxy. And he was an arrogant ass to think he could stop someone like that. Him. Like he was somebody. Like anything he did mattered.

"What do you want?"

A pause. "Why, Jack, I'm quite concerned. You don't sound like yourself. Not at all. Has the apocalypse gotten you down? You and Talia have a fight?"

He bristled.

"What do you want, Luci?"

"I want you, Jack," he said and Jack could hear the smile in his voice. "I want you to witness my success because it's so close. I want you to see your world erupt in flames and Heaven burn. When I ascend to the Thrones, I promise to put out all those fires. When I erase you and your world from existence. It was always flawed and it never should have existed. So take heart, Jack, all the pain will end soon. I promise."

Jack sighed.

"You done? All finished with your lofty speeches and your delusions of grandeur? Because I'm so damned sick of your arrogant bullshit. You wanna destroy the Earth and me? Fine. Do it. At least I won't have to listen to you anymore."

"Jack? Giving up? That's not any fun at all. You may be many things, Jack, but you've always been entertaining. An enjoyable challenge. If you continue to entertain me, I might even spare you. Show you what a truly grand universe could look like—in the right hands."

He glared at the phone. "Your hands?"

Lucifer laughed. "Well, of course, my hands. For millennia I warned my father of the danger His new children posed. That they were pale substitutes for the glorious celestial beings he'd created in those first seven angel days. But as always, He refused my counsel."

"That's shocking," Jack snapped. "Considering that He made you for companionship, not to give him pointers on well—making."

"He created us as warriors. As equals. Then when your kind was created, He treated His angels like they were broken, that His first go at creation had been so flawed. That we had been so damaged that he had to remake us anew. More childlike. Independent of the celestial kingdom so that He could train them properly. Let them discover their power and rejoin Him in the Heavens. To rule over it all. Us."

Jack shifted the phone away from his mouth. "Now, see, Luci, that's where you always get things wrong."

"Me? Wrong?"

"Yeah, wrong. He never tossed away His angels. He meant them to walk beside His youngest. Humans, Luci. I know you think we're gnats, but angels and humans together…damn. We coulda been so good together. Made Him proud. If you'd let go of your pain for a few minutes and talked to your dad face-to-face, maybe He'd see the hurt He caused. And make it right. But you never gave Him the chance. Did you? Too busy trying to prove you're right to tell Him that you just wanted Him to love you."

The line went deathly quiet.

"What's the matter, Luci? Afraid I'm right?"

"Would love to finish this conversation, Jack," Lucifer said finally, sounding a little distracted now. "But I've got preparations to make before sunset. Enochian apocalypse and all that. I'm sure you understand. We'll talk again soon once I've taken the Thrones. Must dash."

The call cleared.

Damn. That had been his last chance to get through to Lucifer. And he'd failed at that, too.

Muriel helped him up from the floor. He slid his phone back into his front jeans pocket and stared at her a moment.

Was it all ending?

He'd loved his time with wings, flying alongside Talia and her squad. Fighting beside the guard. In Talia's squad. Loving Talia with all his heart and soul. Would they do their little memory trick on him soon? Reeducate him? Erase his memories of Talia. Of Muriel and Azrael. Even Berith. Remove his wings and halo. Send him back to the final lines of his formerly fading life. Alone. Forgotten. Facing an overdose.

No matter what happened from here, he couldn't deny that it had been a grand ride. He'd come back from an impending overdose and remade himself on the unlikeliest of shows. Found the love of his life. Saw things beyond his wildest dreams.

He flinched, rubbing his face. It *had* been a grand ride. But he didn't want it to be over.

"Jack," said Muriel. "I've got to go now. But on behalf of the guard, we wanted you to know that we all love you. And hope to see you on the other side."

"When I cross over?" he said, his heart skipping a beat as a spike of cold lanced his spine.

She shook her head. "No, the seventh flight. To stop Lucifer from reaching the Thrones in the upper Heavens."

He felt the chill against his skin dissipating, relief washing over him.

"I don't know what I'm saying here, Muriel," he said, holding out his hands. "But I've loved my time with the guard. And I can't live without Talia. I just hope I'm still here, too, when the seventh flight takes to the skies. To make sure this whole thing isn't over yet. To fight for my happily ever after with Talia."

"I hope I'm there to see that, Jack," she said and rushed toward him, throwing her arms around him in the tightest hug she'd ever given him. "Godspeed, Jack," she whispered and turned away.

"Tell Azrael and the guard that I'm honored they let me fight beside them. And I expect to be invited to the victory party. No matter what, I'm Talia's plus one. Now until forever. And we will be together for that party."

Muriel grinned as she wiped away tears.

"You got it. Be safe, Jack."

"Come back safe, Muriel," he said. "Love you, dudes. Always."

She smashed her eyes closed as more tears fell and blinked through the front door.

That was it then. He was alone now.

For the first time in a year not a single angel hovered around him. And his heart hurt, wishing he could be beside the love of his life and her squad. Beside Azrael and Berith. They were family to him. And he was alone down here while they were getting chewed up in a huge battle that he couldn't help them fight.

Somehow, he had to take down this sixth Traveler and then blink himself up there. Into that battle. Protect the people he loved.

He slid out his phone again. Checked the time. Almost five o'clock. It was less than three hours to sunset. He had a lot of texts to send. Starting with his best friend.

He texted Gianni.

> dude need ur help
>
> Talia's fighting Lucifer's army
>
> u n me last 2 😈 🔥
>
> g2g save her 💔

He sent the text, his eyes stinging. He'd never felt so helpless. Next, he texted Banks.

> dude need ur help

seen the sky? bad shit jn 💨 😾 🙌

my trailer fast

His phone beeped. Gianni.

Jack, omg omw

It killed him to do it, but he found one of Jennifer Collins' emails with the cast's contact information. And looked up Rachel Daniels' number. And texted her.

it's Jack, 🔥apocalypse going down 🙌😾

need ur help to 🪨 it

my trailer now

His phone beeped. Banks.

Holy shit, Jack On my way!

His phone beeped again. Rachel. His stomach tightened.

Jack of course brt

"Zanth!" he shouted as loud as he could. "I know you're still on set. Apocalypse party. My place. Now."

A frantic knock sent him to the door. When he opened it, Gianni practically fell inside, Deemah's Eternean sword on his hip in its sheath. He took Jack by the shoulders.

"Jack..." Pain burned in his kind brown eyes, his calm, easygoing Cary Grant demeanor falling away. "I'm—so sorry. When did Talia leave?"

He tried to reply, but his voice cracked, his face screwing up with pain and heartache that he couldn't even put into words.

"Take it easy," said Gianni in a comforting voice, rubbing his shoulder.

"Gianni," he said finally, talking slowly so his voice wouldn't break again and betray him. "I've gotta—" He pulled in a breath. Held it a moment. "Get to that battle." He shook his head, eyes getting glassy again. "If I don't…I could lose her."

Gianni winced and gripped Jack's arms.

"Dude, she's the love of my life," he said with a hiss of breath. "I've got to be there. The seraphim are all gone—except Seraphina and she's…not a hundred percent." He bowed his head. "My seraphim powers are all that's left after Lucifer blew up High House."

"Oh, God, Jack," Gianni cried. "Heaven's outnumbered?"

Jack gave him an anxious nod. "They need my seraphim powers, dude. But I'm the only one that can locate the Hell princes."

Zanth and Tyler Hughes stepped through the door like apparitions into the trailer, startling the hell out of him.

Gianni shuffled back, pulling the sword out of its sheath. And then he realized who they were. He let out a relieved sigh and returned the sword to its sheath, leaning against the wall.

"Dudes, knock first next time," he said, a hand against his chest.

"Sorry, Jack," said Hughes. "Thought you were expecting us."

He pulled in a heavy breath. "I was. Just not so in my face."

"Forgive me, Jack," said Zanth but her red eyes softened and she moved toward him. "You are distraught, mon ami," she said in a concerned voice. "What has happened?"

Guess demons read emotions like angels did.

He glanced down at his hands, struggling to talk about Talia. It choked him up every time.

"Talia's uh…" He couldn't say it. Couldn't feel that sharp stabbing pain in his heart again. He pointed at the ceiling. "Sixth flight."

Zanth's eyes got big. And then sad.

"She had to leave you behind to fight Lucifer's army," Zanth said in a quiet voice. "They call the sixth flight the Enochian apocalypse because so many angels will give their lives to stop the Army of Dark."

He nodded, smashing his eyes closed. He pulled in a shuddery breath and bit his lip, trying to hold back the moisture filling his eyes with pain. Trying to hold it together.

"I've called Mark Banks and Rachel over to help us take down the last two Hell princes," said Jack, changing the subject. "They should be here any minute. I'll have to call the Watchers back, too. To cover for —Talia. A-and me. For the rest of the cast, too, if they agree to help me." He winced. "But I've got to get up there. Lucifer killed all but one seraph. Talia and her guard have their hands full. They could use my seraphim powers."

Gianni slid his arm around Jack's shoulders and pulled him into a hug.

"Hang in there, Jack. Talia's tough. She'll survive this battle. I'll bet it killed her to tell you goodbye."

He winced, pulling away. He turned toward the wall, eyes smashed closed, the pain of her sudden departure still so raw. Of opening drawers and finding her things…just…gone. Of her just disappearing from his life. God, it hurt! It knocked him to the floor and he was still trying to pull himself up from the blow.

"She uh…didn't," he said with a heavy sigh. "She just disappeared."

"What?" Armand cried, eyes wide as he rushed over to him, a hand on his back. "She just disappeared?"

He nodded, face screwing up into an anguished look as he held in a moan.

"Oh, Jack," said Gianni, rubbing his shoulder. "I'm so sorry. I'm sure she didn't mean to hurt you. It was probably the hardest thing she's ever done."

He nodded, bowing his head. "She sent Muriel to say it for her."

"Then that confirms it," said Gianni, his voice barely above a whisper.

All Jack could do was nod. He understood how painful that had been for Talia, but why couldn't she see how awful he'd feel when every last item of hers had been expunged from his life? Like she'd never existed. Like she was somehow trying to prepare him for her permanent absence.

Didn't she understand that he couldn't lose her? That he'd fight to his last breath to make sure that she survived.

"So, I need a plan," he continued in a shaky voice. "A way to stop this sixth Traveler. Fast. So I can fight alongside her. To keep her and her guard safe with my seraphim powers. They need them right now—more than ever."

"Jack, you want us to fight the Travelers?" Gianni said in a wary voice. "Without you there?"

He turned around, swiping at the tears leaking out of his eyes. "She needs me, Gianni."

Gianni cringed. "Unfortunately, so do we, Jack. We have Zanth and Tyler, but it isn't enough for these Hell princes. We already know that."

Zanth moved beside him and laid her hand on his arm.

"Jack," she said. "I am an archdemoness with a lot of power, but without your ability to track the Travelers, and your other seraphim powers, we would never find them in time."

"I know," Jack said with a groan. "That's why I'm still here instead of taking off for Heaven. But maybe I can call up the trail and then head up to Heaven to save Talia?"

Gianni looked terrified now. "What if we fail to stop them, Jack? What happens?"

He bowed his head, his face screwing up. "Millions of people will die." He sighed. "And it would be all my fault." Finally, he lifted his head, the tears leaking out the corners of his eyes again. "But Gianni... she's the love of my life." He shook his head, holding out his hands. "I can't live without her."

Gianni pulled him into a hug.

"God, Jack—putting you in this kind of position isn't right." He looked over at Zanth. "Zanth, think we could take down two Hell princes without Jack?"

She shook her head. "Non. If they decided to fight us, we would be powerless. They would destroy your world. And Lucifer would grow stronger."

Jack's heart twisted into a knot. He was being forced to choose between his only reason for living and the fate of millions. So unfair.

A curious smile curved across Zanth's face. "But, if we do this right, perhaps Jack Casey can be here for the important parts?"

"What do you mean, Zanth?" Jack asked as Gianni let him go.

Jack wiped his eyes with the sleeve of his blue Henley and stared at Zanth, hoping for some way that he could be in two places at once.

"You get us to the sixth Traveler with your seraphim power. We all try to snatch the payload coin. If we fail, you stay and help us fight it. And then go to Talia. After the sixth flight battle, you return with Talia and the other angels to battle the final Hell prince. Death. The most difficult fight of the apocalypse."

Gianni smiled. "It's all in the timing, right, Jack? We take down the sixth Traveler in record time and then you go help Talia."

It was all he had right now. He had no choice. Maybe if they could con the payload coin out of the sixth Traveler's hands, then he could blink out of there fast. Use his seraphim blink to enter that battle. And protect Talia and the guard. Azrael and Berith.

"We hit this sixth Traveler hard and fast as we can," he said. "Then I blink out."

Zanth nodded. "Oui, Jack Casey. If your other friends help, then maybe we can...*comment tu dis*...how you say—pull this off?"

Someone knocked on the door.

Jack rushed over and opened it.

Mark Banks stood there, dressed in jeans, desert boots, and a faded black Radiohead T-shirt. His sandy brown hair was windblown into messy spikes, worry shadowing his face.

"Banks! Dude, thanks for coming."

Banks looked equal parts concerned and confused as he entered the trailer.

"Looks like a cast party," he said as he nodded toward Zanth and Hughes. "Zoe and Hughes." He glanced toward the kitchen and saw Gianni leaning against the cabinets. "Hey, Gianni," he said with a nod to the taller soap star. "Where's Izzy?"

He pointed over his shoulder. "Next door."

Then he glanced around the space and finally turned back to Jack. "Where's Talia?"

"That's part of the reason I called you over."

His eyes got wide. "Has something happened to her? Is she okay?"

Jack swallowed the huge lump in his throat as his eyes began to sting, but Gianni stepped in and steered Banks over to the couch.

"As soon Rachel Daniels gets here, we'll talk about everything." He lowered his voice and whispered something that Jack couldn't hear.

Banks frowned, leaning against the wall instead of sitting down. He nodded at Gianni and drummed his fingers against the taupe paint as he glanced around the trailer.

"Wow, Jack—" Banks said with a shrill whistle. "You weren't kidding when you said your trailer was upscale."

Jack shrugged. He had no interest in furnishings, especially right now, but Banks didn't know about the apocalypse. But he would.

"Well, I can tell you that Morgan and I appreciated the upgrade. Thanks for speaking up."

"Of course," he said. "It's not my show and I'm not the only star."

Banks gave him a warm nod.

The knock at the door startled him and he rushed toward it.

Rachel Daniels stood there dressed in a faded grey SanFran Confidential T-shirt, black yoga pants, and black sneakers. He couldn't remember the last time he'd seen her without heels and a dress.

"Jack," she cried and hurried inside. "Are you all right? Your text sounded a little frantic. Are you sure about the apocalypse?"

He nodded. "Already took down five Travelers, so yeah."

"Five Hell princes?" Her too-blue eyes got wide as she stared at him. "Wow, Jack—impressive."

Chuckling, Banks stepped away from the wall.

"The apocalypse? Rachel, I hope you brought enough weed to share with the rest of us."

"Dude," Jack said with a sigh. "Bad news. All those sus colors the sky has turned over the past couple of weeks or so…those colors correspond to the plague being set loose on the planet to usher in the apocalypse. By the highest order demons in Hell. Hell princes."

"Are you guys punking me?" Banks asked with a snicker. "Apocalypse. That's too funny, Casey."

Jack sighed. He hated to show proof in such an abrupt way, but Banks needed to know that this shit was all too real.

"Zanth," he said, still staring at Banks. "Can you show Banks here some proof that we're in the fight of our lives and that the apocalypse is real?"

"Zanth?" Banks said with a frown. "Isn't your name Zoe?"

She shook her head slowly at Banks.

"My pleasure, Jack Casey," she said and sauntered over to Banks, looking seductive, a curious smile on her face.

Like she was enjoying this task.

She walked around Banks, sizing him up, and Banks just looked at her and then back to Jack.

"Jack, what are you trying to prove here?"

Zanth stopped in front of Banks, hands on her hips. In a moment, her sultry dark eyes burned bright red, glowing with that terrifying, leering demon grin.

"Holy shit!" Banks shouted, skittering backward from Zanth until he slammed into the wall beside the sofa. "What the hell's going on?"

"Precisely, Mark Banks," she said, tossing her head back, and laughing. "I am archdemoness Zanth, Lucifer's former first lieutenant."

Banks' nervous laughter filled the room as he pressed his back against the far wall.

"Lucifer, huh? This story gets wilder and wilder. You guys are gonna put this on TikTok, aren't you?"

"Non, Mark Banks," said Zanth as she looked him up and down. "I am a real demon and we are really dealing with the apocalypse here."

Rachel yawned and sat down on the couch.

"Banks, she's real," she said in a tired voice. "And the sooner you accept it, the sooner Jack can explain why he called all of us here."

Hughes shoved his hands in his jeans pockets and turned toward Banks who was already freaked out. When their gazes met, Hughes let his eyes glow red.

Banks flipped out. He shuffled backward into the kitchen, slamming into the kitchen cabinets beside Gianni who had reclaimed his calm Cary Grant demeanor.

"What the hell's happening here?" Banks sputtered, backing away toward the sink.

"Dude, relax," said Jack. "Zanth and Hughes may be demons, but they're on our side."

"And just what is our side, Casey?" Banks' face looked bone-white.

Groaning, Jack shuffled toward the kitchen, Banks already backing away from him.

"We're trying to stop Lucifer from destroying our world and Heaven. He's set the apocalypse in motion. Every time the sky turns a strange color, a Hell prince sets out to drop a plague payload on the Earth. We have a day and a night to stop it from activating and killing millions."

Banks held his arms in front of his face, pulling away from Jack as he huddled against the sink.

"Dude, relax," said Jack again and let his wings unfurl to their full height and his halo burn in the late afternoon shadows.

Banks' eyes got so large Jack thought that they might bounce right out of his head.

"Oh, my God!" he cried, lowering his arms. "Jack! You're an angel? Are you—you dead?"

Jack sighed and let his wings flatten against his shoulders. He reached up to his halo and hid its white-gold light.

"No, dude," he snapped. "I'm just an actor that got mixed up with the most beautiful angel I've ever seen."

"Talia?" Banks asked.

He nodded, his eyes beginning to sting. "Long story, but she was forced into a wager with Lucifer and forced to appear on The Cinderella Hour. Sent to Earth to save two souls without her wings or halo. One of those souls was me."

Banks looked shocked. "You? That night you overdosed!"

Jack nodded. Not quite but close enough. "I was supposed to die of an overdose during the filming of the show, but somehow, she saved me."

Banks frowned. "But the wings?"

"Another long story," he said with a groan. "During the final days of filming The Ever After Hour, Heaven tried to hide me from Lucifer after I led him into a trap. He killed me for it, but Talia brought me back before my last breath expired. Then Heaven gave me wings and a halo to hide me from Lucifer, but later, they couldn't remove the wings and halo without harm. So, I'm kinda stuck with them."

"Wings?" Banks said in a quiet voice. "Can you…y'know—fly?"

Jack grinned. "Like Superman, dude. Best feeling ever."

"Seriously?" Banks cried, reaching out to touch the wings at his shoulders. "That's the coolest thing ever, Jack."

Rachel sighed. "Okay, now that you've got the whole angel and demon thing figured out, Banks," she said, annoyed. "Maybe we can get to the apocalypse and help Jack stop it?"

Banks stepped around Jack, glaring at Rachel.

"Why are you and Gianni so damned calm about this apocalypse shit anyway?"

"Because demons kidnapped Izzy on our honeymoon, Mark," said Gianni, his tone matter-of-fact. "I went to Jack for help, only to walk into the most massive demon battle I'd ever seen. But Jack and Talia got Izzy back home. With the help of other angels that showed themselves to me, too."

Banks looked like he'd already heard enough, his expression looking pained.

"So, you've known about this for a while," said Banks.

"Since The Heavenly Honeymoon Hour," said Gianni.

Banks nodded like he'd just read the show's latest script. Then he turned to Rachel.

"And how long have you known?"

Rachel stood up from the couch and stopped in front of Banks, arms folded against her grey T-shirt.

"Since I lured twenty-year-old Jack Casey to Lucifer's beach house to get him hooked on coke and overdose. So I could sell his soul to Lucifer. Like I'd already sold mine."

It took several moments for that painful story to sink in as Banks glanced from Rachel to Jack.

He hated the thoughts of those times, of the blackouts, and the missing memories. Of the flashes of horns and red eyes that haunted his dreams. Of waking up naked in the Breckenridge Suite with no memory of what had happened to him.

Banks looked ill. "You sold your soul, Rachel?" he said finally. "To Lucifer? And then tried to sell Jack's, too?"

She shook her head, staring down at her black sneakers.

"Afraid so. The price of fame. And I'm not proud of it. But Jack forgave me, setting me free from Lucifer's contract."

Banks whirled around and grabbed Jack's arm. "Why, Jack?" he said with a hiss. "Why would you do that for her after all the horrible things she did to you?"

"I just wanted it all to stop and go away," Jack said with a groan. "I just wanted her to stop stabbing me."

His eyes got wide again. "Stabbing you?"

Rachel walked over and rubbed Jack's shoulder. "Jack here sacrificed himself to save Talia from being dragged off to Hell. When she lost Lucifer's wager. He was forced to face me in a cage fight in Hell. Where he forgave me. Releasing me from Lucifer's contract."

Bank's face turned white. "Hell? It's real? And you were there?"

He nodded. "I couldn't let Lucifer take Talia, Banks. I couldn't."

It took a moment or two for this overwhelming information to settle against Banks' reality, but after a few minutes, he seemed calm and resigned to the fact that angels and demons existed. And that they were in the middle of fighting the apocalypse.

"All right," said Banks, holding up his hands. "I get it. I'm in. I'll help you fight these Hell princes, but damn, I'm an actor, not a fighter. Wrestled in high school. Spent some time in martial arts training in college. And for a movie I did."

Gianni clapped him on the shoulder. "Fortunately, we're not planning to fight these bastards, Banks. We're planning to play them."

Banks raised an eyebrow. "Play them?"

Jack nodded. "We've been able to con the payload coins off every single Hell prince and princess so far. And we're planning to continue that tact until we're forced to fight them."

"So, when does this next fight go down?" Banks asked, glancing from Jack to Gianni.

Jack pulled his phone out of his pocket again and checked the time. A little after seven.

"We're less than an hour from sunset," he said. "When that sun goes down, the sky's gonna turn a bright, electric cyan, making night look like day. And it'll stay that way until we either take the payload coin or the Hell prince delivers the payload to its destination. If we're successful, a night and day from now, the sky will return to its standard blue."

"So, right now, we just wait?" Banks asked.

Jack nodded.

Banks moved past him and opened Jack's fridge. He reached in and pulled out bottles of beer until he'd set out six cold beers.

"Then let's toast," he said. "I know I could use a beer about now. Or twelve."

Jack grabbed one of the hefeweizens and twisted off the cap. Gianni slid two beers across the counter to Zanth and Hughes. Jack slid one toward Rachel. He waited until everyone had removed their beer caps and then held his beer in the air.

"To friends good enough to fight beside you during the apocalypse," said Jack.

"I'll drink to that," said Banks.

They all clinked bottles and drank. Jack took a long swig from the icy cold beer, savoring its calming grainy flavor. It didn't have that bitter hoppy taste and he was glad. He hated bitter beer. But the beer helped blunt the razor edges of his grief and for that, he was grateful. He took another swig.

By the time they had all finished their beers, the sky began to change.

Brightening as the sun set, giving the night an eerie nuclear glow that made it look like a bright summer afternoon. Not night.

Gianni patted Jack on the back. "You okay?" he asked in a quiet voice. "I know you're worried sick about Talia, but I'll see this through the whole way, Jack. We all will. And if you need me in this fight to save Talia, I'll be there."

Jack bit his lip to keep the moisture from filling his eyes. He hugged his best friend.

"Means a lot, dude," he said. "Thank you."

He took a deep breath and held it. Summoning his game face. At last, he turned to face the room.

"All right, dudes, let's do this. Party's about to start." He turned to Zanth. "Zanth, tell me again about the next Hell prince."

"The sixth flight has poured out its plague on your world," said Zanth as she set her empty beer bottle on the counter. "That means that the sixth Traveler is making her way to your world."

"Her?" Banks replied.

"Oui, Mark Banks," she said. "This plague is silence."

"Oh, my God!" Rachel cried, holding out her phone to them. "Look at this video!"

Jack squinted. It was small and hard to see.

"What are we looking at, Rach?"

"The Los Angeles River," she said, pointing at the concrete canals that diverted the rivers through and around the city.

But she didn't have to say another word. Jack saw it like a neon sign burning in the dead of night. There were no more rivers. Those canals had gone bone dry in an instant.

All the water had dried up. It was gone!

"The water's all gone!" he cried. "Look...the concrete isn't even damp."

"Jack...where'd the water go?" Rachel asked in a small, tight voice as she stared at him, fear burning in her too-blue eyes.

"The sixth plague has dried up all your rivers," said Zanth. "And there is nothing but silence around you. No ethereal beings to hear you. Or help you." She pointed at the ceiling. "They are being drawn together over your world into a battle that makes the Rebellion look like a cage fight."

Jack's stomach dropped, his heart smashing against his ribs. And Talia would be there. Fighting for her life. Fighting to save Heaven. And his world.

"Let's turn up the volume on this party then," Jack cried and rushed to the trailer door.

He threw it open and pounded down the stairs in his blue Vans. His blue Henley looked so dark against the funky blue sky, only his Levi's lighter.

Gianni rushed out behind him, followed by Zanth, then Hughes, Rachel, and finally Banks.

They stood beneath the eerie cyan sky as Jack glanced around the studio lot, but not a single soul walked the roads and sidewalks of Four Acres Studios. It had gone painfully silent.

"Zanth," he said in a quiet voice. "What sin are we dealing with here?"

"Sin?" Banks replied. "Shouldn't that be plural? This *is* Hollywood."

"Every Traveler presides over a sin," said Jack as he stared up at the sky. "And we use that sin against them to trick, bet, or steal the payload coin."

A faint smile touched Banks' face. "Sounds like fun."

"Zanth?" Jack said as he turned his attention back to her. "It's another Hell princess?"

"Oui, Ronova. Her sin is Lust."

Smiling, Banks rubbed his hands together. "And you call this work?"

Jack tried not to laugh, but Banks had a way of lightening heavy situations, making them seem not so dire. Like now. Jack chuckled. Right now, he welcomed anything that took his mind off Talia fighting a war without him.

"Let's just hope it doesn't get Biblical, dude," said Jack.

Gianni gave him a deep nod. "Exactly. Let's keep the begetting to a minimum. See if we can use this sin against her."

"It'll be easy if she's hot," said Banks, making everyone laugh, including Zanth.

"She is quite beautiful," said the archdemoness. "But remember, lust is not just passion."

"Yeah, it's sex." Banks replied.

Jack snorted, Tyler and Gianni laughing with him.

"Careful, Mark Banks," she said. "You are a married man."

"With a wife insecure enough to brain you from here to Hell," said Rachel.

Banks shrugged. "Yeah, but if I did it to stop the apocalypse, I'm not going to Hell, am I?"

Jack and Gianni looked at each other, smiling.

"You'd better hope you do," said Jack. "It's the only place you could hide from Morgan."

Everyone laughed.

"Lust is a very powerful desire that may not be just sex," said Zanth. "Remember that when you are in Ronova's presence."

As Banks made more jokes about banging a demon for the apocalypse, Jack turned his focus toward the intense cyan color of the sky and summoned his seraphim powers. Until the smoky trail of bright cyan weaved its way through the sky. Sharply south. Back toward L.A.

He frowned, chewing his bottom lip. From the angle, that trail led either toward Beverly Hills. Or Hollywood. Location would determine whether this went well. Or badly.

Very badly.

"Okay, we're gonna have to do this the hard way," Jack said with a groan and glanced at Zanth.

She stared at him. "The hard way?"

"Can't fly," he said with a shrug. "Well, half of us can fly. And you're the only one that can fly and carry a human for any sort of distance."

Banks slid his car keys out of his jeans pocket and held them up.

"I've got you covered, Jack. I'll drive. You navigate."

He turned back to the archdemoness. "Zanth, you and Hughes will have to follow us from the air."

She nodded. "You have Lucifer's mark on you still, Jack Casey," she said. "I will have no trouble finding you."

The handprint on his arm. The one Larry had marked him with after his wedding. It had stopped burning at least, but it was still a beacon to every demon on the planet.

"All right, Banks, you're driving," said Jack. "See you wherever we land, Zanth."

"Be swift," she said as she and Hughes stretched their leathery bat wings and took to the air.

Banks dashed past Gianni's trailer with Gianni right behind him.

"C'mon, Rachel," said Jack, tugging her into a run behind him as they followed Banks around the corner of Studio 22. To the parking lot.

16

THE SKY OVER EARTH BURNED, ANGELS SHOOTING PAST. DEMONS IN pursuit.

Explosions rocked the blackened sky. Smoke rising. Clouds aflame.

The acrid smell of Holy Fire mixed with the stench of hot sulfur. Flashes of red and white exploded as demons and angels fell out of the sky around Talia. She and her squad led the guard through the smoke and fiery debris hanging above the world.

Fallen angels ripped past with shiny black wings resurrected by Lucifer. Hazy, winged demon assassins were shadows against smoke, wings brushing past. Claws raking as they leaped onto the backs of angels that plummeted out of the sky to the ground far, far below. Into stillness.

None of the angels that hit the Earth got up again. Falling from that distance—without divine control—was an angelic death sentence.

Talia thrust her gold shield upward, catching a shadow assassin with a faceful of Holy light.

Knocking it out of the sky.

She turned and sang out orders.

"Squad. Echelon formation. Form around the archangel and await his command."

Clear gold glint of Eternean armor glistened in the thinning rays of sunlight still piercing the smoky haze, choking the skies, and turning the eerie glowing cyan into a thick, inky blackness.

Muriel and Kesien were so close that their wings brushed against each other. Anahera behind her. Deemah in front. Shield-bashing the hordes of wild red demons that flew at them like missiles. Tearing at the tips of their wings. Turning them red and ragged.

"Guard, shift!" Azrael ordered, red-gold swords of Holy Fire in each hand. "Tight wedge formation in squads. Defend Heaven at all costs!"

Squads staggered their positions across the sky, fanning out in front of Azrael and Seraphina in a rush of white and grey wings. Protecting the seraph.

Even Pravuil fought beside them. White sword of Holy Fire gripped in his fist, fury burning in those gold eyes.

The archangel was quickly joined by Archangel Sidriel and Archangel Turiel. And finally, Archangel Sariel appeared, flooding the wedge formation—and the skies—with more death angel squads that overtook the demons. Tangles of long white archangel hair glimmered against the red flash of demons that swarmed around them like starlings.

No matter how many angels joined the fight, the demons outnumbered them at least four to one. The flow of their numbers seemed endless.

Sariel drew a burning white sword of Holy Flame, Turiel swinging one in a wide arc that cut through bursts of demons that launched themselves toward the huge force of angels.

Sidriel somersaulted over top of her leading squads and body-slammed a mass of demons. Turning them to ash.

But more came behind them. Trying to cut through the defensive lines. Slip past them.

Talia winced. To try and reach the portal into the upper Heavens. Her stomach dropped. And the Maker.

Seraphina hovered behind and above them at a safe distance, casting bursts of seraphim light at the endless swarm of demons as a force of fallen angels soared behind them with shiny black wings.

But her bursts were slow. Sluggish. Almost delayed.

Talia knew it was taking every last bit of strength the seraph possessed to defend Heaven. She knew that the seraph would give her last spark of Holy light to hold the Army of Dark back.

"Guard!" Azrael shouted as Berith appeared behind him. "The Scribe is the vanguard. Protect him and Seraphina at all costs."

Berith swung her Eternean sword and blocked two demons with her gold shield of light, shield-bashing them out of the sky.

An angel beside Talia shuddered as his wings caught fire.

Talia tried to smother the flames, but both wings ignited.

The angel screamed as his wings collapsed and he plummeted out of the sky.

Her heart slammed against her chest. Knowing she couldn't help him. Couldn't stop his fall. Or the demonic fire from turning his wings to cinders.

She closed ranks with Muriel and Kesien, Anahera and Deemah shifting closer to the Scribe as another wing of demons rose out of the haze and launched toward them like missiles.

Lifting her shield, Talia bashed two demons careening toward her and her squad.

Light crackled. Demons sizzled. Dropping out of the darkening sky around her.

She whirled around, blocking two more as she summoned a handful of oblivion spheres. Tossing them into the tangle of demons.

Blowing them into a fine red mist of demon goo.

All she could think about as she bashed demons with her shield and flung oblivion spheres at them—murder marbles—was Jack. And how badly she'd hurt him by just disappearing from his life.

She couldn't tell him goodbye.

She couldn't say those words to the man she loved more than her own existence. Saying those words to Jack, seeing the devastation in those sexy pale green eyes, that beautiful face, would have destroyed her.

Like his absence was already tearing her into shreds. She had to survive this battle. For him. All she wanted to do was fly back to that trailer and hold him in her arms for eternity. But Jack and Four Acres Studios felt so far away now. And that realization ached through her.

She only wanted to go home. To Jack. He was her home. And she ached to return to him.

A squad of fallen angels blinked past her. Jet black wings smudged the electric cyan sky.

As they shot toward the Scribe.

"Squad!" she sang out. "Defend the Scribe."

Together, she and her squad blinked past a tangle of assassin demons. Rolled over top of a huge burst of demonic flame. And shot through a column of smoke and feathers.

Floating in front of the Scribe as an angelic shield.

Kesien swung his Eternean sword in a wild arc into the flight of fallen angels. Severing one fallen angel's wing in two.

She fell out of the sky. As more fallen angels and demons flew up behind her.

Muriel shield-bashed another fallen angel. Knocking him backward. Into Anahera. Who shield-bashed him into the approaching demons.

Scattering them like smoke.

Talia leaped over a shadow assassin demon, rolled over top of two fallen angels, and landed beside the Scribe. Blocking a killing blow with her Eternean sword.

More fallen angels lunged for Pravuil. The Scribe thrust his sword of Holy Fire into one fallen angel's gut. Dropping her out of the sky.

Deemah shield-bashed the other fallen angel and Anahera ran it through with her sword.

He collapsed into the smoke and flames and sailed downward like a torch in a shower of black wing feathers.

But three more blinked across the sky in their place.

Talia flung handfuls of murder marbles in their path. They exploded in a shower of gold sparks. Obliterating one fallen angel.

Setting the wings of the other two on fire.

They fell out of the sky, sending up a trail of flames, feathers, and ash as they disappeared in the thick, choking smoke.

"Good job, squad!" Talia sang out. "Keep the Scribe in your sights. Tight Supremes formation."

She felt Pravuil beside her, his hand on her arm.

"Talia," he sang to her in notes that only she could hear. "I've found the memory."

She frowned. "What memory?" she sang in her highest, softest notes.

"The memory of the Omega Rod," he whispered in notes so quiet that they barely reached her ears.

"I don't understand," she said, shaking her head.

She shifted closer. Tossed out more murder marbles as three more fallen angels surged toward them.

"I didn't realize until yesterday," sang the Scribe in a tenor whisper. "That I had seen the last resting place of the Omega Rod. That the memory of it rested within me."

She gasped. Pravuil knew the location of the Omega Rod! Could they get there and retrieve it before Lucifer?

"I sifted through my memories until I found it," he sang in hurried notes. "I just need to—"

Muriel screamed, her sleeve on fire.

Talia lunged for the flames, extinguishing them with a burst of Holy light.

Furious, Muriel wheeled around, shield raised, and bashed two fallen angels in the face. They tumbled out of the sky in curls of thick black smoke, puncturing the clouds with their impressions as they careened downward.

Above them, more fallen angels dropped out of the black clouds on top of them.

Kesien somersaulted over top of Azrael, his sword catching the blade of a fallen angel that had blinked behind the archangel. Halting a killing blow.

Azrael turned, sword of Holy Fire raised, but Kesien bashed it out of the sky.

Still, more descended from the clouds on top of them.

Talia and Muriel linked arms and turned together, blades arcing, and took down two more fallen angels.

But out of the corner of her eye, she saw Pravuil stiffen. His head snapped upward. Toward the Heavens. And he froze, only his wings moving.

Like the seraph was contacting him.

But something felt wrong.

Seraphina had limited power right now and unless communicating with the Maker's Scribe in the middle of an apocalyptic battle was a priority, that wasn't Seraphina.

Turning together, she and Muriel cut down two more fallen angels. And blinked to Pravuil's right side. Whirling around to face another wave of fallen angels with newly recovered wings, shiny and black as midnight.

Lucifer must have used his powers to make those fallen angel wings regenerate! A power only the left hand of the Maker possessed.

"Keep defending the Scribe!" Talia sang out again. "Don't let them get past us to Heaven!"

"Angels! Fall back!" Azrael sang out across the skies. "Squads assemble around me. Defensive phalanx lines. Repel their front lines! Protect the Scribe!"

In a wash of white wings, angels blinked across the battlefield and formed phalanxes at the edge of Heaven.

As her squad tightened formation around Pravuil again, Talia felt the whisper of something dark and menacing nearby.

She glanced around, through the flutter of white wings and gold armor, trying to locate the presence she felt, but all around her, demons and angels filled the skies above the Earth.

"Guard!" Sidriel shouted. "Fall back! Phalanx formations. Push them back. Hard!"

Turiel gathered his guard and placed them in roundel formations between, above, and below the phalanxes. Sariel placed another dozen or so phalanx lines in front of Turiel's guard until a sea of grey and white stood between the Army of Dark and the lowest reaches of Heaven.

The demons gathered into a massive wedge formation and moved together toward the angels trying to hold back this unending tide of darkness.

"They're preparing to rush the lines!" Azrael sang out. "Lock shields. Now!"

The head of the demonic wedge was a concentrated blade of shadow assassins. Fallen angels were the driving force that propelled the assassin demons toward the death angel guards defending Heaven.

"Pravuil?" Talia's soprano notes wafted above the smoke. "Answer me? Are you all right?"

Silence.

Seraphina's Holy Fire cascaded down like molten rain as the huge wedge surged toward them in a shadowy haze and burn of Hellfires. Getting closer as they rode out turbulence and blasts of Holy Fire.

"There's too many!" Anahera shouted, shield raised.

"Hold positions," Talia sang out. "Anahera, check on Pravuil."

"He's not responding!" Anahera's shrill notes pierced Talia's ears, that heavy presence so close again.

"They're cutting through our outer defenses!" Muriel shouted through gritted teeth.

"Bring it, you monsters!" Kesien shouted toward the gathering storm of demons smashed together into a deadly wedge of Hellfires and darkness. Careening toward them like an out-of-control freight train.

A hail of burning arrows cut across the expanse. Slamming into the writhing mass of demons.

Demons fell out of the air by the dozens.

The Watchers unleashed a second massive burst of Holy Fire as Ramiel held position at Heaven's edge behind them.

But the Army of Dark was markedly closer now.

The demons were driving the angels backward. Until soon, the battle would be at the meadow's edge behind Eolowen. She swallowed hard. Until there was nowhere to go. They had to stop them here. At the edge of the Heavens.

Again, Talia felt that malevolent force as the wedge of demons shot across the electric cyan sky toward them at lightning speed.

"Shields forward!" Talia shouted. "Lock arms! And hold on!"

Together, she and the guard locked arms around Pravuil and Azrael. Bracing for impact.

Moments before the demons were close enough to see their red scales, a squad of cherubim blasted overhead and cut right through the center of the massive force.

Splitting it in half.

Talia and her guard cheered as the cherubim banked over top of the broken wedge formation, the demons scrambling to regroup.

"Keep those shields forward and hold the line!" Talia ordered in sharp soprano notes. "Scribe? Answer me!"

Two black wing feathers drifted past her face. She looked up.

Above her. Shielded by dark clouds. A fluid black shadow shifted.

Talia spread her wings wide, rising on the air currents until she was level with the dark clouds floating past.

Concealed in their haze, a familiar fallen angel floated there. She gasped.

Procel the Fallen. Clutching the Book of Secrets to his chest.

He possessed rare angel powers. He'd used the Book of Secrets—and Jack—to break Lucifer's tether. And now, he was using the Book again. Against them.

Her gaze snapped downward. Toward the Scribe.

No! He was using those rare powers on the Maker's Scribe!

Procel leered at her, hand outstretched, pointing downward toward the Scribe.

"It's a shame that you found me, Talia," said Procel.

"What are you doing?" she demanded, calling up another sword of Holy Fire.

"Reminiscing," he said with a chuckle.

A cold chill raked across her wing tips. The memory that the Scribe had just described to her!

She hadn't had a chance to process it all yet. The battle had been too heated. Too close. Even now, the realization sat above her thoughts, trying to sink in that she and Pravuil knew the location of the Omega Rod.

"What do you mean, reminiscing?" She lifted both swords of Holy Fire and shot toward him.

"Reliving memories of the Creation," he said with a wicked laugh, dodging left.

Just out of her reach.

She turned. No. No! Procel was using Transference! He was capturing Pravuil's memory of the Omega Rod.

For Lucifer.

Talia launched herself at Procel, but he blinked out of the cloud. Into a tangle of demons and shadow assassins.

Cherubim shot past. The sky burned as the demonic wedge formation regrouped again.

Talia whirled around. Into a burst of demons.

She tossed a handful of murder marbles at them and blinked downward. Toward the Scribe. Freed from Procel's hold.

She shot downward, hovering beside the Maker's Scribe, the glint of his Eternean breastplate almost blinding.

"Pravuil!" she cried. "Procel used transference on you."

His gold eyes widened, his mouth gaping. "What? Are you sure?"

She nodded, turning, slashing at two assassin demons with her Holy Fire swords. Taking them both down.

"I interrupted whatever he was doing," she said, swinging her Holy Fire swords in a wide arc.

Dropping another fallen angel from the sky.

"But Pravuil, they know," she cried. "They stole your memory."

His face turned arctic pale. "The Omega Rod!"

She nodded.

"Talia!" He grabbed hold of her Eternean breastplate, a desperate glow in his gold eyes. "You must use Transference now. Right now!"

She frowned, slashing at another demon. Sending it free-falling toward Earth.

"What? Why?"

"Because you must have the memory, too. You must find the rod before Lucifer! Hurry!"

She let one Holy Fire sword collapse into a shower of white sparks as she laid her hand against the side of Pravuil's face. And summoned the swirling rush of Transference that welled inside her. She hadn't used this power since she'd awakened it.

Like a crashing white wave of Holy Fire, the power bloomed inside her.

The force rushed down her arm, into her fingers, and spilled onto Pravuil's face and short white hair. The power swirled around him as she reached into the maelstrom of images for the memory of the Omega Rod.

It took patience as her fingers fluttered through the white-hot energy that thrummed against her hand. Until she felt the Omega Rod's image press against her fingertips.

She grabbed hold of it. Pulling it toward her.

The image shot through her fingers, rolled down her arm, and shot up through her chest. Into her head.

Like a firestorm, the image bloomed through her memory.

A dark, forbidding forest shielding markers of the dead behind an old stone church. Buried deep in an old, old grave. Crowned with a weathered marble statue of a weeping angel. And below it, an ironwood casket.

"Brace for impact!" Azrael shouted. "Tight phalanx formations! Shields forward! Hold your ground. For Heaven, angels!"

Talia whirled around, shield raised as Anahera, Muriel, Kesien, and Deemah crowded beside her, wings whispering above the drone of demons approaching. The massive wedge formation cast a black, inky shadow across the Army of Light.

Daidrean slid beside Deemah, shield raised as Cabriawn and his squad blinked in front of Heaven's entire guard of death angels and its four commanding archangels. Into another repelling phalanx line.

"Shields out! Lock arms and hold on!" Talia sang out in crisp soprano notes.

One by one, she and her squad locked arms with each other, crowding together to protect God's Scribe. And hold back the massive force of demons.

Seraphina hovered above the cherubim patrol, raining down Holy Fire.

Demons fell in droves out of the air, but the wedge shot forward. Propelled by every last remaining fallen angel. Driving it like a nail right through Heaven's defensive lines.

Talia held onto Muriel and Kesien with every ounce of strength she had, shield on her wrist extended in front of her body.

"Hold the line!" Talia commanded.

Daylight disappeared, engulfed by the immense shadowy blackness of the Army of Dark, rolling toward them like a massive tsunami.

The clash of Hellfire and demonic flame against Holy Fire and angel light exploded in a crush of brimstone and sulfur. Of Holy Fire and angel light.

The sound was deafening. Earsplitting. Like the world had cleaved in two and rocked off its axis.

Blackness blanketed the skies. Lit by a storm of flaming feathers. Covering angels and demons in a heavy swath of soot and ash. The stench of ozone burned with brimstone.

Talia shifted her wings, trying to clear away the debris.

But it was like tar. It clung to her wing feathers. To her breastplate. To her face.

Gasping, she struggled to free herself from the force holding her back, holding down her wings. Obscuring everything around her.

But her wings caught fire. Burning like a torch with Hellfire.

She screamed as the buoyancy left her wings, the air currents bouncing off as she began to sink through the air stream.

"No!"

"Talia?" Muriel's voice pierced the darkness. "Where are you?"

The weight of the demonic shadows and Hellfires was too much. And she began to drop.

"Muriel, help me!"

"Talia?" Muriel's voice cut through the blackness. "Talia!"

Screaming, she clawed at the air, trying to hold onto her squad, the clouds, anything!

But it all slipped through her fingers as she plummeted out of the sky. Wings burning. Robes aflame. Breastplate burnt and blackened.

She spiraled through the clouds in a burst of charred grey feathers. Sinking through the eerie cyan silence gripping Earth. As the ground rushed toward her.

"Jack!" she shouted.

But the words. The sky. The battle slipped through her fingertips.

She hit the ground full force. Her last thought was Jack as everything went dark. And silent.

17

JACK RODE SHOTGUN IN THE FRONT PASSENGER SEAT OF BANKS' GREY Infiniti X80 SUV. Looked brand-new. Still smelled like leather and money. Gianni rode behind him, Rachel behind Banks as the SUV flew down Olive and merged onto the Hollywood Freeway. Jack hung his head out the window, tracking the writhing cyan trail of smoke that undulated through the eerie electric blue-green sky.

Trailing west. Toward Hollywood.

He frowned. If he ended up in a strip club with Zanth and Rachel, Talia would kill him. Apocalypse or not.

"Please don't be a strip club," he muttered.

Banks gave him a hard look. "Please don't? Jack, are you crazy? The apocalypse is the only defense for ending up in a strip club now that we're all married."

He laid his hand against his chin. "Got a point there, dude," he said. "But Talia would still kill me." He flicked his gaze toward the backseat.

Banks smiled. "You're right. In your case, she'd still kill you."

Gianni leaned between the seats and cast a sideways glance at Rachel.

"She'd definitely kill you, Jack."

"And Morgan would kill Mark twice," said Rachel.

Banks groaned, nodding and they all laughed.

The trail of smoke curved toward the exit for Santa Monica Boulevard.

Banks cut across two lanes and slid into an open spot for the exit as they shot down the off-ramp and careened down Lexington then Saint Andrews onto Santa Monica in what felt like broad daylight because of the eerie sky.

"Where to now, Jack?" Banks asked, weaving between the lanes.

He winced when he saw the smoky trail still curving west. Knowing in his gut where that smoke would lead them.

Hollywood Forever Cemetery.

"The cemetery," he said with a groan.

Banks glanced over at him. "The cemetery?"

Gianni covered his face. "Hollywood Forever, Banks," he replied. "This isn't going to go well, is it?"

"Shit," Banks replied.

That place was so closed. It was way after five o'clock. Jack sighed. And they were about to trespass after he flew all three of them over the fence. To find this demon Hell princess. That place was better guarded than the Pentagon, especially after hours.

"Drive past it," Jack said with a snarl. "There's a strip mall a block or two past the entrance. Zanth, Hughes, and I should be able to quickly fly all three of us over that fence. So we can all get arrested for trespassing after stopping this Hell princess. I can just see tonight's Channel 5 news. Four well-known actors were arrested for trespassing tonight in Hollywood Forever Cemetery. The quartet was found burying their own careers with shovels near the grave of Burt Reynolds. We go live to the graveside services."

Banks and Rachel broke into a fit of laughter, but Gianni looked ill. "God, Jack—you're right. We could tank four careers with this move."

Jack nodded. "All for saving the world. Feel like a hero yet?"

"I feel like I got played."

Jack chuckled and slapped him on the shoulder. "Welcome to my world."

Banks drove past the gated entrance to the cemetery on the left and pulled into a strip mall a couple of blocks away.

They piled out of the vehicle and walked up the street until they located the fence surrounding the cemetery.

"Zanth!" Jack called out in a hushed voice.

It took a couple of minutes before she and Hughes stepped out of the shadows.

"Gotta fly the land lubbers over the fence," he said, motioning toward Banks, Gianni, and Rachel.

"I'll carry Banks over," said Zanth. "Tyler, you carry Rachel. Jack Casey, you carry Armand Gianni."

"Can you use that shadow cover on all of us?" Jack asked.

She nodded and reached toward his face. With both pale hands, she pressed them against his cheeks and then his shoulders.

Shadowing him.

"Dude, let's go," said Jack in a whisper as he motioned to Gianni.

After Zanth put her demon shadow on Gianni, Jack summoned all his strength as he spread his wings and lifted Gianni off the ground. His wings furiously beat the air. He rose ten feet, just above the fence, and blinked over it. Landing hard in the grass. Almost knocking him and Gianni over a headstone.

He and Gianni hurried onto a narrow, paved road as Zanth and Hughes materialized beside him. With Rachel and Banks.

"That was cool," said Banks, grinning.

Jack glanced around until he found the smoky trail again. Leading toward the first crossroad in the cemetery. He shook his head. Demons and their crossroads.

"Trail ends at the first crossroad." He pointed toward where the narrow road they followed crossed the main road ahead. "Right up there."

The six of them hurried along the road's edge, using Zanth's demon shadowing until they got to where the main road crossed an east-west road that bisected the cemetery.

Where a shadowy figure stood. Beside the figure, on the right side of the road, a brand-new, bright blue Ford Mustang parked. The sixth horse in this race.

Jack folded his wings tight against his back as an idea began to trickle into his head.

"Zanth," he said, moving closer to her. "You're surrounded by Hollywood actors. Why don't you pretend that we just died in a car crash or something and you're collecting our souls? We can sell this."

Zanth stopped moving and turned back to him, grinning. "Jack Casey," she cried. "That is brilliant!"

He turned around and motioned everyone closer.

"All right. Change of plan. A little improv."

Banks frowned. "Improv? Cool."

Jack smirked. "We're going to act our way through this," he said. "I've got Zanth pretending that all four of us Hollywood actors just died in a car crash and she's collecting the souls we sold."

Rachel shuddered. "Wow, Jack," she said. "That hits a little close to home."

"Run with it," he snapped.

Gianni shrugged. "I like it. Running with it."

Jack moved toward Zanth, Gianni behind him. Banks wandered beside Gianni, Rachel behind them. Hughes was just ahead as Zanth moved toward the Hell princess, Ronova.

Dressed in elbow-length black satin gloves, a red evening gown with a slit cut up to her demon tail, Ronova had ashen skin like Zanth, a headful of shiny black hair cut into an edgy bob, big red eyes, and full red lips. At six feet tall or so, she looked like a beautiful but demonic 1950s movie star. Jack smelled brimstone and woodsmoke as they approached. Like she'd just stepped out of Hell.

"Bonne soirée, Hell princess," said Zanth as she got close to the demon chick.

"I am Princess Ronova," said the demon in a deep alto voice, a leering grin beneath all that lipstick. "And you are?"

Zanth gave her a deep curtsy. "Eligas, princess," said Zanth, a name Jack didn't recognize.

"I wanted to come here first," said Ronova. "Before I delivered my payload, I wanted to visit all the famous actors' graves." She bowed her head. "Before it all went away. Such a shame." Finally, she looked up at Zanth. "Why are you here?"

So, she'd been visiting famous actors' graves. A fan? He smiled. Or did she have a powerful desire to act burning through those demon veins?

"I am here gathering souls," Zanth said and glanced over at Jack and his cast mates. "A lucrative night. Four Hollywood stars. Sold their souls for fame. And tonight, their contracts expired in a one-car accident."

Ronova's eyes got huge. "Four Hollywood stars? Here?"

She rushed over to Jack and the others. Walking around them. Studying them. Jack held in his smirk. Fawning over them.

Like she was a little obsessed with the Hollywood mystique. But he hoped she didn't recognize him. Because of the bounty on his head. Besides, he doubted there was much love for him among Hell's demons after his short stay.

"Are all of you really Hollywood actors?" she cried.

Jack nodded. "Were," he said. "But what a trip it was! All those movies we made."

"And all those statues we won," Gianni added.

Ronova gasped. "Statues?"

"Oscars, Emmys, Golden Globes, BAFTAs...we had them all," said Jack.

"And the parties," Gianni said in a wistful voice.

"The parties were the best part," Banks added.

The Hell princess gaped at them as she looked them over again, a gloved hand against her mouth.

"I've always wanted to visit Hollywood. Audition for roles. I've always fancied becoming an actress." She bowed her head. "It was my dream."

There it was. The Lust sin. Zanth said it was a powerful desire. That was Ronova's weakness. She desperately wanted to be an actress. Or maybe she just wanted the fame? Or both. They had to play on that. Get the coin somehow.

"Best job in the world," said Jack. "The incredible costumes. The exotic locations. Pretending to be really cool people."

"And all those fans worshipping at your feet," said Gianni. "Hanging on your every word. And getting that Star on Hollywood Boulevard."

Ronova's red eyes turned starry as she hung on their words.

"And all the other stars you meet," said Banks. "Never know who's going to become the next Bogart or Bacall either."

Nice pickup, Banks. Dude noticed Ronova's 1950s-style starlet dress. She had the Hollywood bug bad. Probably had a thing for Hollywood's heyday, too. The legends. They had to push her over the top.

"That's fascinating!" Ronova cried, reaching out and running her hands down their arms, touching their hair.

"Are you an actress?" Jack asked.

That flattery burned her right down to her demon tail. He thought it might just catch fire.

"Me?" She grinned and laid a gloved hand against her chest.

He could see Zanth trying not to choke.

He nodded and stepped closer to her. "Yeah, I'm pretty good at spotting talent. You seem like you've got the chops—and the looks— for this job. Any interest?"

"Me?" she said again, tossing her head back, black hair fluffing in the wind. "I've…dabbled."

"Anything I've seen?" he asked.

She shook her head, covering her face. "Nothing professional. Yet."

He chuckled. She had it bad.

"Y'know," he said, moving closer. "Now that I'm dead, I don't really have much use for my contacts. My agent. I could give you his number, get you an in with him. A last text message before…shuffling off to Hell."

Ronova gasped and laid her hand against his face. "You would do that? For me?"

The drama in her voice was huge and over the top. He fought not to laugh as he pointed at the sky.

"Don't know if it'll do any good though. What with the apocalypse going on and all. Seeing how it's all gonna go up in flames and not exist anymore."

The Hell princess' face fell, the look of disappointment profound.

Sighing, she reached into her left glove and slid out an aged gold coin. She held it out to him.

"Oh, here," she said. "Take it." She sighed and crossed her arms. "I never wanted to end the world anyway. I'll handle any hellhounds Lucifer sends at me. I'm a Hell princess after all." She did a pirouette. "I just can't destroy Hollywood. There's too much fun to be had here. If I don't launch my payload, will you still give me that agent's name?"

Jack reached out and gently took the coin from her hand. He'd give her a real agent's name.

"It'd be my pleasure," he said. "Name's Stanley Albertson at Magicast Talent. I hear he's looking for new blood. Tell him Laren Dumont sent you."

Behind him, Gianni coughed and Banks patted him on the back.

"Thank you!" the Hell princess shouted, grinning.

"Good luck, Ronova," said Jack. "Hope you make it. It's a tough business. If it's your dream, don't give up, okay?"

"I won't!" She pressed her gloved hands to her mouth and blew kisses to them like she was accepting her best actress Oscar. "Thank you. Thank you all."

Jack tensed, fearing she'd launch into an acceptance speech.

She blew them kisses one last time and faded into the shadows.

Jack stared at Zanth a moment, the coin clutched in his fist.

He had it. The sixth flight's payload coin.

"Let's get out of here," he said. "Before we get arrested for trespassing. And become tonight's Channel 5 lead news story."

Under the cover of Zanth's shadow spell, they hurried back to the fence and flew Banks, Gianni, and Rachel over it. When they were over, they ran back to Banks' SUV.

Jack moved toward the passenger side door, reaching out to open it, but the world dropped out from under him.

He grabbed hold of the SUV, his heart smashing against his rib cage, his body free-falling as everything tilted. The pain tore through his wings, through his chest, and shot through his thighs into his feet.

Talia!

He hit the pavement, curling into a ball as everything careened out of control. Accelerating. And everything around him burned.

Gianni's hands grabbed hold of his arms, trying to help him up.

His heart twisted into knots as he felt the massive demonic blow slam against his wings. His body. And everything raced downward.

"Talia!" he screamed.

Then he knew.

Talia had just fallen out of the sky.

18

"Jack, are you all right?" Gianni asked as he and Banks picked Jack up off the pavement.

Rachel pulled open the passenger side door and Gianni sat him down.

His breaths came in gulps, panic washing over him in crashing waves, his heart pumping like an out-of-control piston.

He couldn't breathe. Couldn't halt the waves of piercing pain pounding through his body alongside the overwhelming panic.

"It's Talia," he said, staring past Gianni. "I felt her—I—"

He pushed past Banks, trying to pull himself to his feet and spread his wings.

But Gianni grabbed him and held him down, forcing him to look into the measured calm of his best friend's warm brown eyes.

"Jack," he said in a firm voice. "Jack, look at me."

But he couldn't.

All he could feel was fiery pain burning along his limbs and crackling across his wings.

"Talia!"

He gasped, heaving another breath through the gulps of air as he struggled against Gianni's hold.

"Have to…get to…Talia."

He lurched, his whole body spasming against the fire and the pain, feeling heartsick as he grabbed hold of Gianni's face.

"Dude, Talia fell out of the sky!" he finally shouted. "I've gotta get to her!"

"Jack, where?" Gianni cried, eyes wide, mouth agape as he held Jack on his feet.

Jack's eyes stung with brimstone and sulfur and the heat of Holy Fire setting everything around him alight.

"Gianni, close the door!" Banks. "He needs a doctor or something."

Jack's hand slid away from Gianni's face, the swell of grief beginning to overwhelm the pain, but he tamped it down. Hard.

He had to get to Talia. Now.

"Gotta find her." He gasped another gulp of air. "Before it's too late."

But Gianni and the others weren't listening. They were shouting at each other around him, at Zanth—even Hughes.

"Look at him, Gianni," Banks shouted. "He needs a doctor!"

"He needs an archangel," said Rachel.

"Zanth!" Gianni called out. "Can you help him? He's saying Talia's hurt."

Jack tried to leap out of the SUV again, throwing himself at Gianni, but the taller soap star held him against the seat.

"Easy, Jack—you're injured." Gianni.

"Let me go!" Jack shouted. "Let go! I've got to get to Talia! TALIA!"

Finally, Zanth was beside Gianni, looking unnerved. She reached out, her ashen hand bathed in shadows, and pressed her fingers to his forehead.

Like a spring unwinding, he collapsed against the seat, Gianni with an iron grip on both arms, Banks and Rachel blocking his escape as Zanth cast calming waves of shadow across him.

The darkness made his stomach churn and he wretched, but only air came up.

"Now that you are calmer," said Zanth, glancing at Gianni and then Banks. "Tell us what has happened, Jack Casey."

Gianni leaned toward him, still gripping his arms.

"Jack. What's happened to Talia?"

He sighed, his heart slamming against his ribs. At least Gianni got it.

"Talia's fallen out of the sky," he said, unable to keep the ache out of his voice.

Zanth's face went deadly pale and she exchanged a dire look with Gianni and then Banks.

"Jack," she said in that raspy alto voice, thick French accent soft like worn velvet against his skin. "You know that angels and demons don't come back from that kind of fall."

He gritted his teeth, the moisture filling his eyes.

"No!" he shouted, shaking his head. "No! I feel her! I feel her, Zanth," he said, his voice breaking. "I've got to get to her fast. Before she—"

But he couldn't finish that sentence. Couldn't put those syllables together to form those terrible words. Words that would rob him of the love of his life. Of his happily ever after.

"Jack," she said, pity in her voice. "Angels don't come back from an apocalyptic fall. As it is written."

He slammed his fist against the door. "No! NO!"

A flood of reasons why. Of feelings. Of what ifs burned on his tongue, colliding into a burst of unintelligible ranting that broke when his grief bubbled up like acid to completely steal the rest of his voice. And his words.

"Our rare bond." He struggled to get the words out. "I feel her. Feel her, Zanth! She's fading fast." The tears threaded down his face. "Help me."

God, his voice was so small and quiet that he wasn't even sure Zanth had heard his plea.

"Let me go," he said with a tortured hiss.

He turned his face toward the ceiling of the SUV. Toward Heaven. Toward the Maker, God, or whatever that all-powerful force was that resided above the lower Heavens among Thrones and souls and the Creation's machinations.

"Help her," he prayed with every ounce of hope and faith he had left in his skeptical body.

Yes, it was a completely selfish prayer.

With the apocalypse exploding around them. With hundreds of angels falling out of the sky and he was begging the universe's most powerful entity to spare one single angel of death.

Because he loved her more than his own life.

The moment Gianni relaxed his grip, Jack sprang out of the SUV.

Spreading his wings.

But Gianni and Banks tackled him before he could lift off.

"Jack, it's too dangerous!" Gianni cried. "Talia would never forgive me for letting you get killed like this."

"Sorry, Jack," said Banks.

He fought. He struggled. He swung at his two best friends. But neither one of them let up on their fierce holds on him.

He beat his fists against the ground, asphalt gouging his hands, and cutting his cheek.

Zanth dropped down beside him on her haunches as Rachel and Hughes crowded around her.

"Jack Casey," she said. "It is too late. You cannot save her. You'd never even find her in time."

He shook his head. Hard. Glaring at her. At all of them.

"Resurrect," he growled. "And omnificence."

Her eyes widened.

"You have resurrect? But you must have an angel's full power and gather all those elements first and—"

He violently shook his head. "Seraphim powers. And I'm human—they're already within me."

Zanth's mouth gaped as she stared past Jack.

"Let him go," she said.

Gianni and Banks glanced at each other.

"What do you mean, let him go?" Gianni demanded. "You just said he'd get killed if we let him go."

"Look," said Zanth, pointing behind Gianni and Banks.

They turned as a rush of gold angel light streamed past them.

Jack squinted.

Muriel and Kesien stood behind them, ragged wings unfurled and fluttering in the wind. Dire looks on their ash-smeared faces.

"Muriel! Kesien!" he cried.

Banks let go of him, stepping back as Muriel knelt beside him, Kesien dropping down on his haunches.

"Jack...Talia fell in the battle," said Muriel, tears streaking down her ash-streaked face.

He grabbed hold of Muriel's gold Eternean bracer that encircled her wrist.

"I know," he said, his voice cracking. "I felt it."

Kesien bowed his head, tears dripping onto the asphalt.

"But Muriel, I still feel her out there," he cried. "I feel her!"

Already, Kesien was shaking his head.

"We'd never find her before she expired, Jack. We've looked everywhere, but there are miles and miles of angels and demons littering the Earth right now."

"Kesien, I've got omnificence."

Kesien lifted his head and exchanged a look with Muriel. It was a look of hope. Of one more chance, one more reason that this thing wasn't over yet.

That Talia wasn't gone forever.

"Help me up," he said.

Muriel and Kesien lifted him off the pavement and set him on his feet.

"What happened?" Jack asked.

"The Army of Dark has made it into the lower Heavens," said Kesien.

"We can't stop them," said Muriel. "Only slow them down now. Without more cherubim and seraphim, the lower Heavens are lost."

His heart smashed against his rib cage. Eolowen. The Archive.

"We have to make a last stand at the portal," said Kesien, bowing his head. "If Lucifer gets the Omega Rod first..."

"We intercepted Procel before he could carry the location back to Lucifer," said Muriel. "So, Azrael sent me and Kesien to you. Let's go."

He held his breath a moment. "To find Talia?" he asked.

She nodded. And his heart soared.

This *wasn't* over yet. Not by a long shot.

He turned around and hugged Gianni.

"Thanks for everything, dude," he said. "Hope to see you soon. If not…we had a good ride, didn't we?"

Gianni's eyes got teary and he nodded.

"The best, Jack. Thanks for everything. And dammit, you'd better come back with Talia or I'll never speak to you again."

He smiled as he hugged Banks. "Thanks for being there for Talia. And me. I wouldn't be here if you hadn't."

"Save her, Jack," he said. "We'll work with Zanth to play this last Hell prince when it arrives."

"Or die trying," said Gianni.

Rachel rushed up to him and hugged him. "Godspeed, Jack," she said. "You and Talia belong together."

He hugged her. "Thanks, Rach."

Turning away, he spread his wings wide and nodded toward Muriel and Kesien. With a sharp breath, he held out his right hand, index finger pointing toward the asphalt. Focusing down the maelstrom of omnificence images and data overwhelming him.

Concentrating on Talia.

On the heat of her presence, the warmth of her love that he could never forget, could never let go of—even with her so far away.

Until a faint burst of light, like fireworks, lit the sky toward the west.

"Let's do this," Jack said with a growl and blinked into the apocalyptic, neon-cyan sky.

Muriel and Kesien leaped into the air, wings spread wide, and shot forward, flying on each side of him as he kept a firm hold on his omnificence power that led him northeast.

Toward Griffith Park.

19

to fade and the world began to slowly darken. Except for a strange red glow that hung high above as he followed omnificence over Los Angeles. Into the expanse that was Griffith Park. His exhaustion was growing, weighing on his limbs. Using omnificence like this was expending too much seraphim power.

He didn't care. He had to find her.

No one on Earth besides him knew that that red glow meant that Heaven was burning as the seventh flight climbed on deck, waiting to pour out the final payload. Death. While demons pounded on the portal into the upper Heavens.

Waiting for Lucifer to cave it in with the Omega Rod of Creation.

He had to find Talia and together, they had to find this Omega Rod. Before Lucifer. Before everything perished. Before Talia...he struggled with that thought...before she ceased to be.

Zanth had said that Death's payload was more powerful than the previous six payloads combined. But the seventh Traveler was the least of his worries.

Right now, he had to find Talia.

With Muriel and Kesien still beside him, he banked over the

massive Griffith Park that sprawled across Los Angeles' northwestern corner. Still following the pale golden gleam in the darkening sky.

He glided lower until the grass and dirt materialized out of the cyan glow and the night. But the sight of all the angels and demons made him shudder.

He flew lower, only a few feet off the ground. Feeling only stillness. Hearing only silence.

Cold and stiff demons littered the ground in small craters across the park as he followed the golden glow of omnificence. Leading him toward the observatory peak.

As he approached the observatory's green dome and the hill where people took the famous 360-degree views of the L.A. skyline, his heart hammered faster, his stomach somersaulting.

Angel after angel lay still and silent below him. Trails of grey and black feathers covered the grass like fallen leaves. Confirming the slaughter.

They were everywhere.

It made him sick. He hurled. Throwing up bile as the golden glow grew brighter.

He circled the top of the observatory hill.

In the darkness, faint smears of gold light glimmered like fireflies among tiny bursts of red light. The fading lights of angels and demons as they expired from the world.

It stung his eyes. He wasn't even sure he had enough seraphim powers to save Talia. He couldn't save the rest. But maybe Talia and Berith could?

Ahead, the gold light burned in a column.

He dived toward it.

But his heart nearly stopped.

Lying in the cold, dark grass on the edge of the peak, Talia lay motionless. Silent.

He threw himself into the grass and scooped her into his arms, rocking her as he held her against his chest.

"Talia!" he cried, brushing the hair away from her long lashes, eyes closed.

Trails of gold light streamed down the side of her face. Across her forehead. From her ears. Out her nose and mouth.

Every emotion screamed inside him as he held her, the tears blinding him.

Kesien landed beside him, Muriel in another heartbeat.

"Oh, Talia!" Muriel cried, her face awash in ashen tears, hands shaking as she stroked Talia's hair.

Kesien swiped at his eyes.

She felt so cold. Complexion looked so grey. That ethereal glimmer that clung to every celestial being was fading from her skin. From her wings.

Like a dying firefly.

He had to hurry. Before that last glimmer faded.

He didn't have the power to call back the light from those flashes of illumination like Talia and Berith. And Berith would never get here in time now.

Reaching inside himself, he summoned every last bit of rare angel power—and seraphim power—he had and thrust it forward. Into his hands.

Pulling in a deep breath, he tried to push his shaking and his grief away, focusing everything he had on resurrect.

He'd never used it before. Never even summoned it. But Talia's existence depended on it.

"Lay her on her back, Jack," said Muriel.

With Kesien's help, he laid her in the grass, his heart breaking, the tears a steady drip down his face.

He took a deep breath and summoned the five elements of Creation inside him. And pressed his right hand against her heart.

As the Creation elements roiled inside him, he called up the first drop of water from the Creation. Like the one Talia had pulled from a piece of Aeonium metal used to create the first Heavenly armor.

Sweat beaded across his forehead as he felt the frozen blue orb materialize between the fingers of his right hand.

He thought back to the Garden, when Talia had brought him back from death's edge as she broke Lucifer's tether on his soul.

Remembering where she'd placed those orbs after Muriel told him the story a few times. And each time, it hurt his chest and stung his eyes.

He laid the frozen blue orb against her heart.

And concentrated on the last grain of sand. One that Talia had discovered in the soil beneath the willow tree at Eolowen.

His hands shook when he felt the rough green orb appear between his fingers. He laid it on her stomach.

The gold sheen against her feathers and skin began to darken.

Smashing his eyes closed, he reached inside for the first spark of light. Clawing. Raking. Until a frozen yellow orb appeared between his fingers.

His hands trembled as he laid the sphere on her forehead.

"Hurry, Jack," Muriel cried. "Her light's fading!"

He reached inside for his own breath coming in gasps until he felt another orb between his fingers. A frosty white one. He laid it in the well of her beautiful throat.

And dug for the last element, the lifeblood that had been spilled in the Garden. That had hardened like amber and clung to the grass beneath the felled Tree of Life.

But nothing appeared.

He took another deep breath. Reached for the lifeblood inside him again.

No orb.

"There's no red orb!" he cried.

He could barely see the afterglow of gold light on her skin now. It had already left her wings.

"Find it, Jack!" Kesien shouted. "Hurry! She's almost gone."

"Jack!" Muriel cried. "Her light's going out!"

He glanced down and saw a sharp-edged rock in the dirt beside him.

"Quick!" He pointed at the rock. "Give me that rock!"

Muriel snatched it out of the dirt and slapped it into his right hand.

He gripped it in his fist and raked it across his left wrist. Blood rushed down his arm. He pressed his wrist against the side of her head, where the most light leaked out.

And prayed.

The moments ticked by as the last remnants of light began to dissipate across her skin, her body growing colder and dark.

"Talia, no," he moaned, gripping her hands in his bloodied fingers. "Please…I can't live without you. You have my heart. You've always had it, I—"

Her heart! Was that where the red sphere should have gone?

He thrust his bloodied hands against her heart, leaving his handprint against her arctic pale skin.

A red orb appeared in his hands.

He pressed it against her heart, beside the blue orb.

One by one, the orbs burst, engulfing Talia in blue light. Then a frosty white light. Followed by a rich green glow, like spring grass, that covered her body. The red orb exploded, showering her and him in red light that washed over her entire body. And faded into a pale gold light. It surged over her like water and ebbed.

Until the purest white light he'd ever seen lit every facet and every fingernail. And hummed against her skin.

A gold column of light shot up from the white radiance as Talia's body floated up and hovered in the bright gold light.

Gasping. She opened her eyes.

Her angelic form landed gently in the grass as the gold light disappeared. Leaving her wings and body glimmering with an almost metallic gold afterglow.

"TALIA!"

His voice was barely audible as he crawled toward her and threw his arms around her, smashing his body against hers, holding her so close that he felt the rush of air through her angel heart. Beating with an angel's heartbeat again.

"Jack!" she cried and threw her arms around him, crystalline tears collecting in the grass as she held him.

Oh, God, it was the best feeling he'd ever felt!

Having her back in his arms. Breathing. Heart beating. Voice filling his soul with so many emotions that he was overcome. Could barely breathe. Barely talk. He held her against his chest as the tears leaked out of his eyes in a flood of relief.

"You're shaking," she cried in a weak voice. "Are you all right?"

He closed his eyes as she ran her fingers through his hair. Her touch was all he wanted and he immersed himself in the feel of her hand against his head.

"I am now," he said in a hoarse whisper, still holding her close.

"Muriel?" Talia replied, glancing over at Muriel and then Kesien. "What happened?"

Kesien bowed his head as Muriel wiped away tears.

"The Army of Dark cut through our defenses. We couldn't stop them. We were overwhelmed."

"They've reached the lower Heavens," said Kesien, hands on his hips. "So far, the portal upward is holding."

"By the Maker!" Talia cried as she stepped out of Jack's arms, a hand against her mouth. "The Omega Rod!"

Muriel moved over to Talia and hugged her, but when she let go, she was smiling.

"Talia, we intercepted Procel."

"You got him?"

Kesien nodded and hugged her next. "Before he carried Pravuil's memory of the location to Lucifer."

"We got the Book of Secrets back, too," Muriel added and flexed her wings.

The hint of a smile lifted the corners of her mouth. "Then maybe it's not too late," she said, glancing around at all of them.

When her gaze fell on Jack again, she reached out and gripped his hand.

"Lover, it's not too late!"

"Do you know the location of the rod, babe?" he asked, stroking her hair, aching to just hold her in his arms.

But that would have to wait.

She nodded, her face lighting up, losing the last traces of that horrible grey cast.

"Pravuil insisted I use Transference to capture his memory. I just need to call it up. Everything is so jumbled right now."

A loud thump startled Jack.

He glanced to his right.

As an angel and two demons slammed into the ground beside him. Scattering grey feathers, dust, and red demon scales. A spray of red and gold misted the ground.

"We need to get out of here," said Jack, whirling around as another demon crashed against the grass a few feet away, setting the grass on fire.

Kesien rushed over and stomped out the fire as Talia closed her eyes. He wondered if she was using omnificence to search for Pravuil's memory that she'd somehow collected. Through transference or some other angel power?

Jack felt the roiling of angel powers within Talia. She seemed to be struggling to summon those rare abilities. She was more injured than she let on, from the battle and the fall. Her halo wasn't quite as bright gold as it should have been. Her wings twitched and shifted against her shoulders.

That's when he saw the ragged burned feathers. Could she even fly like that? He knew almost nothing about these wings. They probably reacted differently for angels than they did for humans.

But he noticed that the longer Kesien and Muriel stayed still, the less ragged their wings looked. Like the angel light inside them was somehow healing their wing feathers.

He had a million questions for all of them, but he kept quiet, letting Talia concentrate on her rare angel powers right now. Getting the location of the Omega Rod was the most important thing right now, eclipsing everything. If they didn't get to it before Lucifer, he would destroy the Earth and Heaven both. Couldn't exactly recover from the world and Heaven being destroyed.

But he saw the weakness in Talia's beautiful arctic grey eyes. In the dimmed glow of her gold halo. He'd brought her back from the brink of erasure and she was weak, struggling. Even with her rare angel powers. She wasn't calling them up in an instant like she always had before. She needed rest. Needed time to let all her powers regenerate.

He sighed. Time they didn't have.

A black-winged angel dropped almost on top of him and he shuffled backward, nearly knocking over Kesien.

"Sorry, dude," he said, glancing up at the sky as handfuls of black feathers drifted down around him, some still burning. "This spot's dangerous."

Kesien glanced over at the crushed black wings and red glow surrounding the still figure.

"A fallen angel," said Kesien. "Taking their final fall."

He was right. Every part of this angel's body had gone dark, not even a blush of red or gold light touched the dark, still body now. Black, burning wing feathers continued to drift down from the sky like ash.

"Anything yet, Talia?" Muriel asked, glancing from Talia to the sky.

The seventh flight wouldn't leave for Earth until sometime tomorrow after sunset. Somehow, they had to get the Omega Rod and keep it from Lucifer. Destroy it if they had to—before the sky turned another funky disco color. And brought death to his world.

Talia gave her a slight nod and bowed her head, dove grey wings unfurling.

Revealing all the burned feathers, gaping holes, and tattered edges. He winced. He'd never seen her wings like that before.

But he remembered that night in L.A. when he'd caught her in his arms. The night that Azrael took her wings and threw her out of the Heavens.

He shuddered to think what would have happened if he hadn't caught her that night. Would Azrael have broken her fall somehow? But the archangel had pinpointed exactly where to cast her out so she'd land in the precise location of his shithole studio apartment. At exactly the moment he was out there. Good thing she hadn't landed on one of Bruce's sunbaked dog shit bricks. Or all those Natural Ice cans. Could have been ugly.

"I've got it," Talia announced, her eyes snapping open.

With unsteady movements, she spread her damaged wings wide. Jack moved beside her, his arm around her waist, keeping her on both feet so she wouldn't tip over.

"Babe, you can't fly like this," he said, caressing her soot-covered cheek.

"I have to, Jack," she said, urgency in her clear soprano voice. "We have to get there before Lucifer figures out how to extract that memory from Procel."

She had a point. Procel had probably already alerted Lucifer to his capture—and that he'd successfully stolen the memory.

Now, the four of them were racing the second most powerful being in the universe to a forgotten Creation rod. Whatever that was.

Kesien slid beside Talia on her left and Muriel laid her hands on Jack's shoulders, shifting him away from Talia.

"Sorry, Jack," she said. "But Kesien and I are going to have to hold her on both sides to keep her in the air."

He bristled. "I can do that, too."

Muriel shook her head. "Sorry, Jack, keeping her in the air would exhaust a human. We need you sharp. And all powers at full strength. Seraphina collapsed at the end of the battle—when the Army of Dark broke through. Pravuil and Azrael had to carry her back to Eolowen."

Jack felt ill now. Without a seasoned seraph, the only one left, how would they defeat Lucifer? Now that he had all his powers back?

"All the Death Angel guards fell back to Eolowen with the Watchers," said Kesien as he put an arm around Talia's waist. "Azrael's got the cherubim trying to heal her." He sighed. "But it's taking time we don't have."

"Yours are the only seraphim powers we have left, Jack," said Muriel. "Who knew that the powers that accidentally transferred to you would be the only ones left in Heaven right now. With Seraphina still recovering from her egregious injuries when High House exploded."

Jack glanced at Kesien and then Talia. "If I'm all that's left, an actor, you dudes are so screwed." He motioned at the sky as another fallen angel dropped behind him in a shower of flame and burning black feathers. "Let's take this party somewhere else."

Muriel put her left arm around Talia's waist. "Where to, Talia?"

She turned to Kesien. "Kesien, can you use your angel of death abilities to blink us to the East Coast?"

"The East Coast?" Jack replied. "Seriously?"

"There's an old cemetery there," said Talia, her voice sounding softer than normal.

He chewed his bottom lip. Weaker.

"Tal, you look awfully pale," he said, a hand against her cheek. "You can't fly like this."

She reached out to him and gripped his hand. "Kesien and Muriel will have to help me get there, lover."

He squeezed her hand. "I'll carry you," he said. "For as long as I can."

Her eyes turned glassy. She pulled him close and kissed his lips. He returned her kiss with urgency, wanting only to hold her, but knew he had to let her go.

"According to Pravuil's memory," she said, "there was some long-ago uprising with Lucifer and the fallen angels."

"Which one?" Jack asked. "There've been so many."

"It was the first time that Lucifer warned Heaven that he would regain his powers," said Talia. "Pravuil feared the kernel of truth beneath Lucifer's threats, that he would regain his power and find the rod. So, he and a squad of death angels flew it out of the Heavens. Hid it in the tiniest of graveyards on the East Coast."

"Where?" Jack asked, frowning.

"Duxbury, Massachusetts," said Talia. "There's an unmarked grave in the cemetery with a pocked, worn marble statue of a weeping angel. Buried there in an ironwood casket is the Omega Rod."

"Ready, Talia?" Kesien asked.

She nodded, her face looking so pale.

He closed his eyes a moment, reaching into the deep well of rare angel powers he carried. Mirrors of Talia's abilities. And called up the golden healing light he'd watched her use so many times. He bit his lip, struggling to lift it out of the churning maelstrom of energies. When he finally got hold of it, he felt it seep into his palms and fingers. He opened his eyes, smiling as his fingertips glowed gold.

He reached toward Talia and laid his hands against her bare shoulders. They felt cool and it frightened him. She'd always felt so warm to his touch. He let the gold light trickle from his fingers onto Talia's skin until a golden sheen covered her body.

"Jack, no," said Talia, trying to stop him, but he stepped out of her reach until he'd drenched her in gold light.

"There," he said as the light dissipated. "That should help you feel better."

Muriel frowned at him. "Did you just call up healing light, Jack?"

He nodded. "I had to," he said. "Or she'll never make it to the East Coast."

Kesien spun him around. "Jack, you've never had healing light before," he said. "Where'd that come from?"

Talia looked concerned, too. "Jack, that healing light is a rare angel power that never mirrored in you before."

He shrugged. "Maybe it's a seraphim power? I just reached into my well of angel powers and called up some healing. Before you collapse."

"No more calling up powers, Jack," Kesien said, an edge in his voice. "You need to conserve those energies for Lucifer."

Dude had a point. He hadn't even thought beyond the fact that Talia needed healing.

He bowed his head, feeling his face getting hot.

"Sorry, wasn't thinking. Just trying to take care of my wife," he said.

Talia's hands slid across his shoulders and she pulled him close, kissing the side of his face. "And I appreciate that healing, lover. It will help me get across your world to the East Coast."

With a quick squeeze to Jack's shoulder, Kesien helped Muriel lift Talia into the air. Jack spread his wings, following.

They had to dodge three demons that had fallen out of the sky and a fallen angel.

In a shower of black feathers, Jack laid his hands on Kesien as the tall six-foot-sixish angel of death blinked them into a shower of light that shot across the night sky. Hurtling them across three time zones. To a small, forested cemetery with huge, old-growth trees and dozens of aged, crumbling tombstones.

The air was cold and crisp, smelling like brine, seaweed, and clams as the Duxbury Bay filled the horizon, distant gleam of a lighthouse punctuated by a seagull's mournful call. It was low tide, the sandy beaches cold and windswept as Jack and the other angels passed over a huge oak tree that draped strange elongated shadows of long, dark limbs over the grass and across dozens of old, broken tombstones. The sky's electric cyan color gave the cemetery stones an eerie glow as they flew low over it, searching for the statue of a weeping angel.

The distant red gleam of Heaven burning mixed with the cyan, turning the darkening sky a strange indigo.

They turned graceful circles above the solemn, dark forest that had grown up around these headstones, searching for the weeping angel statue.

"There!" Muriel shouted, pointing toward the southeast.

With Talia balanced between them, Kesien and Muriel flew toward a tall statue that stood almost at the southern edge of the cemetery.

They landed around it, but Jack froze, snapping his arms in front of the angels. Keeping them back.

"What is it, Jack?" Kesien asked.

The gaping, six-foot-deep hole stretched from the statue's base to about ten feet away. In a rectangular shape. That unnerved Jack.

He peered over the edge. At the wooden coffin that had been unearthed and broken open. Shards of ironwood littered the hole and collected like sawdust around its edges.

The ironwood casket was empty.

"Empty!" Kesien cried, his eyes wide.

Muriel covered her mouth, fear burning in her storm-grey eyes as she glanced from Talia to the hole.

With a flutter of wings, Kesien dropped down into the hole and kicked bits of splintered wood and clumps of soil out of his way.

"There's nothing here," he said, his tenor voice sounding like a lament. "Nothing!"

The Omega Rod was gone.

And Jack didn't even know what it looked like. He sank to his knees at the edge of the hole.

Lucifer beat them here. And he'd gotten the Omega Rod.

Now, there was nothing to stop him from breaking through the portal to the upper Heavens. Where risen souls resided. And the Thrones of Creation. He swallowed a pained breath.

And the Maker.

20

Talia realized what happened. Everything had happened so fast. The battle above Earth. Procel. A swarm of demons, the deadly wedge formation, and then her wings were on fire, burning away as she fell from the sky.

She had a vague memory of angels overwhelming Procel.

The fall had shattered everything inside her, especially her heart. As she lay in the cold grass, her light trickling away, she thought about Jack's beautiful face that she would never see again. That she'd never hear his hot caramel voice melting her heart into a puddle. Or never again feel the heat of his body against hers, loving her like no one had ever loved her before.

Things most angels never got to experience. But she'd lived them. She'd loved him. And she'd married him. But she knew in that moment, that she could never have him.

Or keep that happily ever after that they'd fought so hard for.

And just when she thought it was all over, the beautiful heat of his voice warmed her cooling angel light. Rushed through her heart in a blast of flame that kept that angelic core of light burning. Kept her from disappearing forever.

He'd brought her back from oblivion.

And she only wanted to wrap him in her arms and love him, tell him how sorry she was for just disappearing from his life, from his world.

But there wasn't time for apologies or affection. They had to return to Eolowen. Consult with Azrael, the Scribe, and Seraphina while there was still time.

She shuddered.

Before Lucifer arrived with the Omega Rod and broke through that portal.

Somehow, they had to defend the Thrones alongside the Throne angels. She swallowed another shuddering breath.

And defend the Maker.

Throne angels were the most powerful angels in Heaven—except Lucifer. Three Throne angels defended each Throne. Lucifer had to get through all nine of them. To reach the Maker.

"Kesien," she called to the tall, curly black-haired angel of death, unable to hold back the weakness in her voice. "Blink us back to Eolowen."

Climbing out of the empty grave, Kesien stretched out his wings as he hurried toward her and Muriel. Jack rose from his knees beside the hole and moved over to them, glancing over his shoulders. Like he'd heard something.

"Did you hear that?" he asked, glancing around the dark cemetery, the chill of the Atlantic Ocean settling around them as the scent of clams and seawater drifted in from Duxbury Bay.

Like headlights, red eyes began to glow between tree trunks and from behind tombstones. Blinking closer with every movement.

Kesien pulled Jack between him and Muriel as the demon eyes advanced on them, multiplying.

Talia grabbed hold of Kesien's arm as Muriel locked arms with Jack. And together, they blinked.

Against the massing red glow surrounding them, the four of them shot out of the cemetery and launched like a meteor across the night sky. Climbing. Surging through clouds, through the fading apocalypse wash of cyan. Upward. Toward Eolowen and the lower Heavens.

In moments, they appeared on the terrace. The grand hall had been barricaded with barriers of gold light and burned white with seraphim wards. That wrapped around the round room, along the rooftop, the nave, and gleamed throughout the grand hall.

Talia reached out toward the seraphim ward and parted it with her hands and rare angel powers. She held it open, allowing Muriel, Kesien, and finally, Jack to step through. Into the round room.

They cut through it and rushed into the nave. Flying down its length to the room where Azrael had housed Seraphina. Even from here, Talia saw the blue glow from the room. Shielded. So they could enter without being blinded. Or set on fire.

When she stepped through the doorway, Azrael blinked across the room, his face winter-pale.

"Talia! By the Maker!" With glassy eyes and a taut expression, he threw his arms around her and held her.

She put her arms around him, fearing she'd never see him again.

"Azrael," she said in a quiet voice. "It's so good to see you."

He held her out at arm's length as Jack moved closer, looking so lost and frightened. Wrecked.

He'd been through hell.

Her absence and then her falling out of the sky. He'd felt it. Like she'd felt his panic and grief as he tried to get to her. Their bond had been nothing but pain from both sides since she'd collapsed in Muriel's arms, unable to say goodbye to him. She loved him more than her own existence. But she couldn't find the words. Couldn't watch his heart break as she walked out of his life.

In that moment, she'd felt a sense of doom. A deep fear that she would perish in this battle. And she couldn't carry that last image in her heart of him. Broken. Grieving. She'd wanted to hold onto the memory of his stunningly handsome, smiling face and those sexy, pale green eyes that had burned through her soul.

Even now, the hurt clung to his face. Pain that she'd caused. A wound that she needed to heal.

But first, there was Lucifer. And the Omega Rod.

"Jack brought my light back with resurrect," she said, smiling at her gorgeous husband that hovered at the edge of the conversation.

She felt his apprehension. His worry that maybe everything had changed between them. That maybe she didn't want him anymore.

She reached out and took hold of his hand, pulling him into a kiss.

"I love you, Jack Casey," she whispered against his ear. "Now until forever."

His face screwed up and he tried to say the words back, but his voice cracked. He laid his hand against his heart and held it out to her.

She pressed his hand against her heart and kissed him again.

"I'm so sorry I hurt you," she said.

Those pale green eyes glistened with moisture as he tried to summon his game face. But it slipped through his fingers as he wrapped her in his arms and held her against his chest.

"As long as you still love me," he said, pulling in a breath, "I'll forgive you anything, Talia."

She straightened up, staring into those wounded green eyes. Her sudden disappearance still hurt him.

"I've never stopped loving you, Jack Casey," she said.

He smiled, but it quickly faded into that sexy smirk. She reached out and cradled his face in her hands and then kissed him again.

"Talia," said Azrael, motioning over his shoulder. "Seraphina needs to speak to you and Jack."

She nodded, but Azrael gently touched her arm.

"The Omega Rod? Did you get it?"

She shook her head. "Sorry, Azrael," she said with a moan. "Lucifer got there ahead of us."

Azrael winced, turning away toward Seraphina who had resided here since Lucifer blew up High House. Talia gripped Jack's hand and followed, Kesien and Muriel behind them.

Anahera, Daidrean, and Deemah stood guard in the room while Berith tended to both Pravuil and Seraphina.

"Talia!" Anahera cried.

She blinked across the room and threw her arms around Talia.

"It's so good to see you, Anahera," she said in a quiet voice.

"I thought I'd never see you again," said the tall angel of death, her short red hair askew, her face covered in ash, wings burnt and ragged.

A nearby explosion startled her and she jerked her head toward the noise.

"There's fighting all across the lower Heavens," said Anahera as Deemah and Daidrean rushed over to her.

"Talia!" Deemah cried, a hand on her arm. "So glad to see you."

Daidrean nodded, his thick brown hair a shade darker than she remembered, his grey eyes darker, too. "I tried to catch you," he said. "But there were too many demons in my path. I'm so glad you're okay."

"Thanks, Deemah and Daidrean," said Talia.

Claws skittered along the rooftop. Followed by the flutter of wings.

"Talia?" Berith cried, turning away from the Scribe and Seraphina.

She blinked across the room and enfolded Talia in her arms.

"I'm safe, Berith," she said, hugging the redeemed angel of death. "Thanks to Jack, Muriel, and Kesien."

The tension in Berith's face eased when she saw Jack. "Jack, I'm so glad to see the two of you together."

"Thanks, Berith," he said in a tired voice. "It's been a tough day. As long as Talia's beside me, I'll get through it."

She patted his cheek and turned back to Talia. "You look ill." Berith laid her hands against Talia, gold healing light washing over her.

Nodding, she let Berith heal her. She needed it. She was struggling to stay on her feet right now.

Azrael leaned toward Talia and spoke in a quiet voice.

"Seraphina is very anxious to speak to you and Jack."

Tugging on Jack's hand, Talia excused herself from the squad and moved toward the airy, high-ceiling chamber with white stone floors. Each wall had a bookshelf and a tall window between them (warded with white seraphim light). Filled with part of Azrael's collection. Books from every culture and country on Earth throughout the centuries. He didn't have every book ever created, but he surrounded himself with works that either entertained or impressed him. Someday, she hoped to explore this room. If there was a someday. If Lucifer didn't erase Heaven and Earth.

Seraphina's blue shielding light intensified for a moment.

Talia. Jack. To me. Quickly.

Seraphina's commanding voice echoed through her head.

Jolting Jack. He turned toward the blue light, a hand against his forehead as Talia led him closer. Pravuil floated beside the seraph, her form wrapped in blue light. All Talia could see was flowing curly white hair and burning white eyes in a sea of blue light.

Pravuil took hold of Talia's other hand as she moved closer, squeezing it. His gold eyes were glassy, short white hair windblown, white wings shuddering.

"Talia, I'm so glad to see you," he said. "I feared we'd lost you in that fight."

"Thanks to Kesien, Muriel, and Jack, I'm okay."

"Honestly, Scribe," Muriel called across the room. "It was all Jack. We just made sure he was safe until he found Talia."

Pravuil glanced at Jack. "Thought as much," he said, nudging Jack. "Good work, Casey."

Jack couldn't help but smile, but it was fleeting as another explosion shuddered through the lower Heavens.

"Kesien, you and Muriel check the wards, please," said Azrael.

Nodding, they blinked out of the room.

"Is it true, Talia?" Pravuil asked, glancing from her to Jack. "Did Lucifer find the Omega Rod?"

She couldn't halt the pained expression that shadowed her face.

"He got there first, Scribe. We tried to get there before him, but we were just too late."

Jack let go of her hand and began to pace.

"So, what's the plan, Scribe?" Jack asked. "Any minute, Luci's gonna waltz his arrogant ass into Heaven and blow the portal with that rod. And we're all gonna cease to exist."

Jack was right. They were running out of time.

"Jack's correct, Pravuil," said Azrael as he rose into the air, wings in motion. "If I know Lucifer, he'll make a grand entrance. Soon."

Jack pointed toward the ceiling. "We need to get every defense we can carry up to upper Heaven. To protect the Maker."

"And the Thrones," Pravuil replied, his voice a lament. "Those three Thrones run everything in Creation. If they're destroyed, everything disintegrates."

"What about the Throne angels?" Talia asked.

Pravuil shifted position, archangel wings twitching. "There are three assigned to each Throne."

"Just three per Throne?" Jack cried, his eyes wide. "Can they take Lucifer in a fight?"

Next to the Maker, Lucifer is the most powerful being in the universe. Because of his Phoenix Shift, he now has all his powers back. All of them. The Throne angels will fall to Lucifer's power.

Seraphina's voice radiated doom through the room and reverberated through Talia's head.

Jack froze in mid-stride. Her voice was in his head, too. He whirled around, fear burning in those sexy green eyes.

"Then what do we do here, Seraphina?" Jack asked, holding out his hands. "If Luci can crush all of us, how can we fight him?"

With these.

A dozen crystal blue shards floated through the blue light toward Jack. He stared at them but made no move to touch them.

"What are these?" he asked, glancing from Pravuil to Seraphina.

Shards of seraphim power that survived the explosion in the Cloud Chamber.

Jack's eyes got wide, but he still didn't touch them.

"I don't understand," he said finally, shaking his head as he turned toward the seraph.

The concentrated remains of all of Heaven's seraphim power. Excluding my own powers. I am too weak to fight Lucifer. The battle with the Army of Dark drained my energies that were only beginning to refuel. I have nothing left to challenge Lucifer.

Her words were a dire warning that cast a pall over Eolowen. One of Heaven's most powerful angels couldn't stop Lucifer. All that remained were nine higher-order Throne angels, but even they paled against Lucifer's might.

And Jack. The human wild card.

Jack began to pace around the shards, his gaze flicking from them to Seraphina.

"So, we're totally screwed?" he said. "Is that what you're saying?"

He froze in mid-stride, shuddering, his eyes rolling up in his head. The moments dragged on until he gasped and dropped to his knees, hands against his head.

I have removed the failsafe on your seraphim powers and given you the power to open the portal. Use caution, Jack Casey. And the shards. It is our only option.

"The first Holy Fire missile I toss at Luci will get me erased from existence now that he has that rod." He was out of breath, panting as he glared at Seraphina. "None of this is gonna be enough this time. Not these shards. Not my jailbroken seraphim powers. Not even a combined effort between me and the Throne angels." He groaned. "Sounds like a terrible metal band opening for Metallica. Jack and the Throne Angels. Singing their greatest hit, Screaming Death at Lucifer's Hand."

Talia stepped forward, feeling terrified for her husband.

"Jack's right, Seraphina. Sending him to battle Lucifer with only these shards is sending him to certain death."

Talia. You and Jack must stand together with your rare powers. It is the only way to save the Maker. And the Creation.

"Against the Omega Rod?" Talia cried. "How do we fight that? Lucifer's practically invincible with it."

The Omega Rod is a remnant from the foundational elements that collided, exploding into the essential components to create life. Components that created the Maker. Those components contained in that rod are the only thing that can kill a Maker.

The sudden realization made Talia shudder. Lucifer planned to kill the Maker with the Omega Rod.

The rod is shielded. It will absorb all of the Maker's Creation light. The Maker's essence. And without that light, a Maker will cease to exist.

"But you still haven't explained how we can match Luci's power, Seraphina," Jack replied as he stood in front of the shards floating beside him.

Stack half the shards together, Jack. And break them, one by one. You will absorb the stacked seraphim powers. At a steady pace so you do not overwhelm your human body. With these powers combined with your current seraphim powers, you become as powerful as Lucifer.

So, stacking the shards and absorbing their power would intensify Jack's powers?

Except for the Omega Rod. Stay far away from it. It can only kill you if it pierces your flesh.

At last, a smile touched Jack's face.

"Now, you're talking! So, I break half the shards and absorb their power one by one. Becoming Luci's match? As long as I stay out of stabbing range of the Omega Rod?"

Exactly. The shards steadily increase the magnitude of your seraphim power. But you need to either destroy the rod or take it from Lucifer by the time you use the last shard.

A flash of fear ran across Jack's eyes.

"What happens if I go through all twelve shards without getting the rod?" Jack asked, glancing back at Talia.

With that much power, your well of energy will drain quickly without more energy filling it. In minutes, you would become powerless. Then we all perish. Including the Maker.

Jack turned toward Talia and gave her a pained look, but she felt his trepidation. Felt the weight of the situation on their shoulders. It would take both of them to stop Lucifer.

She hurried toward Jack and smashed her lips against his in a desperate kiss. He held her for a moment, returning the heat and fire of her anxious kiss, trying to show her how much he loved her in the only moment they had.

Finally, he let her go and took hold of her hand, fingers entwining with hers.

"Let's throw Luci the worst surprise welcome home party ever, Mrs. Casey," he said, flashing that sexy smirk at her.

"I'll bring the murder marbles," she said, making him laugh.

He turned toward Azrael. "Help us get past that portal?"

Azrael, get them to the portal. Jack can open it now. Godspeed, Jack and Talia.

Azrael nodded and sang out for her squad to assemble.

When Anahera and Deemah flew into the room, Kesien and Muriel followed. Daidrean blinked into the room behind them.

"In case you need another sword," Daidrean said with a smile.

"Thanks, Daidrean," said Talia, patting his shoulder.

Azrael moved over to Berith and kissed her. She hugged him, kissing him hard on the lips, and then moved over to Talia and Jack.

"Come home safe, Talia," she said, worry burning in her storm-grey eyes as she hugged Talia again.

She turned to Jack, tears in her eyes. "And she better not come back without you. Be careful, Jack. I love you like a son."

She hugged him tight and held him for several moments, the tears threading down her cheeks.

He let her go, that smirk burning on his devastatingly handsome face.

"Leave the lights on, Mom," he said and brushed the tears off her cheeks. "But don't wait up."

She ran her hands through his hair and rubbed his shoulder and then let him go.

"Supremes formation," Azrael ordered. "Form on the vanguards. That's Jack and Talia."

Jack laughed at Azrael's formation call as the squad and Azrael surrounded them. Azrael gave the signal. Wings unfurled as all of them rose above the floor and flew into the nave. And blinked out a portal onto the roof.

Into a swarm of demons and angels clashing above Eolowen.

21

Jack resisted the urge to toss a handful of murder marbles at the swarm of demons engaging the guard.

"Leave them, Jack!" Azrael ordered and banked a sharp right.

He rolled out of the path of assassin demons that slipped from the shadows as more angels of death poured out of Eolowen. His wings hit an updraft and he floated above Talia's left shoulder, the squad adjusting to his altitude. Keeping him and Talia in the center of their circular formation.

Below, red demon goo splattered the white stones littered with grey and black feathers. And red and grey demon scales. Holy Fire burned along the white walkways and parks beneath as Azrael swerved below another large force of demons and veered left. Toward the Gates of Heaven. And the Corridor of Pervasive Light.

Its bright white-gold light was still a beacon against the flames scorching the lower Heaven's white stones below. The smoky haze had returned with a vengeance.

Explosions tore across the remaining shiny white buildings below, sending up huge plumes of black and orange smoke that rolled across the sky. Sending waves of turbulence through the air.

Jack braced for the shockwaves, gritting his teeth, and stretching out his arms, stiffening his body to roll with the bursts. The angels rode out the turbulence like it was nothing, but he'd never flown through a war zone before.

With head bowed and a hand over his eyes, Azrael soared through the smoke and debris, his body tilting upward as the smoke darkened the once Parrish-blue skies surrounding them.

Ahead, as they flew past more swarms of demons and flocks of angels, a brilliant gold column of light burned up from the Corridor of Pervasive Light and shot above them, disappearing into the clouds that smelled acrid and gritty with brimstone.

He frowned. He'd never noticed that white-gold beacon before.

Maybe it was the new seraphim power that Seraphina had given him? Allowing him to open the portal into the Throne Room. He'd never seen that beacon before. But Azrael was heading right for it.

A clutch of demons dropped out of the smoke and surrounded them.

Azrael brought the squad in tight, keeping Jack and Talia in the center as they drew Eternean swords and dropped the demons one by one out of the skies. Again, Jack fought down the urge to engage them. And help the squad. But they were doing fine on their own. Especially since Daidrean had joined them.

Talia's wings and body drooped. She looked exhausted as she hovered in the air. He slid his arm around her, letting her lean against him for a few moments. Until Muriel spelled him. They were right. Trying to maintain any altitude while carrying any angel weight was difficult and he struggled.

"Form on the vanguards," Azrael sang out and all five of Talia's squad flew in close, surrounding him and her as Azrael pressed on, toward the gold-white beacon ahead.

In minutes, they closed the distance and the white-gold light loomed, stretching above them as it disappeared into darker clouds.

Azrael banked around the beacon of light, flying in a tight spiral up through the clouds surrounding it. The squad followed and Jack did his best to keep up, to remain beside Talia in case she needed help.

And Jack feared that Lucifer would use her weakness and injuries against him, threatening to knock her out of existence in exchange for his surrender.

The battle sounds softened as they sailed up through clouds that began to shed their storm grey, softening to a creamy dove grey until the beacon halted in a white cloud bank. Where a round, pearly white door glimmered against the soft grey of the clouds.

The entrance to upper Heaven.

Something he couldn't even see until now. Where his grandparents, Myrna and Arthur resided, both thirtysomething when Dad was born. His other grandparents, on the Westwood side, were still around. Earl Westwood was too cantankerous to die. And Bessie was too sweet. But if anyone had deserved wings and a halo it had been Myrna Casey. She had been all angel when she was alive.

They were just past this portal. And he wondered how beautiful the world must be beyond this light, but he wouldn't see that part of Heaven yet. This portal led to the Throne room of Heaven.

It made him shake all over to realize he was about to step into the universe's control room. The thing that held it all together and kept all of it moving and growing and changing. With the most supreme being in the universe at the helm.

It was terrifying and awesome at the same time. And the seal was still pristine. Glowing with an otherworldly light that told him Lucifer hadn't arrived yet.

"It's still intact!" Azrael cried.

He motioned for Jack who flew toward him, laying his hands against the cool, smooth disc that looked like an illuminated white pearl floating in the clouds.

"Jack, you and Talia should be able to slip through the portal with your seraphim power."

Jack nodded and held out his hand to shake Azrael's hand.

"Dude, it's been the greatest pleasure of my lifetime to fight alongside you and the guard. Thank you for everything you've done for Talia and me. You're the best, dude."

Azrael smiled. "A double-dude thank you," he replied. "I'm

honored, Jack. No human has ever transformed almost the entirety of angelic thinking about humanity like you have. So many of you are worth the effort and existence would pale without your presence. It has been my grand honor to know you, Jack Casey."

Then Jack reached out and hugged the archangel. Surprised, the archangel froze for a moment and then hugged Jack back.

His expression was filled with emotion when Jack let him go, those storm-grey eyes glassy.

"But Jack," he said, a hand on Jack's back. "I can't let you and Talia face Lucifer alone. The squad and I have talked it over and we're going in with you. We can provide diversions and protect Talia."

He smiled. That was great news and it took a huge weight off his shoulders. With Azrael and Talia's squad there, he could focus on Lucifer.

"Dude, that's the best news I've ever heard. Thank you."

"All right, squad," Azrael said aloud. "Fall in behind me and wait for Jack to open the portal."

Talia blinked beside him, looking alarmed.

"Archangel, no!" she cried, terror burning on her face as she watched her squad line up. "Lucifer will destroy all of you if you follow us in there."

"He'll destroy us if we don't, Talia," said Azrael, laying his hands on her shoulders. "Lucifer will be concentrating all his attention on the Maker. That's what this is about, Talia. What it's always been about. Lucifer's relationship with the Maker. If he cared about taking down all the angels that didn't side with him in the Rebellion first, he'd have led the Army of Dark into battle himself."

Azrael had a point.

Jack glanced around for assassin demons and sneak attacks. But up here above all the skirmishes and fighting, it was quiet. Regardless, Azrael was right. Luci had no interest in personally destroying humanity or the world right now. Or taking the lower Heavens. He'd seemed ambivalent toward all of it. Focused only on getting that rod. And facing the Maker. His father.

The other destruction would come later. After he'd gotten his vengeance or whatever the hell he was after.

This wasn't about the apocalypse or the Rebellion. This was about Lucifer's relationship with his father. And anyone standing between him and the Maker up there in the Throne room would meet a swift end.

Regardless, Jack planned to be the biggest pain in Luci's ass that he'd ever been. Fighting him seraphim blow for blow until he could take away that rod. Having Azrael and the squad there meant having six potential distractions and six protectors for Talia. A win-win for him.

"Tal, they'll be a huge help for us up there. Distracting Luci when needed while he and I engage in the universe's biggest pissing contest. All so Luci can tell his dad that he was the worst father ever."

Talia glanced from Azrael to Muriel and finally, her attention returned to Jack.

"Will they be safe?" she asked.

"No," Jack said with a chuckle. "Babe, this is Lucifer, remember? But his focus won't be on us. And he won't try to destroy the Thrones first. It'll be dear ol' Dad."

She looked so frightened for her squad and Azrael. She had a good reason to worry about them, but the longer they hesitated and argued about who was going up there, the more time Luci had to breach the portal.

He turned to the archangel. "Azrael, how much more powerful is the Maker than Lucifer—without the rod?"

Azrael thought for a moment. "Without the rod, the Maker has a challenge on His hands—according to Pravuil. With the rod...the Maker can die. That's the difference."

Jack nodded. It was showtime. They couldn't wait any longer and risk Lucifer destroying them on this side of the Thrones.

Reaching out, he laid his hands against the portal and summoned his seraphim powers. In moments, the pearly white portal began to glow with gold light until the surface became liquid. Jack stuck his hand through it and it passed through to the other side.

He bowed toward the portal. "All right, people, let's move. Gotta set up Luci's little surprise party. I'd hate to have him show up early and ruin the surprise."

Azrael ducked under the portal's top edge and passed through the gold liquid, disappearing. Kesien went next. Then Deemah. Anahera followed and then Daidrean walked through the watery surface. Muriel patted Talia's sleeve as she ducked under the top and passed through.

He smiled at Talia. "After you, Mrs. Casey."

She paused to press a quick kiss against his lips that warmed his body and ducked under the curved edge. In an instant, she disappeared through the gold liquid. He glanced around, making sure nothing had followed him, and ducked into the gold liquid.

When he stepped into a short dark hallway, he turned and pressed his hands against the liquid surface. Changing it back to its hard, pearly white shell surface.

He turned around and stared at the massive gold and white doors at the end of the dark hallway. They must have stood twelve or fifteen feet high and the closed doors and doorways were about four angels wide.

He couldn't even see any other passages or doorways that might lead to the place where risen souls dwelled. That meant that Lucifer couldn't see it either.

With slow steps, Jack walked down the short, dark hallway that was part storm clouds and part shadows. But the closer they got to those massive metallic gold and white doors, the more light poured through the clouds as the storm grey began to lighten. The air smelled like ozone and first rain.

And the light that shined around the edges of the doors and underneath them was radiant. Brilliant. Would opening those doors burn all their eyes out of their heads?

"Azrael," he said in a half-whisper and pointed toward the door. "Will the Maker's light blind us if we open that door?"

"Squad, shield your eyes. Muriel, shield Jack's eyes."

"Got it, Azrael," said Muriel.

She blinked beside Jack and reached up, pressing her hand over his eyes until he felt warm light tingling across his face. Obscuring his vision.

"I can't see, Muriel," he said, reaching out to try and find her.

"Good," she said with a chuckle. "That means, the shield is working."

He felt a hand press against his left arm. Azrael.

"I'll lead you to the door, Jack, but you'll have to open the door with your seraphim powers. You still have those shards?"

He nodded. He'd put six in each pocket of his jeans and slid his phone into his back pocket.

"Ready to access," he said.

"Good," said Azrael, his voice sounding distant.

Like he'd turned his head away.

"What is it?" Jack asked.

"I...heard something," said Azrael, still turned away. "Sounded like banging."

Jack felt his heart begin to race. Was Lucifer at the portal? Pounding on it with the Omega Rod?

"We'd better hurry," said Jack.

He reached out toward the doors until his fingers brushed across a huge handle. It took both hands to grab hold of it.

Pulling in a breath, he summoned that well of seraphim powers roiling inside him and focused them on the handle between both hands.

The door resisted twice, but on the third pull, the doors screeched and whined as they responded to Jack's force.

He swung the door open wide, the angelic shield across his eyes making the room look like he wore a blurry pair of cheap sunglasses. That made everything just a little out of focus. But the golden floor was stage-light bright as they followed it inside.

The room was long with an incredibly high ceiling covered in clouds as they walked in a tight group into the brilliant glow of the golden room. Tall walls on either side glowed with ethereal light, shielding whatever cast that incredible glow. Two massive gold-walled chambers hummed and flickered on the left side of the room. One more on the right. Larger than houses.

Those chambers must be the Thrones that Seraphina and Pravuil had spoken about—the ones Lucifer would try to destroy after he killed the Maker.

The noises almost sounded mechanical, but there was a strange cosmic vibration and resonance to them that made Jack apprehensive. Like every planet in the universe would suddenly plummet out of space if he messed with those chambers.

Above one chamber, a holographic-like image of stars burned in the air, like it was a current snapshot of the galaxy or something. Above the right-hand chamber floated another holographic-like image of spheres that looked like planets. Shit-tons of planets. And above the far-left chamber, holographic-like images of humans, angels, and other creatures rotated in a slow, steady gyration above it.

The angels called these places Thrones, but they were more like control chambers that managed all the elements of the Creation.

As they moved closer to the first chamber, a blur of motion and light shot forward, away from the chamber. Toward them.

In a blur of light and wings...Jack shuddered—and eyes—three Throne angels surrounded them. Each set of wings was a different shade of grey. And all of their eyes were filled with Holy Fire. But when the angels halted beside them, he realized that those eyes weren't eyes at all. They were lights. Like sensors. These angels had faces like humans. Two eyes that were filled with Holy Fire. The others were almost like openings or sensors in their bodies that let the tremendous light inside them escape.

But they moved so fast that the lights looked like eyes and the movement made them look like they were just a bundle of wings and eyes. The light blur looked like wheels.

"Halt," said one of the Throne angels, her hair stony-grey, her eyes white with Holy Fire.

Her robes were obscured by her many wings and hidden in the light's brilliance that poured off her.

Azrael opened his mouth and sang notes that Jack couldn't hear.

One by one, the squad followed suit, including Talia. Finally, the Throne angel…moved. In the blink of an eye, she was in Jack's face.

"Who are you?" she demanded. "How has a human entered the Holiest of Heaven's chambers?"

She looked fierce. Pissed. And he had no clever answer or perfectly pitched angel notes to placate her.

"I'm Jack Casey."

She stared at him unaffected. Kind of like the paparazzi before he'd climbed out of the flake gutter he'd been wallowing in before *The Cinderella Hour* cast him as one of three prince charmings. And saved his life.

"I'm carrying almost all the seraphim power left in Heaven," he said. "To protect the Maker from Luci's rampaging bullshit."

Azrael gasped. Muriel snickered.

"Jack, that's a Throne angel," said Azrael, a mixture of surprise and embarrassment in his voice.

"And she hasn't heard the word bullshit before?" Jack turned back to the Throne angel. "Time to ask for some days off if you haven't heard it before."

The whole squad was chuckling now, Azrael glaring at him. Talia just sighed and slid her arm around Jack's waist. He smiled. Accepting him as he was.

At last, the Throne angel smiled.

"Oh," she said. "That Jack Casey."

The squad began to laugh now.

"That's me," he said with a shrug.

"Glad you are here, Jack Casey," she said and her gaze shifted to Talia. "And you must be the angel of death that fell in love with this human."

Talia nodded. "And married him," she added.

"You're not helping your case much, Tal," Jack whispered to her.

Even Azrael was chuckling now.

"The Maker is ahead on The Maker's Throne. We are taking up defensive positions beside all the Thrones. Preparing for Lucifer's assault." She smiled. "Or rampaging bullshit as you called it."

Jack's levity vanished when he heard the frantic pounding echo into the chamber from the short, dark hallway beyond the doors.

His whole body tensed. That was Lucifer pounding on the portal. He was certain of it.

"That's Lucifer, isn't it?" said Jack, backing down the golden walkway.

The Throne angel nodded. "Yes, please protect the Maker. We will try not to let him get past us. If we fail, you are our last hope, Jack and Talia."

"Where is the Maker?" Jack asked.

The Throne angel pointed behind him as the pounding grew louder. More intense.

Jack turned and ran down the golden walkway until ahead, he saw what looked like a glass enclosure looking out over space and time. Earth's galaxy filled the glass-like windows that had an almost golden sheen to them. The view was incredible.

The thumping sound was frenzied now, filling the hallway and infiltrating the gigantic Throne room with its steady blows that reverberated around him in layers.

He hurried down the golden walkway with Talia and Azrael beside him. The squad was only a couple of steps behind them as lights and movements flashed through the chamber.

Nine Throne angels shot onto the walkway. They locked arms and stood three to a row, wings locked together. Blocking the walkway toward the glass chamber of the universe. And the golden Throne that overlooked space and time.

Jack broke into a run, Talia and Azrael a step behind him as he ascended a flight of stairs. Up to the glass chamber of the universe.

Where a figure stood, hands behind their back, dressed in gold and white robes that seemed to float around them like smoke. Their hair was a thick flowing white mane of light that looked part Holy Fire and part sunlight. In constant motion like flames.

When Jack got within four feet of what had to be the Maker, he dropped to his knees and bowed his head.

"Maker," he said in a reverent voice as Talia and Azrael fell to their knees beside him. "Forgive the intrusion."

The squad reached the top of the stairs and slid to their knees.

When the Maker turned around, Jack saw stars in his…her…no, their eyes as the Maker studied him a moment. The Maker didn't look male or female, so using he or she felt…restrictive. They had an almost androgynous look that made them not male or female. A look that made the Maker all the genders. Made sense to Jack since the Maker created men and women and everything in between, supposedly in their own image. Only made sense that the Maker would be just as fluid.

"You do not see my true face," said the Maker. "Seeing it would destroy you because you could not withstand the Creation light it projects. For now, you see a side of me. I have many sides, but at this late hour, I show you the face of my human side because my angel face would also harm you, Jack Casey."

The Maker's smooth voice sounded musical, a harmony of both alto and tenor. It had a deep resonance to it, a lingering vibration that he felt deep in his gut and into his hands and feet.

Jack pointed over his shoulder toward the distant resonance of thumping that grew louder and more destructive as the moments passed.

"Lucifer has the Omega Rod, Maker," Jack cried. "He'll be through that portal pretty quick. And then he's coming here. To destroy you and…well, everything."

The Maker didn't seem alarmed.

"This confrontation with Lucifer has been building since I created humanity. It is time for it to end."

"All of it might end if he gets a shot at you with that rod!" Jack shouted, the pounding louder now. "Maker, he wants to kill you. And destroy everything you ever created."

For several moments, the Maker was quiet, staring out at the universe outside their window.

"Lucifer was my Lightbringer," said the Maker in an almost wistful voice. "My left hand. And he has never understood what that meant.

He has always seen his role as undervalued, overlooked." At last, what sounded like a sigh filled the chamber. "I made…mistakes. Regardless, I must face him."

"Maker, you can't face him when he has that Omega Rod."

The Maker seemed to float through the moments, appearing in front of Jack, Talia, and Azrael.

"He is a part of me. The earliest part of Creation. What I thought was the best of me. My greatest hope. My firstborn. But he became the pettiest and most vengeful. If only I had…"

Jack was surprised. The Maker sounded like a new parent with regrets.

The Maker's voice trailed off and they stared at the chamber walkway as the sound of something smashing reverberated through the space.

"This fight began when I created the first spark of light that became your world," said the Maker. "And the fight will continue to its last grain of sand—unless I face Lucifer."

"What is the Omega Rod?" Jack asked.

"It is the Creation light used to complete the Creation. Used to complete your world and then create humanity."

It all made sense now. Luci planned to end his father with the very tool used to create humans. The creatures that his father chose over angels—at least in Lucifer's eyes.

"That's why Luci chose it as his murder weapon. He intends to destroy every last bit of Creation. Starting with you and ending with humans."

"And I must stop him," said the Maker, regret in his voice.

"Maker," said Azrael, "We've come to stop him with—"

An explosion rocked the chamber, burning bright in the short dark hallway as pieces of the shattered portal blew inward, littering the floor as a tall, blond curly-haired figure stepped through the smoke. Debris crunched beneath his shiny black boots, black General's coat gleaming with two columns of gold buttons linked with gold braid flourishes. His large, glossy black wings cast a forbidding shadow into the chamber. His eyes glowed red with fury and demonic light, a stout glowing cylinder in his hand. It looked like a faceted crystal point encrusted in iron. It glowed with eerie cyan brilliance in his right hand as he slammed the great doors all the way open.

"Hello, Father," he said with a bright, sarcastic shout. "I've brought you a gift." Lucifer smiled. "Your death. Sorry, didn't have time to gift wrap it, but I so wanted to deliver it personally."

Jack winced. Showtime.

22

J ACK WHIRLED AROUND AND CLAMBERED DOWN THE STAIRS, T ALIA AND the squad behind him as Lucifer turned toward the first three Throne angels.

In a blur of light and speed, the Throne angels rushed Lucifer, arms locked, wings in motion.

Lucifer thrust out his hand toward the first Throne angel on his left. An invisible force from his hand knocked the angel halfway across the floor. And froze her in place.

The second Throne angel gyrated around him, tossing bursts of Holy Fire. One of his wings caught fire. The other burned through the black general's coat he wore. The flap fell open, red lining bright against the two columns of gold buttons and gold braid flourishes. He brushed off the Holy Fire and blinked. Slamming his fist against the second Throne angel's chest.

Freezing it in place.

The third Throne angel appeared behind him and rained down Holy Fire like lava on him.

Lucifer blinked out of the bursts that had burned his boots and his general's coat. Gold buttons turned black. Cloth smoked.

Jack reached into his right jeans pocket and pulled out the first six shards.

"Jack!" Talia cried.

She looked horrified as Lucifer body-slammed the third Throne angel against the wall. And froze it in mid-fall.

"You can't fight him, Jack. He'll kill you." She grabbed hold of Jack and pulled him close. "You don't have enough power."

Watching Luci take apart Throne angels like red-shirted ensigns made him shake all over, but what could he do? If he didn't fight Lucifer, the bastard would kill the Maker and everything would get destroyed.

Either way, he was going to die.

"Tal, we can't just stand here and watch him kill the Maker," Jack said, clutching the six seraphim shards in his fist. "I've gotta at least try. Either way, I'm dead, so at least I go out on my terms."

He wanted to hurl. This was it. There was no way out of this fight. And no matter what he did, it would end in the destruction of the world.

"Jack, no—" Talia shouted. "Jack!"

Azrael blinked beside Talia and grabbed Jack's arm.

"Jack," he said, his tone dire. "We fight together."

Jack shook his head. "He'll kill you, Azrael. Berith would never speak to me again." He gripped Azrael's forearms and looked up at the majestic archangel. "You and the squad keep Talia on the stairs. Within range to combine our powers. Defend the Maker if I fail."

He moved out of Azrael's reach.

"Jack, don't!" Azrael called out to him as he ran down the stairs.

Azrael grabbed hold of Talia a moment before she blinked after him.

"Azrael, no!" she shouted, fighting against his hold. "I have to be there to help him. Azrael!"

Muriel and Kesien appeared around her, holding her back.

Jack winced as her scream reverberated through the chamber where he stood at the bottom of the stairs.

Six shards in his right fist. Ready to crush.

Spreading shiny black wings to their full wingspan, Lucifer launched himself across the room. Into the next line of three Throne angels.

They spun around him like tornadoes of Holy Fire. Setting his wings on fire again. Burning his general's uniform.

Smiling, Lucifer backhanded one of the angels with a burst of dark energy that blasted the Throne angel into the hallway. With a wave of his hand, he slammed the doors closed.

Grinning, he grabbed hold of the second angel, freezing it in mid-air. Its myriad wings froze in mid-flutter.

"And for you…oblivion," said Lucifer with a chuckle and thrust the Omega Rod into the Throne angel's chest.

A piercing screech filled the chamber as a white burst of fiery light churned like an out-of-control Roman candle. The burst of heat and light collapsed in on itself and exploded in a metallic gold burst of flames and brilliance. Spraying the walls and floor with gold glimmers of light that continued to twinkle against the gold walls as dazzling Creation light thrummed from the three Thrones.

Lucifer brushed the ashes off his general's coat and then his boots. He glanced at his wings and shook them, dislodging a handful of burnt black feathers that drifted to the floor. They eddied around his boots as he looked up at the final three Throne angels blocking his way to the Maker's Throne.

"Still three of you then," he said, grinning. "I do enjoy a good bonfire, don't you? Shall we wager to see how long the three of you last against me?"

The last remaining Throne angels stood stoic. Unmoved by Lucifer's threats.

Jack's heart twisted into a knot. Resigned to the fact that these Throne angels were about to be erased from existence while protecting the Maker.

He gritted his teeth and grabbed one shard in his left hand. Crushing it.

Not if he could help it.

A shockwave rippled away from him, knocking Lucifer and the

three Throne angels to the floor as a massive sweep of seraphim power shot through his hand and down his arm. Into his chest. And expanded. Growing. Deepening as it mixed into the well of seraphim powers he already carried. Generating a tsunami of energy that thrummed through his fingertips.

Shocked, Lucifer got to his feet, staring past the Throne angels.

"What? Jack Casey? In Father's Throne room?"

Jack grinned, setting himself a few feet behind the Throne angels.

"Surprise, Luci!" Jack cried. "Thought we'd throw you a surprise welcome home party. With murder marbles, seraphim death confetti, and…" He held out his hands. "Failure. So you'll feel right at home."

Lucifer's red eyes narrowed, focusing on Jack now.

Jack wasn't even sure if Luci still saw the Throne angels in his path, now that his hatred had foamed to the surface—like the worst latte ever. Made with two shots of spite, almond milk, and heavy vengeance.

But Lucifer grinned. Making Jack nervous.

"I thank you for the gift, Jack. To think that I get to murder you first and then my father. My joy—and my vengeance—is complete."

Lucifer waved his hand at the nearest Throne angel, freezing it in place. Moving past it, he slammed the second Throne angel across the chamber. Into the massive doors. The Throne angel slid down the doors to the floor in a thick trail of molten gold light. And didn't get up.

The third Throne angel struck Lucifer with several, massive bursts of Holy Fire as it flitted around him, just out of range. Pinning Lucifer to the ground.

Jack lifted both hands in the air, still clutching five shards, and rained down torrents of Holy Fire on Lucifer. Pounding him against the floor.

"Squad! Wards around the Maker!" Azrael ordered.

Jack blinked past Lucifer as the Throne angel surged out of Lucifer's grasp on the left.

Turning, Jack rained down another surge of Holy Fire on top of Lucifer.

For several moments, he and the Throne angel worked in tandem, keeping Lucifer pinned on the floor. But he hadn't been able to knock the Omega Rod out of Lucifer's hands. Dammit!

Somehow, he had to get hold of that Creation rod. It was his only chance to survive this fight. But his odds were off the charts low.

Like a hailstorm, murder marbles pounded Lucifer, each one exploding in a shower of sparks. Knocking him backward. Toward the doors.

"That's my wife!" Jack shouted. "Thanks, honey!"

"Be careful, Jack," Talia called out to him.

In moments, Lucifer recovered. Snatched the last Throne angel out of another surging blink and slammed it against the floor. Freezing it in place.

With the Omega Rod poised in his fist, Lucifer turned to face Jack.

Jack glanced around him. He was alone at the foot of the stairs. If Lucifer got past him, he'd erase Azrael, Talia, and her squad like they were chalk outlines. Then he'd erase the Maker.

He was all that stood between Lucifer and the Maker now.

Again, he unleashed a maelstrom of Holy Fire on Lucifer. Pinning him to the ground.

Lucifer knelt, wrapped his wings over his head and around his body, blocking some of the Holy Fire.

His wings burned. Boots melted. General's black uniform caught fire.

Only when the barrage of Holy Fire ended did Lucifer unwrap the wings from around his body and beat back the flames.

Jack called up a third blast, but it was markedly weaker by comparison.

Lucifer smiled. "Is that all you've got, Jack? And you think you can match me blow for blow?"

Snap! Jack broke a second shard.

"You mean like this?" Jack asked with a smirk.

And rolled two huge balls of Holy Fire toward Lucifer like bowling balls.

Lucifer dodged the first one, but the second one slammed into

Luci's legs from behind. Knocking him to the floor. The explosion threw the King of Hell against the wall.

Lucifer climbed to his feet, glaring as he pounded the flames burning his wings and general's jacket.

And Jack hit him again, catching him from above.

Collapsing under the fire and heat, Lucifer called up a ward as Jack pounded him again with more basketball-sized loads of Holy Fire. Propelling them one after another like missiles.

Until they got smaller and farther apart.

Snick! Third shard cracked in his fist.

As Lucifer leaped into the air, smoking wings spread, and slammed Jack against the floor.

"You call that a fight?" Lucifer demanded. "That was pathetic."

Lucifer's hand rose. But before he could press it to Jack's chest and freeze him, Jack slammed his hand palm up against Lucifer's chest, knocking him across the Throne room.

Lucifer hit the doors hard like a vulture slamming into a plate glass window. He slid to the floor in a heap.

Jack blinked across the room, standing over the King of Hell. And lunged for the Omega Rod.

But Luci was a moment faster.

He rolled away from Jack, spreading his wings. Lifting off the floor, he circled Jack from the cloudy ceiling and dropped Hellfire on him. Burning his jeans and Henley. Setting his wings on fire.

Jack dropped and rolled, putting out the flames. And then blinked into the air. Crushing a fourth shard in his fist.

They flew at each other at dizzying speeds, flinging fire and energy until Lucifer knocked Jack out of the air. He plunged toward the floor.

Talia screamed.

He was inches from the floor when an angel ward lit up around him. He smashed against the floor and rolled, the pain sharp and radiating. But softened enough by the wards that he didn't break anything but his pride.

Struggling to his feet, Jack folded his wings. Turning around.

"Jack!" Talia shouted from the stairs, Azrael still holding her back. "Look out!"

He snapped his fist back, catching Luci in the face.

The King of Hell crumpled, holding his nose as Jack blinked across the room. Back to the stairs.

It took Lucifer a moment to recover from the sucker punch as Jack gathered more bursts of Holy Fire.

Struggling, Lucifer got to his feet and rushed Jack.

The Holy Fire slowed him down, but it didn't stop his advance.

Until Jack crushed a fifth shard and threw a white seraphim ward in Lucifer's path. Lucifer slammed into the ward and bounced backward. He skittered across the gold floor and landed beside one of the frozen Throne angels.

Blind fury burned through Lucifer.

"I'll destroy you, Jack Casey!" Lucifer shouted. "Get out of my way!"

Jack smiled, the sixth shard clutched in his fist. "Not happening." He shook his head. "Luci, go home. You're drunk."

Lucifer ground his teeth together and lunged at Jack, but the seraphim ward held.

Pulling in a breath, Jack crushed the sixth shard in his fist, giving the seraphim ward another boost.

Seven times, Lucifer threw himself at the ward. And seven times, it repelled him, throwing him backward into the floor.

Jack began to sweat, the weakness permeating his limbs. He couldn't hold that ward up much longer. And he doubted that the regular angel of death wards would hold Lucifer back now.

Grinning, Lucifer got up from the floor, wiping away a trickle of dark fluid at the corner of his mouth. He set himself and launched into the air, slamming full force into the ward.

The seraphim ward exploded in a shower of sparks.

Lucifer surged past Jack, knocking him halfway across the room.

Jack slammed against the wall and hit the floor hard.

"Jack!"

Talia blinked past Azrael and appeared beside Jack.

"Jack, how bad are you hurt?" she cried, flooding him with gold light.

The flash of black wings appeared at the top of the stairs to the Maker's glass chamber.

"The Maker!"

Jack scrambled to his feet and pulled Talia alongside him. He blinked across the room. Up the stairs.

Where Azrael and the squad had thrown down angel ward barricades around the Maker who stood in front of their Throne. Facing Lucifer for the first time in millennia.

"Stay back, Lucifer," Azrael replied, his tone dark and threatening.

Jack blinked him and Talia past Lucifer. To stand in front of Azrael.

He pushed Talia behind him and thrust his hand into his left jeans pocket. Freeing the last six shards. He crushed one of them in his right fist and threw down seraphim wards between him and Azrael.

"I can't let you do this, Luci," said Jack, pulling in a lungful of air.

His chest heaved as he tried to catch his breath.

"You can't stop me," Lucifer snarled and slammed his hand against Jack's chest.

He'd been too slow calling up a big seraphim-sized burst of Holy Fire.

Lucifer froze him in place. He grabbed hold of Talia and Azrael. Freezing them where they stood.

The squad rushed Lucifer.

He flung half of them down the stairs. The other two, Anahera and Deemah, he froze in place.

Lucifer advanced on the Maker who stood no more than twenty feet from Lucifer.

As Jack struggled against Lucifer's freeze that held him in place, Kesien and Daidrean slammed into Lucifer, knocking him to his knees.

Lucifer blinked. Slamming Kesien against the glass. Freezing him against it.

When Daidrean launched himself at Lucifer, the King of Hell turned, held up his hand, and repelled the angel of death.

Daidrean careened through the air and slid against the wall. Frozen.

Ten feet from the Maker, Lucifer stopped, Omega Rod in his right fist.

And faced his father.

"Now, it's time for you to die, Father," Lucifer said, barely controlled rage dripping from his words.

A smile curved across his face, those red eyes brightening.

"Why, Lucifer?" The Maker asked. "Why do you want so desperately to kill me?"

"You burned away my wings!" Lucifer shouted. "Extinguished my halo! For daring to tell these simpering humans the truth about their existence! That they were in a prison not a garden! That they were blind to what you really are! That they had free will to choose for themselves! Not live under your iron fist because all of it was only for your amusement. Nothing more."

The Maker shook their head.

Jack struggled against the freezing energy, but he couldn't move. Still, he had five shards left. Gripped in his left hand. Would they be enough to break free of this frozen state?

"You've convinced yourself of much over the millennia, Lucifer. Isn't there a simpler reason why you turned the first humans? A reason that you gave them information that they weren't ready to use? My first creations…and you made them afraid of me." Anger churned the Holy Fire hotter, brighter in the Maker's eyes until the Maker's form ignited with a burst of flame and light. "I loved them, Lucifer! They were my children. I didn't want to harm them."

"You just made more," Lucifer said with a growl. "And they weren't your first children. We were! Your angels." He thumped his hand against his chest. "Me! Your firstborn."

"I never forgot you, Lucifer. Or my angels." The Maker's voice was a steady harmony of tenor and alto notes, but the tension radiated.

Lucifer's upper lip curled into a snarl, the red glow fading from his eyes. Anguish replaced it, his face screwing up into a look of pain and despair.

"You threw me from the Heavens!" Lucifer gritted his teeth and gripped the Omega Rod tighter in his fist as he advanced on the Maker.

Until there were no more than three feet apart now.

"Jack!" Azrael cried. "We've got to stop him!"

Jack struggled. Couldn't move. But his fist was closed around the shards.

Could he crush them all with a flex of his fingers?

Lucifer circled the Maker, fury and hurt turning his eyes a glassy blue. A color that Jack had never seen in Lucifer's eyes before.

"I fell into a pitch-black cavern beneath the Earth! My body broken. My wings gone. And I laid there for hours. Days. Weeks. I called out to you. I begged you to listen. But all that greeted me was silence. Darkness. Cold. So, I became exactly what you wanted." His eyes narrowed, teeth gritted. "A monster." He laughed, a mixture of pain and giddiness in his wounded blue eyes. "And I played my part well. I preyed on your precious Chosen. I tempted them with pleasures beyond their wildest dreams. I gave them exactly what they wanted. I let them do as they desired. And I showed the world, the Creation, their true nature. These creatures that you loved so much! That you discarded me and your angels for! Your firstborn."

The Maker's mouth fell open. It was the first human response Jack had seen from the Maker.

"I loved you, Father!" Lucifer screamed like a wounded animal. "More than my own existence! But you shoved me aside. Relegated me to your left hand. Chose these…these beasts over me. Over your angels!"

Stunned, the Maker stared at Lucifer.

Lucifer was moments away from stabbing the Maker with the Omega Rod.

Jack had to get free. He gritted his teeth and pushed his fingers against his palm as hard as he could.

Until all five shards shattered in his fist.

Jack's body began to thrum with energy. Overloading his human body with too much power.

Melting the freeze around him.

He was free.

He turned toward the Maker. Knowing what he had to do.

"I loved you!" Lucifer's wounded shout filled the chamber with despair. "But you discarded me! You made me what I am. Father. The King of Hell. And I played my part well—like the good son."

Lucifer lifted the Omega Rod. And lunged at the Maker.

Jack blinked forward. Appearing in front of the Maker a moment before Lucifer plunged the Omega Rod toward the Maker's chest.

"Jack, no!" Talia shrieked.

The Omega Rod pierced Jack's chest as Lucifer slammed it forward like a knife at his father.

Jack took the full force of the Omega Rod.

"No," Lucifer replied, glancing from Jack to the Maker, the fury turning his eyes red again. "No!"

"I won't let you kill the Maker," Jack said with a gasp as he dropped to the floor, seraphim forces on overload inside him as the Omega Rod's Creation light began to chew through his body like a churning corkscrew of Holy Fire.

The Maker grabbed Lucifer and restrained him with Creation light, breaking the freezes that Lucifer had cast.

In an instant, Talia was beside Jack, tears running down her face.

"Jack, why? Why!"

The whole squad was beside him. And Azrael.

He desperately waved them off as Throne angels rushed to the Maker's side, taking Lucifer into custody.

"Couldn't let Lucifer destroy everything," Jack said with a wheeze as the seraphim power overload threaded its way through his body.

Toward the Creation light already flooding his body with white light.

"Get back!" he shouted, waving them off. "Overloaded my seraphim powers to escape the freeze. It's all going up."

"No!" Talia cried, grabbing onto him, but Azrael dragged her back.

"Talia! We've got to get clear!" Azrael cried.

"No! Jack…NO!"

But suddenly the Maker was beside him. A hand on his shoulder. Smiling.

"Not this time," said the Maker in that strange harmony.

Jack winced, feeling the warring energies about to collide inside his body.

He gritted his teeth. Bracing for the explosion.

As the unstable seraphim powers slammed into the Creation light.

Jack screamed, smashing his eyes closed as the burn shot through all his limbs and drilled deep into his gut.

But the Maker's hand kept steady pressure against his shoulder, their other hand gripping the Omega Rod.

"Jack!" Talia cried, fighting Azrael's hold.

But nothing happened. No huge explosion. No launching him halfway to Eolowen in pieces.

He opened one eye.

The Maker watched him patiently. Behind the Maker, Azrael, Talia, and the squad watched him in horrified silence.

He opened the other eye.

Glancing around him to make sure he hadn't crossed over into the upper Heavens. He shuddered. Or someplace else. But he was still on the floor of the Maker's Throne room. With the Omega Rod buried in his chest.

And nothing had exploded.

"I didn't explode," he said in a hoarse voice. "Why didn't I explode?"

Still smiling, the Maker patted his shoulder and lifted their other hand.

The Omega Rod separated from his chest. Leaving no wound or mark.

"The Creation light from the Omega Rod, the same light that created you and your kind," said the Maker, "absorbed the overload from the seraphim powers."

Jack frowned, confused. "It did?"

"Angel light and human light balance each other. That's why the Omega Rod didn't kill you. The seraphim power overload saved your life, Jack Casey."

Jack sat up and the Maker helped him to his feet.

"And that strange reaction between angel and human light," said the Maker, "combined with your sacrifice, has…strangely shut down the apocalypse. Returned everything to a steady state." The Maker motioned toward the three Thrones. "A curious system exception that bears investigation. Like this whole incident."

Talia ran to him and threw her arms around his neck. Holding him so tight that he could barely breathe.

"Why'd you do that, Jack?" she demanded, gripping him by the collar of his Henley. "Why!"

He caressed her cheek. "Because I love you. It was the only way to save your world and mine."

"Without you, I have no world, Jack Casey," she said, shaking him. "Don't you ever do that again!"

He laughed. "Hope I never have to," he said. "Last thing I expected was to survive that."

The Maker turned toward the glass chamber, watching the stars.

"Azrael, send Abaddon to Earth to clean up Lucifer's mess. I'll put what remains…out of sorts back together once Abaddon returns."

Azrael bowed his head. "Of course, my Maker. It will be taken care of."

"Thank you," said the Maker.

Azrael and the squad crowded around Jack and Talia as the Throne angels led them out of the Throne room and out of the portal. As a squad, they flew together in patrol formation out of the portal's white-gold light.

Back to Eolowen. Landing in Seraphina's chamber at her command.

The moment Jack stepped into her presence, everything went black and he was on the floor, Talia beside him.

"Jack, answer me! Jack!" she cried.

When the light returned, he struggled to sit up. "What was that about?"

The failsafe is back in place, Jack Casey. To keep you safe again. But know that your seraphim powers are stronger now.

"They are?" he said with wide eyes, glancing at Talia.

You absorbed some of the seraphim power from the shards.

That was unexpected.

"Thanks for the shards, Seraphina," he said. "Saved my life up there. And the world."

"So, Azrael," said Talia, gazing at the archangel in concern. "*Is* the apocalypse over?"

Azrael grinned. "Apparently. Now that Lucifer is in the Maker's custody, the apocalypse is over and we won't have to face the seventh Traveler. Death."

"Good to know," said Jack. He groaned. But they still had a show to film. "And we have a show to finish, Tal."

She wrapped Jack in her arms. "Is it all right to return to Earth, Azrael? To finish filming The Celestial Couples Show?"

"I don't see why not," said Azrael, still grinning. "I'll be in touch soon, Talia. There will be a lot of cleanup over this apocalypse debacle."

Talia spread her wings and Jack unfurled his, stretching them wide. They flew into the nave and blinked onto the roof. In Talia's arms, he held her close as she used her angel of death abilities to blink them back down to Earth. To the City of Angels. From there, they flew back to Burbank. To their trailer.

Barely able to move, he hobbled down the narrow hallway. Toward the bedroom

Once inside, Jack shucked off his clothes. Down to blue boxer briefs, he crawled into bed with Talia, the love of his life.

When he woke up, he found the bedroom empty.

He called for Talia, but like a bad dream, she didn't answer him.

He took a hurried shower and dressed in jeans and a short-sleeved mint green T-shirt. With phone in hand, he shoved open the bedroom door.

"Surprise!"

The dozen or so shouts reverberated through the trailer. Scaring the hell out of him. He froze.

Confused, he looked up, seeing balloons in blues, reds, purples, and greens covering the floor and clinging to the ceiling. Multicolored crepe streamers draped the kitchen cabinets, the walls, and even the television.

He was mobbed by Talia, Gianni and Izzy, and then Banks and Morgan. Jennifer Collins and Steve Kosinski were next. Followed by Herb, Devin Von Fossen, and then Rachel and Eric. Ryder and Claire joined them along with Zanth posing as Zoe alongside Tyler Hughes. And a disgruntled Lare Dumont who grudgingly patted Jack on the shoulder.

"What the hell is all this about?" Jack cried, staring at them with wide eyes.

Gianni chuckled. "Figure it out, Jack."

He glanced at his phone. It was August 8th. He smiled. His birthday. He was 27 now.

"With everything going on," he said with a laugh. "I didn't realize it was already my birthday."

"Happy Birthday, Jack!" Gianni said, patting him on the back.

"Okay, enough about him," Banks said, moving into the kitchen. "Let's cut the cake."

Laughing, Jack turned around.

A huge, double-decker sheet cake with white and blue icing that read, Happy Birthday, Jack Casey, sat on the counter. With twenty-seven metallic gold candles that Talia and Izzy lit.

"Make a wish, Jack!" everyone shouted.

Grinning, he approached the cake, wishing for good friends and his and Talia's happily ever after. Then he blew out all the candles in one shot.

Izzy cut the cake and everyone crowded around the kitchen counter, grabbing forks and a slice of cake. Jake savored his piece of cake as he leaned against Talia, hoping that for just a little while, everything would be okay. Now that Lucifer had been captured and the apocalypse was over.

But when he glanced into the bedroom, his stomach dropped.

Azrael, Kesien, and Muriel appeared in the room. Looking solemn.

He exchanged a worried glance with Talia.

"Okay, people," Herb shouted. "Finish your cake. Filming starts at ten sharp today."

"Be right back," Jack said, excusing himself.

Talia was beside him as he stepped into the bedroom. She came in behind him and closed the door.

"Azrael," said Jack. "Hey, Muriel. Kesien. How are things this morning?"

The archangel sighed and held out something to him.

"A birthday card? Dude, you shouldn't have!" Jack's smirk didn't lighten the archangel's mood.

Muriel smiled. "Today's your birthday?"

Jack nodded. "Just turned 27."

"Happy birthday, Jack," said Muriel with a fist bump to his shoulder.

"Yes, Happy Birthday," said Kesien.

"Thanks, dudes."

When Jack looked at the thick piece of ivory paper, he couldn't help but frown. It was in the Maker's Scribe, Pravuil's handwriting. With a bright metallic gold wax seal.

Jack Casey and Talia,

In two human weeks, your presence is mandatory at the apocalypse tribunal where Lucifer will be sentenced.

Seraphina

Jack's mouth fell open. He stared at Talia and then his gaze shot back to the archangel.

"Jury duty?" he cried. "You're calling me and Talia to Heavenly jury duty? On my birthday?"

Muriel couldn't hold back her smirk.

Jack sighed. Worst birthday present ever.

Azrael clapped him on the shoulder. "Sorry, Jack. The Maker wants you and Talia there to decide Lucifer's fate."

The archangel sighed and didn't meet Jack's gaze.

Jack squirmed.

"What else aren't you telling me?" Jack demanded as he cast an anxious glance at Talia.

"Spill it, Azrael," Talia said, hands on her hips, glaring at the archangel.

"The Maker also…wants to—discuss this…relationship between an angel of death and a human. Your relationship with Jack, Talia."

Jack felt his stomach drop into his feet. It was the worst thing Azrael could have said to him. Especially on his birthday.

"Sorry to crash your surprise party, Talia." Azrael fidgeted and turned to Jack. "Sorry, Jack. Happy Birthday."

Azrael, Muriel, and Kesien blinked through the ceiling and out of the bedroom.

He glanced at Talia who looked frightened. And she was shaking.

He slid his arms around her, holding Talia against his chest as her wings wrapped around him. She slid her arms around his waist and laid her head on his shoulder.

It looked like Lucifer wasn't the only one on trial here. His and Talia's marriage was also on trial.

The fight was still on for his and Talia's happily ever after. And he'd throw everything he had at it—including his acting career and his seraphim powers—if that's what it took to stay with Talia.

The End of THE ENOCHIAN APOCALYPSE SHOW: A Game of Lost Souls, Book Eleven

The story continues in…

THE ANGELIC ANNIVERSARY HOUR: *A Game of Lost Souls, Book Twelve*

Forthcoming!

Novels by Lisa Silverthorne

Standalones:

ISABEL'S TEARS

LANDFALL

PACIFIC BLUE TATTOO

A Game of Lost Souls series:

THE CINDERELLA HOUR

THE PRINCE CHARMING HOUR

THE EVER AFTER HOUR

THE FALLEN HEARTS SEASON

THE RISING SPIRITS SEASON

THE ETERNAL SOULS SEASON

THE ROYAL WEDDING HOUR

THE HEAVENLY HONEYMOON HOUR

THE DIVINE NEWLYWEDS SHOW

THE CELESTIAL COUPLES SHOW

THE ENOCHIAN APOCALYPSE SHOW

Curse and Crown series:

THORN & BLADE

The Spiral series:

BETWEEN

REPRISE

AVENGE

The Resurrectionist Papers

GRAVE RECKONING

Short Story Collections

THE SOUND OF ANGELS

THE MAGIC OF ORDINARY THINGS

TIMELESS

Science Fiction Writing as L.S. Silverthorne

Standalones:

REDISCOVERY

Experiencing True Purple series:

RECOMBINANT, Book 1

HELIX, Book 2

SPLICE, Book 3

FORTHCOMING!

A Game of Lost Souls series:

The Angelic Anniversary Hour, Book Twelve

The Perdition Picture Show, Book Thirteen

Curse and Crown series:

Storm & Steel, Book Two

Dagger & Flame, Book Three

The Spiral series:

Ruin, Book 4

Descent, Book 5

The Resurrectionist Papers:

Corpses Delicti

Stiffed Again

Cease and Deceased

SCIENCE FICTION WRITING AS L.S. SILVERTHORNE

Experiencing True Purple series:

Cipher, Book 4

Renascence, Book 5

ABOUT THE AUTHOR

LISA SILVERTHORNE, an award-winning bestselling author, has published 25 novels and 150 short stories and novelettes in many genres. She is the author of *A Game of Lost Souls* series, *Experiencing True Purple* series, *The Spiral*, *The Resurrectionist Papers*, and a new series, *Curse and Crown*. She lives in Las Vegas, Nevada.

Before you go, you are invited to please leave a **review of this book**!

Reviews are a wonderful way to help an author. They are also an exciting opportunity to share your honest thoughts with other readers, so **please post yours,** in as many places as possible!